Hell's
Hoofprints

LESTER DENT LIBRARY
VOLUME 3

Hell's
Hoofprints

The Complete *Western Trails* Tales
of Lester Dent

Edited by Gene Christie

With an introduction by Will Murray

2009
Normal, IL

Contents

Introduction

Will Murray

Lester Dent (1904–1959) made his reputation in pulp magazines like *Doc Savage* and *Black Mask*. When he began writing in 1929, the recent exploits of pioneer aviator Charles Lindbergh had catapulted the pilot hero to the forefront of pulp fiction. And so Dent's first stories centered around dashing barnstormers. From there, he expanded into the mystery and detective field, where he made his mark as a writer.

Dent is not usually associated with the Western. But it was a genre that he knew well, having grown up the only son of what he later called "chronic pioneers" in the days when people still traveled by covered wagon.

Born in La Plata, Missouri, young Lester was only four months old when his parents moved to Broken Arrow, Oklahoma, where cattle could be driven to market in Tulsa in a single day.

But Oklahoma did not work out. After one too many tornadoes, the Dent family relocated to Wyoming. The Johnson County Cattle Wars were yet fresh in some memories, and cowboys still drifted up from Texas to work the ranches at branding time. It wasn't the old Wild West, but it was still plenty rough.

The cowboy bunkhouse was usually awash in pulp magazines like *Argosy* and *All-Story,* and here Dent's youthful imagination was set afire:

> I never read such wonderful literature before.
> The minute I got through helping dad put out a prairie fire
> or skin a bear or whatever boring, everyday, humdrum duty
> I had to go through, I would rush to the bunkhouse and read
> pulp magazines in which people really got active.

When neighbors moved too close for comfort, Dent's father Bern and his brother's family loaded up their covered wagons and broke a trail across the Big Horn Mountains to settle in Pumpkin Buttes, Wyoming, an arid wasteland of greasewood, sage and sandstone spires surrounded by the Black Hills and the Belle Fourche badlands, and within riding distance of Devil's Tower. Here, on the 4-J ranch, Lester spent his teenage years. He came to hate it. Ferocious blizzards dogged the winter and every summer seemed to bring drought. Worst of all, Lester had no children his own age to play with. He often said the loneliness was almost unendurable.

Yet when he talked about those hard and lonely times, it was to joke, "Punch cows? Of course, I punched cows. All up and down the Wyoming slopes I punched cows. Every time they punched me, I punched them back."

Fortunately for Lester, when it came time to go to high school, the Dent family returned to La Plata so their son could receive a traditional education. And when it was time to strike out on his own, Lester moved back to Oklahoma, where he felt most at home. The truth was Dent saw himself as an Oklahoman more than anything else—and his thick Oakie twang backed him up.

Curiously, when Dent first began writing for the pulps, and was living in Tulsa, he shied away from Westerns. In later years, he joked:

> Shucks! I was raised on a ranch! Now wouldn't I be crazy to go writing about something I knew all about? I never been north of southern Alaska, but I write wonderful stories about the North Pole. You're crazy if you think you're going to get me to write about Pumpkin Buttes, Wyoming. I've already seen Pumpkin Buttes . . .. There are Wall Street secretaries writing stories about cattle rustlers that haven't seen a pick-pocket, whereas we really had cattle rustlers in Wyoming. And I can tell you about the time the ranchmen formed a posse and took out after a bunch of horse thieves. The horse thieves retreated to a place called Hole in the Wall, famous outlaw hideout, and fought off the posse for three days. When they got bored the horse thieves chased the posse off. It really happened that way. Maybe that's why I can't write Western stories. I might tell the truth.

But in mid-1931, the Great Depression was crushing the pulp magazine industry. Circulations were collapsing. Editors stopped buying. Times were so hard that Dent temporarily abandoned New York City, where he had been a contract writer for Dell, and retreated to his economic security of his parents' La Plata farm to figure out his future.

Pulp magazines were simply living off their inventories. Many were folding. Dent piled up rejection slips. The Western pulps were the hardest hit. Yet in some way, Lester found a receptive market in A.A. Wynn's pulp chain, which had emerged from the ashes of a Harold Hersey enterprise. In November, Dent peddled his first successful pulp Western, "Dusty Trant—Road Agent," to Wyn's *Western Trails*. In short order, editor Harry Widmer snapped up two more. Lester was back in the big city as one of Widmer's star writers. And Westerns had made his comeback possible.

The cowboy story had been ridden into the ground by six-gun super-heroics and fast-draw clichés. Editors wanted something new, chiefly better characterization. As A.A. Wyn described it:

"The hero doesn't have to be a gun-wizard; he can be a man who has certain clearly-defined character traits, and through these oddities he is able to overcome the obstacles in his path. The trouble with the majority of the Western stories that fail is that the characters are not sufficiently emphasized to become real; they are mere gun-dummies."

As defined by one editor, a gun-dummy was a "hero who is simply a zero with a name and two spitting Colts and a Stetson . . .." In other words, a steel-eyed stereotype.

If it was to survive, the regulation pulp Western needed new blood like Lester Dent. The struggling market was hungry, so Lester kept turning them out. He began filling the pages of Wyn's *Detective-Dragnet* and *Flying Aces* as well. He grew so prolific that the title story of this collection was printed under a pen name because it shared the issue with another Dent story. Dent took only one break. In the summer of 1932, with childhood friend Louis "Jasper" Madison, he toured the Western United States, camping out and prospecting for gold in Arizona, California and Death Valley. Thanks to a wave of Depression joblessness, a new gold rush was on. But they panned out only a small bottle of gold dust. Still, Dent picked up enough Western color and lore to feed his plot-hungry imagination for another round of Western sales.

All through 1932, Lester Dent toiled as a prolific Western fictioneer. Nearly all of his sagebrush yarns were printed in *Western Trails.* Some were supported by background letters in the magazine's Stampede column—a few of which were authentic, others clearly tall-tale recollections of Dent's youth. One brought the following response:

> I just finished reading Stampede and was surprised to see the name of Lester Dent in it. Bill, I always thought those letters were a lot of bunk, but I've known Lester Dent since he was 12 years old, also know those cousins, Ted and Paul Norfolk. In fact, I've known their mother before Ted was born.
>
> To prove that I know him—I lived near neighbors of his and the Norfolks in Gillette, Wyoming, when Paul got his hand torn all to pieces, picking up a dynamite cap.
>
> I know Lester knows his West or ought to. I enjoyed his story.
>
> I'd like Lester to see this letter, if possible.

The note was from Mrs. Joe Hartzog of Roosevelt, Oklahoma.

Dent's "The Sudden-Disaster Gent," was also singled out in agent August Lenniger's 1932 *Writer's Digest* article, "The Western Story," for its vivid, individualistic style and authentic characterization as an example for other Western pulpsters to follow.

Once the demands of *Doc Savage* grew to be too much to freelance elsewhere, Dent dashed off a final pair of cowboy stories for Street & Smith's new *Pete Rice Magazine,* and happily abandoned the genre. A.A. Wyn continued publishing new stories by "Cliff Howe" for years after—converting a personal pen name into a de facto house name.

Most pulp Western writers of the Depression consisted of what some derisively called "Hudson River cowboys"—Eastern pulpsters who cribbed their knowledge of the West from movies and pulp magazines.

Lester Dent was the real article, however. He could ride like an Indian and bagged his first antelope with a .22 rifle when he was just eight. And he knew the territory. As his wife Norma once put it, "He was a *Westerner."*

Yet pulp readers, influenced by the Wild West wonderland they saw depicted by Hollywood, demanded magazines that dramatized the never-never land version of the Golden West. A professional pulpster, Lester Dent gave them what they wanted, but with the real flavor of the fierce frontier in which he was reared. He also followed the *Western Trails* slant: Widmer preferred a mystery element in his range-and-ranch stories, and Dent duly complied. And just for variety, the occasional Mountie tale was offered. Dent did a few of those, too, at the end of his *Western Trails* phase. After having a cowboy yarn in almost every monthly issue for a solid year, he probably needed the change of pace.

All of these deserve special mention. "The Frozen Phantom" was later adapted for the first issue of *Ace Super-Mystery Comics* in 1940. "Snow Ghost" was the start of a series featuring the spectral Silver Corporal. The sequel, "Death Cache," was never published in Dent's lifetime. Presumably it was submitted to *Western Trails,* but rejected for reasons unknown. Perhaps Harry Widmer was phasing Mounties out of his magazine. Dent closed out his *Western Trails* phase with a handful of Western fact articles, which are also included here.

But to fully appreciate the stories that comprise this first-ever collection of Lester Dent Western yarns, you have to know that in his letters to Harry Widmer, Dent often spoke of writing a "Bill Hart Western," or a "Wallace Beery Western"—meaning that he was modeling his salty cowpokes as much upon the top box-office Hollywood versions as he was on the wranglers he actually had known. But, as you will notice, Dent rarely depicted a matinee-idol hero, but true sons of the West in all their raw, sunburned glory. This sometimes got him into trouble with his editor, who once warned him to back off using such "unpleasant, repulsive" characters.

Repulsive—or realistic? You decide. But fans of the immortal Monk Mayfair will recognize in colorful characters like Craggy Storms and Andy Frost the makings of the future Doc Savage character. Dent knew what he was doing.

A funny thing about Lester Dent's aversion to Westerns: He tried breaking into the slick magazines from about 1936 onward, and was relentlessly rejected. Not until the post-war Western TV boom did he at last succeed, cracking first *Collier's* and then *The Saturday Evening Post* in 1948 and 1959, respectively.

Both stories were authentic Westerns. One was adapted for the top-rated *Wagon Train* show, and was based on a harrowing experience from Lester's childhood experience on a wagon train. Dent took a swing at scripting an episode of *Gunsmoke,* only to discover that it was not an open market. A third script done for *Zane Grey Theater* also failed to sell.

Finally, when Lester Dent built his La Plata home in 1941, to commemorate his childhood he decorated the basement bar area in a Western motif. Above the bar he hung pulp cover paintings he had acquired over the years—including several that had graced issues of *Western Trails* featuring stories like "The Gun Quest."

·····

Dusty Trant—Road Agent

The hard-jawed ranny on the polka-dot black read menace in that lass rope swish in the darkness at his side. His hands turned into two tendon-wrapped claws and traveled for the .44 irons leathered to his thighs. His spur wheels sang on the polka-dot black's flanks.

The rope settled over his shoulders, tightening with a bullwhip crack. Plucked off the saddle, arms pinioned, he turned slowly over in space so that he crashed on his shoulder in the trail dust.

"Grab him!" a voice squawled.

Greasewood fluttered as men pitched for his squirming frame. The ranny kicked both feet, connected and sent a shadowy figure floundering back with arms and legs limber as strings.

"Keep 'at rope tight!" the voice yelped.

The ranny rolled, pumping, and freed his arms. He pawed to get the rope off his head. But it caught on his nose, tightened there; grinding his lips, crowding his jaws apart. Somebody kicked his feet from under him.

A man jumped on his stomach with high-heeled boots. The ranny's breath gushed squealing through his teeth. His stomach muscles writhed up in agonized knots. His heels beat a tattoo. His fingernails dug through the trail dust at the hardpan.

Three men sprawled atop him. Two clamped his arms. One got his feet.

"Strike a light!" the spokesman ordered.

A match whizzed on a pants leg and was transferred, fizzing, to a grime-stained palm. The puncher who held it was long of arm, bandy of leg, with little flesh on his bones.

Near him, hunched forward, another man stared and sucked his lower lip between his upper lip and teeth. He was fat. His red-veined eyes were too far below his brows. His nose was too small. The lower part of his face was big and stuck out.

"His pan ain't nohow familiar at close range, Leery!" grunted the fleshless man who held the match. "He don't ride with no spread in these parts."

The fat man stopped sucking his lower lip. It flopped down like lifeless rubber, showing big teeth and pale, bloodless gums.

"Just the monkey we need!" he said. "Search him!"

The hard-jawed ranny contracted slowly, taking great breaths into his lungs, and explosively straightened. The men who held him grunted and swore and flailed about. Leery grabbed his lower lip with his teeth, ran around and kicked the ranny in the top of the head. The ranny lay quivering and helpless while the fat man rifled his pockets.

The right pants pocket disgorged a handful of silver and gold coins and a tight roll of greenbacks fully an inch thick. The pocket of his sweat-stained checkerboard shirt held a cloth sack of tobacco and papers, along with matches.

"He's sure heeled with coin!" muttered the bony puncher.

"Roll him so I can get in his hip pocket," said Leery.

The four on the ground heaved about some more.

Leery pulled a folded, soiled paper from the ranny's left hip pocket. He unfolded it, then suddenly let go his lower lip.

"Listen to this!" he chortled, and read haltingly: "Five thousand dollars reward. Dead or alive. Dusty Trant, bank robber, cattle rustler and killer. Height five eleven. Weight one hundred and ninety. Big jaw, light blue eyes; hair coarse and the color of sagebrush. Knife scar from corner of right eye across temple. Dangerous gunman. Signed, Ban Haines, Sheriff, Crosswater, New Mexico." Leery laughed and held the poster with both hands stuck out straight in front of him. "Does this picture look like him, Bonesy?" he asked.

The fleshless Bonesy struck another match.

"It's him," he said.

"Search him again!" said Leery. "Them bad hombres sometimes keeps a derringer in their sleeve or a toad-stabber slung down between their shoulder blades."

Leery got the hard-jawed ranny's .44 irons and crowded them in his tight belt. Holding the match in one hand, Bonesy pinched inquisitorial fingers along the ranny's arms, slapped over his body and felt in his boots.

"Cleaner'n a whistle," he said.

Leery hunkered down and peered into the hard-jawed ranny's face. His bloodshot eyes rolled in a repulsive leer.

"Is your handle Dusty Trant?" he demanded.

In a low, cold, ferocious voice, the hard-jawed ranny said two short, explosive words.

"Whatcha goin' to do with this hombre?" uneasily queried Bonesy.

"Do?" asked Leery. "What'd we catch 'im for? Ain't he exactly the monkey we're needin'? Seein' he's Dusty Trant, the five-thousand-dollar outlaw, it oughta be easy to persuade him to help us. He'll be dang willin' to drag it outta the country afterward."

Bonesy shook his match out, his face suddenly startled.

"Ps-s-s-t!" he hissed uneasily. "What's that?"

A coyote yipped and wailed in the distance. To the northward, a creek frog was croaking. The breeze made a faint whining moan in the greasewood.

"Ps-s-s-t!" repeated Bonesy. He sidled away in the darkness, to be gone only a moment before his laugh rattled out, relieved.

"It's that hombre's polka-dot black!" he said. "The durn bronc came back. Wait a minute and I'll catch her. Whoa, girl! Whoa, there. Whoa, you crowbait!"

Bonesy came back leading the snorting, bit-champing black.

Paper tore and a match flared fitfully as Leery improvised a torch from the leaves of a checkbook.

"Let 'im up!" he ordered.

Instantly the ranny blasted off the ground and landed on a puncher, fists pumping. They rolled, fighting. Blows popped. Dust rose up in a cloud.

"Help!" bawled the puncher. "Ow-w-w! He's killin' me!"

Leery dragged his six-gun out and leaped into the dust cloud, holding high his checkbook-leaf torch. The gun barrel chopped viciously. The hard-jawed ranny collapsed atop the puncher, quivering as before.

The puncher rolled him off, floundered over on his hands and knees, got to his feet unsteadily.

"That coyote is gonna be hard to handle!" he said.

"I'll handle him!" said Leery, his words thick and unclear. "Hogtie him onto that polka-dot bronc!"

They lifted the hard-jawed ranny to the kak on the back of the polka-dot black and strung a lass rope under the barrel of the bronc, tying him there. Then they led five horses out of the greasewood, mounted and rode. They went toward the north, where the creek frog was croaking.

Soon Leery fleshed his spurs and shot ahead. When on the point of dying in the distance, the drum-rattle of his horse's hoofs ended abruptly and his voice came faintly across the greasewood flats.

"Over here!"

The others rode to him, stopping under a wad of black that was a cottonwood tree. Somewhere near, a trickle of water over a small falls made a steady musical sound like tiny hammers beating tiny anvils. Leery seemed to be standing in his saddle.

"Get a rope. Here's a limb." He struck a match and touched it to another checkbook torch. "Kick that monkey in the face!" he barked sharply.

The hard-jawed ranny, lying across his kak horn, hands hanging down limply, was tearing at the knots in the lass rope that held his ankles. The puncher who had taken the beating struck him in the face with a fist, jarring his whole body, then settled a rope about his neck, noosed it snug, tossed the other end of the rope over a limb and hauled until the ranny was pulled up straight in the saddle.

"Tie the end around the tree," said the fat man. He rode over, sucked in his lip and leered in the fitful flame of his makeshift torch.

"Now supposin' I fan yore nag with my hat?" he asked.

The hard-jawed ranny stood on his boot toes in the skirted stirrups to ease the tension of the rope about his throat. He licked his lips wet, then peeled them off his teeth in a snarl.

"Speak your piece!" he said.

"I'm speakin' it!" snarled the fat man. "You're gonna pick between two things, monkey. You can get married, or you can see how much that rope will stretch before yore head comes off."

The polka-dot black stamped uneasily, irritated by the rope which ties the hard-jawed ranny's feet under her barrel. "Whoa, honey-girl," said the ranny. Then he eyed Leery bleakly, asking, "What are you talkin' about, toad-face?"

The fat man sucked in his lip and blew it out with a harsh, angry sound. He drew back his fist and threw it against the hard-jawed ranny's mouth, knocking him over so that only the rope about his throat supported his weight. The ranny's breath in his throat was like sheets of sandpaper rubbed together.

"Listen close," said Leery. "You're gonna be a jasper named Dan Seabuck an' get spliced in marriage. After that, you can ride." He leered. "If you like yore bride, you can take her along."

"Whoa, sweetheart!" hoarsely whispered the hard-jawed ranny to the polka-dot black.

"Take yore pick!" said Leery.

"Try wagglin' your chin some more!" suggested the ranny.

"That's all you need to know. You just be Dan Seabuck. When you see yore bride-to-be, tell her you're the kid old Luke Showalter thought so much of when he was livin' down in Texas, before he came to Wyoming."

"Whoa, lover!" the ranny breathed raspingly to the black.

"I'm waitin', monkey!" said Leery impatiently. "D'you wanta see yore wife-to-be, or see how stretchy that rope is?"

"You're a pip," snarled the hard-jawed ranny. "Why didn't you say it was somethin' like that you wanted? Get this rope off my neck before my damned hoss jumps!"

Bonesy loosened the rope end from the cottonwood trunk and snaked it off the limb. He shook the noose big around the ranny's neck, shook it down over his chest and yanked it snug. Then, with expertly-tossed half-hitches, he trussed the man's arms to his sides.

"That'll hold him," he said, satisfaction in his voice.

The hard-jawed ranny tilted forward in his kak and glared at the fat man. The scar on his right temple looked raw and livid as the ravelings of blood that drooled from his mouth.

"You're makin' the mistake of your life!" he said.

"Haw, haw!" roared Leery. "Put a hackamore on yore jaw an' ride!"

Saddle leather made rosined squealings as the half-dozen horses racked through the night, leaving the greasewood flats and traveling over rolling, sage-whiskered hills. The bawling of a distant cow came down the wind. The heavens acquired a great, shapeless gash of silver as the cloud canopy parted. A big-eyed moon looked through the gash, deluging the Wyoming range with lactescent, gentle light. A horse stumbled and the rider cursed the animal.

"Why pick on me?" asked the hard-jawed ranny abruptly.

"Haw!" laughed Leery. "You was the first stranger to come along."

The cloud gash widened in the sky. Stars joined the moon, a freckled scattering of them. With a great snorting and arching of backs, the horses slid down into a gulley, then went up the other side with more snortings and frog-like, jerking leaps. Dust sifted over the riders.

The red squares of lighted windows appeared ahead, scarlet dapples on one of several shadowy humps that were ranch buildings and corrals squatting close to the range.

"Good-lookin' spread," said the hard-jawed ranny unexpectedly.

"Yea—brother," said Leery.

"What's it worth?"

"Half a million, maybe. You don't care what it's worth. Shut up!"

They unhorsed at the corral. Blankets and kaks were flung over the lodgepole pine railings and bridles hung on the kak horns. Horses rolled with loud grunting and tail swishing in the corral dust.

Bonesy untied the hard-jawed ranny, who stretched and stamped his muscles loose and said nothing. His eyes became faintly warm in a cold, hard face when he saw his polka-dot black tied to the outside of the corral with the saddle still cinched in place.

Leery broke the ranny's big .44 irons and sent cartridges spattering in the dust, then picked the ranny's belts clean of slugs and gave him back his guns.

"Act nice, monkey!" he said. "And you'll live a while." He slapped his guns with his palms. "Get tough, Mister Dusty Trant, and you'll collect a flock of lead, pronto!"

The hard-jawed ranny jutted his face forward. His brows pulled into beetling knots over steel-glittery eyes.

"You talk a lot with that mouth, don't you?" he said.

Leery grabbed his lower lip with his teeth. He shucked both guns out and crammed them into the hard-jawed ranny's belly.

"For twenty-three cents less than two bits, I'd give you a lead injection!" he said. "I can get five thousand for you dead. Go to the horse tank and wash the blood off your chin. Then we'll go to the house."

The ranny walked to the wooden horse tank and sloshed some water into his face. He pulled out the front tails of his shirt, wiped his face on them, and poked them back into his pants. Then he stared at the fat man. Wrinkles gathered at the corners of his eyes. The ends of his hard mouth twitched up, putting a cold, satanic smile on his lips.

"Do I look like a bridegroom?" he asked.

"You look all right," said Leery. "Don't let it slip your mind that you're Dan Seabuck."

They went toward the crouching black mass of the ranch house. The building was of logs, a story and a half high. A porch was slung upon two sides. The lighted windows were downstairs, all in one room.

"Lefty!" shouted Leery.

There was silence for a moment, then two men came down the steps from the porch, walking slowly, arm in arm, in close proximity. One was short, with a black beard, uncut hair and a flushed face.

The other man was fully seven feet tell. His startlingly long black overcoat, buttoned from throat to knees, hung upon his bony shoulders as on a coathanger. He was bareheaded, his face long, sunken, his lips bulging over big teeth. Three raw, red scratches started in his hair and slanted down to the collar of his black overcoat under his left ear, blackish beads of dried blood sticking to the deeper parts of the scratches. Under his arm he carried a quart whiskey bottle about a third full, and a thick book with yellow covers and green leather corners.

Alcohol odor rafted ahead of the short, bearded puncher and the tall, black-overcoated man.

"Pie-eyed!" snarled Leery.

"Like fun we is!" protested the bearded puncher.

The tall man jutted a bony forefinger at nothing in particular, squinted at the finger, then moved it carefully so it pointed at the hard-jawed ranny.

"Is that him?" he asked. "I wouldn't have his job!"

Lefty suddenly doubled, his laugh blowing out alcohol fumes, and pointed at the scratches on the tall man's skull-like face.

"You would've taken it a while ago!" he said. He doubled over again with gales of loud, spasm-like alcoholic laughter, poking a finger repeatedly at Judge. "He got to foolin' with her. She shore clawed him. I had to pull her off!"

Leery frowned at him.

"The hell you ain't drunk!" he said.

He stamped past the two men and up on the porch, shoved the door open and followed it into the lamplit room.

"Keep away from me!" a woman shrilled in a voice that was more threatening than frightened.

Leery turned and beckoned.

"Come in, Mister Dan Seabuck!" he said loudly. "And meet Miss Telsa Showalter."

The hard-jawed ranny walked through the door.

A girl stood with her back pressed to an old-fashioned china closet. One end of a rusty tug chain, the whipple-tree end, was padlocked about one of her ankles. The other end of the chain was stapled to the floor. Her right hand, held stiffly in front of her, gripped a pair of sharp-pointed scissors. She was tall. Her blonde hair was drawn so tight it stretched the skin of her forehead and knotted on the back of her head. Her eyes were cobalt blue, her face a little shiny and her lips pale. Except for the hand that stiffly held the scissors, her body drooped loosely.

"Dan Seabuck!" she said. Both her mouth and words trembled. "I'm glad you came."

The hard-jawed ranny fingered the grips of his empty .44's. His eyes smouldered hotly beneath slitted lids. His neck swelled with muscle until its diameter was greater than his head.

"You fat buzzard!" he said to the fat man in a low, crunching voice.

Leery grabbed his guns. "I've got a crawful of yore cracks, monkey!" he snarled.

The girl's face whitened. "Be careful, Dan!" she said.

The hard-jawed ranny made his face slack and emotionless. His neck collapsed to its normal size.

"Danged if this ain't a puzzle!" he said softly.

"The lawyer's letter didn't explain much, did it?" queried the girl, color mounting her cheeks. "This fat toad is Leery Showalter, my cousin. As the letter said, Uncle Luke Showalter willed the ranch to me, providing I marry you within a year. If I don't, it goes to the other heirs, and Leery is the only other heir."

The hard-jawed ranny looked at the girl, at the floor, and finally at the fat man. Laughter smouldered in his hard eyes.

"That sounds crack-potty," he said.

"Luke Showalter thought a lot of you, Dan," murmured the girl. "I think—I know he wanted a man like you in the family. He was old—and I suppose it seemed to him the only way to get what he wanted, even if I had never seen you. Anyway, the will is legally airtight. If any of us try to break it, the property automatically goes to the Cattleman's Home at Laramie."

The hard-jawed ranny's mouth rolled inward until it was a taut, bluish line. Hard gouts of muscle gathered in front of his ears.

The fat man leered at the girl. "You've misjudged me, Miss," he said. "You thought I was gonna make you marry me. But you oughta know I wouldn't do that, and even if I did get the idea, it'd only land me in a lotta trouble. You can marry Dan Seabuck here. That's what I call danged generous, me not makin' no trouble for you. But I'm that way, I am."

The girl looked at the tug chain securing her ankle.

"Too bad about that," smirked Leery. "But you was gonna tell the sheriff a lotta lies about me tryin' to make you marry me."

He grinned toothsomely, unlocked the padlock that held the chain to the girl's ankle, then walked to the door and conversed with Bonesy and the black-coated Judge. His whispered words reached none but the two he addressed. Bonesy nodded and left. Judge grinned, his lips skinning off the bulge of his big teeth.

"Shore," he said loudly. "I can splice 'em now, an' fix the license when I get back to town. But it'll cost you—"

Leery placed a hand across Judge's mouth, the fat, blunt fingers digging into Judge's sunken cheeks.

"You old goop!" he snarled. "Go ahead an' marry 'em!"

Judge stowed his quart whiskey bottle in a pocket of his long, tube-like black overcoat and opened his yellow book. His hands shook, his knees did not hold still; all of him seemed to be drunk but his voice. He turned a few pages, then began reading a civil marriage ceremony.

"T'hell with this!" croaked the hard-jawed ranny. He took a step forward, placed one hand in Judge's face and shoved like he was slamming a door. Judge skittered across the floor, long legs pumping in his overcoat like pistons. The back of his head hit the wall with a thud. His lips puckered over his bulging teeth as if threaded with a drawstring. He fell forward on his face and did not move, although his breath came loudly.

"Now—!" The ranny's mouth rolled into its thin, bluish line and he said no more than the one word.

The fat man and the four punchers had covered him with six-guns.

The girl breathed in loudly, and when she exhaled the sound was as if something fluttered wildly in her throat. The hard-jawed ranny spoke to her without taking his eyes off the guns.

"You're not this dumb," he said.

"I know you're not Dan Seabuck," she agreed. "But what can I do?"

Leery laughed loudly and answered the question.

"Nothin'!" he said. "We'll go ahead with the ceremony when Judge wakes up."

The girl looked at the hard-jawed ranny, saw the gouts of muscle bulging up in front of his ears again. Her face became sallow, as if no blood was left under the skin.

"That won't be necessary," she said.

She inserted two fingers in the front of her dress and drew out a letter. Walking to the table, which held the oil lamp, she dropped the letter on the oilcloth cover.

"Read that!" she said.

Eyes uneasily wide, Leery spread the letter out. Followed by gun muzzles, the hard-jawed ranny sidled over until he could read the missive:

Miss Telsa Showalter:
    The letters addressed to Dan Seabuck have reached my hands. I am returning them herewith.
    I regret to inform you that Dan Seabuck died six months ago.
                                        Sincerely yours,
                                        R.Q. LYNN

The sheet bore a letterhead which advised all that R.Q. Lynn was an attorney-at-law in Windy Creek, Texas.

"I've had that a month," the girl told Leery. "So I knew why you wanted me to marry this man. You knew I couldn't get a divorce before the year was up."

"Uh—um," grunted Leery uncertainly.

The hard-jawed ranny walked toward the door.

"Now that the beans are spilled, I'll be leavin' you," he said as he walked.

"Freeze up, monkey!" Leery snarled sharply. "The sheriff will be here in about an hour."

The hard-jawed ranny pivoted stiffly. "The five thousand, eh?" he said.

Leery smirked. "The five thousand."

"What are you talking about?" shrilled the girl.

The fat man laughed. He jerked the reward poster from his pocket and sailed it at the girl.

"Take a look at what I get besides the ranch, sister," he said. "If you raise a row about bein' held prisoner out here, I guess that much boodle will fix it up."

The girl's eyes grew big and wetly glistening as she unfolded the poster and read.

"Say—" Leery drawled. "If you knowed this monkey wasn't Dan Seabuck, why was you willin' to marry him?"

The girl looked at the recumbent form of Judge, her eyes protruding a little, the flesh working about her mouth.

"I planned to have him help me fight you," she said.

The fat man laughed easily.

"Hell of a lot of he'll help you," he said. "Bonesy's gone for the sheriff. In an hour they'll be here. Dan Seabuck is dead, so you can't marry him. That gives me the ranch. It looks like you're outta luck, sister."

"It may look that way to you," said the girl. She folded the reward poster, extended it and added, "Here—take this!"

Leery reached for the poster.

The girl's hand flicked sidewise and knocked the chimney off the oil lamp. At the same instant, she blew her breath gust-like across the flame, extinguishing it.

The lamp chimney shivered on the table. With the sound, the hard-jawed ranny reached the unconscious Judge's side. He stooped, ran his hands under the man's coattails, his fingers finding a short-barreled Colt.

"Block the door!" Leery yelped.

The hard-jawed ranny's Colt gushed a V of flame—one arm jumping at Leery's voice, the other at the black profile of a man which had appeared in the silver rectangle of the door. The profile in the door tied its arms across its middle and sat down on the threshold.

The room crashed scarlet with gun lightning. The hard-jawed ranny jumped sidewise. While he was in the air, a bullet picked flesh off his left ribs, high up. He landed gently, feet wide apart—and battered against the girl. She caught his arm and they traveled across the floor, wrapped in a suddenly ugly calm.

Judge breathed noisily. The man in the door made a whimpering sound of agony.

The ranny found a doorknob. He pulled softly, then gave a sudden wrench and shoved the girl through.

"They're goin' upstairs!" bawled Leery.

Without following the girl, the hard-jawed ranny crashed the door shut. Bent almost double, he scuttled along the wall. Beyond the door he had closed, the girl went up a set of stairs on all fours, pounding the steps with her fists to give sounds of two persons ascending.

Guns belched, filling the room with a cracking, flickering roar, as of a dozen thunderstorms unleashed. The ranny folded down on his knees beside the outer door. His right hand explored about the man who lay there and found two guns.

Still on his knees, he twisted and shot. A man fell and threshed on the floor.

"He's still in here!" barked Leery.

Window panels broke tinkling and wooden crossbars splintered as a man pitched head-first outside. Another instantly followed. The remaining man, somewhere in the room, was silent.

"Keep quiet in there, Lefty!" yelled Leery's voice from outside. "We'll get him if he comes out."

A stifled, dog-like yelp came from across the room.

The hard-jawed ranny jutted his guns out and soft-footed forward. His eyes were getting used to the darkness.

The choking yelp came again.

Suddenly the pale square of another window was blotted out amid the splintering crash of glass. A man thumped on the ground outside.

"You crackpot!" squawled Leery. "You oughta stayed in there!"

"Bugs in you!" retorted Lefty, his voice very sober. "I got the hiccups!" And he gave a dog-like yelp.

The hard-jawed ranny scuttled softly to the window through which Lefty had plunged. There was a vegetable garden on that side of the house and the three men had evidently taken shelter among rows of tomato plants.

A bullet came in the window and plaster fell off the opposite wall, rattling on the floor. The ranny glanced through the outer door, past where the dead man lay on the threshold. The moonlight beyond the porch was bright enough to reveal the separate leaf stalks in sagebrush clumps. He found the door that led upstairs and let himself through.

Instantly a match scratched and a red glow spread at the top of the stairs.

"Careful!" he said.

The girl was turning the reward poster slowly, watching it burn as he issued from the top of the stairs. She dropped the black cinder while little patches of it still glowed redly and stepped on it.

The ranny went to a window, tried unsuccessfully to raise the sash, and tapped out a pane with a pistol barrel. A bullet struck the window, showering glass into his face. He backed away, brushing off his face and shirt. The left side of his shirt was getting soggy.

He opened a door and crossed an attic-like room to a window that overlooked the vegetable garden.

The foot portion of a boot stuck out in the moonlight between two rows of the tomato plants. He pointed his pistol at a spot four feet above the boot top, then shook his head dubiously and aimed at the boot itself. It jumped a yard with his shot—an empty boot alone—proving it was a decoy, for simultaneously a bullet came through the window from the garden below and stirred his hair. Another, aimed lower, dug a cloud of splinters out of the window sill, ricocheted and hit him in the chest.

The ranny sat on the floor. His hands went to his chest, exploring the bullet hole. A couple of inches to the right, above a rib, a tumor-like welt had been raised by the ricochet slug, lodged harmlessly. He got up from the floor, entered the other room and gave the girl one of his guns.

"I bit an old one!" he said dryly. "I'm goin' back downstairs. You stay here."

He descended cautiously. The room did not now seem so dark to his eyes. Judge was stirring and groaning. Keeping close to the wall, the ranny went to Judge's side, felt for the fellow's jaw with a toe and kicked it solidly. Judge was unconscious again.

Upstairs, the girl's gun cracked. The ranny shot through the window at the flash of a six in the garden, but missed.

"Shoot the girl, too!" snarled Leery in the night outside. "We can tell the sheriff that damned outlaw did it!"

The hard-jawed ranny began prowling from window to window. His face was white and drawn and dead-looking, except for a feverish spot around either eye, and his hands were sweaty, although his face was dry.

He was still prowling from window to window nearly an hour later, when three men arrived at the ranch.

They were plainly visible in the moonlight as they pulled to a stop near the horse corral. One, who rode a gray gelding with black stocking feet, was big, bony, a mutt-like fellow. With him were a red-faced man on a strawberry roan, who rode with his stirrups too short, and Bonesy.

The hard-jawed ranny called the girl.

"That him?" he asked.

"Yes."

"Who's the other?"

"His deputy."

The ranny stared at the sheriff, his eyes sardonic. The officer's head was turning slowly, watching someone crawl toward him. The ranny craned his neck, but could not see the man or men who crawled.

"Why didn't you go to the sheriff with this in the first place?" he asked the girl.

"No chance," she said. "Leery was friendly as a fat, grunting pig at first. When I told him where to get off, he chained me to the floor. I've been there a week. He would have married me himself—but that would have been a little too raw. He thought he would marry me to someone else. His men would back him up—swear I did it willingly."

The ranny watched the sheriff get off his gray gelding hastily and put the horse between himself and the ranch house. The deputy followed suit.

"The sheriff know Dan Seabuck's dead?" he asked the girl.

"Not unless he's learned it in the last couple of minutes."

A grin picked at the corners of the hard-jawed ranny's mouth.

"Who's this Judge I pushed in the face?"

"A justice of the peace—drunken bum!"

The grin pulled the ranny's lips off his teeth.

"Yell at the sheriff and tell him you're comin' out," he said. "When you get out, tell him I'll surrender when I see Leery and the other two give up their guns."

"But—"

"No but!" said the ranny in a voice grating and harsh. "Drag your skirts out there!"

The girl came over, grasped his arm above the elbows and her fingers sank into his flesh like claws. The pumping of her heart was audible.

"You won't fight them?" she asked.

The hard-jawed ranny pulled her hands off his arms, turned her around gently and gave her a push toward the door, saying, "Drag it!"

The girl called shrilly and got an answer in the sheriff's booming tones before she went outside.

The hard-jawed ranny felt on the floor until he discovered a hat that had been dislodged in the gunfight. He tried it on, finding it rather tight. Standing stiffly upright, he placed the short-barreled Colt he had taken from Judge on top of his head, then pulled the hat on firmly.

He sat down on the floor then and drew off his right boot. Into it he inserted a hand. There was a ripping sound as the boot lining came out, and he withdrew several papers and a number of greenbacks of high denomination. The greenbacks he returned to the boot. The papers he stowed in his shirt pocket. Then he pulled the boot back on, stood up and stamped, then went to the door.

Leery and the other two punchers had joined the sheriff. Their voices, and that of the girl's, were an angry, argumentative babble. Leery and his friends seemed reluctant to surrender their guns. Suddenly the sheriff threw down on them with his sixes and his deputy collected the disputed weapons.

The hard-jawed ranny stepped over the body on the threshold, called out and tossed away one of the sixes that he had taken from the dead man. The girl had the other gun, so, excepting for the Colt in his hat, he was weaponless. Walking mechanically, so as not to dislodge the Colt, he re-entered the room and lit the lamp.

The sheriff and the others trooped inside, the officer carrying the pistols his deputy had taken.

Leery's lip had been split by window glass. The other two had weathered the fight with lesser glass cuts and one had a bullet hole through the fleshy part of his forearm, which he had bandaged with a dirty handkerchief. Leery poked a cone-shaped finger at the hard-jawed ranny.

"That hombre's the outlaw!" he yelled. "He leaded down two of us while we was tryin' to hold him for you!"

The hard-jawed ranny stood bent forward a little, elbows bent, hands palm uppermost in front of him, eyes under the brim of his hat brightly focused on the sheriff's gun hand. He hardly changed his position as the sheriff frisked him for weapons—missing the hat.

"Do I get a say?" he asked.

"No reason I should believe you, I guess," said the sheriff. He jerked his head at Leery. "But go ahead. I wouldn't believe that hombre either, not on a stack of Bibles."

The hard-jawed ranny took from his shirt pocket the papers he had removed from his boot and gave them to the gangling officer. The latter placed the pistols he carried on the table while he read the papers.

"Enough proof there?" asked the ranny after two full minutes.

The sheriff laid the papers on the table.

"I guess there is, maybe," he said. "There's your birth certificate, your army papers and some newspaper clippin's showin' your picture and your name and tellin' how you won rodeo prizes. Yep, you're Dan Seabuck!"

"The hell he is!" shrieked Leery, his voice so filled with rage that some of his words were only shrill squeaks. "He's Dusty Trant, the outlaw with five thousand dollars on his scalp."

The sheriff frowned. "Keep yore hair on," he said. "I'm gonna run in the whole kiboodle of you, I guess. I'll find what's what that way, maybe."

The hard-jawed ranny still stood with his hands palm-upward in front of his stomach.

"That's an idea," he said softly. "But would you do me a favor first, sheriff?"

"Depends on the favor."

"Let me get married—right now."

The sheriff's mouth became a round hole as his jaw sagged. The hole grew elliptical and closed.

"This is a funny time to get married," he said, "But yore reasons are good, I guess. They are if you're Dusty Trant. Go ahead."

The hard-jawed ranny pivoted, not too suddenly, until he was eyeing the girl. His face was hot and red.

"I think you better marry me," he said.

The girl caught the inside of her lips with her teeth. Otherwise her face remained blankly emotionless. She nodded slightly.

"All right."

The hard-jawed ranny shuffled to the recumbent Judge.

"Wake up!" he said harshly.

He kicked Judge lightly on the apex of his cranium. The long, cylindrical black overcoat writhed as Judge stirred his long legs. The ranny put one booted foot on Judge's face and moved it with a circular motion. Judge groaned loudly and pawed at the boot, finally pushing it away and sitting up.

"Get up!" said the ranny. Judge stared stupidly. The ranny lifted a foot, and with care not to jar his head, kicked Judge lightly in the nose. "What you waitin' on?" he asked.

Judge stumbled to his feet, got his yellow book with the green corners and began turning pages, swiftly and one at a time.

Leery was standing to one side. Suddenly he screamed.

"My cousin don't marry no outlaw!" he shrieked, his tone mad. "Not while I can stop it!" His hands extended for the guns on the table.

The hard-jawed ranny twitched his head backward sharply. His hat skittered down over his nose. The short-barreled Colt inside it bounced off his big jaw. His hands, ready in front of his stomach, moved just enough to catch the Colt.

He held the gun ready to fire for an appreciable interval—until Leery grabbed two sixes off the table and whirled. Then the Colt blew out lead and noise. Leery's knees folded so that he sat down and fell over against a table leg, then twitched and fell away from the table to lie very still and black in the shadow under the table.

But long before he had completed these motions, the short-barreled Colt had exploded again. Bonesy, leaping for the guns on the table, seemed to forget what he wanted to do. He crashed into the table so that the chimney-less lamp fell over, but did not break. Putting both hands over his mouth to stem an ugly flood, he gently lay down on the floor.

The hard-jawed ranny flicked the Colt muzzle over the sheriff and the others, all but the girl.

"Damned if I wouldn't stand right still," he said. His left hand reached out and set the smoking lamp upright. With stiffly flowing, catlike movements, he disarmed the sheriff and the deputy. Then he kicked the stupidly blinking Judge in the rear middle of his long tubular black overcoat so hard the tall man crashed against the wall and fell down on the floor.

"Get busy and marry us!" he said harshly.

Without moving from where he had gotten up off the floor, Judge began reading the civil marriage ceremony in a high-pitched, rapid voice.

The girl's "I do" was clear, but weak.

Judge looked up uneasily.

"It's here you put on the ring," he said. "Ain't you got any?"

The hard-jawed ranny licked his lip. "Get it over!" he snarled.

Judge finished swiftly. As the ranny nodded, "I do," he pulled the girl around so that she faced him, but not enough that she blocked the muzzle of the Colt.

"Go get my polka-dot black nag," he ordered. "She's saddled and tied to the hoss corral. Do it as quick as you can."

The girl left, and was back and calling to him from outside in something near two minutes. In the interim, the ranny kept a bleak gaze on the sheriff and the others, saying, when the sheriff muttered, "Dry up!"

When the girl called, he stooped swiftly and, from the person of the lifeless Leery, removed a tight, thick roll of bills and some silver and gold coins, which he pocketed.

Then he herded his prisoners outside and made them stand in a line in the moonlight.

As he took the reins of the polka-dot black from the girl's fingers, she swayed forward until the upper part of her body pressed against his. Her knees jointed and she started to slide down to the ground. The hard-jawed ranny caught her left arm savagely, a little below the shoulder, and pushed her out at arms' length, all but lifting her off the ground.

"You can divorce me anytime," he said harshly. "I'm leaving my papers so you can get the ranch without trouble from Leery's heirs."

Twice the girl's lips made certain movements, no sounds coming forth. The third try, she said:

"You—you're really Dan Seabuck?"

The hard-jawed ranny laughed hollowly, a sound like a rock rattling in a coffin.

"That's right," he said. "But Dusty Trant more places. That's why, when I got your letter, I had a pal write you Dan Seabuck was dead. Later I got to thinkin', and decided to drop around."

"Do—you—have—to—go?" The girl put a space between each word and after she finished, the flesh around her mouth twitched.

"You make it easy!" said the hard-jawed ranny, croakingly.

He swung up on the polka-dot black and his spur poked. The mare snorted and ran away through the moonlight.

• • • • •

Gunslick Roundup

The red-headed girl moved her leg and drew the .30-30 from her saddle sheath. She rocked the hammer back, slanted the rifle muzzle over the cut-bank and aimed carefully.

In the creek bed below her, the big puncher with the brassy face shook his lass off the fat shorthorn steer he had just snaked out of the quicksand. He coiled the rope, waded into the shallow water and kicked the steer in the ribs. It grunted, did not stir. It had given up, as fat steers will. The puncher got two flat rocks from the shallow water. He put the end of the steer's tail between his knees, pinched the tail between the flat rocks and rubbed up and down briskly, "tailing" the animal. The steer bellowed softly as the tail began to smart. Suddenly it got up and staggered out of the water, away from the quicksand.

The brass-faced puncher looked at the brand on the hip of the steer, then quickly at the similar brand on his white-stockinged dun saddle bronc rein-anchored at the edge of the water.

"Stewpan," he said, as if mildly surprised.

"It's the frying-pan for you, bronc forker!" rapped the red-headed girl. "And hell-fire if you don't claw sky *pronto!*"

The puncher's big hands turned into hard claws in which the rocks hung loosely. His thin stomach became thinner, his thick shoulders thicker. The knots and ridges of muscle in his brassy face swelled. His bleak, almost colorless eyes jerked under thick brows as he looked up at the red-head.

Lurid flame suddenly filled the pipe-like gullet of the .30-30 and a clap of powder noise jumped down the cut-bank. The brass-faced puncher's hat fell on his head, lit in the creek, and water came in through two small new holes in the crown, slowly filling it.

"The next one may swat you in the eye!" said the redhead. "Put'm up, cowboy! Put'm up!"

The man in the water slowly pushed his hands out until they were as far as they would go on the ends of rigid, thick arms. The rocks made two wet plunking noises in the water. His rigid arms carried his hands above his head until his thumbs touched.

"Hogtie him, boys!" ordered the redhead.

A blocky dark-haired man and a bowlegged apish man came from behind her and slid down the cut-bank, spurs digging loose rivulets of gray clay that poured ahead of them, leather chap wings flapping, the six-guns in their hands jerking about unsteadily as they balanced themselves.

"Lift his hardware, Henry," said the redhead.

With a right hand that had two fingers brown with cigarette stain, Henry shucked out the brass-faced puncher's guns and tossed them into the creek. He looked at the puncher intently, then swabbed his lips with tongue and looked relieved, as if suddenly deciding what he had thought would be a disagreeable job was going to be very pleasant.

"Stand petrified!" he said harshly. His lips opened an oval as he grinned, showing swollen, lead-colored gums and yellow teeth as short as nail heads. His solidly block-like body seemed to settle and broaden as he made his right hand into a fist and sank it in the brass-faced puncher's stomach, below the belt.

The puncher sat down in the water. His arms collapsed above his head so that his hands fell down. He slumped over sidewise and the breath going out of his lungs made a loud gobbling noise in the water.

Henry sheathed his gun, took the puncher's left wrist in both hands and dragged him out on the bank. Water came out of the puncher's nose and mouth.

The red-headed girl slid down the cut-bank, balancing the .30-30 in supple, browned hands. Her face was evenly tanned, her eyes the blue of gun steel. The bit of a grim, lipless line into which her mouth was pressed took little from the prettiness of her features.

Henry got the brass-faced puncher's rope, dropped it over his shoulders and yanked it tight, trapping his arms.

The redhead came and stood close to the puncher, looking down at his brassy face, her small nostrils moving in and out as she breathed.

"Know who I am, Mister Stewpan rider?" she asked.

The flesh around the puncher's mouth was yellow and bloodless looking. He managed after a great effort to sit up. His lids came together tightly over his bulging eyeballs. They did not part as he said thickly:

"I don't give a damn, sweetheart."

The redhead put her foot against his head and shoved. He fell over sideways, slackly, as a sack of grain might upset.

"I'm Graya Hunger, owner of the Walking Bug," she said without emotion. She flicked the .30-30 muzzle at the stubborn steer. "When we ran that herd of Stewpan dogies off Walking Bug range this morning, I sent notice it wouldn't be healthy for the next Stewpan rider we caught. Also that I have word Dint Smith will be here today or tomorrow. Didn't Mag Spain pass the news along?"

The puncher struggled feebly until he was sitting up again, but the blockish Henry jerked the rope and he fell over. He did not say anything.

"What's your name?" asked the redhead.

The puncher's head rolled on the sand loosely, like a brass ball, until his gaze focused on Henry.

"You can go to hell, you!" he said hoarsely. He rolled his head until his eyes rested on the girl. "And you can go with him, darling!"

The redhead dropped the .30-30 in the crook of her arm, the muzzle pointing at the ground in front of her feet. She took her lower lip between her teeth. She shuddered.

"I don't want to watch it," she said. "You know what to do, boys. I'll go get our horses."

She turned and climbed the cut-bank, following an angling course, high-heeled riding boots dislodging clay that came down the slope with dry rustling sounds. She disappeared over the edge without looking back.

Henry walked to the white-stockinged dun bronc with the Stewpan brand, tied the reins to the saddle horn and hit the horse's tender nose a terrific blow with his fist. The dun reared backward and ran away with a great beating of saddle bags against saddle skirts.

Henry jerked the brass-faced puncher to a sitting position. Standing in front of the puncher, he swung back his right boot and drove it at the big man's stomach. The puncher got his wrists and hands in front of the boot. The boot tore the back of one hand and upset him. Henry kicked him in the ribs and the neck. The puncher tried feebly to grab Henry's boot. Henry stamped the grabbing hand into the sand, skinning and bruising it. The puncher's lips crawled away from his teeth in a grimace of ghastly agony.

Henry leered at his apish companion. "He likes it!" he said. "It makes him grin!"

"D'you reckon we're makin' a mistake?" queried the apish man uneasily.

"Naw," said Henry. "Couldn't be. This is a chance to get solid with the girl. And I'm gonna like bouncin' this hombre around!"

He kicked the brass-faced puncher in the face. The puncher's head and shoulders shook loosely with the impact. Henry took a handful of his hair and lifted his head.

"Aw, hell!" he complained. "He's out!"

The brass-faced puncher opened his one eye that would open. The eyeball moved jerkily, peering up at a metallic bowl of sky. A thin formation of clouds was in the sky. Below the clouds, seven buzzards sailed on stiff wings.

One of the puncher's knees twitched, then bent slowly and brought his foot up. He moaned softly. His hips heaved and he rolled over.

He was alone in the creek bed below the cut-bank.

Pushing with his hands, his elbows raised grasshopper-wise, not lifting his body, he crawled for the water. When he lay in it, he splashed the liquid in his face, feebly at first, then with more vigor. By the time he was clean of drying blood, his legs could support him shakily.

He waded deeper into the creek, avoiding the gleaming smoothness of the quicksand, until he reached the spot where his six-guns had fallen. He ducked several times, got them both, then stumbled to shore and fell down on the hot sand. He broke both guns and strewed the cartridges in the sand.

After that he lay on his stomach, head pillowed on his arms, eyes opening and closing slowly. By the time the sun had dried the cartridges, his eyes were bright and there was a healthy glow in his hard, brassy face. He reloaded the sixes, pointed one at the sand and stroked the trigger. The gun jumped and sand flew up in a cloud. He formed a soundless "O.K." with his lips and holstered the guns. He walked in the direction the dun bronc had taken.

But he went no farther than to climb up out of the creek bed. He stopped there in the mesquite that bordered the Arizona range.

Distant half a mile, two riders, men, were chasing the white-stockinged dun, one twirling a rope. The rope snared the dun. The two men then rode toward the creek, leading the animal. Their horses, the brass-faced puncher saw as they came near, were both branded Stewpan.

They reined up before him and one of the pair squinted down. The fellow was thin, long, and as he moved in the saddle his body seemed flexible, without bones anywhere. It was as if he were made of rubber. His fingers were limber, restless.

"We heard a shot," he said.

"There's nothin' wrong with your ears, then," the brass-faced puncher said unsociably.

"About half an hour ago we saw some Walkin' Bug rannies ridin' away from here," added the limber man.

Without answering, the puncher eyed the other rider. The fellow's hair was so fair as to be almost white. He was in his early twenties. His face was boyishly pink-cheeked, his body slender without being skinny. The fair-haired man wore two guns—not slung on his thighs, but belted tightly to his waist. And his hands seemed never to drop below his waist.

"I'm Mag Spain," the limber man said harshly. "Who're you?"

The brass-faced puncher moved his gaze from the boy to Mag Spain's showy Mexican saddle.

"Saddler," he said shortly. "Bill Saddler."

"Cowpoke?"

"When I work at it."

"Where you from?"

The puncher moved his gaze to the boy and said tonelessly:

"You don't give a damn about that."

Anger showed in Mag Spain's slitty eyes. He inclined his head toward the white-stockinged dun bronc.

"Where'd you get the dun?"

The fair-haired boy's face was flushing redly under the brass-faced puncher's steady stare. The puncher spoke without removing his eyes from the boy.

"Jumpin'-off place named Lindo. 'Bout forty miles away."

"He's one of a bunch we sold in Lindo last spring," said Mag Spain. "So the Walkin' Bug outfit mistook you for one of my riders?"

"That might explain it."

Mag Spain squirmed his limber body in the saddle. He smiled under his angry slits of eyes.

"Why didn't you tell 'em different?"

"Wasn't worthwhile."

"They wouldn't have believed you, eh?"

"No," the puncher said, staring steadily at the boy.

The boy suddenly tilted forward a little in his saddle, elbows bent, hands hanging splayed in the air above his waist.

"What the hell, bud?" he asked in a low, cold voice. "You near-sighted?"

Long ropes of muscle slowly ridged out under the bibless overall pants that clung wetly to the brass-faced puncher's thighs. His stomach stopped moving as he breathed and became still and hard. At the end of arms down rigid at his sides, close, to his guns, his big hands dangled loosely.

"Don't get yourself hurt, son!" he said harshly.

The boy's upper lip lifted off even white teeth in a chill, bitter smile. "Maybe you know me, but—?" he asked.

Nothing about the brass-faced puncher moved but his lips as he answered softly:

"I've heard of you, son. You're Boy Irons. You're supposed to be poison."

The boy stopped smiling and his lips pulled thin over his teeth.

"You're askin' for somethin' you won't like, brother!"

Mag Spain held up a hand. Uneasiness had joined the anger in his slitty eyes.

"Stop it!" he said. "Boy, stop it! You too, Saddler!"

Without taking his gaze off the puncher, Boy Irons said:

"One more crack and he'll be pickin' lead outta himself."

Mag Spain made smoothing gestures with his hands. He spoke to Boy Irons in the tone a trainer might use on a dangerous animal.

"Now, now, don't be so touchy, Boy. What them Walkin' Bug rannies did to this hombre has got him hot under the collar. He's not responsible. And I'm not payin' you—" His hands abruptly became motionless and his voice harsh. "Boy, are you sure you know this Dint Smith by sight?"

The boy, not moving his hands or eyes, said:

"What kind of a sap do you take me for?"

Mag Spain's face registered relief.

"Then you're sure this hombre isn't Dint Smith?"

"Hell!" said Boy Irons. "Ain't you got me hired to kill Dint Smith on sight?"

Mag Spain started and frowned. "All right, all right," he growled hastily. "I'm not payin' you to fight every cowpoke we meet, either." He moved his gaze to the brass-faced puncher, smiled widely with his lips, put his left hand on the saddle horn, put his right on top of it, and asked: "Saddler, want a job?"

The brass-faced puncher took his gaze off the boy.

"No," he said.

Mag Spain licked his smiling lips.

"What are you gonna do about what them Walkin' Bug rannies done to you?"

The brass-faced puncher's mouth hardened. His pale, thick brows drew together. "I'll fix 'em!" he said harshly.

Mag Spain smirked and patted the top of his left hand with the palm of his right.

"I thought you would feel that way," he said. "But you're takin' on somethin', Saddler. That red-headed girl who owns the Walkin' Bug has written down in Mexico and hired one of the orneriest gunslingers there is, a killer named Dint Smith. Dint Smith is so fast, them that knows says there's only one hombre has a chance of beatin' him—Boy Irons, here. I don't know whether this Dint Smith is at the Walkin' Bug yet, but if he ain't, he will be in a day or two."

The puncher rubbed his bruised jaw.

"Throw in with you and get help with the Walkin' Bug—that what you're tryin' to say?" he demanded.

"That's it. And you'll get two hundred a month for doin' it. What do you say?"

"Them's gunhand wages."

Mag Spain smiled. "It's gunhand work you'll do, Saddler."

"Let's talk about it some more," said the brass-faced puncher.

"All right," Mag Spain said agreeably. "I own the Stewpan. I've got nine thousand herd of prime beef trailin' from my summer range in the mountains to my winter range. It's been a dry summer and the only route I can trail my beef where there's water is through the Walkin' Bug range. That damned redhead at the Walkin' Bug says I can't go through. I say I will. It's government land."

The puncher's brassy face had become loose and stupid looking as he listened.

"The redhead got much of an outfit?" he asked.

Mag Spain hesitated. "Runs several hundred head."

The stupidity want out of the puncher's metallic face. It was coldly alert as he looked at Mag Spain.

"What the hell, brother!" he said harshly. "D'you think I'm simple? Why not come out and say you aim to guzzle up the Walkin' Bug's dab of grass with your nine thousand beeves, and that the Walkin' Bug has hired a smokepole-slinger to keep you off, and that you've hired this squirt here to down him?"

Mag Spain's face became flushed and ugly.

The boy raised in his saddle, hands poised small and pale above his waist.

"I think we've fiddled around long enough with this rooster!" he said.

"Be careful, son!" said the brass-faced puncher harshly. "You're fixin' to have the sun shine through you."

"Now, now," said Mag Spain indulgently. "You've got nothin' to gain by smokin' Saddler, Boy. After all, it's better if we get the cards on the table. Saddler's not dumb. And we can use another gunhand. I'd like to hire him if you'll leave him alone."

Boy Irons looked with pale, expressionless blue eyes at the puncher.

"All right, but tell him he better not try to ride me," he grated.

Mag Spain smiled at the puncher. "Leave Boy Irons alone, Saddler," he said. "If you get him mad, somebody's liable to stop a flock of bullets."

The brass-faced puncher answered harshly without taking his gaze off the boy.

"Keep him away from me, then! I don't like him! I'll kill him if he cuts up with me! I'll kill him!! I'll shoot his guts out!"

"Now, now!" said Mag Spain. "Boy Irons is all right. He just don't like to be stared at. But don't forget, he's bad, Saddler. We've got enough beddin' between us to fix you up. Come on."

The brass-faced puncher growled in his chest and mounted. They rode at a gallop, twisting to follow such open spaces as appeared in the mesquite growth. The sun was low on the evening horizon, so that upright clustering stems of organ cactus threw shadows for hundreds of feet. As they left the valley in which the creek ran, grass disappeared from underfoot. The mesquite grew stunted, gnarled. They clattered among rocks, the horses blowing, and crossed a divide.

They passed to the right of a crumbling, deserted shack that stood disconsolately in a bed of weeds and crazily slanting, wireless fence posts—the abandoned dream of some dry farmer foolish enough to tackle the sun-baked Arizona range.

The bleak, dry range smouldered red with twilight as the spike of a distant mesa speared the sun. A beef herd of several hundred sleek animals came into view.

"Them Walkin' Bug rannies stampeded that bunch today," Mag volunteered.

The brass-faced puncher said nothing in reply.

A waterhole glistened wetly about a mile beyond the beef herd. Close by it squatted an adobe shack and the crawling ring of a brush corral. Several hundred yards to the north a horse cavvy of a score or so of animals grazed.

"We're campin' in the shack for a few days," said Mag Spain.

The adobe shack had become a low, black wart in the darkness as they rode up. Mag Spain dismounted and handed his reins to Boy Irons. The boy rode toward the waterhole, leading Spain's mount. The brass-faced puncher rode slowly after him.

The moon was rapidly silvering away the first gloom of night. A coyote wailed in the distance. The brass-faced puncher dismounted a couple of yards from where Boy Irons stood and let the white-stockinged roan wade out and suck up water.

Boy Irons watched him silently. His fair hair in contrast made his boyish face seem almost black in the gloom. He looked at the puncher, then pivoted slowly on his heels, sweeping the vicinity of the waterhole with sharp eyes.

When he had done looking, Boy Irons made a clucking sound with his tongue and the roof of his mouth. He came over and stood, small and boyish, beside the big puncher.

"Well, Dint Smith," he said softly. "I'll bet that after our show, the last thing Mag Spain will suspect is that we're workin' together to annex his beef. What went wrong with your angle?"

The brass-faced puncher yanked the rope to keep the dun from wading out deeper in the waterhole.

"My saddle bronc broke a leg in a badger hole," he said. "The only hoss I could buy on short notice to replace him was this Stewpan dun. The Walkin' Bug outfit saw the dun and mistook me for a Stewpan ranny, just like I said."

"Why didn't you tell 'em who you were, boss?"

"I got a sock in the belly and let myself get mad!" said the brass-faced Dint Smith.

After a bit, he said: "It won't gum your play, nohow."

"The girl was with them when they jumped you, wasn't she?" asked Boy Irons.

"Uh-huh. Her and some jasper she called Henry and a little ape of an hombre."

"Henry's her foreman," said Boy Irons, his voice suddenly bitter. He turned his head to look around them again in the moonlight. His voice was casual again as he added: "The redhead is—a spunky little devil."

Dint Smith's brassy face got rough with muscle welts. His pale, thick brows sank down over his eyes.

"What the hell—what the hell?" he asked harshly.

Boy Irons coughed softly. "Nothin', boss," he said. "Only this Mag Spain is a crummy no-good. He's tryin' to put the girl out of business and glom the Walkin' Bug range. His nine thousand beeves will clean her winter grass and she'll have to pull out."

"Go ahead!" growled the brass-faced puncher when Boy Irons hesitated. "Get it all outta your craw!"

Boy Irons moved his shoulders downward. "When I came up here, I didn't know this girl owned the Walkin' Bug," he mumbled.

Dint Smith pushed his brassy, knotty face forward. "When you came up here, it was because I sent you!" he snarled hoarsely. "You were to hire out to this Mag Spain so we'd have an inside man in his outfit. That was all you were to do, too! From what I seen of that redhead, she can take care of herself. Are you gettin' chivalry, kid? If you are, you'd better start travelin'!"

Boy Irons was silent. His breathing made swishing sounds in his nose. When fully a minute had passed, the brass-faced puncher put the palm of a big hand on Boy Irons' face and shoved it back roughly.

"Forget it!" he said. "You haven't ridden the owlhoot trail long enough to get hard to the game. Why'd Mag Spain hire me?"

Boy Irons cleared his throat with a growling noise.

"To keep you from smokin' that rat, Henry, who's foreman of the Walkin' Bug. And the little ape, too."

"Why's he worryin' about their health?"

"They're both on his payroll."

The brass-faced puncher laughed harshly and said: "He's stealin' our stuff, eh? Now I savvy plenty why friend Henry beat me up. He knew I wasn't a Stewpan rider, and saw a chance to get in solid with the girl by doin' some stompin' on somebody she thought was. What else has Mag Spain done?"

"He ran off a bunch of Walkin' Bug dogies this afternoon. Drove 'em south, hazed 'em good and left 'em runnin'. They'll be in the desert and dead of thirst before they stop."

The brass-faced puncher made a sick sound of disgust with his throat.

"Where's Mag Spain's cattle?"

"There's about five hundred here—that bunch the girl stampeded off her range. The rest are in the big herd, about twenty miles back."

"Where's his men spotted?"

"There's nine riders with the big herd. Nobody but Mag Spain and me here. We brought the five hundred on ahead. Mag Spain wanted to throw 'em on the Walkin' Bug range and see what the redhead would do."

The brass-faced puncher laughed harshly again. "That's hunky-dory!" he said. "I thought it sounded like a good bet when this Walkin' Bug owner wrote and hired me for a gunhand. I didn't know until today that a girl owned the outfit, however. She forgot to put that in her letters. But what the hell! My merry men will be up from Mexico in a couple of days, kid. They're as sweet a spread of cow thieves as you ever saw. We'll egg this range war along by liftin' beef from both outfits, like we planned. Each will blame the other for the rustlin'. We'll clean the range of beef. Don't get tender-hearted, kid. Outfits that hire gunhands to fight their range wars deserve about what they get. And that goes for the redhead, too."

Boy Irons took off his hat and turned it slowly in his hands. The top of his light-haired head was like half a snowball in the moonlight.

"I've met the redhead—a couple of times," he ventured slowly. "She don't know I'm workin' for Mag Spain. The girl is—I like her, boss."

The brass-faced puncher's arms became rigid bows at his sides. "Hell's fire!!" he snarled. "You playin' that on your harp again? You can't get senti-mental in the cow stealin' business, son! Maybe you got bellyful?"

Boy Irons lifted his eyes from the hat. His face looked unwell. His lips pulled apart in the middle as he made a weak smile.

"It's danged near empty," he said hoarsely. "I ain't put nothin' in it since mornin'. Let's go chow."

A loud rattle of hoofs caused the brass-faced puncher to open his eyes to bright, warm sunlight the next morning. He yawned, threw back the soogan under which he had slept and sat up. His eyes were heavy with sleep as he watched Mag Spain slide off a lathered, blowing bronc and anchor the animal with dropped reins. Spain was carrying a brass-slide telescope. He was excited, and was not doing a good job of keeping his agitation off his face.

"I got a hurry-up job for you, Saddler," he called. "I'll throw you some breakfast together while you yank on your clothes."

The brass-faced puncher slowly worked his legs from under the soogan and stood up. He stretched and yawned and scratched himself. He put on his hat first, then pants, shirt and boots. He strapped on his guns.

"Where's the squirt?" he called.

"Boy Irons is out scoutin' for strays from that little herd you saw last night," Mag Spain replied from inside the adobe. "You ready to eat?"

"Nope," said the puncher. He walked toward the waterhole.

The white-stockinged dun bronc stood with hanging head and swishing tail in the brush corral. A magpie, cawing excitedly, flew up out of the mesquite. A rattler buzzed beside the waterhole and the brass-faced puncher broke a chunk of dried mud from the edge of a horse track and threw it at the snake as it squirmed into a prairie dog hole. He grinned at the dog hole, then his eyes got hard and metallic and he looked toward the adobe.

"Somethin' has busted loose," he told himself as he sloshed water into his face. "Mag Spain is some riled. He's suddenly decided he wants me away from here *pronto.*"

When he returned to the adobe, Mag Spain had dished breakfast onto a rickety table and was waiting impatiently. The brass-faced puncher ate bacon and syrup-covered flapjacks off a tin plate, washing it down with coffee from a tin cup. He took his time. He swabbed the tin plate clean with a flapjack and pushed the flapjack into his mouth.

"Get your bronc, Saddler," said Mag Spain abruptly. "Take them horned critters you saw last night and throw 'em back with the big herd. There's enough grass and water here for the strays Boy Irons finds."

Irritation darkening his brassy face, the puncher hooked his thumbs in the beltless waistband of his pants.

"I'm not ridin' herd today," he said shortly. "And don't be too surprised if I don't ride herd any other day."

"Now, now, Saddler, I'm boss here!" Mag Spain said, his eyes suddenly ugly. "You keep that in mind."

The puncher pulled his pale, thick brows down and made his mouth surly.

"Who the devil do you think I think you are?" he asked harshly. "You're not payin' me two hundred a month to ride range. You can like that, or not like it and go to hell! I didn't ask you for the job."

Mag Spain worked his mouth open and shut. Before he could say anything, the roll of distant hoofbeats reached them on the morning air. He swore softly.

"It's too late now, anyway!" he snarled. "The redhead is coming. I saw her from the divide with my telescope and wanted to get you away before they got here. Listen, Saddler, there's two men with her, the pair who stomped on you yesterday. Now I ain't ready for no shootin' yet, so you lay off them two."

The brass-faced puncher looked at Mag Spain from under lids drawn down to hide the humor in his eyes. He made a growling sound that contained no words, stamped to a corner and sat on an empty wooden canned corn box with the solid gray adobe walls at his back and partially at his two sides.

Horses clattered up outside. Saddle leather squeaked. Mag Spain went to the door.

"Good mornin', Miss Hunger," he said. "This is a pleasure."

"I knew it would be," said the redhead's voice. "Hadn't you better invite us in?"

"Now, now, the shootin' iron ain't necessary, really," protested Mag Spain.

The redhead followed a large blue-steel six-gun into the adobe. She stopped on the threshold, her eyes, angry and narrow in a flushed face, twitching from side to side.

"Sit still—you!" she said sharply to the brass-faced puncher. "Or you'll get worse than you got yesterday."

Mag Spain smiled and the smile spread until all his ugly face was a-grin. His mouth opened and a laugh came gobbling out.

"After you've cackled," said the redhead. "You can get your bronc."

The block-like Henry and the apish man came in the door and stood behind the girl. Henry saw the brass-faced puncher. His jaw fell down. He glanced swiftly at Mag Spain, seemed about to say something, and changed his mind. The apish man stood on widespread feet, saying nothing, no surprise in his simian face.

Mag Spain has shut his lips on his laugh.

"Huh?" he said.

"We tracked the rider who drove my beeves into the desert," said the redhead huskily. "The tracks led here. I'm taking you in to talk to the sheriff about it. I happen to know you're one of the things our sheriff don't like. Running off my cattle will sound like rustling to him."

Uneasiness filled Mag Spain's slitty eyes, but went away with his loud laugh.

"Now, now, you can't frame me like that," he chuckled. "You ran your own horned critters into the desert and expect your rannies to lie and say I did it. Ain't that right, you two?"

The apish puncher said nothing. Henry pulled his uneasy gaze off brass-faced Dint Smith, blinked stupidly, caught his cue and laughed.

"Sure, Mag—Mister Spain," he said. "That's what she done. She's payin' us two rannies gunhand wages to run off her beef, then swear you rustled it. But I guess we ain't the kind of fellers who can be bought like that."

The redhead stepped swiftly to one side, so that she faced everybody in the adobe. She took her large blue-steel gun in both hands.

"So they're both working for you!" she said to Mag Spain. She pointed her gun at Henry. "Get out of that door, so I can walk out of here without turning my back to you!"

"Now, now, you'll have to stay," said Mag Spain. "You've tried to frame me on a serious crime, so I'll have to hand you over to the sheriff, instead of you handing me over."

He took a step toward the redhead. She moved her blue gun from Henry to Mag Spain. Henry leaned over and chopped down with the edge of his right hand, knocking the blue gun from the girl's fingers.

Mag Spain rushed the redhead. She kicked him in the shins, stuck her fingers into one of his eyes, but he kept coming and put his arms tightly about her.

"Hold her for me," he ordered.

Henry grinned and took the girl in his arms.

Mag Spain stepped back and stooped for the girl's blue gun. His fingers were almost on the gun when he pulled them away. He straightened. Tears were leaking from the eye the girl had gouged. He rubbed the eye, not with an instinctive gesture, but one that was deliberate, as if he had just thought that the motion might be a good idea. Cunning came into his face. He licked his lips as if tasting something he liked.

He drew a handkerchief from his hip pocket. He dropped it over the grip and trigger of the blue gun. He picked up the gun, fumbled with it and wheeled casually to confront the brass-faced Dint Smith.

When he faced Dint Smith squarely, hot flame squirted out of the blue gun. Almost simultaneously, a red spark and a roar of powder came from the muzzle of the six-gun that had suddenly appeared in the brass-faced man's hand.

Mag Spain shivered, his entire body shaking as with the ague. The blue gun, the handkerchief that wrapped it smoking, flew from his fingers and rolled across the floor. He fell loosely forward. He struck the dirt floor, dust gushing from beneath him.

The brass-faced puncher stood up, holding both his six-guns jutted out in front of his hips.

"He thought quick!" he grunted at the white-faced, shuddering girl. "He planned to tap me with a slug from your gun, then swear you done it."

Henry, with the red-headed girl clamped to his chest, suddenly twisted so that she was between him and the brass-faced puncher.

"Let 'im have it!" he yelled. Holding the girl with his left arm, he swept out his gun with his right.

The redhead flipped her legs to one side, then the other, exposing Henry's booted feet. The brass-faced puncher's big hands trembled with his gun roar. His first two bullets knocked Henry's left leg from under him. Henry fell down on the floor on his back, pulling the screaming girl atop him. His gun tongued flame.

The apish man squatted on widely spread feet and unlimbered his guns.

The brass-faced puncher pitched sidewise, his guns roaring. Adobe jumped off the wall behind him. Puffs of dust sprang from the floor beside Henry. The apish man squawled hoarsely and flopped sidewise. He collided with the table; it upset and he fell over it. Hot squirts of acrid powder fumes filled the room. The place bawled with sound.

The apish man knocked the table away from him, almost to the feet of the brass-faced puncher, and started to get up. Dust puffed off the front of his shirt in two places and he no longer tried to get up, but sat there, head hung forward, eyes staring sightlessly down between his knees.

Suddenly the brass-faced puncher shot off both guns at once. Henry's head lost much of its shape and his gun arm fell down laxly.

The red-headed girl flopped off him and lay motionless.

Brass-faced Dint Smith lowered his guns and liquid ran out of his right sleeve. He frowned at the hand, holstered the gun it clasped and held the hand over his sleeve.

He went and looked at the girl, bending over, but not touching her body. He straightened and walked to the door and looked out, his face hard and sullen. He cursed harshly, then went back and took a handkerchief from his hip pocket. He wiped his right hand and, fixing his teeth in a corner, tied it tightly around his arm, above the elbow.

By that time the sullenness had gone from his face. Walking with purposeful swiftness, he went to the brush corral, got his rope off his saddle, snared the dun, saddled and led the animal back to the adobe.

The girl had not moved. He felt of her wrists, slapped them, and slapped her face. He took her by the shoulders and shook her. His brassy face was not so brassy.

He put the girl's blue-steel gun in his pants pocket. Carrying the girl, he went outside, picked up the reins of the horse which bore a saddle that was unmistakably the girl's and mounted the dun.

With the unconscious redhead held in the saddle with him, he rode south, keeping the dun in a gallop, yanking the girl's horse along behind him. Heat beating up from the bare range made perspiration ooze on his face. A covey of sage chickens rose in front of him with a great roaring of wings. Three times jackrabbits sprang away with long leaps. The yelping of a prairie dog town stilled as he rode through it.

He reined up in front of the abandoned dry-farmer shack he and Boy Irons and Mag Spain had passed the night before. The adobe walls of the place were crumbling, much of the dirt roof had washed off, leaving the yellowish mesquite brush which supported what remained sticking out like partly buried skeletons.

Inside, a bunk still stood against one wall. A rickety table tottered on three legs in the middle of the floor. He deposited the girl on the crude dusty slats of the bunk. He felt her wrists again, shook his head and, sitting on the bunk edge, inspected the flesh wound in his right forearm.

A snort from one of the horses outside jerked him erect. Feet clattered on the sun-baked earth and Boy Irons flung through the door. His face was ghastly and pale except for muddy spots in either cheek. He made a harsh whizzing through his teeth. He saw the girl and, still flinging forward, croaked: "Damn you!" His hands turned into a grayish blur at his waist.

The brass-faced puncher jerked a big hand at the rickety table, flipping it through the air. Boy Irons' bullets splintered wood as it came toward him. The table hit him, drove him against the wall beside the door.

The puncher pitched against the table, crushing Boy Irons between it and the wall. His right fist swept up to Boy Irons' pale jaw, bounced away. When he stepped back, Boy Irons fell down slackly between table and wall.

The brass-faced puncher took the girl from the bunk, carried her some fifty yards from the shack and laid her in the net-like shade of a mesquite clump.

Returning, he lifted Boy Irons, sat him against the wall, then slapped his face three times very hard. He went out to the dun, got a whiskey bottle from a saddlebag and poured what whiskey was in the bottle down Boy Irons' throat. Boy Irons' eyes opened a little. The puncher lifted him and he could stand, propped by the wall. "Can you hear me?"

Boy Irons nodded slightly.

"Why'd you try to smoke me?"

"I saw you just as you got here with her," Boy Irons mumbled. "I didn't know what you was gonna do. I guess I kinda went ding then. I been meetin' her almost every day lately. She, well—I asked her to marry me. And she kinda indicated the answer would be yes. I was crazy to do that, too, I guess. She don't know I was workin' for Mag Spain. And she don't know I'm an outlaw."

The brass-faced puncher made a noise in his throat.

"You ain't workin' for Mag Spain now," he snarled. Harshly, swiftly, he told Boy Irons of the killings. "The girl fainted. There's not a mark on her, so she'll come out of it pretty soon. I was bringin' her over here so she wouldn't be mixed up in the hoorah when the bodies are found. You didn't give me time to tell you that. Listen, Boy: This whangjam will stir up the country until we can't rustle anybody's beef. I'll have to meet my gang of cow thieves and take 'em back to Mexico."

Boy Irons nodded vaguely and mumbled: "I guess that's what we better do."

Brass-faced Dint Smith's voice came a low roar.

"We? It ain't 'we' no more, kid! This is the kiss-off for you and me!"

He jammed a hand inside his shirt, pulled out several letters and crowded them into the waistband of Boy Irons' pants. He put a finger against the letters.

"It'll raise hell with your playhouse if the girl finds out why you've been workin' for Mag Spain," he growled. "I ain't got no record on this side of the line. Take these. They're the letters the redhead wrote me when she hired me. She don't know I'm Dint Smith. Tell her you're the gunhand she hired. Tell her you were gettin' the lowdown on Mag Spain before you came to work for her. She hired me as her foreman. You can be that, or her husband, or I don't give a damn what."

He stopped and waited for Boy Irons to say something. Boy Irons said nothing. His smile was inarticulate.

The brass-faced puncher shoved his fist against Boy Irons' smiling mouth.

"Damned sap for luck!" he said thickly. "Make her a good husband!"

He went out and got on the white-stockinged dun bronc and rode south, not looking back at the red-headed girl trying to sit up in the shade of the mesquite shrub.

· · · · ·

The Sudden-Disaster Gent

The pewee-sized gent was not much to look at. But it was evident he was a lot to look out for. His knobby hands had tendons like Colt barrels and hairs as big as shingle nails. Somebody had stood on his nose in the past. The rest of his face looked like it had been walked on many times. Catawampus across the top of his head, his hair had a permanent part. His neck resembled a bundle of wire hawsers on which the skin had been painted.

The undersized puncher made a yawping sound as he yawned. He stretched beneath the soogan and tarp of his bedroll. Lids came apart over one bleak, yellowish eye, but slitted as the morning sun flamed into a sleepy eyeball. The eyeball rolled sluggishly. It rested on something under a gray sagebrush a few feet away—

"Hell! Whew!" he whizzed through his teeth.

A young woman sprawled under the sagebrush. Thin cotton rope bound her, wrist and ankle. A bandana handkerchief gagged her. Her feet and hands were small, shapely. She had curly brown hair. Her eyes were closed and had long lashes. The bandana gag was pushing against her nose, but it was probably snub anyway.

She had not been here when he bedded down the night before.

The sawed-off puncher said again, harshly, through his teeth: "Hell! Whew!"

His face began to turn gray. He soaked his lips with his tongue. From under his pillow he pulled cartridge belts and two black Colts and cinched the guns to his hips without getting out of the bedroll. He found his boots under the tarp, stuffed his feet into them. He looked at the palms of his hands, saw sweat. He wiped the sweat on his pants.

A frightened jackrabbit sailed out of the sagebrush—abruptly—saw him, took greater fright and skittered off madly in a different direction.

The undersized puncher shivered slightly. He drew the soogan up over his head and pulled on his hat under it. Wrapping the heavy soogan about him until only his eyes showed, he stood up.

"Whew!" Sweat came out on the puncher's homely face.

He walked quickly toward the waterhole a score of yards away.

"Not so swift, brother!" bawled a voice in the sagebrush.

The peewee ranny frog-jumped for the gully in which the waterhole lay. He landed on hands and knees in foot-deep water and mud. Flinging off the soogan, jerking partially erect, he went up the gully in a boiling maelstrom of water. He glanced back at the spot where the bound form of the girl lay.

Two men were charging for the gully, taking long, spraddling leaps. One was a great solid giant of a fellow whose face was an unsmooth mass

38

of bones and whose upper lip was divided like that of a rabbit. He carried two six-guns.

Beside him ran an elongated, stringy man. The morning sun flashed on the nickel-plated star pinned to his flapping vest. Rigidly out in front of him, he held a Winchester.

The peewee-sized ranny rolled his right-hand Colt over the gully rim, driving three bullets in front of the pair. They flopped into the sage, guns returning gulps of flame and noise.

"Salt him, bronc peelers!" bawled the stringy sheriff. "Unravel some lead!"

Leathering his Colt, the peewee ranny gave attention to picking his boots up and setting them down. He got out of the water, plugged through mud, hit hard sand. Lead made squawkings and whuppings over his head. Earth, dried grass and sage stems fell into the gully by bucketfuls. There seemed to be a half-dozen men pushing lead at him.

He dodged into a side draw, left the metal storm behind. The side draw narrowed, sank, a wiggling gash, in sandstone. He looked back at brown messy tracks his muddy boots left. His tongue between his teeth, he climbed the side of the draw. At the top, flat in runty sage and pale Spanish bayonet, he pulled off the muddy boots, put them under his left arm and slid back into the sandstone gash. His sock feet leaving no marks, he ran on, away from the muddy trail that indicated plainly he had left the draw.

A few rods farther and he doubled into another gully. That one petered soon, spitting him out belly-down on the Spanish bayonet and sage and cactus cankered top of a hill.

He slithered forward, arms, stomach, legs collecting cactus that stuck to him like big green ticks. Reaching the crest of the hill, he peered over. Both knotty hands splayed for his Colt grips.

A dozen yards down the slope a man perched on a mealy-nosed roan horse and held the reins of five other horses.

The man rode a side saddle. One of his legs was not as straight as the other. His hair was salted with gray over the ears, although he was not much older than thirty. A cigarette stuck to the corner of his mouth. He was coaxing a mean-eyed, flea-bitten sorrel bronc to eat sugar out of his hand.

The peewee ranny jutted a Colt in front of each yellowish eye.

"All right, camp-tender! Hang onto them broncs and don't make no gestures that might cause a funeral!"

The man in the side saddle looked up—did not spill any of the sugar from the palm of his hand.

"So you done an Indian on 'em," he said around his cigarette. "I kinda figured from the amount of gun talk that you hadn't laid down and turned up your toes peaceable-like."

"Skin yourself! Do it with two fingers!"

When the man in the side saddle had drawn his gun with two fingers and dropped it, the undersized puncher squirmed over the hilltop and stood up.

"They wanted a corpse, huh?"

"Four of 'em probably figured that'd help. The sheriff, not bein' on the inside like the others, might've been satisfied with somebody heavy enough to stretch hemp."

The peewee puncher showed his teeth in a cat-grin "They was tryin' to make it look like I kidnapped the girl, huh?"

The other man chuckled dryly and squinted smoke out of his nose.

"Maybe *you* call it tryin', but it strikes me they done the job up tight. You're over your hat in trouble, Mister Craggy Storms."

The peewee ranny's jaw fell down. He pulled it up with a snap and said:

"Get loose from the crowbait!"

The man slid off the side saddle, favoring the one of his legs which was not as straight as the other. When he advanced to hand over the reins of the horses, he moved with a shuffle and skip gait.

"What do they attract your attention with?" asked peewee Craggy Storms.

"Drink, poker chips and food, in that order. Once I got a check that said Skipper Edwards on it."

"Wise guy, eh? Skipper Edwards! Never heard of you. How'n hell'd you know my name?"

Skipper Edwards shook his head. "You're fixin' to talk yourself full of holes. Better drag it. Them gun jaspers'll be here in a minute."

Craggy Storms pulled on his boots, singled out the mean-eyed, flea-bitten sorrel and hairpinned the animal. He squinted down at Skipper Edwards.

"You ain't a bad Johnnie."

"Much obliged," said Skipper Edwards dryly. "But I keep bad company, cowboy. Better put your tail in the air and travel. It's open season for Craggy Storms."

The peewee ranny put his tongue between his teeth, took it out to ask: "Fork a bronc for the Slash Circle?"

Skipper Edwards raised his shoulders up and let them fall.

"I don't fork a bronc. I ain't forked one since a Boche potato-masher spoke its piece beside me in France. I'm the Slash Circle cook. That is, I cook when Miss Vicks Cox is at school in Des Moines. Other times I'm just kinda the Mexican Joe around the place."

"Vicks Cox the girl that was tied near me?"

Skipper Edwards' face hardened. His lips got thin and blue.

"They drugged her, damn them!" he said in a low hoarse voice. "She didn't know what they were doin'. Her own half-brother did that to her. The lousy pup!"

Little Craggy Storms leaned over the saddle pommel.

"Can't visit no longer. Don't think they saw me good. It'd help if you hadn't either."

Skipper Edwards grinned slightly. "All but the sheriff saw you when they planted the girl. But they're not supposed to have until they got there with the sheriff. So nobody's seen you if I haven't. I'll say you sneaked up when my back was turned. Better make it look real."

Craggy Storms nodded. "What's Cox's handle? What's he look like?"

"Split Cox. Big, bony, can't-whistle jasper."

"Got a harelip, huh! I saw him, then. Why don't he want me to take over the Slash Circle?" Instantly after he had finished the question, Craggy Storms stood up in the saddle, strained his ears, then said: "Never mind. Stand still while I make it look real."

Leaning over, he swung the barrel of a Colt against Skipper Edwards' head. Skipper Edwards shut his eyes and stood blindly in the path of the gun. After he had been hit, he fell backward stiffly.

Craggy Storms stuck spurs in the flea-bitten sorrel, the bronc leaped away, the other horses, led, loping in its wake. Craggy Storms doubled, became shapeless over the saddle.

He covered four or five hundred yards before a yell rang from the top of the hill. A rifle bullet moved past with a shrill squeal. Craggy spurred down into a draw. Hauling the led broncs close and reaching out, he tore off the bridles, one after another. The freed horses ran on at top speed.

Craggy Storms threw the bridles away, then bent his efforts to herding the horses northward, where he knew lay the cowtown of Git, Wyoming.

Something wet hit the back of his hand. He felt, discovered his face running with perspiration. He laughed and swabbed it with his sleeve.

"Kind of a warmish country!" He put two fingers in his left hip pants-pocket and took an envelope out.

MR. C. CUSTIS KING,
MEXICALI, MEXICO

He put the envelope betwixt his teeth while fishing for tobacco and papers. The tobacco was soaked, the papers damply gooed together. He put them back and drew a letter from the envelope.

Dear Mr. King:

I beg to advise receipt of your letter saying you have taken over the Slash Circle ranch as payment of a debt, but that you are unable to take charge yourself and will send a man named Craggy Storms to run the outfit for you.

Your letter also asks dope on the Slash Circle.

I regret to say that during the last few years the ranch has lost money steadily, due to the range not being good, dry summers, bad winters, the blackleg, etc.

The former owner of the Slash Circle, the man you got it from, has not lived here for seven years. During that time, I have been foreman. I am considered a good cowman, so I am sure the ranch cannot make money.

However, it might be sold to some outfit. If you wish, I will be glad to undertake the selling. That way, you can save the expense of sending your man, Craggy Storms, up here. Knowing the markets, I could get you a better price than a stranger.

Trusting you will sell instead of losing money by trying to operate the Slash Circle,

I am,

Yours truly,

E.A. Cox
Foreman, Slash Circle Ranch
Git, Wyoming

Craggy Storms returned the letter to the envelope and the envelope to his pocket. He grinned all over his homely face and made a *tsk! tsk!* sound in the roof of his mouth.

"Range ain't what she should be, summers dry, winters bad, dogies got the blackleg," he said harshly to the flea-bitten sorrel. "So Split Cox says the Slash Circle won't make no money for nobody. Just the same, he's goin' to pains to see I don't take charge. Bronc, it's too danged bad we didn't get to talk awhile longer with the Johnnie who rides the side-saddle. We'll have to get hold of him again, or somebody else, and find out why Split Cox don't want us around."

He yelled, waved his arms, hazing the bridleless horses.

Some three hours later, he sighted Git from the crest of a ridge. The cow-town was splattered against the side of a hill. He headed the horses away from Git and got them running. He dismounted, removed the bridle from the flea-bitten sorrel and sent the animal pounding after the others. The bridle he dropped in a handy prairie dog hole. He slid into a draw, found a level spot between narrow, steep banks that almost met overhead, and lay down on his back.

The long day had reddened and darkened to black night before Craggy Storms left the draw.

He walked to Git and entered the cow-town without, he believed, being observed. He clumped down a broad sidewalk, crossed a street in which dust was deep enough to run into his boots, sidled carefully between horses that were thick along a hitchrack, and parted two swinging doors over which a sign said:

SAM CROW'S RECREATION PARLOR

The place was lighted by three pear-shaped electric bulbs dangling from the ceiling. It had a long bar to the right. Dice, faro, poker, casino, seven-up and keno games took up the floor space. Craggy Storms went to the bar. A pale man came and wiped a towel on the bar in front of him.

"I hanker to wild up," said Craggy Storms. "See if you got my brand of mule sweat."

The pale man grinned, put a thick-bottomed whiskey glass and a bottle on the bar and leaned his elbows behind them.

"Guess you heard 'bout the kidnappin'?"

Craggy Storms poured a glassful of the stuff in the bottle into a cavernous mouth, batted yellowish eyes twice before he said: "Ain't got the lowdown on it yet."

The pale man flicked his limp towel across his shoulder.

"Split Cox's half-sister, just back from school in Des Moines, was kidnapped from the Slash Circle last night. They rescued the girl before she was hurt any, but the varmint who done it got away. Sheriff and the Slash Circle Johnnies been huntin' him all day. But they don't know just what he looks like. None of 'em saw him good. Girl didn't see him. He drugged her."

"Hell! Oughta string a polecat who'd do that!"

"Dontcha worry, brother—they will. Split Cox ain't so well thought of by some, but Miss Vicks is only his half-sister, and she sure is popular."

A bowlegged man, banging a silver dollar on the bar, called loudly for bug juice and the pale man went to wait on him.

Craggy Storms hitched his belts, got a fistful of bologna and brown bread from the lunch bowl and went over to watch a poker game.

He took a chair against the wall, next to an open window where it was cool, and where he could keep an eye on the front door as well as listen to the gossip at nearby tables. He rolled a cigarette, got it working, hooked his toes behind the front legs of his chair and leaned back.

He was finishing the bologna and bread when the swinging doors swelled inward to let a thick-bodied man through. The thick-bodied man peered about from under lids pulled down over uneasy, watery eyes. His lips were meaty. He wore one gun.

"That's one of them Slash Circle Johnnies now," said a man at a table near Craggy Storms.

The thick-bodied Slash Circle rider worked slowly among the game tables, seemingly observing the play. But as Craggy Storms watched the man's progress, the corners of his mouth sank downward a little and his yellowish eyes began to burn like balls of hot sulphur in his homely face. He unhooked his toes from the chair and let them hang down, touching the floor.

The breeze through the open window at his elbow blew squirming horizontal worms of smoke from the cigarette sticking to his lower lip.

The thick-bodied Slash Circle rider stopped abruptly in front of him. The fellow licked his lips.

"Ain't I seen you somewhere previous, feller?" he asked in a voice meant to carry.

Several men looked up from nearby tables.

Undersized Craggy Storms lifted a face that was sleepily stupid except for the hot yellow smouldering in his eyes.

"Take a walk, sweetheart!" he said harshly. "You're monkeyin' with sudden disaster!"

The thick-bodied Slash Circle rider's knees bent so that he squatted a little. His lips pulled together.

"Damn my eyes! You're the Siwash who got away from us this mornin'. You're—"

The three lights went out—suddenly. Black dark gushed into the place.

"Nail him!" bawled the thick-bodied man in the sepia abyss. "He's the varmint who kidnapped Miss Vicks!"

Craggy Storms put his feet flat on the floor and raised off his chair. But before he could stand upright, a great hard arm came through the window behind him and took him around the neck. The arm jerked him back against the sill of the open window. A big hand rasped down his side, plucked the Colt out of his right holster. The Colt twice jetted flame and powder noise. Then the hand dropped the gun on the floor and the great hard arm released Craggy Storms' neck. Whoever had reached through the open window and taken hold of him went away. It all happened in splits of seconds.

The three lights came on, squirting pale whiteness.

Craggy Storms shucked his left Colt and trained it on the crowd. He hunkered down and got the other gun.

His lids were peeled off yellowish eyes that were hot and mad. His face was a twisted, ugly purple mask on which old scars showed like child-scribbled chalk marks.

"Stand gentle!"

In front of him the thick-bodied Slash Circle rider lay on his face on the floor. The fellow's hips bucked up feebly a time or two before they got still and his fingers uncurled to lie flat on the floor.

The swinging doors bulged, admitted a man into the place, a great giant of a man whose face was an unsmooth mass of bones and whose upper lip was divided like that of a rabbit. Split Cox! He stopped and, not moving thumbs hooked in his belt, asked a question.

"What the hell? What the hell?"

A man who had stiff arms up pressing against his ears answered: "One of your rannies recognized this varmint as the kidnapper and got a couple of windows in himself for his trouble."

Split Cox raised big shoulders a little. Thumbs pulled out of his belt and the palms of his big gloved hands pressed flat against his belly.

"That's skookum!" he said harshly. "We'll give the heel a chance to drop his flame-throwers. If he don't, we'll splash him all over the walls!"

Unexpectedly, through the open window behind Craggy Storms, a six-gun banged three times: The three lights overhead blacked out with a smatter of glass and a snarling play of green electric fire.

Craggy Storms pitched sidewise. His elbows jerked, knocked two men down. Somebody's gun gushed a yard-long plume of flame. Somebody else bawled fear. Chairs and tables upset.

"He's makin' for the door!" a man yelped.

Craggy Storms snapped back against the wall. He found a window. This one was closed, the glass slick and cool to his fingers. He holstered his Colts, wrapped his arms about his face and dived headlong through the panes. He landed on his arms and chest in a cloud of glass and splinters. A dim figure skipped to his side.

"This way! Quick!" hissed Skipper Edwards.

Craggy Storms jerked erect. He sprinted away in the rear of buildings. Skipper Edwards, trying to follow with his gliding skip gait, rapidly dropped behind.

"Hell and all!" Craggy Storms whirled, caught Skipper Edwards below the hips, flung the man across his shoulders, then ran on away from the bawling, hell-in-a-box inside Sam Crow's Recreation Parlor.

"Gee a little!" Skipper Edwards grunted. "Slash Circle broncs are tied to the livery stable corral."

Craggy Storms changed his course, said: "Talk fast, cowboy!"

"Split Cox didn't get along with that ranny who was just salivated—he'd been askin' too big a cut of Split's stealin's. Split jobbed him. Told the ranny to go in and accuse you of bein' the kidnapper. Told the ranny he'd shoot through the window if you drew. Instead, another Slash Circle puncher pulled the light switch, Split Cox reached in the window, got your gun and shot the ranny. He's got you stuck with a murder now, besides the kidnappin'."

"Why, cowboy? Why?"

"'Cause he's stole most of the Slash Circle stock. Every fall he puts his brand, the Hard Knot, on the Slash Circle calf crop. He's been doin' that for seven years. Now his herd is bigger'n the Slash Circle. If you'd take over the Slash Circle, he knows there'll be some questions about this year calves bein' branded Hard Knot and runnin' with Slash Circle cows. Besides, if you take the Slash Circle, he won't have any range to run the stuff he's stole. He wrote this feller King you're workin' for, hopin' to buy the Slash Circle cheap. That didn't work and he's tryin' to run you outta the country."

A corral, snorting broncs anchored to its bars, swelled up in the darkness.

"Here we are."

"What's your next play, Edwards?"

"It's out the bailiwick for me. Split was kinda leery of my story this mornin' about not seein' you. Now he'll know I shot out them lights. I ain't much good as a fightin' man, so I'm rollin'."

"Why've you stuck this long?"

Skipper Edwards blew out a brittle laugh.

"The hombre who used to own the Slash Circle was a no-good. He left the country after he killed his wife. I didn't worry too much if the Slash Circle didn't make a profit when he had it. I'm no good as a range hand. Can't ride nothin' but a side saddle on account of my leg. I ain't even a fair cook. So my job meant considerable to me, feller. But she's gettin' too raw. I'm draggin' it."

Craggy Storms counted the broncs. Four of them.

"One ranny at the Slash Circle with the girl now, huh? Where's the Slash Circle from town?"

"Yes." Skipper Edwards gave terse directions. "But you better show some brains and blow, feller."

"I'll blow!" Craggy Storms said thickly. "I'll blow hell out of them! They can't fog me! I'll blow hell out of them! Yes, I will!"

He untied one of the broncs. wheeled the animal away from the corral rails, stopped in front of Skipper Edwards. "Girl know her half-brother's been slappin' his brand on the Slash Circle calf crop?"

"No." Skipper Edwards said it thickly.

"She the reason you been stayin' with the Slash Circle?"

Skipper Edwards lifted a face that, even in the gloom, showed mad twistings of pain.

"You go to hell!" he said hoarsely and walked off.

It was past midnight when Craggy Storms sighted, close to the black range, red pins that were lighted windows in the Slash Circle ranch buildings.

The trail snaked across a creek, the banks of which were hairy with willows. He left the bronc tied in the willows and went afoot across a greasewood flat toward the red pips.

One lighted window was in the ranch house, the others in the bunkhouse. No stir of life was in the ranch house when he circled the squatty building. He stalked to the bunkhouse, a couple of hundred feet away.

A tubby, bat-eared man sat in the bunkhouse, snapping cards down on a table between an oil lamp and a flat bottle of whiskey. He was alone. The door was open.

Craggy Storms removed his boots. He walked into the bunkhouse on his sock toes and took the tubby, bat-eared man's throat in both hands. The bat-eared man did not look up until fingers were in the flesh of his throat. What air was in his mouth blew out a fine spray through his teeth.

Craggy Storms upset backward the bat-eared man and the chair in which he sat. They came to the floor without much noise. Craggy Storms got on the man's chest and put his legs around the fellow's plump shanks and the chair so that the lower part of him was helpless. He held his breath and pressed rigid, quivering arms against hands almost buried in the man's throat. When the bat-eared man hit him on the ear with a fist, Craggy's pressure increased. The bat-eared man's struggles got weaker.

After three or four minutes, his arms fell down limply on the floor.

Relaxing, Craggy Storms straightened the tubby, bat-eared man out and tied him wrist and ankle with a lass rope off a saddle lying beside the door, then poured whiskey in his mouth. When the fellow groaned, Craggy Storms got a big German sock out of a dusty pair of overshoes under a bunk and stuffed it in his mouth.

"Can you write?"

The bat-eared man glared at him. Undersized Craggy Storms laughed.

"Sudden disaster has overtook you, feller! Why t'hell d'you think I squeezed your gullet instead of hammerin' your conk with a six-gun if it wasn't to show you there's ways and ways of dyin'? You write out a confession and sign her. Then be prepared to tell the sheriff about it."

"I think," said a feminine voice abruptly from the door, "he'll gladly tell the sheriff about it!"

Craggy Storms turned his head and looked into the round black eye of a Winchester barrel and past it into the face of the young woman he had seen tied beside him that morning. Her face was pale, determined. The Winchester hammer was crouched back and her finger was curled against the fang-like trigger.

The bat-eared man spat the German sock out of his mouth.

"Watch him! He's the varmint who carried you off last night!"

The girl betrayed faint puzzlement.

"So you came back to try again. I don't understand this. I never saw you before. Why did you do it? What was that talk about confessions?"

The bat-eared man heaved on the floor.

"He'll spring a pack of lies on you, Miss Vicks! Get me loose and I'll handle him!"

The girl looked at Craggy Storms intently. "Drop those guns and be careful! I don't think you'd be very heavy on my conscience if I shot you!"

Craggy Storms hesitated. "Will you listen to something then?"

"I'll listen."

Craggy Storms dropped his guns clanking to the bunkhouse floor. The girl untied the tubby, bat-eared man. The bat-eared man got up, took a chair and broke it to pieces over Craggy Storms' head and shoulders. Craggy Storms slumped down loosely on the floor.

"Sudden disaster! I'll sudden disaster you!"

Craggy Storms was lying on his back on a table when he opened his eyes. Two oil lamps in wall brackets and curtains on the one window that he could see told him he was in the ranch house. He said something thickly unintelligible and sat up.

Split Cox, waiting beside the table, hit him in the face with a big fist, knocking him off the table. Split Cox carefully stood him on his feet, knocked him down again with a short blow to the stomach, then took his shoulders and slung him loosely back on the table.

He said harshly: "I'd sure like to string you up! But I guess the law'll do it anyway."

Craggy Storms rolled dull yellowish eyes between slitted, pain-racked lids. The tubby, bat-eared man stood back of the table. The girl sat on a chair with her hands folded in her lap. She was watching Craggy Storms, but when he looked at her, she glanced away. No one else was in the room.

Split Cox put the tip of his tongue in the divided place in his lips.

"We sent a man after the sheriff," he said. "He'll be here pretty soon now."

Then Skipper Edwards, holding two six-guns in front of him, came in the door with a skipping-jump and said: "Put 'm up!"

The bat-eared man lifted his hands while his mouth fell open and his lips made sucking movements. Split Cox held his big hands in front of his stomach and stared.

Craggy Storms sat up, took his right leg with both hands and swung it—then the other—off the table top.

"You happen around at the handiest times," he mumbled thickly.

Skipper Edwards said: "I got to thinkin'. So I got on the deck of my bronc and set sail. Been waitin' outside the door for you to wake up." He waved his two guns at Split Cox. "Get 'm up, damn you! I'll blow your head off!"

The girl's eyes came open wide. Horror filled them and all her face.

"Oh!" she screamed shrilly. "Oh! You mean it! You'd kill my brother! You would!"

She flung at Skipper Edwards, striking hysterically. He tried to shove her away with his right hand, saying: "Now, honey, watch out! Watch out!"

A black six-gun was small in Split Cox's big hand as he drew and fired. Skipper Edwards yelped and his gun spilled out of his left hand. The girl squealed and her hysteria went away as suddenly as it had come and she flung herself back as abruptly as she had flung herself forward.

Split Cox threw a chair that knocked Skipper Edwards down, then leaped and kicked the other gun out of Skipper's hand.

Undersized Craggy Storms slid off the table and stood on weakly shaking legs. The bat-eared man hit him in the face with a fist and he fell down. Then he kicked Craggy Storms under the table, upset the table and continued kicking him until his body only shook with the impacts. After he stopped, Craggy Storms lay face down on the floor, lips drawn fixedly off his teeth.

His bony face dark and sullen, Split Cox looked down at Skipper Edwards. The blue of Skipper Edwards' shirt sleeve between elbow and shoulder was getting red.

"Damned swell of you to come around," said Split Cox. "I been wonderin' how we was gonna shut your trap. But you fixed that; you sure did." He jerked his head at unmoving Craggy Storms. "He'll kill another man before the sheriff gets him. He'll kill you tryin' to get away, then get killed himself. That'll settle all of it. The whole works."

The girl brought her hands to her mouth and put the tips of her fingers between her teeth.

"What are you talking about?" she cried around her fingers.

Split Cox looked at her. He separated his rabbit lips over his teeth. "I guess you gotta know all about it. You gotta tell he sheriff this runt shot

Skipper tryin' to make a break. He grabbed my gun, see. And he shot Skipper, see. Just like this!"

He pointed his six-gun at Skipper Edwards' forehead and pulled the trigger. But Skipper Edwards twisted and the lead tore a hole through the floor where his head had been. He clawed wildly at Split Cox's legs with his good arm.

Split Cox backed up hastily and kicked him. Skipper Edwards upset on the side of his wounded arm. Split Cox drove his boot toe solidly against Skipper's jaw. Skipper rolled over on his back and was still.

Split Cox again slanted his six at Skipper Edwards' forehead.

"'Betcha he don't duck this'n!"

"My Heavenly Father!" screamed the girl. *"What have I done!"* She flung herself across the gun arm, knocking it aside, seizing it with her arms and both her hands.

Split Cox shook his gun arm. He cursed. The girl screamed again, shrilly. He doubled his left fist and hit two blows on her back. "Leggo, you damned brat!" The girl got the thumb of his gun hand in her mouth and bit it. Split Cox roared at the bat-eared man:

"Pull her off! Bop her brains out!"

Undersized Craggy Storms got up weakly from the floor. He reached out blindly to the table, picked up the table and staggered with it against the bat-eared man. The latter upset so that he sat down on the floor.

Craggy Storms, making shrill noises with his mouth, raised the table the full length of his arms overhead and brought it down on the bat-eared man's head. His great weakness and the great effort of swinging the table caused him to fall down.

Split Cox looked around. He gave a bawling sound of rage. Making a great bony block of his free fist, he brought it against the nape of the girl's neck. She collapsed off his gun arm onto the floor.

Craggy Storms put his right hand under the table, brought it out almost at once, holding one of the bat-eared man's guns. He gave a high, mad laugh and worked the trigger with his finger.

Split Cox put his left hand, open fingered, over his stomach. His gun lifted slowly. Something seemed to knock his chest back a little between his shoulders. When his gun was straight out in front of him, he let it fall to the floor. He took his hand from his stomach, put it down, feeling for the floor, then fell flaccidly atop the hand.

Craggy Storms unclasped his fingers from the bat-eared man's hot, empty gun, put his face on the floor and shut his eyes tightly.

A stringy man with a nickel-plated sheriff's star on his vest came, breathing heavily as if he had been running, and stood in the door.

Craggy Storms stretched stiff, sore muscles to get the full benefit of the morning sun that pressed warmth against the log side of the Slash Circle ranch house.

The stringy sheriff walked out of the ranch house and sat on the bench beside him.

"Bat-ears spilled the beans," the sheriff said. "After that, and after what you and Skipper Edwards and Miss Cox told me, the ranny who came to town after me thought he had better empty himself too. So he did. The girl just signed a bill of sale returning to the Slash Circle all the cows her brother stole."

Craggy Storms squinted at the sheriff, wrinkles nearly hiding his brightly alert, yellowish eyes.

"Then I'm clear?"

"Looks like it. The coroner just finished his inquest over Split Cox's body by givin' you a vote of thanks."

Somebody called the sheriff from inside the ranch house and he went in.

Craggy Storms got up and walked stiffly to the horse corral. He took a rope off a saddle hanging on the top rail, singled out a long-legged blue roan bronc and dallied the rope onto the horse. He put the kak on the animal, cinched up, and led the bronc toward the ranch house,

Skipper Edwards came out of the ranch house, his wounded arm in a sling, and hopped toward him. Skipper's face was excitedly flushed. Words tumbled out of his mouth while he was yet a dozen yards away.

"I don't savvy this a-tall! Sheriff just handed me a paper that says I've been deeded a half interest in the Slash Circle and authorized to run the ranch."

Craggy Storms took hold of the saddle horn and tested the cinch for tightness.

"What's the matter? Ain't you ready to quit cookin' fur a livin'?"

Skipper Edwards' mouth worked up and down at the ends.

"I—I've—I feel like a kid who's just seen Santy Claus," he said. "But this deed—was signed by King—the man who sent you up here."

Homely faced Craggy Storms grinned thinly. "King signed the deed," he said.

"But—the hell! Then you're King?"

Craggy Storms flipped the reins over the roan's neck.

"This King hombre," he said harshly, "he's no good. He's an outlaw. His scalp is price-tagged from Montana to Mexico. So when King won this ranch in a poker game, he thought a jasper named Craggy Storms had better come up and see about it. Now Craggy Storms has gotta be gettin' along before somebody starts lookin' for the feller named King. If you get what I mean."

Skipper Edwards said slowly: "I savvy—King."

Craggy Storms swung into the saddle "You got my address in Mexico. Might mail me an invite to the weddin'. Kinda like to have it, even if I can't come."

Skipper Edwards reddened. "Aw!" he said. "How'd you know?"

Craggy Storms' face was suddenly wistful. "I didn't." he said harshly. "I was just wonderin'."

· · · · ·

The Gun Quest

The gent rode hunched over his kak horn, always with his right hand tangled far forward in the mane of his black cayuse. The night was warmly black around him. Hot wind pushed into his face.

Overhead, thunder thumped and gobbled, and occasional lightning glared into the sage-walled Wyoming range trails

Scenting something the wind carried, the black cayuse threw its head. The rider, detecting the move with the hand tangled in its mane, pulled up and listened. Silently, he spilled out of the saddle. Quieting fingers on the bronc's muzzle, he led it aside up a sand-floored gully.

Lightning glare splattered whitely upon the man as he crouched, waiting—a great nemesis of a figure, nearly seven feet tall, bowed legs making him appear wider at the knees than at the shoulders, bones thinly sheathed with flesh that looked as hard as petrified wood. His clothes were faded and nondescript, the attire of a sifter, a range tramp, a rider of the chuckline.

His two wood-gripped, triggerless .44s filled holsters that were not tied down and had the bottoms cut off so that the barrels projected through. The guns were minus front sights. The hog hide of his Cheyenne tree saddle was gummy with dust sticking to recently applied oil.

He listened, one hand a claw on the muzzle of the black bronc, as a rider who had been behind trotted abreast and passed. Then he relaxed, thumbs hooking restfully in the beltless waistband of his pants. His thin rip of a mouth made a grin.

"Just a bronc peeler—"

Shots cracked down the trail, sending gun noise tumbling in a sudden roar. Hoofbeats rattled in wild flight. The clatter came abreast and descended into the gully.

A voice, low, grinding with pain, pleaded: "Whoa, girl—whoa—!"

Sand scattered as the rider spurred into the gully. The gent with the sifter look leaped aside, reached up and by blind guess trapped a man's throat and arms in his great bony hands. A loose bundle, the rider came out of his kak.

Lightning blazed upon them. The second man was also tall, but his flesh was not as hard and there was more of it. And his chest had received at least two gun slugs. In the brief skyfire flash, his eyes, glittery with pain, traveled the sifter's great length.

"Long Shorty Sims—from the Utah country!" he croaked.

The sifter gent clapped a hand down and tilted a .44 without unleathering it. His voice was an ugly rumble deep as the thunder above, but lower; it carried little farther than his arms could reach.

"Yeah. You got me pegged—but I never seen you before, fella!"

The wounded man made words by jerks. "I've seen—Long Shorty Sims' map on posters—in the Utah country. Ten thousand, dead or alive."

Long Shorty Sims, who looked like a sifter, took the guns of the stranger who knew him. Jumping down the gully, he fanned lead among the trail at the bushwhacker spread.

From two places metal came squawking back, showering him with dirt. He thumbed at the flashes, then scuttled a retreat. The wounded man was hanging to his kak horn by his hands, head drooping.

Long Shorty rumbled: "Who you, fella?"

The other hauled his head up: "Name—Brad Daggert."

Long Shorty slitted his eyes in a lightning flicker. "Seems I recollect a Brad Dagger in the Utah country who was worth a couple of thousand, too."

"That's right."

His voice a roar that hardly got out of his lungs, Long Shorty Sims asked: "Them other jaspers the law?"

"Nope." The other forced the word out twice. "Nope."

Leaping up the gully bank. Long Shorty shot once at random, then pitched aside. Lead from two guns ripped through the sage. He fired at the powder stabs and made a man yelp.

The second bushwhacker called: "Creased?"

"Hell, no—but he plumb ruined twenty dollars worth of hat!" snarled the other. "He's shore tough—I bored him twice in the wind box."

Long Shorty coasted down the gully side on his heels and gathered up the reins of the two broncs. He hooked an arm around Brad Daggert.

Through a gurgling, Brad Daggert said: "Thanks, pard. But 'tain't no use. I'm buckin' out."

Long Shorty stripped open his rip of a mouth and wet its edges. "Tough break, Daggert. Maybe they was after me. Even my corpse is worth that ten thousand, shipped back to Utah."

"Nope." Brad Daggert was about gone. His arms moved spasmodically.

Long Shorty abruptly splayed fingers over the dying man's hands—for Brad Daggert had clawed a gun out of his shirt. Long Shorty wrenched and got it, a tiny six. He thought Daggert wanted to shoot himself.

Losing the gun seemed to excite Daggert. He gulped fragments of sentences that didn't quite make sense.

"That gun—Del Payne—Keyhole outfit down the trail—" His voice became too faint to understand.

"I didn't get much of that, fella," Long Shorty said gently.

Brad Daggert made no attempt to repeat.

Long Shorty lowered him and felt of his wrists. He unfolded from the gully bottom like a carpenter's rule as he got up.

"Takin' the gun away didn't keep him alive long," he grunted softly.

He stowed the little six in his pocket, bent down again and searched. In a pants pocket dead Brad Daggert had some silver and a buckskin poke gold-heavy for its size. Long Shorty hesitated, left the silver and took the poke.

Leading his black cayuse, he retreated up the gully a hundred yards. He tied the bronc to a sage root in such a manner that it wouldn't be likely to raise its head and nicker. Confident the two bushwhackers were unaware of his presence, he went silently back.

One of the killers had just found the body.

"Here he is—deader'n a door nail!" he yelled.

"Search him, Speed," his companion called from neat the trail.

A dozen yards from them, concealed around a bend in the gully, Long Shorty Sims stared as lightning licked above. He wondered if the pair would see his tracks. He relaxed a bit—cows had recently used the gully bed as a trail. His tracks would go unnoticed in the welter.

"He ain't totin' no little shootin' iron with gold handles!" suddenly barked the bushwhacker who searched.

"Hell he ain't! You sure?"

"Come here and frisk him yourself, Shag."

Long Shorty Sims took from his pants pocket the tiny six Brad Daggert had carried, stared at it as sky fire cracked. It had gold grip plates.

Shag, apparently having searched the body himself, growled: "Nope. It ain't here. We've wasted some lead."

"Damn the luck!" Speed cursed. "Let's roll our freight. It's gonna rain pitchforks in a minute. That'll wash our sign away."

"The boss will have a worm when he learns we didn't get it," Shag complained. "C'mon! We'll leave the body in the trail where somebody'll find it."

They moved away, stumbling under the weight of dead Brad Daggert. Long Shorty followed, curious to get a good look at the pair. But he didn't get it until they had deposited the body in the trail and were on their horses. Even then he learned little. They were two squat hombres who hunched like bullfrogs in their kaks.

Long Shorty Sims went back and hairpinned his black cayuse and rode down the trail, taking the same direction as the bushwhacker pair, Speed and Shag. But he traveled slowly enough that there was no likelihood of his overhauling them.

Lightning stretched a snake of sizzling flame from the sky to the range, filling the air with the odor of ozone and scorched sage. The heavens were full of bumping thunder now. After a bit, the clouds opened and rain came in hissing sheets.

Off to the right, a lightning-burst revealed a shack like a scarlet box. Long Shorty rode to it and found a deserted line shack. He pulled off, dropped the tool chest from the black bronc's mouth and took bridle and kak and corona saddle blanket inside. He started a fire in the sheet-iron stove, using matches he shook out of a flat whiskey bottle. Leaving the stove lids off for the night, he skinned his wet clothes.

Crouched beside the stove, he inspected the gold-handled six-gun. It was a .32 with an engraved barrel, worth possibly seventy-five dollars. Hardly enough to kill a man for.

A hot iron had burned "Brad Daggert" near the top of the buckskin poke. He opened it, saw it held a little gold dust, and, hefting it, rumbled: "Worth maybe three hundred."

Shaking his heap, he prepared to get some shut-eye. "Don't make sense, them bushwhackin' a man for this. I'll turn the stuff over to this Del Payne hombre at the Keyhole—I guess."

CHAPTER II
The Praying Gent

A hot sun had finished half its morning climb when Long Shorty Sims rode up to the Keyhole ranch. He had not seen a cow or horse with the Keyhole brand. The place had a run-down look. Rails were dropping out of the horse corral. The feed shed was a canting ruin. Broken panes in the bunkhouse windows were plugged with gunnysacks.

The roof of the log ranch house sagged and the logs needed chinking. Swallows swooped and zoomed about the building, and their mud nests clung under the eaves by the score. A man was perched like a sunburned bullfrog on the opera house, the top rail of the rickety corral. He had almost no neck. His thin nose rested far down in the huge V that was his mouth.

Long Shorty stared at him from the back of the black cayuse. "Where's Del Payne?"

The bullfrog roan grunted: "In the house!"

Long Shorty continued to stare, adjusting the fellow's voice to something fresh in his memory. This was one of the bushwhacker pair! The one named Speed!

The bullfrog man put his hands on the corral rail, close to his gun grips, and clipped: "Ain't you got ears? I said in the house!"

Still staring, Long Shorty thumped: "Why get riled about it, fella?"

The bullfrog's body seemed to settle and widen on the rail. The ends of his mouth drew up under his heavy-lidded eyes. For fully a minute he said nothing. Then he took his hands off the rail, slowly, and removed makings from his shirt pocket.

"In the house," he repeated.

Long Shorty neckreined the black about and rode slowly to the ranch house. He could hear a man's voice rumbling inside.

A woman broke the rumble angrily: "I don't want your sympathy, Mister Praying Squent! And I've told you not to come around here! Get out!"

All the lower part of Long Shorty Sims' face seemed to turn to teeth as he made a fierce grin. He dropped the reins and put heavy feet on the porch. At the sound, squeaking swallows boiled from the mud nests under the eaves.

A woman came to the door. She was twenty or so, blonde, tall, and a bit too slender. She wore a percale house dress and one hand held a small black, double-barreled .44 derringer close to her waist. Her face was strained and pale.

She stared at Long Shorty Sims, mouth open, eyes widening. Then she cried: "Darling! My husband! I'm so glad you came!"

Then her arms entwined Long Shorty's neck. She kissed him furiously.

Over her tangled hair, he saw a man appear in the door. The fellow wore black-spotted white angora chaps and a snow-white hat with a tremendous undented crown. His vest was white and black calfskin; his guns were pearl-handled in tooled, silver-mounted holsters. His eyes were brown and softly calf-like in a cherubic, infant face. A baby-faced range dude.

The blonde stepped back; said: "Come in."

The baby-face backed away to let them in. No one else was in the room.

Long Shorty, eyeing the dude, rumbled: "You Prayin' Squent?"

"Right." Baby-face held out his hand. "I'm glad to meet—"

Long Shorty, ignoring the hand, said: "Get out!"

Praying Squent's brows lifted. His cherubic mouth puckered. "But—"

Long Shorty's fist, a square block of bones, hit the puckered baby mouth. Praying Squent clapped both hands to the brim of his white hat. Angora chaps churning, he traveled backward through the door, across the porch and fell on his back on the ground. He did not lose his hat off his head. Frightened swallows fled with shrill cries.

Baby-face started to put his arms above his head.

Long Shorty, hands holding both guns, still in their holsters, rammed out in front of his thighs, thumbs fan-ready on the hammers, crashed: "Don't do it!"

Praying Squent lowered his hands. His voice ugly, he began: "You damned—"

"Shut up! Get your bronc! Drag it!"

Tears bubbled out of baby-face's eyes. His voice suddenly whining, he started to raise his hands above his head in a pleading, praying gesture. "Feller, I don't see why—"

"Dry up! Get away from here!"

Praying Squent arose, stumbled to the corral, forked a pinto bronc and rode away. The bullfrog man on the top rail did not move and apparently took no notice of Squent.

Long Shorty Sims took his hands off his guns, used them both to wipe off beads of perspiration which had suddenly come out on his face.

He eyed the girl. "He keeps a trick gun in his hat, eh?"

She nodded. "Yes. It goes off when he mashes down on the top of his hat. He has killed more than one man by putting his hands in the air and praying for mercy. That's where he got his name—Praying Squent."

When Long Shorty continued to stare at her, she suddenly rubbed the back of her hand across her mouth, lifted the derringer suggestively and said: "Don't get any wrong ideas, cowboy!"

"You're a plumb stranger to me," Long Shorty frowned. "Why'd you grab me like that?"

She hesitated, then said: "I thought it might help if Squent thought I already had a husband. I'm afraid of him."

Long Shorty blinked. "Why'd you think I'd play the part?"

The girl studied him, coloring a little. "You look fairly decent."

His coldly humorous laugh at that sent swallows away from the eaves in a cloud. "I'm ornery and crooked as hell!"

She frowned faintly, then asked, almost pleadingly: "You looking for a job?"

Long Shorty stopped his laugh. "Huh?"

"I need another gunhand. I had two. But Praying Squent just rode over to tell me—to tell me one of them was found dead in the trail this morning." Her voice shook and seemed on the point of breaking. "The other is afraid of Squent. I need one who isn't."

Leathery skin gathered in great wrinkles all over Long Shorty's face as he frowned.

"What's the layout?" he asked.

"I want Praying Squent and his U-Bar outfit kept away from me. We'll tell everybody you're my husband. Would a hundred a week and a thousand bonus if you do what you're told interest you? It'll last maybe a month, maybe less."

He raked a jaw with tremendously long fingers. "Well, the job sounds like one with possibilities."

"But you don't kill Praying Squent!" the girl said sharply. "He wants this ranch and I want him to have it. But he's going to pay me for it. Twenty thousand dollars. That's why I want him alive. You get your thousand when he comes across."

"From what I've seen, this spread ain't worth five hundred!"

The blonde stiffened a little. "You don't worry about that! Praying Squent will pay twenty thousand and be glad to do it."

"Yeah?" He was skeptical.

"He will, all right. I—I think he did for my gunhand, Brad Daggert, last night. Brad was carrying a little gold-handled six-gun. When Praying Squent got that, right away he was sure this place was worth twenty thousand. I thought he'd try to get the gun, but I didn't think he would—he would kill my—kill Brad Daggert to get it."

She gulped out the last. Her eyes became wetly swimming. Her shoulders heaved.

Long Shorty went over to her, put his long arm around her, said soothingly: "Now, now, crying won't help it—"

A small hardness gouged his stomach. He looked down and saw the derringer jammed into his midriff.

The blonde, not sobbing now, assured him: "You said this job has possibilities, cowboy. It has. One is a tunnel through you."

Purple-necked, Long Shorty took his arm from around her and stepped back. He grinned foolishly. "I kinda like your style."

The blonde lowered her stubby, big-barreled derringer. A little color came up from the collar of her percale dress. "I guess you didn't mean anything. But we understand each other. And I like the style you used on Praying Squent. It's worth money to me."

"Well, maybe it's for sale. But I gotta know things first. Who are you?"

"Del Payne. I inherited the Keyhole from my uncle. When I came here, I found Praying Squent had practically put my uncle out of business and one of Squent's U-Bar rannies had even killed him in what the sheriff called a fair gunfight. Squent wants the Keyhole. He owns about all of the county anyway. I've simply decided he will pay what the Keyhole was worth originally before he gets it and I sent to Utah for my—for Brad Daggert and hired another gunhand to fight him."

When she stopped, Long Shorty frowned at her. "Where does the gold-handled gun come in?"

"You better forget about that." She spoke sharply, decisively.

Long Shorty spread his hands open flat against his shirt front. Under them, he could feel the gold-handled gun and the poke of dust he had taken from Brad Daggert.

"You ain't gonna trust me, then?" he asked in a hurt voice.

"I never saw you until you came onto the porch a few minutes ago," Del Payne said coldly. "Why should I?"

The corners of Long Shorty Sims' mouth twitched downward. On the point of telling her he had been on hand at the killing the night before, he changed his mind. There was something queer about this.

"All right, all right," he said. "Where do I bunk?"

She pointed to a door at one side of the room. "You'll have to stay here to make it look like you're my husband, There's a spare room. I'll introduce you to my other gunhand now."

She went to the door and called to the bullfrog man on the corral: "Come here, Speed!"

Speed slid off the corral rail.

"Want him to think I'm your husband?" Long Shorty asked softly.

"Yes. What he don't know won't hurt him. You're—you're Sam Payne from now on."

The bullfrog man came up.

"My husband, Sam Payne," said blonde Del Payne. "Sam, this is Speed Hullbeck, our bronc peeler."

Long Shorty Sims eyed Speed—one of the bushwhacker hombres who had killed Brad Daggert. He stripped his lips off his big teeth in a benign grin and said: "Glad t'meecha, fella."

CHAPTER III

NIGHT TRAIL

Long Shorty Sims usually slept like a bear trap, the slightest sound acting like a ton of bricks on the pan of the trap. But Del Payne knew how to wrangle groceries, and Long Shorty, who had eaten nothing at all for two days, had gorged unreasonably at her noon and evening chuckpiles.

Too much grub must have made him logy. For something was slithering along his arm under the bedcovers when he awakened sometime that night. He knew what it was at once. A snake! A rattler, possibly, although he hadn't heard it rattle. He had no desire to hear it; a rattler's inclination to rattle and bite come together.

He kept perfectly still, cold wetness oozing on his forehead. He had been rattler-bitten on the arm once. It had made him sicker than he cared to think about. If that snake sank fangs in his ribs—it was his left side, close to his heart—

The serpent was acting restless. With its squirming, something brushed and made crinkling sounds on his shoulder. He abruptly understood. The snake had a paper tied to its tail! And it was becoming enraged because the paper had caught on the bed clothes!

Ever so gently, Long Shorty extracted his right arm from the covers. Bringing it over, he clapped it down where the snake's head should be. Simultaneously, he exploded—rose straight up and hit the floor in the middle of the room, with the snake left behind in the bed.

He found a match, raked it afire and moved back to the bed. The tail of a diamondback stuck wriggling from the coverings. He picked up a chair, put it on the reptile. Then he removed the paper tied to its tail by string. The paper bore two pencil-printed words:

CLEAR OUT

Long Shorty swept his triggerless .44 irons from under the pillow and ran a hot glare around the room. The floor was carpeted thinly with brittle cornflake breakfast food. He had borrowed a box from Del Payne and sprinkled it there so no one could approach the bed without stepping on the noisy flakes. But nowhere were the flakes crushed as if a person had walked into the room.

He glowered at the stirring tail of the snake. Its rattles had been removed. The reptile could not have climbed onto the iron bedstead from the floor. He tilted a glance at the ceiling. Solid. He went to the window. It was open a bit from the top. He looked out into the clear, bright moonlight.

A rain barrel stood beside the window. Near it leaned a long pole made of thin strips split from cedar fenceposts and spliced together with haywire.

"So that's the way they got it in!" he grunted.

He went back, drew on his pants, girded his gun belts, and stepped into his worn boots. The tiny gold-handled six-gun went inside his shirt with the buckskin poke of gold dust. With the chair, he executed the rattler and, opening the lower sash of the window, tossed it out. He eased his gangling seven-foot length through after the reptile.

The swallows were silent, roosting under the eaves. From a nearby waterhole, frogs and water bugs sent up a steady clamor. A little range owl poured out a quavering hoot and mosquitoes made a shrill, undulating whine.

He approached the bunkhouse. Near one corner he folded down and explored the darkness. His fingers found a thread—something else he had borrowed from Del Payne—and he followed it, stretched tautly from sagebrush to sagebrush at a height a little less than a man's knees. The thread, unbroken, passed in front of the bunkhouse door and to the other corner. The door was the only exit from the bunkhouse and he was sure Speed had been asleep when he put the thread there.

He looked through a window, the sash of which was nailed in place, and made out the form of Speed. Stealthily, he went inside. He felt of Speed's boots. They were not warm as if they had been worn recently. Speed's feet projected from his bedroll and there was no fresh dust on them.

Speed apparently had had nothing to do with the rattler.

Frown wrinkles all over his face, he started for the log ranch house. Halfway there, he wheeled and ran to the corral. Onto his black cayuse he flipped corona blanket and Cheyenne tree kak. He led the bronc a couple of hundred yards because he knew the animal, full of oats, would buck when forked. He mounted and held his teeth tight-pressed while the horse vented steam by bucking the sunfish and an infinitely worse backshuttle.

During the day Del Payne had told him the location of Praying Squent's U-Bar ranch. He rode toward it, the black in a dead run.

A windmill, spearing above a hill mossy with sagebrush, was his first glimpse of the U-Bar. The ranch buildings lurked in a clump of cottonwoods. There was the inevitable small, round horse corral and a bigger corral, egg-shaped, with dehorning chutes and dipping vats at the narrow end.

Three lighted windows were red panels on the wad of shadow that was the ranch house.

Long Shorty walked his bronc as he came nearer and soon discerned a star-faced roan under the cottonwoods, anchored by dragging reins. He dismounted, approached the roan and explored with his hands. The cayuse was lathered and still blowing from a hard ride. A gunnysack was tied to one of the kak strings.

Long Shorty scowled and settled his guns solidly on his thighs. The rattler had been carried in that sack.

He stepped back and watched the house. It was a frame building, held a couple of feet off the ground on brick pillars. A tomcat came out from under the house, saw him with green fireball eyes and scuttled back, tail uplifted.

Then the ranch house door swiveled open. The man who stepped into it nearly filled the lower half of the light oblong. His shoulders were enormous, with an apish slant; his hands were low-dangling and hairy as dog paws; his hair was long and fuzzily black, concealing his ears.

He called into the room: "That skinny hombre's probably doin' some strong thinkin' right now!"

The voice was that of the man who had helped Speed kill Brad Daggert!

Praying Squent's chuckle drifted out into the night, "Or travelin'! Good work, Shag."

Shag closed the door and came toward the star-faced roan. Because he had been in the lighted ranch house, he did not discover Long Shorty in the shadows under the cottonwoods. As he reached for the reins, Long Shorty stepped forward and hit him.

He had the rattler in mind, and he wanted to hit hard enough to get some satisfaction without breaking knuckles. So he landed his blow in the upside-down V of softness above Shag's belt buckle. Shag collapsed in his middle. A roar of breath came out of his mouth. He started to sit down.

Long Shorty clicked his other fist on the gorilla man's jaw, then swooped and got one hairy wrist. Dragging Shag, shucking out a gun with his free hand, he ran to the door and kicked it.

Flapping inward, the panel struck Praying Squent's face. He must have heard the two blows and been about to open it. Squent was still stumbling backward, hands over his bruised nose, when Long Shorty came inside.

Long Shorty jutted a triggerless, wood-stocked six and ripped: "Unbuckle 'em!"

Praying Squent's hands fluttered, then floated around in front and loosened his cartridge belts. His gaudy sixes clanked to the floor. His brown calf eyes rolled longingly toward his white hat, well out of reach on a table.

Long Shorty spilled Shag in a chair and felt the man's wrist. There was a chance that sock had killed him. But it hadn't. Lifting the shaggy hair, Long Shorty looked at Shag's ears. Both had the tops cut off.

Long Shorty showed his teeth in a brittle grin at these marks of a horse thief. Shag wore that load of hay on his skull to hide them.

He eyed Praying Squent and said: "Well—my guessin' was close."

Squent did not reply.

Long Shorty drew out the paper that had been tied to the rattler tail and sailed it at him.

"Figured we might have a sing about that," he suggested.

Squent looked at his guns on the floor and at his white hat on the table, still saying nothing.

Long Shorty bolstered his gun and thumped: "Take a load off your legs, fella!"

His cherubic face a fountain of rage, Praying Squent perched gingerly on a chair edge. There was a purple smear around his mouth where he had been hit that morning. The door had bloodied his nose.

Going to the door, Long Shorty listened for sounds from the bunkhouse. Hearing none, he came back, sat down and rumbled: "After this Shag jasper put that varmint in my bed, it sorta come to me that me and you had better get together and make medicine."

"I dunno what you mean," Squent grated.

Long Shorty scowled. "You're a liar. But we won't chew the fat about that. What I come over to say is that we might be able to do each other some good."

A foxy look abruptly came over Praying Squent's chubby face. He relaxed a bit, spread his fingers on his knees and tilted forward in his chair. "Meanin' what?"

Long Shorty, thumping his words slowly, said: "Meanin' I ain't no more Del Payne's husband than you are."

Praying Squent's mouth opened, then his jaws worked as if chewing something good.

"You ain't, huh?" he muttered. "She hadn't mentioned a husband and I was some surprised when you turned up. Well—tell me some more."

Long Shorty scratched a horny palm suggestively.

"How much do you want?" Squent asked.

"Del Payne hired me to keep you away from her and is payin' me a hundred a week. I'll two-time for you at the same price—and you pay me five weeks in advance."

"Hell I will!" Squent cackled unreal mirth. "You've already told me all I want to know."

"Hell you will, eh?" Long Shorty's stick-fingered right hand jerked—and was suddenly palm-down on his knee, a big, stripped six under it, the sight-less barrel gaping an iron tunnel at Praying Squent.

He inquired: "Fella, didya ever see how a man's face heals after it had been chopped into beef with the end of a hogleg barrel?"

Squent showed less uneasiness than Long Shorty expected. Suddenly he knew there was ugly iron back of that baby face. Squent was not the whimpering jellyfish he pretended to be.

"Besides, there's a little matter of a six-gun with gold handles," Long Shorty added. "We might get together on that."

Squent's eyes lifted out as if pulled by strings. He skittered to the edge of his chair, hands hanging down.

"That gun!" he barked. "D'you know where she keeps it?"

Long Shorty put elaborate surprise on his bony face. "So help me! Del Payne thinks you got that gun off Brad Daggert's body and she's some worried. Ain't you got it?"

Squent collapsed back into his chair, his face bloated and puffy. "I dunno nothin' 'bout Brad Daggert's dyin'. And I ain't got that gun. She's lost it, huh?"

"She acted like it."

"She's a damned liar."

"Well, she ain't trustin' me too much," Long Shorty agreed. "Maybe she's still got it."

"In the drawer, a tin box." Praying Squent twitched his head at the table. "Get it."

Long Shorty got the box, saw the money inside. He gave the box to Squent. The latter counted out five hundred—leaving very little in the box— and passed the greenbacks over.

"I want that gold-handled gun," he gritted. "You work for me, cowboy, and if you get it, I'll pay you a thousand more."

Long Shorty kept surprise off his face and stowed the wad of currency in his pants pocket.

"Why you want it?" he asked.

"That's not your business!"

Long Shorty brought the triggerless, sightless six-gun up, a bony thumb second joint holding the hammer half-rocked back.

"It's your money I like and not you, fella!" he boomed softly. "And I'm some particular about knowin' what I'm doin'."

Praying Squent sneered. "You already know what you're doin'. You're double-crossin' the girl."

Long Shorty's bony face rammed forward. "I'll double cross whoever it pays me to double-cross, and you better paste that in your bonnet, fella! I'm crooked as hell. Why do you want that gold-handled flame-thrower?"

"It's worth money to me, that's all." Squent's voice was firm.

Long Shorty glowered at him, wondering if gun-barrel work on the baby face would bring what he wanted to know. He doubted it. And one yell would arouse the U-Bar rannies from their bunks.

He stood up and dropped his six in its bottomless holster. "I'll keep an eye peeled for the flossy gun, then. So long."

Backing outside, he pinned the nigger bronc and rode away. When he had gone a couple of miles, he told the bronc disgustedly: "Well, you black mess of crow meat, we still don't know why that little gold-handled gun is so important."

He caressed long fingers over the five-hundred roll in his pants and crashed out a chuckle: "But we got paid for the varmint in our bed, anyway!"

CHAPTER IV

FIVE HUNDRED INVESTED

Dawn was smearing scarlet on butte tops when the black cayuse single-footed up to the Keyhole horse corral. Long Shorty unsaddled and hung kak and corona and bridle on the top rail. Swallows were sweeping around the log ranch house eaves as he stepped on the porch. He went in—jerked to a stop.

The stubby black derringer was big-mouthed under his nose. Back of it, blonde Del Payne glared hot-eyed and thin-lipped.

"Unbuckle your guns!" Her voice was almost a sob.

Careful to make no jumpy moves, Long Shorty let his arsenal fall, then asked innocently: "Didn't you sleep good?"

"It's lucky I didn't! I heard you leave your room. You went to the bunk-house to make sure Speed was asleep, then rode off. I followed far enough to make sure you were going to Squent's U-Bar. So you're working for him! You took me in, all right! Get back on your bronc and ride!"

"Sure I went to see Squent." Long Shorty's lungs pumped out a chuckle. "That ranny of his'n who carries a load of hay on his skull to hide his ears put a worm in my bed."

The blonde's eyes said she didn't understand.

Long Shorty let her follow him into the room where he had slept and showed her the dead rattler outside the window. But she still held the derringer muzzle on him as they came back.

"I told you not to kill Squent!" she snapped.

"I didn't. We just had a pow-wow." He fished the five hundred out of his pants. "The lollygaggin' ended by me collectin' this to get that little gold-handled gun for Squent."

The girl, saucer-eyed, gulped: "He hasn't got it?"

"Nope."

"But Brad Daggert had it! And Praying Squent must have killed him. I don't see—" Her voice trailed off.

Long Shorty waited for her to go on. She didn't. He looked at the wad of greenbacks and shrugged.

"You ain't runnin' short of lucre are you?" he asked.

She batted her eyes at him. "How did you know?"

"I didn't." He twitched his shoulders. "I was guessin'."

"I was—was wondering how I would pay Speed tomorrow." Her voice wavered. "I haven't a cent."

He shook the fistful of money. "In that case, we'll let Squent pay him."

Blonde Del Payne's lips worked in between her teeth. A little knot traveled up and down her tanned throat. Her hand lifted, hesitated, then went out and took the five hundred.

"I'll pay you back when—when Praying Squent buys the Keyhole," she said steadily. "But why—why give me this money?"

"Because I don't like that baby-faced jasper!" Long Shorty ground hotly. He put his forearm across his shirt front, feeling the tiny gold-handled six in his pants waistband. "Why is the gold-handled gun so important?"

She looked at him. Crescents of moisture appeared around the lower lids of her eyes. She shook her head. "I can't tell you."

Long Shorty put what he thought was a saintly smile on his homely face and urged: "But I'm kind of a partner of your'n now, ain't I?"

The girl bit her lips, then released them to gulp: "I—I wish I could trust you!"

Then she whirled, ran into her bedroom and slammed the door. Through the wooden panel drifted a tearing sob.

Staring steadily at the door, Long Shorty made a cigarette and got it working. With the first gush of smoke he shook his head wonderingly. He went to the door, buckled on his guns and shoved the holsters down on his thighs with an angry ram.

Outside, swallows were sweeping into their mud nests in clouds. Long Shorty eyed them—and became suddenly hard of face.

It looked like the birds had recently been scared away from the eaves.

"Now I wonder!" he muttered. "Was somebody listenin' to us?"

He ambled out to the horse corral, leaving a dotted line of gray smoke puffs. The black bronc, exploring the corners of a feed box, threw its head and blew a snort at him.

Long Shorty scowled at the cayuse. "Bronc, you're blowin' your breath at a goop who just spent five hundred frogskins for some information and didn't get it." He climbed to the opera house. "Now why'd she run off cryin'?"

He made another cigarette. Putting the makings back, he hitched the gold-handled gun under his shirt so it would not dig into his ribs.

"I'd give a pretty to know why Prayin' Squent wants this gun," he declared thoughtfully. Puzzled puckers gathered over his eyes, one above the other, until even his scalp was wrinkled.

Seriously, he consulted the black bronc. "Hoss, you reckon we better sell this gun to Squent for a thousand iron men? Us crooked hombres has gotta look out for ourselves. And it seems this Del Payne wants him to have it." He grinned widely. "Now, there's a real gal, bronc. She's got good sense, too. She shows it by not trustin' me and you a'tall, a'tall."

The black horse stood with hung head and swishing tail. Long Shorty, sweeping the horizon idly, suddenly became blank-faced. A horseman had appeared momentarily in the distance, spurring across a hollow between two low hills.

"Speed Hullbeck!" Long Shorty spat.

He vaulted off the corral rail, scooped up bridle, kak and corona, and ran for the bronc.

CHAPTER V

SOME DOUBLE-CROSSING

The gorilla-like Shag was recovering slowly from the effects of the two punches he had received. He was perspiring freely. From time to time he worked his jaw tenderly with his blunt fingers.

"Oo-o-o!" he moaned. "My ribs is broke!"

Baby-faced Praying Squent stood erect from examining Shag's chest.

"You're all right!" he snapped. "Quit bellerin'!"

"He hit me when I wasn't lookin'! And I been feelin' worse an' worse all mornin'!"

Squent went into another room and came back with a flat bottle of Old Crow. He suggested: "Here, get drunk and you'll be okay."

Shag swigged from the bottle and revived enough to be low: "I'll kill that skinny hombre! I'll pull his head off!"

"No, you won't!" There was none of the baby-face in Praying Squent now. His voice was an ugly rending. "Not until I give the say, you won't. That hombre is tryin' to get the gold-handled gun for me."

Shag dropped his jaw in surprise. His gaze went through the open door and he said suddenly:

"Here's Speed!"

Speed Hullbeck dismounted and came into the U-Bar ranch house. He discovered the Old Crow bottle and took it out of Shag's fingers without waiting for a invitation.

Praying Squent ripped: "Haven't I told you to stay away from here or that girl will get wise you're workin' for me?"

Speed drank from the bottle before he replied: "Yeah—you have. But I got somethin' you'll want to know. That husband of Del Payne's told her this mornin' that he had been over here and you gave him five hundred to get the gun for you, and he gave her the money. I was listenin' outside the window and heard 'em."

Praying Squent stamped like a maddened bull and roared: "Gave her my five hundred, did he! Damn him! Maybe he's her husband after all! Hell's fire! They just plain rooked me outta that five hundred!"

Speed scratched what neck he had. "Not her husband, eh? I thought they was talkin' kinda funny for man and wife. Maybe that explains it. He tried to get her to tell him why you wanted the gun, and she wouldn't. And another thing—she ain't got the gun. I heard her say Brad Daggert had it the night we got him."

Praying Squent stopped in front of Speed, his eyes ugly. "That's something for you to explain!"

"Explain—hell!" Speed spat accurately at one of the many cracks in the floor. "I searched Brad Daggert and didn't find it. Then I called Shag and he searched, too. And didn't you have your whole spread of rannies go over the ground around where we shot him to see if he had hid it? Daggert wasn't carryin' the gun that night."

Shag, buttoning his shirt tenderly over his ribs, growled: "Now I guess you'll lemme give that skinny hombre what he's got comin'!"

Praying Squent got a glass and rage shook his hand so that he spilled whiskey on a crack in the floor as he filled it. He emptied the liquor down his throat.

"You can get him, all right!" he raged. "But not until I say go. I've got that gent pegged. He's just a gunhand, but he's wise that the gold-handled six is worth a lot, and he's lookin' out for himself. He tried to find out from me why I wanted the six. He's double-crossin' everybody."

"Then why let him go around stickin' his bill into things?" gorilla-like Shag wanted to know.

"Because he might get hold of the little six," snapped Squent. "The girl has probably got it yet, even if she told him she hadn't. And if he gets it, and is too dumb to figure it out, he may bring it to me. I offered him a thousand for it. The minute he gives it up, we'll blow him to hell!"

"Yeah," Speed suggested. "And if he figures out what the gun is?"

"Then we'll follow him to the spot."

"We tried to follow the girl and Brad Daggert often enough," Speed laughed harshly. "Where'd it get us?"

Praying Squent sloshed more whiskey down his throat, then glared at Speed. "You smeared that all to hell. Just like you smeared this Brad Daggert killin'! I told you not to get Daggert until you were sure he had the gun!"

"You don't like my style, eh?" Speed hung his hands to his belt by his thumbs. "I saw the girl and Brad Daggert handlin' the little gun and overheard why she wanted to hold onto the Keyhole, didn't I? I helped bushwhack Brad Daggert when he was headed for the place, didn't I? If you're not satisfied, supposin' you pay me the thousand you owe me and I'll drag it."

"Gettin' scared, huh?"

"Yeah, I'm gettin' scared. I ain't none too hot about this. That skinny jasper is onery'rn a corral of bobcats. And that girl is bad medicine. I'd rather fight six men than her. She keeps that damned little black hogleg in her hand all the time. Whenever I'm around her, I'm wonderin' if she's wise to me. She'd blow a hole in me if she knew I was a gunhand you sent over there for her to hire when you heard she had brought Brad Daggert in from the Utah country and was lookin' for another."

"I like the gal, myself," Praying Squent smirked.

Shag gave his opinion. "Your likin' is gonna get you all covered up with dirt."

"I'll take the fizz and spit out of the heifer!" Praying Squent chuckled.

"Well, do I go on workin' for you?" Speed demanded.

"You do."

"I'll be movin' then." Speed clumped outside, spur chains rattling across the cracks in the wooden floor.

And under that floor, whence he had crawled in time to hear, through the cracks, most of what had been said, gangling Long Shorty Sims lay perfectly still and wondered if anybody would think to stoop and look beneath the house. Against that possibility, he worked both sixes out.

His lips soundlessly formed: *Damn my brand of luck! I don't know yet what that gold-handled gun means!*

Speed Hullbeck mounted and rode away. Shag retreated to the bunkhouse with his bottle of Old Crow.

Long Shorty Sims listened long enough to become convinced Praying Squent was not going to talk to himself. Then he inched out from under the ranch house. He got into a wash without discovery and made his way down it and down the small canyon into which it emptied to the spot where he had left his cayuse. The bronc's barrel between his knees, he rode.

Puzzlement wrinkled his face. He whistled soundlessly. His fingers stroked his jaw in exasperation. He took out the gold-handled six-gun, inspected it.

Ejecting the cartridges, he studied them. They didn't look like they had been disturbed. Just to make sure, he pulled the lead out with his teeth and found nothing inside but powder. The gold butt plates were fastened in place with two screws. He broke his fingernails trying to loosen these. They were too tight. Suddenly, he put the gun back inside his shirt and hauled the black cayuse up.

"I'm beginnin' to see the light!" he ejaculated. "Del Payne wants Squent to have this gun, I'm bettin'. Well—we'll just bring this to a head!"

Wheeling the bronc, he galloped back to Praying Squent's U-Bar.

Squent met him, suspicion on his baby face. But he made no hostile motions.

"Huh—you back?" he growled.

"I wanted to tell you early enough that you could go to the bank and get my one thousand," Long Shorty said amiably. "I want it in cash, fella."

Praying Squent, brown calf eyes protruding, yelped: "You've got the gold-handled gun?"

"Nope. But I know right where she is."

"Where?" Squent got it out like a cough.

"In Speed Hullbeck's bedroll in the Keyhole bunkhouse," Long Shorty fabricated blandly.

That gave Praying Squent a shock. His mouth clopped open and shut as if he had a hot buckshot on his tongue. He made a wordless spluttering.

"I saw him put it there this mornin'," Long Shorty continued glibly. "Speed had been out somewhere durin' the night. His hoss was hot as if it had been fogged hard. Speed hid the gun and a little buckskin bag of somethin' heavy in his bedroll."

In a bawl, Squent said: "The double-crosser! Damn him! He searched first and got the gun when—!" He pushed the rest back down his throat.

"When he killed Brad Daggert for you, huh?" Long Shorty finished.

Squent's hands fanned slightly on a level with his hips.

"You're talkin' too much for your own health, feller!" he snarled.

"One thousand frogskins is a powerful gag," Long Shorty suggested. "Be sure and have it in cash, like I said. I'd have brought the gun, only Speed was stayin' around the bunkhouse like he might be watchin' it. You want me to fetch it, or will you come after it?"

"Bring it!" Instantly after he said that, Squent changed his mind. "No, don't do that. I'll go back with you and get it."

"Have you got my thousand in cash?"

"Oh, hell! I'll pay you as soon as I can ride to Gillette after the money. It's more'n half a day's hard ride there and back."

"Guess again, fella!" Long Shorty shook his head stubbornly. "I don't trust you no farther'n I can jar this old world by stompin' on it. It's my thousand iron men on the line or you don't get the gun."

Praying Squent scrubbed the back of a hand across his mouth while he thought.

"Did the girl say anything to you about sellin' the Keyhole?" he questioned.

"She said she was afraid of you, but that she'd be damned if she'd take less than twenty thousand if you tried to buy her out," Long Shorty replied evenly. "If she wasn't scared, I don't think she'd sell."

"Yeah. That's the price she sprung on me the other day." Squent seemed satisfied he was being told the truth. "And the dump ain't worth spittin' on."

"What interests me is my thousand in cash, fella."

Squent snarled, "I'll bring it!"

"And you'll come after the gold-handled gun yourself?"

"I'll come, or I'll send Shag."

Long Shorty frowned. "If you send that Shag monkey, tell him to leave his shootin' irons behind, or I'll cram 'em down his throat. So help me Noah, if I don't!"

"Shag won't bother you!"

"You're damned right he won't!" Long Shorty scowled. "I'll bother him, what I mean!"

He spurred the nigger bronc away, riding twisted on one leg to watch Praying Squent until he was out of gunshot. When he turned, his sudden, fierce grin threatened to push his ears together on the back of his head.

Before he was out of sight of the U-Bar, he saw Praying Squent's pinto cayuse leave the cluster of ranch buildings and gallop northward toward the cowtown of Gillette.

"Goin' after my thousand—and probably after the twenty thousand to give the girl so she'll sign a deed to the Keyhole so nobody'll ask him questions about ownin' the outfit."

66 LESTER DENT

Long Shorty's laugh tumbled across the range and sent prairie dogs in the town through which he rode yipping down their holes. "He took the bait, hook, line and pole. There's sure gonna be civil war in the polecat family!"

Back at the ramshackle Keyhole ranch, Long Shorty scouted for Speed. Not finding him, he went to the girl with questions.

"I've got about twenty head of cows," she said wryly. "I found one bogged in the quicksand and came back and sent Speed down to get the critter out."

Long Shorty eyed her narrowly. "You really want to sell the Keyhole?"

She looked at him queerly. "Yes—for twenty thousand. Why?"

Long Shorty grinned with genuine humor. "I just wanted to be sure."

He went to the bunkhouse wondering if she had followed him on his last jaunt to Praying Squent's U-Bar. Probably not. The Belle Fouche, a spring-fed trickle of water where the cow must be fast in the quicksand, lay in the opposite direction.

In the bunkhouse, he planted the gold-handled revolver and the poke of gold dust. A muslin tick filled with hay was between the bunk slats and Speed Hullbeck's tarp-swathed bedroll. He put the stuff there, hesitating over the gold. But the poke had Brad Daggert's name burned onto it and would help cinch Praying Squent's suspicions, so he put it with the tiny gun.

That done, he got some saddle oil and, rubbing the gummy dust off his kak, applied a fresh coat. After that, he killed time cleaning his stripped-down .44s

Speed returned for the noon meal. The girl said almost nothing and did not eat with them. Afterward, Long Shorty followed Speed to the bunkhouse. When they were inside, he leaned against the doorjamb and broke into conversation. "For a long time, now, I been hirin' out to different parties who needed a gunhand."

Speed looked at him suspiciously.

"Is this a history class?" he growled. "Or you tellin' me somethin' you want put on your tombstone?"

"Neither. I'm gonna settle down one of these days and when I turn in my chips, it'll be from old age and they'll probably put on my tombstone, 'A lovin' husband, father of a big family and a respected neighbor' or somethin' like that." He shut his eyes and smiled dreamily, then jerked them open. "But what I started to orate is that my, um—career—has made me kinda sympathetic for the gunhand breed. I hate to see one of 'em two-timed."

"Well—whatcha chokin' on?" Speed grunted.

"On this!" Long Shorty said smugly. "Prayin' Squent promised me five hundred mint berries to croak you. Now a hombre who'll only pay five hundred for a job like that ain't entitled to service for his money, the way I look at it. So I figured I'd put an owl in your hat."

Speed hunched down as the import of the words dawned on him. He looked more frog-like than ever.

"The dirty—!" he squawked. "He tell you why he wants me dusted off? "

Long Shorty shrugged his shoulders, sure now that his lie was sticking. "Nope. Only him bein' that kind of a cheapskate, I figure he owes you more'n that and thinks it's a cheap way to pay off."

Speed stared at him coldly. "Just who the hell are you anyway, Mister Know-so-much?"

Long Shorty made his bony face innocently blank. "Just a crooked jasper tryin' to wriggle through this world without gettin' stomped on."

"Prayin' Squent send you here in the first place?"

"Yeah." Long Shorty thought of something else that might help the story he was weaving out of a fertile brain and added it: "I got the gold-handled gun for Squent, you know. The girl tried to make me believe Brad Daggert had it, but I found where she was hidin' it last night. Anyway, she saw me take it to Squent this mornin', and I had to tell her I had flimflammed him outta five hundred bucks and give her the money before she'd believe me. Don't think she's missed the gun yet. Dunno whatin'ell will happen when she does."

Long Shorty hoped that would lull any suspicions Speed might have about the talk he had overheard that morning. Apparently it did.

"When does Squent want me fogged?" he asked ominously.

"Tonight. He's comin' over to buy the Keyhole. When he has it—your number is up." Long Shorty pushed his hat back on his head and scratched coarse, faded hair down over his eyes. "Funny 'bout that little gold-handled gun. Nobody's told me why it's so hell-fired important. But when Prayin' Squent got it, right away he decided to pay twenty thousand for the Keyhole and get rid of you. What's there about the gun that'd make him do that?"

Speed gave him silence.

"If that gun is worth jack to Squent, it oughta be us, too," Long Shorty put persuasion in his voice. "Maybe we can make some medicine of our own."

Speed pulled his mouth ends up under his eyes and grated: "I ain't got no idea what that gun means, feller!"

Taking his back from the doorjamb, Long Shorty grinned at him. "Well, in that case, I guess you can take care of yourself."

He went out and wandered to the corral to feed his nigger bronc oats.

"Now there's a grateful stinker for you, bronc," he said disgustedly. "I put him wise he's bein' double-crossed, and yet he won't tell me a thing. Are we ever gonna learn why Squent wants that flossy gun?"

The cayuse blew a snort. Long Shorty chuckled: "That's right—insult the great brain of the feller who is your meal ticket. You're gettin' just like these other polecats around here."

CHAPTER VI

"DONE AS HELL!"

The afternoon dragged itself into wherever time goes. As the hour for the evening meal approached, Long Shorty sat on the corral top rail, the highest spot around the Keyhole he could occupy without attracting suspicion. His eyes were alert.

As dusk spread crimson glow, a lamp reddened the ranch house windows and the girl came to the door with a call: "Come and get it!"

Speed came from the bunkhouse, but Long Shorty waited a bit. When he did leave the corral, he went to the bunkhouse and sidled around it.

In the knots of sagebrush crouched Squent and gorilla-like Shag.

Shag scowled. Squent looked a question.

"You got my thousand?" Long Shorty demanded.

"I got it!" Squent snarled. "But I want that gun first!"

"Speed is eatin' supper. Go in the bunkhouse and get it. His bunk is right in front of the door."

Praying Squent nodded and sidled around the bunkhouse. After a while he came back. Evidently he had the gun.

"The double-crossing toad!" he gargled. "Here's your thousand."

He passed over a wad of paper money. Long Shorty took it, eyes and hands alert. He watched Praying Squent and Shag scuttle off in the sage. Then, tucking the roll of currency in his pants, he ambled in and ate supper with gusto.

Speed slouched back to the bunkhouse, sullen, muttering to himself.

The girl looked after him curiously. "Now I wonder what's biting Speed?"

Long Shorty sopped his plate clean with a biscuit and poked it down his throat. He stood up and jerked his head. The girl followed him out on the porch where they could be sure nobody overheard their talk.

The swallows were quarreling in their mud nests under the eaves. The red flush of dusk was gone and clouds blotched the sky overhead, making the night rather black. Coyotes caterwauled from hilltops. In the distance a cow mooed.

Long Shorty eyed the girl and said : "Things are gonna happen around here before long and I better show you how the cards are stacked."

"I don't get you," she murmured.

He pulled air into his lungs. "Did you know Speed is workin' for Squent?"

She nodded calmly. "Yes. I had Brad Daggert make sure of that before I put him on my payroll."

"I'll—I'll be hornswoggled!" Long Shorty exploded. "It looks like I been doin' a lot of unnecessary worryin' about you! Seems like you know what you're doin'."

Del Payne reached out impulsively and took his big hands.

"I'm sure it'll come out all right, even if Praying Squent didn't get the gun," she said. "In a few days I can make other arrangements."

Long Shorty frowned. "He's already got the gun."

"What?"

"I'll tell you the whole thing," Long Shorty said swiftly, "I was near Brad Daggert when he was bushwhacked by Speed and Shag. I took the gun and a poke of gold dust off him before Speed and Shag searched him. They didn't know I was around—don't know it yet. The next mornin', I came here to give you the gold-handled gun and poke of dust.

"But the way things turned out, and me bein' a crooked jasper by nature, I decided to hold onto them until I found out what this was all about. Then I got to—well, I got to worryin' about you—"

He stuttered and reddened.

"Anyway, today I told Prayin' Squent that Speed had the gun and was holdin' out on him. He believed it because Speed had searched Brad Daggert first and could have taken the gun. Then I slipped Speed word that Squent was gonna dust him off to keep from payin' him for killin' Brad Daggert.

"While you were eatin' supper, Prayin' Squent got the gun and poke of dust from where I had put it in Speed's bunk. He'll be back any time now to buy you out, unless I'm wrong. After that, I'll be some surprised if him and Speed don't start eatin' each other up."

The girl's voice was a brittle rasp: "You say—Speed and Shag—killed my—killed Brad Daggert?"

Long Shorty nodded slowly. "They did."

"Brad Daggert was—" Del Payne's voice broke. "Brad Daggert was my brother. His name was—Bill Payne."

Then, before Long Shorty could untangle his tongue, she spun and stumbled into the house.

The gaunt puncher stared after her. Bewilderment twisted his long face.

He went out to the corral and perched on the top rail, staring morosely at his black bronc.

"This is sure a puzzle, cayuse!" he complained. "But I'm kinda relieved to learn Brad Daggert was her brother. She was showin' a lot of grief over his passin'. And, bronc, she's sure a spunky little moharrie."

The black bronc slept on its feet, showing no interest.

Long Shorty had been on the corral rail nearly two hours when hoof-beat sounds came tumbling across the range. He hurried to the ranch house and waited on the porch, peering through the night. Riders were approaching at a gallop. They came into the aurora of lamplight shed by the door. Two of them. Attracted by the sound, Speed came from the bunkhouse.

The horsemen dismounted—Praying Squent and Shag. They crowded into the ranch house. Long Shorty and Speed followed them.

Blonde Del Payne appeared in her bedroom door, her eyes red, the black derringer jutted out in front of her.

"I told you to stay away from here!" she snapped at Squent.

Praying Squent tilted his white hat over one eye and smirked: "Now, now! I'm here on business. I wanta buy the Keyhole."

Del Payne flicked her eyes at Long Shorty, then back at Squent.

"You know my price—twenty thousand," she said in a firm voice.

"I've got the cash," Squent stated.

Long Shorty had moved over until the room's one solid log wall was at his back. Speed also stood apart, his ugly face sullen and uneasy.

"I've got the deed," Del Payne said steadily. "I'll sign it over to you. Let's see the color of your money."

"There it is!" Praying Squent dropped a bundle of paper bills on the table.

Del Payne got a folded document from a drawer and set pen and ink on the table.

Long Shorty licked the rim of his big mouth and breathed heavily. When that deed was signed, hell would split wide open. Praying Squent wouldn't let that twenty thousand go and he wanted the girl. He thought Speed had double-crossed him and would try to kill him. Speed, convinced this number was coming up, was crouched, guns ready for Squent.

The girl counted the money. She speared the pen into the dark bottle and scratched her name on the deed transfer. At Praying Squent's grunt, Shag scribbled his signature as witness.

The Keyhole was sold.

Long Shorty put his back to the log wall, feet well out in front so he wouldn't fall down easily when lead hit him, put his hands flat and open over his wooden .44 grips.

He thumped: "Well, school's out! Drag it, you sagehens!"

Praying Squent lifted a hand to adjust his hat, changed his mind and held the hand out foolishly in front of him.

Speed settled closer to the floor. Shag glared and shifted so Squent was not in his line of possible fire.

Squent began: "I ain't don—"

Long Shorty's roar crashed in the room. "Yes, you are! You're done as hell!"

Squent's cherubic hands started quivering and Long Shorty wondered whether he'd better feed him first lead—or leave him to Speed.

Speed settled that. He must have thought that number of his was about up. He drew. And Squent saw him—went for his own gun.

Squent was a little the faster. His gun ran out a scarlet tongue. Speed's body loosened. As he collapsed down, he twisted so that he fell with his face away from Squent. And he didn't move afterward.

"Don't hurt the girl!" Squent screeched. He wheeled his gun muzzle toward Long Shorty. "Get him! Cut loose—"

Del Payne emptied one barrel of her derringer at the oil lamp—blew it into a cloud of glass.

CHAPTER VII

THE INVITATION

Out of the holster bottoms Long Shorty's stripped .44s gushed at gorilla-like Shag—who had his gun nearly rolled when the lights went out.

Shag squawled. In the lurid powder glare, Shag was invisible, feeling on the floor for the gun he had lost out of his bullet-ridden right hand.

Long Shorty folded down and lunged forward. One hand floated up and got the twenty thousand in bills off the table. He crammed the money into his pants.

Del Payne screeched and emptied the other barrel of her derringer. Near where she had screeched and fired, Squent cursed and retreated.

Long Shorty thumped: "Get out—girl!" Then he jumped away from a crackling storm of lead which came at his voice.

He twisted and crouched low, thumbs wagging off the iron hammers of his jumping sixes. One gun went empty. He skittered sidewise for the door that led to the kitchen. Flame squirted at him and his hat lifted off. He didn't shoot back when he heard the man who had fired change his position.

He pitched back into the kitchen, hunkered down and, gripping the barrel of his empty gun betwixt his knees, clicked cartridges into it with one hand.

A couple of yards from him, in the kitchen, a gun banged and a pellet grazed his neck. The gun sounded like a firecracker—a short-barreled iron.

"Hey—be careful!" he rumbled.

"Oh!" gasped Del Payne. "I nearly shot you when you came in. Did you—get Speed?"

"Uh-huh," grunted Long Shorty softly. "Your brother is paid for."

In the other room Praying Squent yipped: "I hear the girl and the tall hombre in the kitchen! Get around back, Shag. Evidently he was behind something that would turn bullets and was not afraid of his voice drawing lead.

Long Shorty hopefully fanned lead at his voice, however. Hot metal came back at him, chunking into the log kitchen walls like tossed mud balls. The flashes showed him that Squent was behind the dining room heating stove.

That gave Shorty an idea. He reloaded his other six. Then he found the kitchen stove. It was still warm. He yanked it away in a shower of falling pipe and soot and skidded it across the door.

Bang! A bullet squealed into the kitchen.

"That came from outside—back of the house!" Del Payne gasped.

Long Shorty grabbed a frying pan and tossed it over the stove so that it lit just beyond, close to the door. Lead splashed on the stove. He flexed a thumb—once.

"Dang!" he grunted. "That feller sure is hard to kill!"

Bang! Bang! Shag, outside, shot twice into the kitchen window. His metal came close.

Long Shorty rumbled words that were soundless. "About the next time I blaze away through the door, that booger will pour it to me!"

He found Del Payne in the gloom and dragged out the roll of bills Praying Squent had paid for the Keyhole. He thrust them into her hands. "I'm goin' out and stampede these cusses. While the fireworks is on, you get out, grab a bronc and fan it away from here." She made no answer.

Impatient, he demanded: "You got it?"

"Yes," she said, her voice a wisp in the darkness. "I'm sorry—sorry I caused this."

Long Shorty strained his ears in the ugly quiet around the ranch house. He found her hands and squeezed them.

"That's all right," he mumbled. "I dunno what you done. But we ain't got time to talk it over. You drag it when I open my keg of nails in there."

"There's no other way?" Her voice was choking.

"Not that I see," Long Shorty said harshly.

She kissed him then, furiously. Arms around his neck, pulling his face down to hers. Then she released him abruptly and recoiled in the darkness. Listening, he could hear her breath sounds.

He drew air into his lungs slowly, put elbows tight against his ribs, sixes speared out, and made for the door. About to hurdle the stove, he held back, swabbing his lips with a tongue that felt round and hot. He could feel sweat on all his face.

He croaked: "Hell—I'm losin' my taste for lead!"

A bullet splashed hot air in his face.

He leaped aside and eyed the splotch of dirty gray that was the kitchen window. Then he slithered along the wall, feeling for the shelves above where the stove had stood. He found them, located a couple of boxes a little larger than full Bull Durham sacks. He sniffed one, discarded it and sniffed the other, then breathed: "Peppered!"

He tore off the top of the box, ascertained it was nearly full, then returned to the door. His six-gun tilted and blew lead into the other room. A flame tongue licked back at him. He flung the open pepper box at the flash.

The girl's derringer popped. Outside the kitchen window Shag gargled cuss words that showed he was nicked again. Inside the other room Squent sneezed. Again he exploded air through a tickling nose.

Long Shorty hurdled the stove, streaking flame from his hips at the sneeze sounds. Lead burned Long Shorty's hip a little. Squent's sneezing abruptly turned into a rattling gasp. He sighed loudly and his body fell on the floor.

Long Shorty pitched out into the cloud-blotted night. Shag burned powder at him as he ran along the log side of the ranch house. He fanned a slug back. Shag yelped and sat down. He fired again as he hit the ground, but he was rattled and his slug went popping off through the sage. There was light enough to disclose his form faintly. He was aiming once more. Long Shorty shot him—once.

Fitful light flared inside the house, then Del Payne came out on the porch, still carrying the match she had lighted. Her face was white.

"Squent is—is through," she said jerkily.

Long Shorty entered the house, struck a match and searched Praying Squent. He found the gold-handled gun.

"What is this thing, anyhow?" he asked. "Why did Praying Squent want it and why did it make him pay twenty thousand for the Keyhole?"

"There was a map inside the handle of the gun," Del Payne said in a strained, weary voice. "It marked the location of what Squent thought was a gold mine on Keyhole land."

"Thought?" Long Shorty questioned.

"There was no gold—only what my brother and I planted there. It was a plot. You see, Squent broke my uncle and had him killed. I—we conspired to let Speed overhear enough to make him think there was gold. We knew he would go to Squent and knew Squent would pay a high price for the Keyhole. I—my brother and I thought Speed would steal the gun. But they— they killed—my brother—to get it."

Long Shorty nodded thoughtfully and felt of the wound on his hip.

"You are hit?" Del Payne asked sharply.

Long Shorty shook his head. "Don't even need bandagin'. Well, I better be draggin' it."

"Where are you going?" Del Payne's voice was low.

"To Canada, reckon." His voice thumped hollowly in the darkness. "I'm losin' my appetite for this owlhoot trail. I'll have to settle down to ranchin' in Canada, I guess."

The girl seemed to think that over.

"I'll be in trouble—if I stay around here." Her voice was full of huskiness. "Do you think—I had better go to Canada, too?"

"I was tryin' to get up enough backbone to invite you!" Long Shorty boomed.

· · · · ·

Hell's Hoofprints

Buildings were black boxes along the darkened cowtown street.

The thrown knife came from behind one of them. Krill heard the swish of the blade—too late to duck.

Chuck! The sound was dull, ugly. Pain sloshed across Krill's chest like scalding water. One hand a claw over the knife hilt, he lunged, gained the shelter of the next building. Hurtling onward around the corner, his right hand shucked out the one silver-gripped six-gun he wore. Near the rear, he listened.

Silence seeped at him from every side. Overhead, clouds were plastered on the moon. He bent forward tense, eyes strained. His faded blue shirt was greatly oversize, though he was a gaunt giant of six and a half feet. The shirtsleeves hung loose as sacks on his long arms.

The knife was clinging in the shirt fabric like a splinter. The gash it had opened in his chest was shallow. He fingered the blade, discovering it was a scant three inches long, heavy, curved.

To the left a horse snorted softly. He concentrated on the sound with eyes and ears. A corral sprawled a couple of rods distant, two big Bain freight wagons clots of gloom near it. In the corral, the horse snorted again. It sounded mildly alarmed.

Silent as a trickle of campfire smoke, Krill approached the corral. Sagebrush was underfoot and he felt out the location of the clumps before each step. Then something crinkled softly under his boot. He quickly reached down and picked up an envelope. On the point of throwing it away, he changed his mind and crammed it into a pocket.

Overhead, a cloud, black and lowering and shaped like a bull buffalo's head, slowly skinned off the moon, allowing pale silver light to spill down.

Staring intently, Krill discerned what had alarmed the horse, a figure crouched beside the rider board of a freight wagon. He waited. The form did not move for some time, then it shifted a bit to better see the rear of the buildings.

His mouth a hard gully, his long body a stiff bow of tendons, Krill took two quick steps. His arm hooked around the dark form. He brought it against his chest with a vicious yank—and an astounded grunt rushed out of his lungs.

"Hell—a woman!"

He cupped a hand tightly over her mouth.

The moonlight, rapidly becoming brighter, disclosed that his capture was young and slender, her figure as firmly supple as a cat's.

She wrenched, struck at him and tried to scream through her nose.

"Behave!" Krill said, his voice dry, humorless.

For a moment all was silent. From a nearby saloon came the banging of a piano.

She continued her struggles, Krill holding her as effectually as though she were a bunny rabbit. Convinced of her helplessness, she loosened submissively in his clutch.

He flashed the short knife in the moonlight so she could see it, asked: "Why'd you stick me with that?"

Her eyes widened at the wet stains on the blade and she shrank from the spreading moistness on his oversize shirt. She tried to say something, and he released her mouth.

"I didn't!" She wrenched, trying to free herself. "Let me go!"

Krill pulled a piece of notepaper from a pocket, let her read:

> Adam Krill:
> Hear you want to buy a cow outfit. I have exactly what you want. Meet me in front of the Three Aces saloon at ten o'clock tonight and we'll have a talk.
>
> Joe Baker

Krill pulled the girl's face close to his, said bitterly: "I'm a stranger in town, and I never saw you before. Did you make a mistake, or have I got some friends here I don't know nothin' about?"

She returned his stare, eyes blank, as if she were puzzled.

"If you think you can get away with anything as raw as this—you're crazy!" she hissed abruptly. "It won't work!"

Krill's eyes, fixed on the girl, rolled like balls of pale blue quartz as he shook his head. "You're talkin' riddles. All I wanta know is whether you made a mistake when you tried to knife me, and if you didn't, who hired you. Who's Joe Baker?"

"There's no Joe Baker in this country," she snapped angrily. "You're hurting my arms!"

Krill growled. "Let's have the truth!"

She parted her lips, said softly: "I am sure—" Her voice lifted suddenly to shrill: "Help! Help Help!"

The shrieks splintered through the moonlight like an armload of glass shattering on stone.

The piano in the saloon stopped in mid-chord. Excited punchers and townsmen shot through the bat-wing doors as if blown out. They milled, seeking the source of the screams.

"This way!" a man bawled in a voice that was an owl-like hoot. He charged the corral with bowlegged leaps.

A dozen feet from Krill and the girl, he brought up. He was a tall, angular man whose hat rested far back on his head, exposing his face to the moonlight. He had a round head with big eyes which wrinkles encircled like rings, making him look owlish.

He whipped out a six-gun, hooted: "Unbuckle the hardware, you damned woman grabber!"

Krill stood on hard feet, his left arm down stiff at his side, the loose sleeve around it in folds. He dove a glance at the end of the big Bain freight wagon and decided one jump would take him there.

"Skin, yourself—quick!" snarled the owlish man.

Quietly, Krill unbuckled his gun belt, using his right hand. His left arm remained rigidly down. He seemed to settle a bit and the folds of his oversize shirt pulled apart as his chest filled with air. His gun belt slapped the ground at his feet.

A split of a second later, hot flame lashed from his left hand. The hand had not moved to a perceptible degree—but it suddenly held a spouting black .38 revolver.

The owlish man bawled and twitched his gun hand up as if snakebitten. His six-gun, struck by a .38 slug, cartwheeled forty feet. But it had not covered a quarter of the distance before Krill was sheltered by the freight wagon, left arm and gun resting across the load-boards.

"Don't nobody get spookish!" he said in an ordinary tone.

"He grabbed me!" the girl shrilled. "He sneaked up behind me and grabbed me!"

A man in the rear of the crowd rumbled angrily.

Krill's homely features became gray and solid.

"Don't go jumpin' at conclusions—or makin' passes at your ironware," he said. At the girl, he flung harshly: "Tell 'em the rest of it! Tell 'em how you threw that knife at me after you or your friends decoyed me in front of the Three Aces with that note."

"Oh—you liar!" she shrilled.

Krill tossed the short-bladed knife out so that it stuck hilt-up in the ground in full view.

"Somebody named Joe Baker sent me a note to meet him and somebody heaved that toad-stabber at me when I got there!" he said in a loud voice. "I skinned around here and found this girl skulking."

He allowed time for that to soak in. Then he walked, heavy-heeled, from behind the wagon and confronted the crowd. His right hand made a fist from which the thumb protruded stiffly. He jerked the thumb at his blood sodden shirt, then at the girl.

"That's how it was. Maybe she made a mistake—maybe she didn't. I was tryin' to find out when she squawked."

The girl strode over and confronted him. Her slender body was rigid. Anger—if it was not anger, she was an excellent actress—caused her arms to quiver.

"I think I know what your game is, and I think I know who hired you, stranger!" she bit off. "But it's not going to work and I'd advise you to get out of town while the getting is good. This part of Wyoming is not healthy for your kind. You belong over in the Hole-in-the-Wall country!"

That out, she wheeled and stamped away, her pretty features a mask of rage.

From a composed face, Krill's eyes followed her, but his neck slowly became hot and purple. The Hole-in-the-Wall was Wyoming's toughest outlaw hangout.

The owl-voiced man slouched forward, lowered: "You better take Miss Aaron's advice, hombre! We got no use for gunslick gents around here!"

Krill stared the fellow slowly up and down, the hot purple spreading from his neck to his lower jaws. He rammed his right hand into his pocket with a hard, malevolent gesture and words came tearing out of his chest like angry animals.

"Listen—pop-eyes! Rollin' a gun on me a minute ago was a natural mistake, but it won't be no damn mistake the next time. And you better be ready to back up any leavin'-town talk you make!"

The owlish man wheeled on the crowd, hooted: "Throw down on 'im, some of you gents! We ain't gonna let him bother a girl like Zola Aaron and get away with it!"

"Dag nab it, wait a minute!" A man sidled out of the crowd. He was beaten by age and weather, his eyes almost lost behind brows that were like whiskbrooms. He wore a pair of drooping, tobacco-stained moustaches of tremendous size.

"Dag nab it, Owl Sutter!" he continued shrilly. "Ain't you kinda pushin' this too far! The gent got a knife throwed at him and he thought Zola Aaron done it. It's natural he'd do somethin' about it!"

Owl Sutter glared at him, hooted: "Stickin' up for this gunslick gent, eh?"

The weathered old cowman hooked his thumbs in his pants waistband.

"I'm stickin' up for fair play." He gestured at Krill with a jaw which had the flinty look of a bronc's hoof. "Besides, I've heard of this gent. He's known some wide on account of that fancy draw you just seen. He's Adam Krill from down in the Middle Park country. He used to be a cattle association detective down there, one of the best."

He extended a hand, open, edgewise, at Krill. "That right?"

Krill eyed the shriveled old cowman, then took the hand and shook it. "That's right. I quit the cattle association and came up here with the idea of goin' into the cow business."

"They call me Dagnabit Addison around here," said the old cowman. "I figured you was Krill. You got Zola Aaron wrong. She didn't throw no knife at you," he chuckled. "Maybe she'd shoot a man. But she'd get out in front of him to do it."

Krill wet his lips, looked at the crowd, said: "Maybe I made a mistake. Somebody else could have tossed the sticker and ducked back to the street." He shifted his eyes to Owl Sutter and they got narrow and ugly. "Maybe *you* made a mistake, too?"

Owl Sutter stared at Krill, then dropped his eyes to inspect the open palms of his own hands.

"Maybe I did—if Dagnabit Addison says you're straight," he said with bad grace. "I've heard of Adam Krill. If you're him, I guess I did make a mistake." He lifted his eyes suddenly and his voice became more hearty. "No hard feelin's, huh?"

Krill nodded. "No hard feelin's."

"I'll buy a drink," Owl Sutter said.

The crowd, some laughter in it at the way things had turned out, flowed back into the saloon. Owl Sutter amongst it.

Krill grinned dryly at Dagnabit Addison. "Thanks, old-timer. I won't forget you got me out of that."

The ancient cowman chuckled. "You wasn't in much danger, dag nab it! Owl Sutter is as popular as the itch around here. He ain't long on guts and he was talkin' big because three or four of his waddies were in that crowd." He tugged at an ear that was a leathery tuft. "Funny Owl Sutter would stick up for Zola Aaron. Her and her kid brother ranches on one side of me and Owl Sutter's spread is on the other side. I happen to know Zola Aaron thinks Sutter is lower'n mouse meat."

Krill scowled. "The funny part is who threw that sticker at me."

"You're plumb mistaken if you think it was Zola Aaron," declared Dagnabit Addison. "I know that gal. I'm gonna sell out to her as soon as she ships enough stock to pay my price."

"There's another thing funny about it." Krill bent over, pulled the knife from the dirt and tapped the short blade with a forefinger which was lean as a six-gun barrel. "Notice how short this blade is? Anybody would know it's too short a thing to kill a man with by throwin' it at him. And somebody named Joe Baker called me here with a note."

Dagnabit brought a hand up and milked his tobacco-stained moustache. "Dag nab my soul!" His voice sounded startled.

Krill eyed him sharply. "Got any idea what's behind this, old-timer? The girl acted like she thought I was tryin' to put somethin' on her."

The old cowman gave his moustache a tug, seemed to think deeply and reach a conclusion, said: "No Joe Baker in these parts. But I don't figure Zola Aaron threw that knife at you. I've known her since she was a baby. When she was born, old man Aaron figured she was just about the last word in nifty womanflesh, so he named her Zola because it was the farthest name down in the Z list he could think of. And dag nabbed if about everybody don't think he was right."

Krill separated his lips, but not his teeth, to say emphatically: "I don't!"

An hour later Adam Krill, undressing in his hotel room, happened to think of the envelope he had taken from Zola Aaron. He removed the paper it held, spread it out, read:

> Miss Aaron:
> I got something to talk to you about secret. It concerns Owl Sutter. Meet me at the corral back of the Three Aces Saloon about ten o'clock tonight.
>
> Dagnabit Addison

Krill dragged makings from his shirt, spilled tobacco in a paper and made the paper into a cylinder. He sat on his bed streaming slow smoke from his nostrils.

After thinking for a long time, he put an opinion to voice: "Kinda figured the old-timer was actin' too innocent. I'll bet the old cuss knows what's back of this. Writin' on this looks like the other."

Immediately after he said that, his face registered shock and his lanky frame rammed up stiff on the bed. He yanked the cigarette out of his mouth and stared at it with unseeing eyes.

He muttered violently: "Hell's fire! Did somebody decoy that girl there, then throw the knife at me hopin' I'd cut loose some lead and salivate her by mistake?"

Getting up, he wrenched on the clothes he had removed, something savage in his motions. He tied a thin silk thread to his black .38 and, drawing the gun up the left sleeve of his oversize shirt, tied the thread snugly around his chest. He swelled his chest slightly, making sure a very deep breath would break the thread and allow the gun to drop down his sleeve into his hand.

He left the hotel and made a quick round of streets and saloons, asking the same two questions over and over.

He learned Zola Aaron had ridden out of town for her ranch, the Saddle Horn, accompanied by her sixteen-year-old kid brother and her two punchers. Her parents had been dead some years, a man explained.

No one had an idea where old Dagnabit Addison might be.

Krill stamped back to his hotel, undressed, went to bed.

The sun had heated to near ninety degrees the butte-rimmed bowl in which Sundance lay when Adam Krill left his hotel the next morning. He ambled to the livery stable, no hurry in his movements, dumped about a gallon of oats into a nosebag and entered the corral at the rear of the establishment where he was keeping his blue roan saddle bronc.

His first glance at the horse was casual, but it suddenly became a stare that was intent and startled. His lips made a soundless whistle and an "I'll be damned!" that was sharp, explosive.

Hanging the nosebag over the roan's ears, he stepped back and studied the horse narrowly.

It had unquestionably been ridden hard during the night. Dried lather and alkali dust was like whitewash on its flank and barrel.

Krill lowered his gaze, frowned, then advanced and gave the roan's right rear a gentle kick. As the horse lifted its hoof, he caught it.

A strange shoe had been nailed on the hoof during the night, the job so cleverly done that the shoe had the appearance of having been there a long time.

Krill dropped the hoof, slapped the roan, clucked: "Get over, boy!"

The horse moved, disclosing the prints of the strange shoe were startlingly unlike those left by the other three shoes. It had square calks where the others had round calks; around the inside was a series of deep nicks.

Krill eyed the corral gates. Taking the roan and returning it secretly would not be hard. The roan was a top rope horse, a well-broke animal that anybody could ride.

Krill gave his hat a twirl, then manufactured a cigarette and got it working. He left the livery stable and was walking rapidly toward a restaurant when he met Owl Sutter. The fellow grinned widely, if not genuinely, and spoke a civil greeting.

"Seen Dagnabit Addison this mornin'?" Krill asked him.

Owl Sutter nodded. "Yeah—just a minute ago, when they took Zola Aaron's kid brother to the doctor's office. Dagnabit was with the crowd."

Krill sucked deeply off his cigarette. "What's the matter with Zola Aaron's kid brother?"

Owl Sutter carefully looked away from Krill and said: "They found him where he must have dropped off his horse about a mile from town. He was shot and unconscious, but the doc said he may wake up enough to tell who leaded him."

Krill dropped his cigarette and stepped hard on it. "Anybody ridden to notify Zola Aaron yet?"

"Not yet. Think the sheriff's waiting to see if the kid knows who shot him."

Krill eyed Owl Sutter, seemed about to say something, but apparently reconsidered and said something entirely different: "Thanks. That's too bad about the kid."

He watched Owl Sutter enter a saloon, then wheeled and went back to the livery stable with long, quick steps. He exchanged bridle for nose-bag, swung blanket and Brazos tree kak on the blue roan, cinched up, got his Winchester from the livery stable office and spurred out of town.

He already had an idea of the country's lay. Zola Aaron's Saddle Horn ranch was fourteen miles north, Dagnabit Addison's spread seven miles farther. Owl Sutter's outfit beyond that.

Krill's blue roan topped a hill and the Devil's Tower, the gigantic natural monolith of stone that was a landmark to all of northeastern Wyoming, jutted up in the distance. He rode fast, rarely slowing below a gallop. As successive miles dropped behind, he watched his horse intently.

"Whoever took him last night rode hell out of him!" he decided aloud. Then he cursed savagely.

The Saddle Horn—house, bunkhouse, sheds, corrals, hay lots—speckled the gentle southerly slope of a hill. Krill rode directly to the log ranch house, dropped the reins of his weary and blowing horse and ran toward the door.

Twenty feet from it, he halted to stare at hoofprints imprinted thickly in the dust.

Prints of a shoe with square calks and nicked inner edges were prominent—the strange shoe nailed on his blue roan during the night!

Krill flung into the Saddle Horn ranch house like a gust of rowdy wind.

A man, a Saddle Horn puncher, was spread face-up on the floor, arms outflung like a mounted, scarlet-bodied butterfly. He had been shot three times in the lungs and had died slowly.

Across the room, bullets had torn the upper panel out of a door. Krill kicked the wreck ajar. Across a chair in the bedroom beyond lay the second Saddle Horn ranny. Lead had punctured his head from ear to ear.

Eyeing the body, Krill said aloud and bitterly: "Whoever done it put that trick shoe on my bronc. I'll bet he was dressed like me and left enough life in the kid brother for him to get to town and say I done it. But—what the hell is the motive for this?"

Without raising his voice perceptibly, he called: "Miss Aaron! Miss Aaron!"

Silence made answer.

Moving with plunging speed, Krill searched the kitchen and another bedroom, but did not find Zola Aaron. Going outside, he walked abound the house in widening circles until he ascertained the departing killer had ridden westward—leading another horse.

Krill swung aboard the roan and followed the departing tracks. The range was dry, dust-coated, and the passing of the two animals had knocked dust off sage and grass, leaving a darker swath occasionally discernible half a mile ahead. He rode as fast as the weary roan could travel.

The tracks traveled a straight line to the Belle Fouche river. At a small cut-bank, the trail of one animal stopped. But the tracks of the strange shoe angled away in the direction of Sundance.

Krill dismounted, peered over the cut-bank. Water was less than six inches deep below, flowing over a yellowish-gray bottom that looked firm and smooth as concrete.

Unstrapping his lass rope, he dropped the metal hondo into the water. Slowly, it disappeared beneath the seemingly solid bottom.

Krill tugged. It took all his strength to draw the rope out. Quicksand! No telling how deep the stuff was, for the torn edge of the cut-bank was the only trace of the horse that he could plainly see had been forced to jump into it.

Absently, Krill gave his black hat a twirl. He coiled the rope and strapped it on his saddle. His cheeks had become feverish and his breath came and went through tightly pressed teeth.

"It's cinched onto me!" he said thickly. "Neat as hell!"

Then old Dagnabit Addison, erecting in the shallow gully in which he had crawled close, squawled: "Grab sky! Grab her high up!"

Krill stretched his arms stiffly above his head. Dagnabit Addison approached, his big single-action six-gun alert, took Krill's silver-gripped six and got the black .38 out of Krill's sleeve by breaking the silk thread that went around his chest.

"I seen you talkin' to Owl Sutter and followed you!" the old cowman ground harshly. "Guess you got orders to come back and make sure there was no sign left of what you done. Didn't figure on her kid brother bein' alive, did you?"

Krill moistened his lips, asked: "Did you send Zola Aaron a note last night?"

"Dry up!" Dagnabit Addison's voice was guttural with rage. "I oughta salivate you, you buzzard!"

"In my shirt pocket," Krill said steadily. "Get it."

"You can't finagle me, you sheep tick! Zola Aaron's kid brother was almost able to talk when I left town. When he does, there'll be a posse after you. I'll just hold you 'till they get here."

"There's somethin' in my shirt pocket with your name on it, old-timer," Krill said patiently. "Get it. Maybe it'll help straighten this out."

Dagnabit Addison hesitated, then put his six-gun in Krill's stomach and got the envelope Zola Aaron had carried the night before. He read the contents once. Twice. He coughed softly, rubbed his moustaches back with horny knuckles, folded the note slowly.

"I took that away from the girl last night," Krill said levely. "Did you send it to her?"

"Nope." The old rancher shook his head, then began to curse steadily with a horrible, grinding rage.

Krill interrupted in a tone louder than the old man's cursing: "That mess last night was a trap somebody set hopin' I would kill the girl. When that didn't pan out, the killer knew it would look like I had a grudge against her, so he took my bronc and raided the Saddle Horn. I been framed, old-timer. Framed high, wide and handsome."

Dagnabit Addison eyed him, bit savagely at the center hairs of his moustache. Abruptly he holstered his guns.

"I begin to savvy this!" he said hoarsely. "Get your shootin' irons, Krill. I'm gonna take a chance on you. From what I've heard, guess a feller couldn't find a better gent to take his chances on. I figured there was somethin' queer about what happened last night. Fact is, I wondered if somebody hadn't tried to fix it so you'd kill Zola Aaron by mistake. That's how I come to stick up for you last night and be watchin' you and Owl Sutter this mornin'."

Krill swallowed, asked: "You think Sutter is back of this?"

"Sure I do!" The old cowman swore vibrantly. "But provin' it is somethin' else again, dag nab his grayback infested soul!"

"Why would he want Zola Aaron killed?"

Dagnabit Addison explained rapidly, bitterly: "My ranch is between his range and Zola Aaron's. Two years ago I borrowed some money from Owl Sutter and gave him a mortgage on my spread. After that, I began having bad luck. Somebody run some blackleg critters onto my range and I lost about half my stock. Then my supply of hay burned and I lost a lot of money buyin' feed.

"A prairie fire ruined my winter range last year. I never been able to prove anybody had a hand in them things, but a month ago Owl Sutter let me know he was gonna take my ranch if I didn't pay off when my notes are due about Christmas time. Dag nab his dirty heart, I offered my place to Zola for the amount of the mortgage. And she's gonna buy me out as soon as she ships this fall. So—with her dead, Owl Sutter would get my spread."

"Your outfit must be worth a lot, old-timer?"

"If a man had the money, about ten sections could be irrigated and turned into prime hay land that'd be worth a million. That's why Owl Sutter wants it."

Krill nodded vaguely and, making a cigarette and smoking it slowly, walked for a hundred feet along the tracks left by the departing square-calked horseshoe. He studied the impressions, sometimes on hands and knees. Coming back, he followed the same procedure with the tracks approaching the quicksand hole.

He asked suddenly: "Owl Sutter ever shine around Zola Aaron?"

"Yeah." Dagnabit Addison nodded. "He tried to get her to marry him. I heard she promised to shoot him if he didn't keep away from her."

Krill asked: "Ain't you wondered why he brought the girl to this quick-sand hole?"

Dagnabit Addison stared at the ground. Tears coming out of his faded eyes filled the wrinkles in his leathery cheeks.

"I ain't thought about it," he said hoarsely. "Anybody who'd do a thing like this is a crazy man, Krill. Plumb crazy! I guess a crazy man would do things without reasons for 'em."

Krill, pointing at the hoofprints, said: "The tracks leaving here are a little deeper at the fronts, as if the bronc was carrying more weight."

The ancient cowman started; elation overspread his seamed face; he smacked a horny palm against his thigh. "You mean he drove the bronc in the quicksand to make it look like Zola Aaron was dead, then carried her off somewheres?"

Krill said: "That's the way it looks."

"We gotta find her!" Dagnabit Addison started to run for his horse, wheeled back. "Dang it, Krill—I'm gettin' old and my eyes is in no shape to ride sign or shoot. You hunt for her. I'll take your bronc and lead the posse off in the other direction. They'll follow the prints of that square-calked shoe."

Krill asked: "Can you prove where you spent last night, old-timer?"

Dagnabit Addison squinted, said too emphatically: "Sure I can! I was in a poker game until daylight with a couple of pards of mine."

"You're a damned poor liar!" Krill said softly. "If that posse catches you, they're liable to hang you higher'n hell."

Dagnabit pulled his moustaches soberly. "I don't think so. I can outtalk 'em. But if they catch you, Krill, you ain't got a chance. Go ahead and take my bronc. It's the only thing we can do."

Krill pressed his lips together tightly. He took off his hat and wiped his forehead with the back of one hand. He replaced the black .38 in his sleeve and, not looking up from tying the string about his chest, said: "Thanks, old-timer. Thanks—a lot."

Thickly, Dagnabit Addison said: "Hell—you're wastin' time."

Krill ran for the spot where the old man had left his horse. The animal was a dappled gray, a big-barreled cayuse with a promise of endurance.

Mounting, he saw Dagnabit Addison spurring the weary blue roan northward.

Krill followed the trail of the square-calked horseshoe southward toward Sundance. It was a plain trail and he rode it fast.

Half an hour later the tracks crossed a ridge, the top of which was a ledge of stone fully half a mile long and varying from a few feet to several yards in width. Krill pulled to a stop on the ledge, dismounted, bent close to the stone and squinted.

The thing he looked at was a pale brown string of burlap that might have come from a gunnysack. Straightening, he twirled his hat absently, ran his eyes thoughtfully up and down the ledge.

He pinned the dappled gray again and, though the square-calked trail continued beyond the ledge straight and plain, rode up and down the slab of stone, watching its edges.

Near the west end he found crushed cactus where a horse had left the rock. That confirmed his suspicion—the killer had wrapped gunnysacks on the blue roan's feet to conceal the horseshoe prints and ridden off to hide the girl, later returning to the stone ledge to remove the gunnysacks and continue on to Sundance.

The trail of gunnysack-wrapped prints was much harder to follow. It kept to cowpaths and angled off across rocky ground at unexpected times. Bent stems of sage, mashed grass and cactus, overturned stones, dust brushed off sage and greasewood—Krill read them all like a draftsman reads his blueprints.

The sun coasted to zenith and started down. Repeatedly, he flushed jackrabbits and sagehens and, once, a big timber wolf that had three furtive coyotes traveling with it. The country became rougher, the Wyoming badlands of the Black Hills. A herd of antelope sprang away ahead of him with tremendous, bouncing leaps, white feet flashing in the sun. Dwarfed pine trees began to spot the hilltops dark green.

It was midafternoon when Adam Krill came to the end of his trail. A cabin, ramshackle, sod-roofed, huddled among runty pines which furred the sides of a deep, waterless canyon.

Krill spilled out of the saddle and circled the cabin cautiously. He looked in the window. A flour-sack curtain obscured the interior. He tried the door. Locked. He hit the panel with a shoulder. It battered him back. He knocked the glass out of the window with his six-gun, crawled inside.

The place, evidently a line shack, was stocked with canned tomatoes and corn, a side of bacon and some flour in a three-gallon lard can. It had been used not so long ago.

There was—he saw it when he lifted his eyes—an attic of poles and crudely hewn planks. There was no opening. Mounting the rickety table, he beat against the attic flooring until he found two boards that were loose. He grasped the edges of the opening made by their removal, chinned himself and climbed up.

A moment later he lowered Zola Aaron into the cabin. She was bound to a fence post, the ropes encircling her form and the post like a mummy's wrappings. She was gagged. She was also unconscious.

He untied her, took a can of the tomatoes, shot a hole through it and trickled some of the juice between her lips and on her face. He rubbed her arms briskly. There was a welt in her wealth of brown hair; she was either unconscious from that or the tightness of her bindings.

She opened her eyes at last, shuddered and shut them tightly.

"You're all right now," Krill said gently. "Take it easy—"

Zola Aaron had seized his six-gun and jammed it against his side. Holding the weapon pointed at him, she pushed herself away from him on the floor, then got to her feet.

"I'll kill you!" she screamed hysterically. "Make one more and I'll kill you!"

Patiently, Krill said: "You're makin' a mistake."

"Mistake!" She laughed wildly. "Do you think I don't know you because you were masked last night? Think I don't know it was you who shot my brother and my two punchers and knocked me unconscious and brought me here?"

Krill's quartz-like eyes were filmed; perspiration was a mist on his face; his breathing was in short spurts, as if his lungs hurt.

"You think—it was me?" he asked, the words coming in two jerks.

"I *know* it was!" shrilled Zola Aaron.

Owl Sutter, stepping sidewise and forward so that he came from outside to the center of the cabin door, said: "Now, ain't this nice!"

He came in and crossed the floor rapidly, reaching for the gun Zola Aaron held, his own six-gun trained on Krill.

Krill yelled: "Don't give him that gun! Don't—he's the man that killed—!" He stopped when he saw Owl Sutter had Zola Aaron's gun.

Owl Sutter laughed harshly, said, "You'd buy old Dagnabit's ranch, would you!" and struck the side of the girl's head with his open hand, knocking her across the cabin. She fell into a bunk backward, struggled out of it and stood staring at Sutter. Then understanding blanched her face.

"Oh!" she choked. "You—you wore a mask and did it! And I let you take my gun!" Her legs seemed to lose all their strength, letting her down on the floor.

Krill had lowered his hands—both were rigid at his sides. Air came into his lungs in a slow rush, swelling his ribs against the string that held the black .38 in his sleeve.

"I saw old Dagnabit Addison follow you and I trailed along," Owl Sutter smirked. "I saw you two meet and figured you had seen through my quick-sand trick. Now I'll just plug you and say I done it tryin' to capture you. Then I'll use your gun on the girl and say you done it. That'll fix all—"

He discovered Krill's swelling chest. His jaw shot down; his eyes protruded as if air had been pumped behind them. Apparently he still didn't know where that gun had come from the night before, but he associated Krill's swelling chest with it and he was terrified. His six-gun jutted forward and exploded.

The sleeve gun was in Krill's hand and tilting up when Owl Sutter's slug hit and broke his left arm. The shock spun Krill slightly; the .38 caromed off the wall behind him like a billiard ball.

Zola Aaron screamed and sprang up from beside the bunk. Owl Sutter half-wheeled and raised his silver-gripped six-gun to shoot her.

A chair stood within reach of Krill's right foot. He kicked the chair—there was no time to throw it—he kicked it at Owl Sutter. The chair hit Owl in the chest, knocked his arms aside.

Going down, Owl fired. His bullet made a trench of agony across Krill's neck.

Jumping and lashing madly with his feet, Krill kicked both the guns out of Owl Sutter's hands. One nipped through the door. The other bounced off the wall and stopped near the girl's feet.

Krill leaped for the latter gun.

Owl Sutter ran for the one outside.

They reached the weapons about the same instant. Owl Sutter fired his when it was hardly off the ground. The bullet passed so near Krill's ear that the air closing after it was a sound like a stick breaking.

Krill pitched sidewise to better his aim. He fired, but fell over the chair at the same instant and missed. Rolling, he reached the door and banged it shut to keep Owl Sutter from killing Zola Aaron.

Silence descended like something solid.

Krill gritted at the girl: "Get behind the stove, where he can't hit you from the window!"

Zola Aaron obeyed quickly.

Straining his ears through the crash of his own pulse, Krill heard—

A Winchester shot! Outside the cabin Owl Sutter gave a shrill bark of terrified surprise and fired back. The Winchester smashed again, the slug slapping the cabin logs loudly.

Then Owl Sutter ran away from the cabin.

A shrill voice began swearing steadily, disgustedly and came nearer. Krill plucked open the door.

Old Dagnabit Addison, hopping toward the cabin and flourishing his Winchester, wailed: "Dag nab it if I ain't gettin' too old to shoot, even! He got plumb away!"

Zola Aaron began to sob wildly, hysterically. Krill went over to her, put his arm that was not broken around her, palm pressing flat against her back.

He said gently: "Don't act like that, dear. Your brother wasn't badly hurt. Don't act like that."

Dagnabit Addison, hopping into the cabin with a trouser leg hauled up to inspect a fresh bullet hole in his stringy calf, howled: "Dang his soul! I was scoutin' from a hill for the posse and seen he had been watchin' us, so I trailed him. I'd have got here sooner, only—"

A spattering of distant rifle shots sounded, tossing echoes in the canyon like a roll of faint thunder. They came again, a flurry of possibly a dozen, and the echoes died away into nothingness.

Old Dagnabit Addison licked his lips like a tomcat skulking away from a goldfish bowl.

"Like I started to tell you," he said softly. "I'd have got here sooner— only I stopped to nail that trick hoss shoe on Owl Sutter's bronc. The posse wasn't far behind me. Dag nab it, I'll bet two bits they saw the tracks that shoe was leavin' and plumb salivated Owl!"

· · · · ·

Fear Ranch

The puncher was long and lathy, somewhat mulelike of face. He was shaking brown tobacco flakes onto a brown rice paper when it happened.

Two shots banged, filled the canyon with clamor like rocks in a rolling barrel. A woman's cry, a frightened wail like a hurt puppy, splintered into the thumping echoes. Then hoofs beat a mad rattle.

The puncher's piebald gelding spooked at the uproar and tried to buck. He kept the animal's head up so it could only prance, grunted: "Whoa, you jughead!"

Around a bend in the canyon popped a small, dappled gray bronc. A woman folded over the saddle horn, looking back. Her right hand quirted the gray steadily. Her left hand, holding the reins slack over the gray's whipping mane, also gripped a short Winchester.

A hundred feet from the lathy puncher, she turned her head and saw him. She pulled up, jerked the Winchester against her shoulder.

She was young, twenty or less. Her small cowman's boots and corduroy riding skirt had seen a lot of use. A black John B., nearly new, was jerked low over her eyes. Below it, her features were fixed, pale as a sculpture in marble.

"Keep your hands away from that gun!" she snapped, then demanded coldly: "Hanging around to see that your friend did a good job?"

A shocked look overspread the puncher's face. He said: "You got me plumb wrong!"

The girl glanced uneasily over her shoulder, gestured with the Winchester barrel at a gully that gashed the canyon wall to their left. "Ride in there!"

The puncher frowned, moistened his lips.

"Hurry up!" she ordered.

He forced his snorting piebald into the water-torn rent. The girl followed, alert.

"That's far enough!" she warned. "You ride for the Lazy-N, don't you?"

His frown became a scowl. "What give you that idea?"

She rammed the Winchester at his face, gritted: "Answer my question, cowboy!"

"I'm a stranger in this neck of Wyomin'," he said in a voice anger made brittle. "My name is Titus—Sephus Titus. An' I ain't ridin' for nobody right now. Fact is, I'm huntin' a job."

The girl eyed him steadily. "Somebody took a couple of shots at me a minute ago. There was only one man, I think."

Titus stared at the Winchester muzzle, color inching up in his neck. "Then you better cut out this foolishness an' let me scout around for whoever it was bushwhacked you."

The girl continued to eye him, then shrugged, holstered her Winchester.

"Maybe I made a mistake," she admitted. "Running into you that way, I thought you were with the man who shot at me."

Still scowling, he asked: "Which side of the canyon did the shot come from?"

"The right! But there's no use following him. He probably rode off when he saw he had missed me. That's the kind of an outfit the Lazy-N is— shoot from ambush, then run."

He eyed her sharply. "You're sure it was a puncher from this Lazy-N? You see him?"

"No," she admitted. "But it must have been some of them. Either the owner, Pike Jiggins, or one of his hands. We've been having trouble with them."

He neckreined his piebald around. "I'll see what I can do. I dunno what this is all about, but shootin' at a woman takes that hombre out of the human class an' makes him plain varmint. Season's always open on them. There oughta be a trail where he rode away."

"Wait—please!" A sharp note of pleading was suddenly in the girl's voice.

He twisted in the saddle to look a question.

"I—I would rather you rode part way home with me," she said haltingly. "I—well, I'm afraid. He might try again."

Titus stared at her, his homely face mirroring none of his thoughts. "Sure—maybe I'd better do that instead."

The girl nodded up the gulch. "We'd better go that way."

They rode in a trot while the cut narrowed and the steep sides decreased in height. A bit later they were among the rough cactus-and-sage crusted gray hills of the Little Powder brakes. The girl reined west.

"Mind tellin' me what this is all about?" Titus asked.

She looked at him a moment. "I guess you're entitled to an explanation. I'm Carla Norbeck. My stepfather, Mad Hatters, owns the High Hat outfit. Somebody has been holding up our punchers and beating them, and even shooting some of them, although none have been killed."

She paused, then added bitterly:

"The purpose of that was to scare our hands into quitting, of course. It worked. Day before yesterday one of our men got shot in the leg. We had the sheriff out, but he found nothing. Then, yesterday, this masked man shot into the kitchen where our cook was working. He drew his time and left."

"Masked man?" Titus interrupted.

"Yes—the man who does it always wears a black raincoat and black mask. We have no proof he is from the Lazy-N. Pike Jiggins has a bad reputation, though, and we've had trouble with him before. This masked rider has succeeded in scaring all of our hands but one, Baldy Wade, into quitting. We're in the middle of the haying season. If we don't get our hay put up, the winter will wipe us out."

Titus did not look up from the cigarette he was making.

"Jiggins is low-down mean!" the girl said angrily. "He owns about sixty sections of land he got by driving homesteaders out of business after they proved up, forcing them to sell out to him. He would like to get the High Hat. And, well—he wanted to marry me. I guess this trouble started when I turned him down."

"You figure the masked man is maybe Pike Jiggins?"

"That's what we're going to find out—as soon as we get our hands on somebody riding for the Lazy-N."

Titus glanced at her sharply, put a match to his cigarette and drew in slowly, watching the girl from the corner of an eye. His appraisal, mildly interested at first, became puzzled when he noted she seemed strangely uneasy. Her face was still as pale and strained as it had been in the canyon.

He was still wondering about that when two riders appeared ahead. The girl scrutinized them eagerly.

"Good!" she gasped. "That's my stepfather, Mad Hatters, and the one puncher we have left, Baldy Wade."

The two men reined their broncs about, came through the sage at a gallop. They pulled up a dozen feet away.

Titus, lifting a hand, palm out in the Indian sign of a friend, said: "Howdy—"

His greeting ended in a startled croak as both riders suddenly drew guns and leveled them at him.

The girl's Winchester leaped from the saddle scabbard, gouged his side.

"Lift 'em, cowboy!" she advised frigidly.

Titus pushed higher the hand already up, hastily elevated the other beside it. His mouth opened wide, then shut hard without letting out words.

One of the two men grated: "Frisk 'im, Baldy!"

The man called Baldy dropped off his horse. His was a form once tremendously powerful, now shrunken to a great, stooped framework of bone and wrinkled, ash-colored skin. Above his ears, his head was a gray, hairless knob; below them, his face was covered with reddish gray beard which was coarse and long as a mane. A few scattered hairs made eyebrows over eyes that were a pair of deep wrinkles filled with glitter.

He relieved Titus of an ivory-handled six-gun and removed a .38-55 Winchester from the untanned cowhide sheath under the stirrup. His hands slapped over Titus' person. Stepping back, he shook his head.

"That's the size of it. He ain't packin' a hideout, Mad."

The hand with which Mad Hatter flung the reins over his bronc's head twitched as if palsied. In dismounting, he all but fell, so uncontrollably did a nervousness jerk his body about. He was a tall man, near forty, not fat, but rather padded by good living. His face was startlingly pallid for a cowman. His eyes were bloodshot and their lids fluttered with an uncontrollable nervousness. When the girl spoke, he started as if struck.

She said: "He sure fell for it!"

Titus turned his head, saw she was looking at him and made a pained scowl. "Whatcha mean, ma'am?"

"Nobody drygulched me. I fired those two shots myself. We wanted you, but we didn't want any gunplay."

Titus pushed back his worn brown hat. "You mean that bushwhackin' was all a—a story?"

"And a pretty good one, don't you think, Mister Lazy-N Rider?"

His mouth and eyes pictured surprise. "Huh?"

"Oh, we know you're a Lazy-N ranny!" snapped the girl. "You told me you weren't riding for them. You liar! We were watching the Lazy-N and saw you get your piebald out of their corral and ride for the High Hat."

Titus blinked. "You saw me do that?"

"We did! You're not denying it, are you?"

"I don't reckon there'd be much use," he grunted.

Baldy yelled suddenly; "Don't—you fool!"

Bang! The bullet passed so near Titus' ear that it made a distinct click. His head sank instinctively into his shoulders; his gaze swiveled around.

Smoke was curling pallid gray strings from the muzzle of Mad Hatter's six-gun. Baldy had one shrunken claw of a hand fastened to the gun. With the other he warded off the fist with which Hatter mauled him.

"We don't want a killin'!" Baldy shouted angrily. "There ain't been none yet an' we don't wanta start it!"

Hatter snarled: "Leggo my gun! Damn the Lazy-N! They've beat up, shot and run off my rannies! Why'n hell shouldn't I shoot him? Why'n hell shouldn't I?"

Titus vaulted off his piebald, leaped for the pair.

"Hold on, cowboy!" snapped Carla Norbeck.

Titus halted, slanted a lowering eye at the girl. Her face had paled more; her eyes were horrified globes.

"Keep back!" she warned over the Winchester muzzle. "Baldy can handle him."

Baldy, straining furiously, got Mad Hatter's gun. The instant he had it, Hatter ceased struggling and stood, arms and legs trembling like reeds in a wind.

Baldy looked at Titus, his eyes nearly invisible in the wrinkles.

Titus said: "Thanks, feller."

In a guttural, enraged voice, Baldy said: "You go to hell!"

"Plug him, Baldy!" Hatter snarled.

"You're loco!" Baldy yelled at him. "We plug him and the whole Lazy-N spread will land on us with the sheriff. We'll do what we planned to do when we trap him—make him tell us who the masked rider is and sign a statement to that effect."

Mad Hatter licked his twitching lips, said viciously: "I'll help you! I can make him talk!"

"You will, like blazes!" Baldy grunted. "You'd bash in his head or some-thin'. You ain't in no shape for a job like this. You take the girl and ride back to the High Hat. I'll make this jasper talk."

"Yes, dad, let's go home," the girl chipped in. "Baldy can— Baldy knows best."

Hatter glared at Titus. "Do it right, Baldy! Pay him back for what the Lazy-N done to our punchers."

With shaking hands, he threw the reins over the head of his bronc. His manner of getting on the horse seemed to entail great effort, as if he were incapable of directing his own movements.

Titus kept his gaze on the girl while she swung aboard the dappled gray, waiting for her to meet his eye. When she did not and he saw she was not going to do so, he said:

"I dunno whether to hold this agin' you or not. Hoss sense says I oughta. But I guess I ain't no hoss, because I kinda like your nerve."

The girl did not look at him and did not reply.

Titus' words enraged Hatter more. He snarled: "Beat him until he's raw meat for insultin' her, Baldy! Show him the Lazy-N is gonna get back as good as they give!"

He and the girl rode away.

Loudly, so they could hear him, Baldy ordered: "Pin your cayuse, Lazy-N hombre! Ride into that canyon!"

Titus boarded the piebald. They rode in a fog of cold silence until the canyon walls tossed up sheer sandstone about them. The gash veered abruptly, let them into a sharp-angled job which enclosed them on all sides.

Baldy pulled up, grinned, handed Titus his six-gun and Winchester.

"You oughta be an actor, fella," he said. "I was kinda afraid you'd let on you knowed me." Titus holstered his ivory-handled six with an angry gesture, slapped the Winchester in the saddle sheath.

He scowled, said: "When I talked with you in Sheridan, you told me Mad Hatter was worried, but you didn't say nothin' 'bout him bein' plumb crazy!"

"He's got worse since he sent me to hire you," Baldy muttered. "This masked man has about got his nanny. I never saw anything quite like it."

"Why'd you pull that wild stunt a minute ago? Why not tell Hatter and the girl I'm the jasper Hatter sent you to hire to get this masked hombre?"

Baldy peered furtively about the canyon rim. "I had a damn good reason. Let's talk fast. How come you didn't get a job on the Lazy-N, like we planned?"

"They was full up. Jiggins said they'd laid off four hands yesterday."

"You reckon they knew you was a trouble-buster we'd hired to clean this mess up?"

"Nobody knows me on this range." Titus squinted thoughtfully. "You know, it's kinda strange, but when I asked Jiggins about chances of gettin' work at the High Hat, he cussed and ranted and said two of his rannies had been shot by a masked man. He seemed to think the gent in the mask was a High Hat hand."

Baldy abruptly drew his six-gun, fired it into the ground.

"What the hell?" Titus barked.

"Tell you in a minute!" Baldy said swiftly. "Jiggins is that masked rider, or one of his men is. When we had the sheriff out to see about our men gettin' shot up, Jiggins told the sheriff he'd had the same trouble. He's just fixin' up an alibi for himself. Nobody else has got a reason to do these things to the High Hat."

"You learn anythin' by watchin' the Lazy-N?"

Baldy shot another anxious look around the canyon lip. "Not a dang thing."

Titus tilted forward in his saddle, asked savagely: "What the hell is eatin' you? You act like somebody is watchin' us!"

"I think there will be before long. This masked hombre was trailin' us. I saw him sneakin' through the brakes a couple of times while we was followin' you."

Titus swore. "Then that's why you didn't tell Mad Hatter an' the girl who I was? You wanted it to look to this jasper like you all thought I was a Lazy-N ranny and was holdin' me up?"

Baldy grinned fiercely. "That's the idea. Now I'm gonna ride off, leaving you behind lookin' like you been tromped on considerable. I'm bettin' he'll come up to have a look at you, out of curiosity. When he does, cut down on him!"

Titus grunted, dropped off his piebald, began dashing dust on his clothing.

"I told Carla Norbeck my right name," he said as he worked. "How come she didn't know I was the jasper Mad Hatter sent you to Sheridan to hire?"

"She don't know Hatter had me hire anybody. Of course, she'll tell him your name and he'll know he made a mistake about you. No harm's done."

"There danged near was when he tried to plug me!"

Baldy scowled. "The rattle-brained old goop! Maybe that'll teach him not to be in such a damn hurry to shoot people."

Titus flopped on the earth, right hand under him, gripping his gun, the other arm and both legs twisted grotesquely. "There's quite a difference between Hatter and that girl. He's her step-daddy, huh?"

Baldy's voice suddenly became scratching. "Yeah. Him and Jim Norbeck went off to the war. Jim Norbeck was killed in action. That's a damn war for you. Fellers like Jim stop machine gun slugs, while jaspers like Mad Hatter don't get a scratch, Hatter done his fightin' in a swivel chair in Paris, I heard. Anyway, he come back an' married Jim Norbeck's widow. She died 'bout five years ago. That's how Hatter got his outfit. By marryin' the widow of Jim Norbeck."

Titus eyed Baldy curiously. "You don't think a hell of a lot of Hatter, do you?"

Baldy scowled. "He ain't no part of a man. You saw the shape he's in. He's that way because he's plain scared. His backbone is limber as a dead rattler. I wouldn't be stickin' with the High Hat if it wasn't for Jim Norbeck's girl. She needs somebody to take care of her. Mad Hatter ain't no man for the job. That bushwackin' trick was a sample of how little he cares what happens to her. He thought up the idea of her leadin' you to us. I let her go through with it 'cause I knowed she wouldn't get hurt with you."

"This oughta fool that gent in the mask," Titus said.

Baldy swung on his horse. "I'll ride far enough to make him think I'm goin' to the High Hat. It may be an hour before I get back."

He spurred down the canyon.

Titus' face was thoughtful as he watched Baldy depart. He listened, casting his eyes about alertly. In the distance a bull bawled several closely joined roars of deep sound. Small yellow-headed flies with bites like jabbing needles began to swarm about.

Some time later a scattered cloud of sage chickens went over the canyon rim with a rushing drone of wings. Titus stared at the spot where they appeared, wondering if something had frightened the birds. His eyes widened as a pebble rolled down the canyon side.

Some seconds later the phenomenon repeated itself. He scowled, swore softly. Then he realized somebody was throwing the pebbles from behind him. His knowledge came too late.

"Just hold that pose, sleepin' beauty!" advised a rasping, metallic voice.

Titus rolled his head—not too quickly. A man stood a few yards away—a tall man enveloped completely in a black raincoat and a black sack of a mask. His hands were gloved and each held a blue Frontier .46.

"Get up!" directed the masked man. "An' leave that gun you're layin' on stay where it is."

Titus wet his lips, scowled, decided it would be better to comply. He stood up. "I'd have sworn a rabbit couldn't sneak up on me. You must be part ghost."

A chuckle rattled in the depths of the sepia mask. "Yeah, I am sort of a ghost at that. But I seen through your 'possum scheme."

The masked man sent a shower of cartridges out of Titus' gun, tossed it away.

"You workin' for the High Hat?" he asked.

Titus stared at the fellow, trying to decide what sort of a person was behind the mask. The man's voice sounded aged. His body looked thin, wasted.

Titus noted the man's riding boots were embroidered with green hearts, then said: "T'hell with you, sonny!"

The black raincoat made a rubbing sound as the other shrugged. "I got here in time to hear you an' Baldy talkin', so I know who you're workin' for."

The chuckle crackled in the mask again. "Like you said, I *can* get around on this range like a ghost in the house where he was raised, even if this is the first day I've been able to ride. You can tell Mad Hatter that."

Titus sneered: "You're talkin' locoed."

"It won't sound locoed to Mad Hatter. You tell him the bullets he put into the ha'nt two months ago didn't do the job." The masked man's voice became shriller. "Tell him I'm gonna make him die by inches. Tell him I've thought of lots of ways of doin' it in them two months I nearly died from the cripplin' he give me. Then you can get out of the country. This ain't nothin' for strangers to mix in. I ain't got no hanker to do you damage."

Titus grated: "I'll take care of myself!"

"I'd hate to have to hurt you. But I won't have my plans spoiled."

The masked man backed away rapidly. Fifty feet distant, he called: "You give Mad Hatter my message about the ha'nt! That's the only reason I had a talk with you."

The man wheeled, leaped out of sight around an angle in the canyon.

Titus gritted, "Damned if this makes sense!" and raced to his gun. He loaded it, ran to the spot where the masked man had vanished. A narrow cleft slanted upward. He climbed. Halfway up, he heard a flurry of hoof sound.

Swearing, he descended, mounted his piebald and spurred down the canyon until he found a spot where he could ride out. He galloped back, hunting a trail. He found it without difficulty—the hoofprints of a madly running horse.

He followed the sign, surprised at the speed he was able to make. No effort had been made to guide the animal onto stony ground where no hoofprints would have been left.

He covered a mile, two. Then, pulling up suddenly, he jerked a brass slide-telescope from one saddlebag. He used it, then reared back like an opera singer to let profanity boil out of his lungs.

Far ahead, he had seen the horse he was following. It was still running full tilt. It bore neither saddle, bridle or rider—and it was running only because scared of a lass rope tied to its tail.

Reining about, Titus galloped for the canyon. He met Baldy Wade sitting his horse on the gash rim.

"Didya get 'im?" demanded the whiskered High Hat foreman.

"Get—hell!" Titus snorted sheepishly. "He sneaked up on me like I was no more'n a sagebrush. Then, when I tried to follow him, he tied a rope to a bronc's tail to keep it spooked and runnin'. Like a ninny, I followed the hoss—givin' him plenty of time to clear out."

Baldy growled: "Damn the Lazy-N!"

Titus fished out makings and got a cigarette working. "You know, that masked jasper's actions was sure locoed. He could have salivated me, but instead he seemed plumb worried for fear I'd get hurt. Somehow, that don't jibe with the Lazy-N crowd."

Baldy tugged wrathfully at his beard. "It's gotta be the Lazy-N! Ain't nobody else got a reason for pickin' on the High Hat."

"Maybe," Titus admitted. "But this masked gent as much as said Mad Hatter shot him and left him for dead two months ago, and that he hadn't been able to ride until today."

"The hell he did!" Baldy exploded. "That's about when Hatter started gettin' the jitters. This masked jasper give you any clue who he was?"

"Nope. Just said for me to tell Hatter the ghost of the man he thought he killed two months ago was gonna ha'nt him plumb to death."

"I'll be a sonofagun!" Baldy muttered. "This is gettin' to be a danged deep, black mystery."

Titus gathered up his reins. "I'm gonna scout some before night makes it darker. You tell Miss Norbeck I ain't no onery Lazy-N yahoo like she thinks, will you?"

"Sure."

Baldy wheeled and rode in the direction of the High Hat.

Titus, setting his piebald at a gallop, made for the Lazy-N spread of Pike Jiggins. He rolled and smoked successive cigarettes, pinching each out between a bony thumb and forefinger before he threw it away. His homely face was thoughtful, but only mildly puzzled.

It took him nearly an hour to reach the Lazy-N establishment, ramshackle sheds, corrals, dipping and dehorning chutes and fenced haystacks that clustered about the low bunkhouse and ranch house.

Dismounting, Titus strode into the bunkhouse. He had learned that afternoon that Jiggins had only four riders. All four of them were in the bunkhouse. They gave him a greeting of surly silence.

Titus grinned bleakly at them, ran his eyes over their feet in search of a pair of boots with green embroidered hearts, such as the masked man had worn. Finding none, he asked: "Where's Jiggers?"

"House," one grunted.

Titus strode to the ranch house.

Pike Jiggers was a squat man, ruddy of face, soft of hand. His mouth was square, lips big and solid. His eyes, small, turtle-like, crowded close to his spongy nose.

He said sourly: "What're you back for? I told you we ain't hirin' no hands!"

"Oh, I ain't havin' any luck," Titus explained innocently. "So figured I'd like to put up here for the night."

"We ain't got room for you."

Titus looked at Jiggins' boots, saw they had no green embroidery. "Sure, if you feel that way about it."

He turned to go, then seemed to think of something. "I ran into your masked friend this afternoon."

Jiggins' little eyes popped like beads. He roared: "What?"

Titus was astounded at the effect of his words, but his mulish face remained inscrutable:

"Sure," he said. "The feller who's been shootin' your rannies."

"There ain't—" Jiggins bit that statement off—his very haste showing he had been about to declare none of his punchers had been shot. "Where the hell'd you see him?"

"About ten miles west of here."

Jiggins rubbed a hand across his solid lips. His little eyes narrowed, acquired a cunning expression. "Did he get around pretty spry?"

Titus showed by no sign that the query surprised him. He said: "He looked spry enough to me. He had a couple of guns and I didn't inquire too close into the state of his health. But he said somethin' about bein' in shape to finish some business he had with the High Hat. Told me to pass Mad Hatter the news if I got a chance."

Jiggins looked at his hands with a disinterested expression that was plainly assumed. "He say when he was gonna transact this business?"

Titus thought swiftly, picked a reply at random out of a prolific brain.

"Sure. He said to tell Mad Hatter it'd be tomorrow."

A tightening of Jiggins' mouth showed the words gave him a shock. He scowled. "Why'd he tell you all that?"

"Well, I told him I was headed for the High Hat scoutin' for a job," Titus explained blandly. "He gimme that as a message. But I decided not to go there huntin' work. I don't want no trouble."

Jiggins glowered, said: "Well, you can't stay here tonight. We ain't runnin' no hotel for range bums."

Titus glared, roared, "Range bum, huh!" and hit Jiggins in the mouth with his right fist. He cut his knuckles. Jiggins staggered backward. Titus, following him closely, clipped his left to the man's fat jaw. The blow made a sound like a loud handclap.

Jiggins struck the floor a dead weight that shook all the house. He breathed noisily, but did not move.

Titus, making a dusting motion with his hands, roared again, "Range bum, huh!" and stamped outside.

He forked his piebald and rode in the direction of town until he was out of sight, then altered his course for the High Hat. The sun was hanging about its own width above the horizon and fat cattle were already beginning to bed down for the night.

After he had ridden a while, he began to state opinions aloud, as if he wanted to hear how reasonable they sounded.

"Pike Jiggins as much as said none of his waddies had been shot, which proves he was lyin' about that the first time I seen him," he declared. "And he was plumb interested in learnin' this masked hombre was up and about. That means he knows a lot about that jasper he ain't tellin'. And it means the masked gent has really been laid up."

He swore softly, then grinned: "Now I wonder if my lyin' about the masked jasper goin' to finish his job tomorrow was the right thing?"

He grinned more widely. "Poppin' Jiggins that way oughta get him in a frame of mind for some action, anyhow."

Pulling up suddenly, he sat rigid in the saddle for fully a minute while his face became gladly alight.

"By crackey—it's come to me! Just about the whole danged thing!"

With his spurs, he poked the piebald into a gallop. The sun, lowering, balanced a bright ball on the horizon. Off to the right, a small herd of antelope appeared, running swiftly. They saw him, veered away in greater fright.

Titus watched them out of sight, lips pursed for a whistle that didn't sound. "Them beasties don't spook none at sight of a cow. That means they saw a man on hossback—somebody trailin' me."

He neckreined the piebald to the left, made for a high knoll. Atop it, he stopped.

Taking a pencil and a notebook from his pocket, he wrote:

Mister Masked Man:

It seems that Pike Jiggins has been playing masked rider while you was laid up. Somebody dressed in an outfit like your'n has been trying to put the High Hat out of business and Jiggins has spread word around that the same party has been bothering him.

I wouldn't be surprised that Jiggins has some dirty work he'll try to pull before tomorrow.

The Jasper Who Didn't Catch the Ghost

Chuckling low mirth, he tore the sheet from the notebook, dismounted, made a little pile of rocks and weighted the paper on top. Mounting, he rode on.

A mile distant, he halted and focused his telescope on the hill. He had not watched long before the man in the black raincoat and mask rode to the spot where the note lay. The fellow bestrode a roan horse, bareback, guiding the animal with a rope hackamore.

He got the note, read it. Then he waved an arm, mounted and went out of sight at a gallop.

Titus laughed softly. "I dunno where that gent is, but he's got the earmarks of a white man. That's more'n can be said truthful for Pike Jiggins an' Mad Hatter."

He urged the piebald for the High Hat.

Darkness had seeped over the range before he reached the ranch. Calves in a corral were bawling lustily. Unperturbed by the sound, a couple of small wild ducks of a species that summered in the Wyoming range country swam on a water hole near the corral, making ripples that shimmered in the increasing moonlight.

Titus unsaddled where Baldy was graining work horses in a corral. He grained his piebald with the work animals and made for the ranch house at a fast walk, leaving Baldy to finish choring.

Carla Norbeck had changed to a figured house dress which fitted her shapely form admirably. Her hair, darkly brown and luxuriant as a sable pelt, was drawn down and made into flat whorls over her ears.

"Baldy told me who you are," she said. "I'm terribly sorry for the way I acted—and for what my—what my stepfather nearly did."

Titus grinned. "That's all right."

"I saved some supper, if you're hungry."

"I could eat you!" he declared admiringly.

"You must be hungry!" she laughed.

"I wouldn't have to be to do that. You look sweet as an ice cream sundae I ate once in Sheridan."

"Whew-w-w!" she gasped. "Baldy said you had more nerve than any man in Wyoming! I believe him."

"It ain't that. I'm just able to tell which is the prettiest girl in Wyomin' when I see her. I'm an expert that way."

"You must have had lots of practice," she said archly.

"Nope." Titus got out of that smoothly. "I just discovered today what an expert I am."

She said: "You better eat your supper, cowboy!"

"Sure," he agreed. "Sit down with me. I wanta talk to you—about business. Do you know anybody besides Pike Jiggins who could have a grudge against Mad Hatter?"

The girl seated herself. "No one."

"That's funny. Pike Jiggins ain't the only one that's got designs on your stepfather."

"What do you mean?"

He grinned at her. "I'm not sure enough yet to start talkin'. But this afternoon I done a couple of things that should start some fellers thinkin'. Sorta started rockin' the boat. If I rock it hard enough, maybe it'll upset."

"What you're saying doesn't make much sense," she said, perplexed.

"That's on account of you. Just lookin' at you sorta makes me dizzy."

She stood up, color in her cheeks.

But before she could say whatever she intended, Baldy poked his head into the room.

"We heard somebody comin'," he said. "Sounds like about five riders."

"Daggone!" Titus muttered in a shocked tone. "It looks like I've plumb upset the boat with the first rock!"

He blew out the lamp, grasped the girl by the arm, shoved her toward Baldy. "Don't let whoever it is know I'm here!"

Baldy stared wonderingly. "You got an idea who it is?"

"Pike Jiggins and his gunhands, maybe! Hurry up. I'll stand by in case somethin' happens. They don't know yet that I'm workin' for you, so they won't expect me here. Where's Mad Hatter?"

"Just got in from takin' a walk down to the haystacks. He don't know you're back. I'll tell him."

Titus hesitated, said: "Don't tell him. He's nervous and might give me away. Get in the other room."

The girl and Baldy, swallowing their questions, went into the other room. Peering through the door, Titus saw Mad Hatter come in a moment later and crouch by the window, trembling, peering toward the approaching sound of hoofbeats. He seemed in the last stages of fear.

Titus drew his six, gave the cylinder a spin and replaced it loose in the leather. He plucked a dozen cartridges from his belt, enough for two reloadings, and held them in his left hand.

Outside, Pike Jiggins' coarse voice hailed: "Hello the house!"

"What d'you want?" Mad Hatter quavered.

"Just a peaceful talk!" Jiggins shouted. "Can we come in?"

Titus breathed, "Peaceable—hell!" and hefted his six uneasily.

Mad Hatter apparently considered, then said: "Come in. But don't start nothin'!"

Spurs clattered. Heeled down in the dark kitchen, Titus saw Pike Jiggins and his four sullen punchers stalk into the other room.

"What you got to talk about?" Hatter snarled.

Jiggins twisted his square mouth into a grin. "Just hold your hosses, fella. Our visit is plumb friendly, like I said. It's about that masked gent."

"The masked—" Hatter shrieked. "What about him? Where is he?"

Jiggins leered, said: "C'mere an' I'll show you." He walked to the table, whipped a folded paper from his pocket. "Look at this!"

Hatter jumped forward, bent over the paper.

Jiggins, not looking at his four men, shouted: "All right, boys!" Then he seized Hatter's gun from his holster and struck the man a swiping blow across the temple. Hatter reeled across the room, making squealing sounds of fright and agony.

The other four men pounced on Baldy. The old cowman freed his six, pumped a shot that hit nobody. Then three hands leeched to his gun wrists.

Titus, in the kitchen, filled his throat with silent, tearing oaths, because he could not shoot into the melee without likelihood of hitting Baldy.

A gun barrel made an arc, stopped with a thump on Baldy's hairless head. He collapsed.

One of Jiggins' men lunged, seized the girl. After a short struggle in which he received a long scratch across his face, the man pinned her arms.

Jiggins seized Hatter, propelled the quaking man to the table and jammed his face against the paper.

"Blank!" he sneered. "Just a trick to get your attention while we grabbed you!"

Hatter began to blubber words. "Pike—what're you tryin' to do? You ain't gonna hurt us, are you?"

"Naw, we ain't gonna hurt you!" Jiggins leered. "We're just gonna salivate you an' old Baldy. That won't hurt—for long!"

"Me! Me!" Hatter screamed. "You—you can't do a thing like that! They—they'll hang you. The sheriff knows we been havin' trouble. You—he'll know it was you."

Jiggins sneered a laugh. "No, he won't. Because we're gonna capture the murderer. Only he's gonna be killed gettin' captured."

"What—what do you mean?" Hatter whined.

Jiggins slammed the trembling man down on the floor and kicked his groveling form.

"We know all about the masked man who started scarin' you to death a couple of months ago," he leered. "We know all about how you shot the feller with a hideout gun you was carryin' an' left him for dead. We know that because we found him an' nursed him back on his feet. He told us about it while he was delirious."

"You found—" Hatter's voice was a terrorized shriek. "He's alive, then!"

"He sure is. Alive an' rarin' to settle with you. We know why, too. We know how you killed a man in Paris durin' the war an' hung the blame onto him. He was visitin' you at the time. We know he served more'n ten years on Devil's Island for it, then escaped an' come back an' found you had managed to get him reported killed in action an' had married his wife."

Carla Norbeck stiffened in the clutch of her captor. Her eyes widened until the whites showed a ring; her lips parted. She gasped:

"Oh! Oh—you mean—my father is—is he alive?"

"Sure he is, honey," Jiggins leered at her. "Jim Norbeck is alive because we kept him from dyin' after this stepfather of your'n shot him an' left him for dead. He's the masked rider."

The girl said a low, throaty, "Oh—oh!"

Jiggins looked at her. "Turn me down when I offered to marry you, will you? Well, you'll find that was the damndest mistake you ever made."

Hatter's teeth, chattering, sent out loud clicking noises. He sobbed:

"Take the girl, Pike, but don't kill me! Take her! I won't say anything! I'll get out of the country and never say a word. I'll hafta do that, or Jim Norbeck will kill me for what I done to him in France. Please, Pike, you don't have to kill me." He was on his knees, fingers picking at Jiggins' clothing.

Titus gnashed his teeth in the kitchen, pointed his gun at Hatter and all but dropped the hammer on a cartridge.

"Not a chance," Jiggins sneered. "We've got Jim Norbeck to take the blame for this killin'. We'll make it look like he went crazy an' salivated all of you, then killed himself. We'll fix it to look like the girl was so ashamed she drowned herself somewhere. I'll make her write a note an' everythin'. That's what we kept Jim Norbeck alive for—kept him alive until we could run your cowhands off so there wouldn't be so many of you to salivate."

"Please—please—" Hatter foamed. "Pike—you—"

"Let's get this over!" one of Jiggins' men urged.

"Sure," Jiggins agreed. "We'll pop the two men off now an' take the girl—"

He didn't finish—because a man clad in a black raincoat and a black sack of a mask leaped into the room from the outer night, a six-gun jutted before him.

Titus kicked the kitchen door open. His six blew lead into the right leg of the man who held the girl—and who would be likely to use her for a shield.

The man howled, clawed for his gun. Carla Norbeck whipped free, dropped to the floor. Titus' six loosened another thunderous breath of metal. The man who had held the girl collapsed down like a sack emptying itself.

Masked Jim Norbeck fired at Jiggins. The latter shot back a full second later, then sat down foolishly on the floor. The masked man's gun banged again. Jiggins jerked as if stung somewhere, the gesture tossing his gun away. Then, somewhat awkwardly, he fell over on his side.

Titus fanned a slug at one of the men standing over Baldy. The fellow gave a dog-like bark, jumped sidewise. Titus, charging headlong into the room, fired at him again and missed.

The other Lazy-N puncher beside Baldy held two guns. Both ran out crimson tongues.

Titus felt one slug do something unimportant to his leg, heard the other smack the wall beside him like a big fist. His thumb flexed across his six-hammer again.

The two-gun man tried to jump for the door. At the second leap, he veered, dived onto the table, slid across it like a flung garment and landed atop the body of Jiggins. His arms beat madly, his guns striking the boards like clubs, but not discharging.

The surviving man gained the door, went through it. Then he made a fatal mistake. He stopped outside, his body sheltered by the wall, and shot back around the doorjamb.

Titus, calculating the thickness of the plaster and weatherboarded wall, shot into it at the spot where the man's chest should be. At the third fan, his gun gave him an empty click. But the man outside had already begun to pitch across the door. He landed on the threshold, an inanimate bundle.

Pivoting, Titus saw Mad Hatter clutching wildly for the weapon dying Jiggins had dropped. He realized what the man was going to do—threw his empty six. The heavy weapon hit Hatter's shoulder.

The man shrieked, but scooped up Jiggins' gun as if his very life depended on it. He slanted it at masked Jim Norbeck.

The weapon was almost level before Norbeck's gun crashed—once.

Hatter sighed, lay down loosely.

In the tomblike silence that followed, Jim Norbeck croaked through his mask: "It's—finally—done."

Feet dragging heavily, he backed for the door. Then he stopped. "I can't stay around here as Jim Norbeck, even if I got acquitted of this. I'm an escaped prisoner."

He moved another halting step for the door, stopped again, looked at the girl. "I—I gotta go away. I'd kinda—I'd kinda like to know you—ain't thinkin' bad of me."

Tears were in Carla Norbeck's eyes. Her mouth trembled. Her crying gasp, "Oh—my father!" was a throb of emotion. She flung herself into his arms.

Brokenly, between long, wrenching sobs, she said: "I'm—I'm going with you!"

Jim Norbeck slowly stripped his mask off. His face, once that of a handsome man, was seamed by the intensive suffering he had undergone. He shook his head slowly.

"You can't do that. I'll be ridin' the owlh-oot trait." He looked over at Titus. Then he kissed her hungrily, turned her, shoved her toward the lathy puncher.

"Take good care of her, fella," he said. "I knowed you was all right this afternoon. And it was your note made me follow Jiggins here."

Titus enfolded the sobbing girl in his arms. He dampened his lips, eyed Jim Norbeck. "Let us know your address. Figure we may get you cleared of that murder charge. Hatter confessed, sort of."

"Thanks," Jim Norbeck said thickly. "I—well, thanks. I'm figurin' on you to kinda look after things. I guess it'll maybe be worth your while."

Titus looked down at the girl's head, said: "It sure will."

Stepping swiftly backward, Jim Norbeck vanished into the range darkness. A moment later, hoofbeats battered out, then receded.

Old Baldy, regaining consciousness, rolled his eyes until he could see Titus, with Carla Norbeck crushed in his arms.

"I dunno what the hell happened!" the old cowman mumbled weakly. "But it musta turned out all right."

· · · · ·

Trigger Trap

The freckled girl in the calico sun bonnet used both hands to squeeze the cutting-pliers. *Pin-n-g!* The barbed wire parted with a whang like a broken fiddle string.

Crouched in the sage fifty yards from her, the shabby puncher breathed, "Why, daggone her! I'll put a stop to that!"

He squinted across his Winchester sights. His battered gray felt hat, a wire threaded in the brim seam to make it retain some semblance of a shape, got in front of his aiming eye. He gave the wired brim a twist, moved the Winchester barrel a fraction of an inch.

The girl brushed her bonnet back so that it hung by the strings knotted about her sun-bronzed throat, gripped another barbed wire with the pliers. Her hair was a hue of fresh hickory ashes.

Wham! The shabby puncher's Winchester exploded.

The girl screeched, flopped face down in the sage. Her dun bronc spooked and bounded away a score of feet before dragging reins stopped it.

Leaping erect, the shabby puncher charged toward where the girl had dropped. He lifted high in the air hurdling a sagebrush, craning his neck to catch sight of her.

She had crawled to the nearest fencepost, was fumbling with a rifle. The rifle breech mechanism was hopelessly shattered.

The puncher grinned, slowed his pace. He was six-foot three. Straightening his bowed legs would have added another inch. His face was long. His snub nose had a few freckles. He stopped a couple of yards from the girl.

She threw her broken Winchester down, got up to face him angrily. "You—you ruined my rifle!"

"Uh-huh," he admitted. "Not bad shootin' for fifty yards, if you was to ask. Stood it against the fencepost to keep it handy, didn't you?"

She glared him up and down. His worn trousers had a jaggedly torn hole in the right knee, his right shirt sleeve was torn between elbow and wrist. Fence staples in his trouser pockets had worked sharp iron points through the cloth.

"Circle-Dash line rider!" she said contemptuously. "One of Boots Mena's tramps!"

He scowled faintly. "Well, I ain't seen you before, but you been described to me. You're Fay O'Reilly, the hank o' hair who runs the OR."

"What do you mean by shooting at me?" she snapped. "In case you don't know it, they hang men for shooting at women in this neck of Wyoming!"

"Yeah?" he inquired sarcastically. "An' what do they do to a shemale who rides another outfit's line fence an' cuts it every dozen rods? Anyhow, I shot at your rifle, not you."

"You're darn right I'm cutting your line fence!" she told him wrathfully. "I've got most of my cattle on Circle-Dash range, and I'm going to throw them all on. Boots Mena started that prairie fire that burned off my range. He thought he'd put me out of business, Well, I'm running my beef on his range, and I'd like to see you stop me!"

"I been fixin' this line fence all mornin' where you'd cut it," he said dryly. "I'm all-fired tired of it. You gotta stop."

"I have—have I!" She made a sudden dive for the Winchester under his arm. He held the weapon high in the air, out of her reach. She made an angry, sputtering sound and slapped his left cheek smartly with her right hand.

He grunted, tossed the rifle away. Then he seized her, enwrapping her slender form in his long arms. She bit his right arm. He trapped her head with a big hand, held her teeth together so she could not bite his lips, and kissed her.

When she kicked his shins, he kissed her again. Then he let her tear herself away.

"You're going to wish you hadn't done that!" she exploded.

"An' you're gonna wish you hadn't monkeyed with the Circle-Dash," he snorted. "We're about losin' our patience with you."

She glared unutterable disgust at him, then wheeled, ran to her dun horse, mounted and spurred off. He watched her until she was out of sight.

When he turned away, a rider and a led horse were approaching him.

The rider was short, fat. His torso, arms, legs, neck—fat bulged his range clothes everywhere. He had a round, bronzed, pleasant face, humorous eyes. He rode a Roman-nosed bay.

The led horse was a blazed sorrel. Big fencing pliers and a come-along for stretching barbed wire were tied to the saddle whang strings.

The fat puncher pulled up. He laughed, and all the bulges in his clothes shook.

"You sure let yourself in for somethin', Wick. That Fay O'Reilly will just naturally have your hide for kissin' her that way."

Wick grinned, but not heartily. He put his old hat on, bent the wired brim into shape. "Daggone, Spindlin'! She don't look like the female bobcat everybody says she is. Sorta expected a rip-snortin', prong-horned devil instead of a nice-lookin' little girl in a poke bonnet."

Spindlin' squinted at Wick's cheek. His plump bulges quaked again with mirth. "She sure left her mark. You can see right where ever' finger hit."

Wick frowned soberly. "I sure hated to grab her that way, but it hadda be done."

Spindlin' sobered suddenly. He put his fat hands on his fat thighs and blinked quizzically. "Figured you was just gettin' even for her tryin' to grab your gun, an' for that fence work she's caused us this mornin'."

"Nope." Wick untied the pliers and come-along from his saddle. "Wanted to make her madder'n ever at the Circle-Dash."

Spindlin' continued to blink a moment. When Wick turned toward the wires the girl had cut, the fat puncher slid off his bay, got in his path.

"Wick, I don't savvy you a-tall. I write an' tell you about this range war I'm mixed up in, an' a week later you show up an' ask Boots Mena for a job." Spindlin' ran his eyes up and down the gangling, shabby, sun-baked cowhand. "You show up lookin' like a dang tramp. You tell Boots Mena you're broke an' frightful hard up for a job. Hell! You got more money than Boots Mena himself."

Wick dogged the come-along to the barbed wire, began to tighten it. He said nothing.

"Now you make a crack about keepin' that gal mad at the Circle-Dash," continued the fat puncher. "What's your game? Tryin' to help things along so they'll kill each other off?"

Wick swore as the come-along slipped and a wire barb tore a new hole in his right shirt sleeve. "Won't nobody get killed off but Boots Mena, Spindlin'. That girl has got Boots right. She's gloomed onto his range as bold as can be. An' he can't gun-haze her off because the sheriff warned him that if he did, it'd be just too bad. She's got the sheriff on her side. An' her grain' off Boots' range is sure gonna break him. He's got the Circle-Dash mortgaged to the hilt."

"That gal is doin' the world a favor if she puts Boots Mena out of business," Spindlin' said solemnly.

Wick grinned. "I aim to see that she does it. But I bet she thinks she's gonna buy the Circle-Dash when Boots sells out, or the sheriff does it for him. Well, she ain't. I'm gonna buy the Circle-Dash."

Spindlin' extracted tailor-made cigarettes from a vest pocket. "Figured it was somethin' like that. Well, you know me, Wick. I'm with you from taw. Especial against this no-good Boots Mena. They sure scraped the kettle when they made him."

"Yeah." Wick made a gesture with his left shoulder. "Here comes the pride o' the West now!"

Two riders, topping a saddle between two nearby buttes, were approaching.

Spindlin' looked, made a long sound with his tongue and upper lip to indicate infinite disgust. "Boots Mena an' his foreman, Ole Bates!"

The two riders came up. Boots Mena pulled his horse to a halt, and before he spoke looked down at his feet. They were shod in boots of such a soft, expensive quality as to be striking even in a country addicted to vanity in footgear. A grasshopper had been mashed against their shining surface. He produced a handkerchief, carefully wiped off the stain. His body looked thinly unhealthy. His face was long.

Ole Bates, foreman of the Circle-Dash, was blue-jowled, squint-eyed, squat and muscular.

Boots Mena gave his boot a last rub, stowed his handkerchief, piled his bony hands one atop the other on the saddle horn. He spoke in a voice which seemed to toll like a funeral bell.

"Both you men have expressed a willingness to make a little money on the side. Am I right?"

Wick finished splicing the ends of the barbed wire held in the come-along. "You're right."

"I want you two men to take a dozen head of my cattle and change their Circle-Dash brands to Fay O'Reilly's OR brand." Boots Mena nodded slightly at his foreman. "Ole Bates will show you what ones to take. You will blot the brands clumsily enough that they can be told as such. After dark, you will throw the dozen cattle in with the beef stuff Fay O'Reilly has turned onto my range."

Wick detached the come-along, made it into a bundle. "Then you go to the sheriff an' claim the girl has been rustlin' your stock, eh?"

The bony, sombre-faced man stared at his gleaming boots intently. "I shall take the matter up with the Cattle Association. But I will be generous. Very generous indeed. If Fay O'Reilly takes her stock off my range, I shall not press charges."

Wick laughed dryly. "You're pretty clever. You're afraid to pull somethin' like that on the sheriff, so you're goin' to the Cattle Association. You know they'll raise hell with any sheriff that ignores a rustlin' complaint."

"Our sheriff is not a just man," Boots Mena tolled.

Wick looked at the fat puncher. "What about it, Spindly? Will we do it?"

Spindlin' scowled. "C'mere! I wanta talk to you."

The fat ranny waddled away a dozen yards, waited for the gangling Wick to amble up.

"Listen, Wick!" he said in a low, savage voice. "You ain't gonna do this, are you? Hell a-mighty! It'll mean the ruin of that girl. She can't fatten any stock if she don't have the use of this range. An' I happen to know she's got money borrowed just like Boots. She's ruined if she don't ship a lot o' fat stuff this fall."

The gaunt puncher studied holes in his shabby shirt, "Just how honest are you, Spindlin'?"

"I ain't very damn honest on occasion, an' you know it. But that ain't got nothin' to do with it. The girl is doin' humanity a service tryin' to clean out that long-faced skunk. I ain't gonna hinder her."

Wick looked at Boots Mena and Ole Bates, made sure his voice could not reach them. "What I mean—are you too honest to double-cross Boots?"

"You know daggone well I ain't. There's nothin' I'd rather do."

"Then we'll go ahead and blot the brands." Wick smiled wolfishly. "We'll also catch some o' Fay O'Reilly's calf crop an' slap Boots Mena's Circle-Dash on 'em. Then we'll go to the sheriff, say Boots propositioned us to try to lay a rustlin' on the girl, an' claim we've noticed Boots has been brandin' the girl's calves."

Spindlin' scratched his plump jaw. "Boots will swear we branded his stuff without him knowin'. He'll try to make it look like we're workin' for the girl."

"We'll lie ourselves black in the face an' claim it wasn't us blotted the brands."

Spindlin' grinned. "This is kinda involved. But I'm for it." They walked back. Wick said, "We'll do it."

Boots Mena's horse threw its head, champed foam. Some of the foam splattered the man's foot covering. He cursed the bronc, wrenched on the cruel curb bit.

"Good," he growled. "Ole will show you the stock. I'm riding back to the Circle-Dash."

He wheeled, spurred away. Wick whanged the fencing tools to his saddle, then swung into the rig.

Ole Bates growled, "We might as well ride this durn fence a ways, seein' as how it's been cut every few rods," and reined west.

They single-footed along briskly. Calves with a herd of white faces put their tails in the air and dashed about briskly at sight of them. They reached a draw which held water, paused to let their horses drink.

Half a mile beyond the draw, they found the line fence cut.

Ole Bates cursed peevishly, looked at the sun. "Boss wants this fence fixed, but my time's gettin' short. Wick, you stay here an' splice it up. I'll take Spindlin' an' show him the critters you're to blot the brands on. You can come on when you get the fence fixed. It's just over the hill."

Wick scowled at the severed barbed wire, dismounted. The other two galloped on, veering away from the fence.

Picking up a wire, Wick saw pliers had cut it. He made a smoke, pondering lazily. "Now I wonder if that moharrie just rode on ahead an' continued cuttin' this fence so her beef can get onto Circle-Dash range. She's spunky enough to do that."

He was untying the come-along when the crackling roar of shots came tumbling across the range.

Wick wrenched his Winchester from the dried cowhide saddle sheath, leaped away from the horse and looked in the direction Spindlin' and Ole Bates had gone. Both men had wheeled their broncs, were spurring madly down the boulder-cluttered side of a butte.

Ole Bates was slumped across the saddle horn, swaying with every leap of his mount.

Spindlin' twisted in his saddle to fan his six-gun at the rocky summit of the butte.

From the butte top, rifles hammered back at him. The fat puncher lurched, dropped his gun. Another volley of lead came from the butte.

Spindlin' waved his arms crazily, spilled out of the rig. His horse made a dozen leaps, then went down in a flurry of legs and stirrups. Neither man nor animal got up.

A rifle slug snapped savagely into the sage near Wick. The gaunt puncher leveled his Winchester, saw no target, did not fire. He swung onto his blazed sorrel, spurred to intercept fleeing Ole Bates.

The two men reached the shelter of a deep gully almost together.

Ole Bates' left sleeve was crimson soaked. "It was that OR outfit!" he yelled. "They cut down on us without warnin'. The girl was with 'em!"

Wick scrambled up to the gully lip. A rifle bullet cut tops from sage near him. He hunted vainly for a target. The ambushers on the butte were well hidden.

Ole Bates groaned loudly, fingers clenched about his arm. "Where's Spindlin'? Did they get him?"

"Looks like it," Wick said grimly. He selected a boulder on the butte crest and glanced a Winchester slug off it. The shot was not answered.

"I saw 'em plain," Ole Bates moaned. "It was that OR spread. Hey, tie somethin' around my arm. I'm left-handed. Can't do a thing with my right hand. Damn! This hurts!"

Wick slid down to the gully bed, opened the squat foreman's left sleeve. The wound was a clean tunnel, wide of the bone. He tied the foreman's handkerchief tightly above it to stem the crimson flow.

"Let's get outta here!" Ole Bates gulped. "They may be surroundin' us!"

Wick eyed the fellow, saw he was trembling and scared, spat disgustedly.

"You ride to the Circle-Dash for help," he grunted. "Have 'em send a man for the sheriff. I'll cover your getaway."

"But you—"

"Spindlin' an' me has shared a bed roll more'n once. I'm stayin' here to make medicine with the buzzards that salivated 'im!"

"Maybe I oughta stay too." The foreman's burly knees began to shake.

"No! I'll go for help. That'll be better."

The man scrambled back onto his horse, prodded with his spurs, went pounding down the gully.

His face grim, his faded eyes wintry, Wick goosed another cartridge into his Winchester. He worked up the gully side, digging in his high boot heels for footing. Flattened at the top, he stared for a long time at the butte summit.

There was no movement there.

Shoving the Winchester ahead of him, Wick wormed through the sage. The Wyoming spring had been rainy and the stuff had grown rank. A cactus bed detoured him. Grasshoppers flew out of his path with a great rattling of wings. Overhead, the sun and sky was a hot coal in a bowl of heat.

Spindlin' lay open-eyed in the sun glare. His arms were half akimbo, fingers digging at the hardpan. He was dead.

When Wick had made certain the fat puncher was dead, he crawled on toward the butte crest. No motion, no shots came from there. He heard pounding hoof beats of rapidly ridden horses, as though the dry-gulchers were departing. But he continued to crawl, using as much caution as before hearing the sound.

Nobody was atop the butte, or visible among the brakes beyond it.

Wick turned, ran down the butte side to where Spindlin' lay. The fat puncher's horse was lifeless. Wick unsaddled the animal, used the saddle blanket to cover the man's body.

He crouched there, long face stormy, for several seconds. His lips hard, blue, snugged tightly against his teeth. Suddenly he cursed, leaped erect, sprinted for his blazed sorrel in the gully.

"Damn fool!" he berated himself savagely. "Played right into their hands!"

He made the back of his sorrel with pony-express mount, reined the bronc down the gully, using the spurs. His eyes, probing the ground ahead, discerned where Ole Bates had quit the little canyon. He followed the trail.

Going over a ridge he lost it, but found it on an alkali flat beyond. Hoof-crushed cactus aided, as did sun glitter from freshly shattered mica fragments which strewed a hilltop.

He rode into a region of jumbled washes. Ole Bates' trail led him into a flat-bottomed wash.

He rounded a bend, came face to face with ash-blonde Fay O'Reilly. She held a rifle and had him covered with the weapon before he saw her.

"Unbuckle your gun belt with your left hand!" Her eyes were cold blue pools in the depths of her sunbonnet.

Wick stared at her, making no move to comply. "Did you see the men who shot Spindlin'?"

She made a small, meaningful gesture with the Winchester barrel. "Unbuckle your cartridge belt!"

"You followed us after I caught you cuttin' fence. Can you identify the jaspers who shot 'im in court?" He asked it earnestly.

She hesitated, said, "I was behind you. I didn't see them."

He ignored her gun and looked past her up the wash. "I gotta get Ole Bates, then. How far ahead is he?"

"Drop your gun!" Her Winchester cocked with an oily click. "Get off your horse."

He scowled at her, then remembered something. He had ruined her Winchester—but now she had a rifle. He looked intently at the weapon.

"Ole Bates' rifle!" he grunted. "You stopped him!"

"I roped him off his horse," she admitted grimly.

Wick did not unbuckle his gun belt. He slid out of the saddle. The girl retreated a pace, keeping the Winchester muzzle aimed at his chest. Her head moved to a position where the sun slanted hot light against her face. Her lips were pallid. Her eyes were dry, scared, but recently shed tears were wet below them.

"Poor kid," Wick said sympathetically. "It scared you pretty bad when you realized what they'd done, didn't it?"

She said nothing in a half-frightened way.

He gestured vaguely at the horse tracks in the gully bed. "I was tryin' to catch Ole Bates. He left me—before I saw through their scheme."

She did not lower her rifle.

"Spindlin'—the ranny they shot—was my best friend," he said, tight-voiced. He told her he had planned to buy the Circle-Dash when Boots Mena was forced to sell, told her how he and Spindlin' had planned to egg the range war along, told her how they had expected to double-cross Boots Mena. He finished, "An' that's why I kissed you—to keep you plenty mad at the Circle-Dash."

She retreated, still keeping him covered with her Winchester. "Ole Bates is up here." She nodded up the wash.

The Circle-Dash foreman lay face down on the wash bed, roped hand and foot. Wick turned the man's face up, slapped the blue jowls twice savagely.

"Guessed the truth when the bushwhackers rode off!" he grated. "If they had been the girl's OR hands, they'd have stuck around to finish us off so nobody would've been left to go to the sheriff. But they didn't, because they were Boots Mena's Circle-Dash waddies."

He swore, struck Ole Bates in the face. "It was a frame-up. You was to let 'em shoot you in the arm, then swear they was the girl's riders. You left me fixin' that fence so I'd see Spindlin' killed!"

Ole Bates rolled his head, moaned. "They was her OR hands. I saw—"

Wick took his throat and choked him into silence. "You saw Circle-Dash rannies, an' you're gonna tell the sheriff you did!"

The squat foreman coughed three times. "I ain't!"

Wick stood up, went to his blazed sorrel and drew his Winchester from the cowhide scabbard. Coming back, he stood over Ole Bates. "If you won't tell the truth, it don't leave me but one thing to do," he said coldly. "You'll have to be salivated. Then I'll go to the sheriff an' claim Circle-Dash men got both you an' Spindlin'."

The foreman rolled his eyes, breathed noisily.

Wick backed a couple of paces. He aimed the Winchester at Ole Bates' temple. "Won't powder-burn you from here. The slug will go right through your head, so nobody'll be diggin' it out to identify my gun."

Ash-blonde Fay O'Reilly gave a gasping moan, ran wildly at Wick. At the third step her knees began buckling. Her face was drained of color, her eyes frenzied. After the fifth step she fell on her face.

When Wick did not as much as look at her, the foreman pulled his lips off blunt teeth and screamed shrilly. He writhed, gibbered.

"I'll tell the sheriff!" he whimpered. "Boots Mena hadda get the girl to keep her cattle off his range somehow. He figured he'd get her out of the way by layin' a killin' on her, so he could run her stock off. So he and his hands arranged with me to bring Spindlin' to that bluff, an' leave you behind where you could see us. Boots Mena and his men plugged Spindlin'! I was to swear it was the girl and her hands done it. I'll tell the sheriff all that! Honest I will!"

Wick lowered his Winchester and went to the girl. She had fainted. He inspected Ole Bates' bonds, tightened the ropes, then carried the girl a hundred feet down the wash and rubbed her wrists until she was awake.

She made a choking sound, recoiled from him.

"That was plumb low-down of me," he told her contritely. "I should've let you know it was just a bluff."

"Oh." Fay O'Reilly got the horror out of her eyes. "I—I should have known that. Did he—will he tell the truth?"

Wick slanted a violent stare at Ole Bates. "He said so. I don't know. He'll try to deny it when he's safe with the sheriff, but I'll try to throw enough of a scare into him that he won't dare."

She grasped his hand impulsively. "I'll never be able to thank you enough for this!"

He became uncomfortable. "I ain't no Sir Galahad. I expect to get paid by buyin' the Circle-Dash cheap." He clenched his right fist, eyed the whitening knuckles. "That ain't all of it, though. Spindlin' was my best friend. I'm gonna see that the skunks who salivated 'im get plenty of justice!"

"I—I had better go to the sheriff with you," she said jerkily.

"I reckon so." He went back to Ole Bates.

The foreman's horse was up the wash with the girl's. Wick put the blue-jowled man on the animal, first untying him and searching him for weapons.

"I'm gonna leave you untied on account of your arm," he growled. "Better not try a get-away. You won't make it."

Ole Bates rode ahead. Wick and the girl followed him, riding abreast when they could, the girl dropping behind as the wash narrowed. They reined west, toward the trail which led to town, forty miles away.

Wick, seeing Ole Bates moving his arms, spurred up even with the man. The fellow had only loosened his belt.

Dropping back again, Wick kept his Winchester ready. From time to time, he glanced covertly at the girl. He had never liked freckles, having some himself, but he decided hers were rather nice. He liked me way she rode, too. She caught him watching her. He colored, hastily fronted his eyes.

He was just in time to see Ole Bates tumble headlong off his horse. The foreman's spurs dug the animal as he fell. The bronc reared, plunged away. The reins were wrapped about the saddle horn.

Wick started to spur after the animal, saw Ole Bates leap for a boulder. His Winchester flung up and banged. The foreman sprang into the air as the bullet spaded hardpan from under his feet, shot his hands up.

"I fell off!" he wailed. "Bronc shied an' I fell off on account of my bad arm."

"It looked to me like you dived off." Wick stared after the foreman's bronc. The animal was too far away to catch, and still running.

Ole Bates' belt was still unbuckled. Wick buckled it, tied the man's hands, lifted him onto the brazed sorrel and climbed up behind him. The gaunt puncher's face was puzzled at what had happened.

"Another of them stunts'll be the end of you!" he promised grimly.

They rode forward two hours and the girl, pointing, was saying, "Look! That dust!"

Wick peered past Ole Bates' shoulder. The dust, a shapeless plume of it, denoted riders to their right and ahead. He turned his gaze. More dust was being raised by other riders to their left.

"They're tryin' to cut us off from town!" he growled. "Boots Mena has found out we're wise to him, somehow. He knows he's sunk if we get to the sheriff."

Suddenly he grunted savagely, knocked Ole Bates out of the saddle, pounced on the man. "That bronc of yours would go straight to the Circle-Dash! Did you tie a note to the saddle for Boots Mena?"

"You know I ain't got nothin' to write a note with," the blue-jowled foreman whined.

Wick glowered at the fellow. His eyes searched over the foreman's squat body, coming to rest on the belt buckle.

"So that's it!" he gritted. "You used the prong of your belt to scratch a message on the pommel of your saddle."

"I didn't—"

The rest of the foreman's lie was a wailing and rattling of teeth as Wick shook him. The gaunt puncher swung his captive back on the sorrel, mounted and barked at the girl, "They're ahead of us enough to cut us off. We'll have to back track."

They reined about, used their spurs. A quarter of a mile and several rifle bullets traveled near them with long squeals. Wick shouted at the girl; they veered into a canyon.

Wick inspected his horse and the girl's.

"Our broncs are tired," he grunted. "We can't outride 'em. These brakes are a better place than any to make a stand."

The girl nodded, pulled up.

Wick flung Ole Bates to the ground. He tied the reins of his bronc to the horn of the girl's saddle. Writing a note saying they were cornered by Boots Mena and his Circle-Dash hands, he tied it to a whang string of her saddle. He dropped the bridle off her horse, lashed both animals with it. They spooked and ran away.

"If the broncs get through, so much the better," he growled.

With his Winchester, he prodded Ole Bates up the canyon. The girl trailed, watching the rear.

Came shots, yells from the direction the horses had gone.

"That's that," Wick grated. "They stopped the broncs."

"Where—" The girl's voice was shrill, but with excitement rather than hysteria. "Where are you going? There's an abandoned prospector's tunnel about half a mile ahead."

"We're headed for that," Wick told her. "Boots Mena uses a cabin beside the mine for a line shack."

He gave the girl his revolver, sent her on ahead with Ole Bates, and dropped back. As soon as she was out of sight, he plucked the cartridges out of his belt, pocketed them and threw the belt away.

Hearing a rock rattle behind him, he fired at the sound. Then he ran back to join the girl and her prisoner.

"Your belt!" she gasped when she saw it was gone.

He did not look at her, but said, "I dropped it—didn't have time to pick it up. It's tough, but the cartridges in the Winchesters are all the ammunition we've got."

"Oh! There's only three shells in my gun."

He shook his head slowly. "And two in mine."

Before them appeared the black mouth of the abandoned mine. Judging from the enormous pile of rubble before the hole, the unknown gold hunter had penetrated quite deeply into the canyonside before giving up his quest. A heavy door at the entrance gaped ajar.

The shack beside it was ramshackle, of inch planks nailed to a two-by-four framework.

"Only five shells!" Wick grunted. "And that shack won't turn lead!"

He shoved Ole Bates to the door of the rickety structure, then steered him away, toward the tunnel opening.

"There's canned grub in the shack!" he rapped at the girl. "Grab it. We'll hole up in the mine, try to keep them away!"

The girl ran into the building. Wick waited an instant, then prodded blue-jowled Ole Bates with his Winchester muzzle. "You stay right here. I'll help her!"

He stepped backward, joined the girl. But almost at once he leaped outside again. As he had expected, the foreman was sprinting away.

"Stop!" Wick roared. Ole Bates only ran faster. Wick flung up his rifle, aimed wide of the racing man, fired. He shot again. The foreman did not look back, but zigzagged madly from side to side.

Ash-blonde Fay O'Reilly sprang to the shack door. Wick seized her Winchester, pumped two shots out of it. Then another!

"You've used all our ammunition!" shrieked the girl.

Wick flung into the shack. He ignored the canned food she had gathered, picked up an oil lantern and shook it. Kerosene gurgled in the magazine. Pitching across the shack, he seized half a dozen empty salt sacks from a corner.

"C'mon!" he grunted.

Out of the cabin, they raced to the mine tunnel. The bore slanted downward steeply. Loose rubble covered the floor. It smelled of coyotes. Evidently the animals used it for a den.

Wick leaped and slid down to where the passage abruptly became level.

The girl, careening after him, choked: "We haven't any ammunition! And if we did, they wouldn't try to rush us. They'd set off a charge of powder, cave in the tunnel mouth."

Wick's chuckle was a metallic rattle. "We've got plenty of ammunition! What I said was to make Ole Bates think we didn't have. I want them to come into this mine to kill us, thinkin' we're helpless."

"But there'll be at least half a dozen of them. We can't—"

"I'll show you my scheme!" Wick grunted.

Back into the tunnel another hundred feet they crept. Wick struck matches. The bore forked.

Doubling close to one wall, Wick stripped off his vest, wadded it. He poured the kerosene from the lantern on the fabric, kneading it to saturate thoroughly. Finding he had plenty of kerosene, he unraveled the salt sack seams to get the string, then added them to the fuel pile.

He levered two shells out of the Winchester, twisted out the lead with his teeth and poured the powder into the rifle barrel. He put a third leadless shell in the breech. Then he planted the rifle so the muzzle rested on the oil-sodden sacks, attached his string to the trigger and walked backward.

When he had the string placed, he returned and cocked the Winchester.

"That'll give us a light behind them," he said grimly. "Talk about your snipe hunts!"

He crept back to the end of the string as he loaded his six-gun with the cartridges he had removed from his belt and pocketed.

Almost at once, Boots Mena and his Circle-Dash hands were clamoring at the tunnel mouth.

"Go in after them!" tolled Boots Mena's funeral bell of a voice. "They are without ammunition!"

Somebody muttered doubtfully.

"A-course they're outta shells!" rasped Ole Bates. "Gimme a hogleg, somebody! I'll lead the way in!"

Wick found the girl's arm in the darkness. "Go back. Find a place where you won't be hit."

She hesitated. "I can—"

"Don't argue about it!" he growled. "When this thing starts, I'll be throwin' lead at everything that moves around me. I don't want to drill you by mistake."

From the tunnel maw Boots Mena tolled, "All right, gentlemen! In we go! Ole, you will lead."

"Gentlemen!" Wick gritted. Then he discovered the girl was still beside him. "Go back, dang it!"

He could hear her rapid breathing over the clatter of rubble as men came down the slanting tunnel.

"I—" The girl stopped, then went on impulsively. "I hope we get out of this, Wick. I mean—well—" She gripped his arm with a clutch almost fierce. "Be careful, dear!"

Wick blinked, temporarily forgot the potential death coming down into the mine, and reached out an arm to embrace the girl. But she had gone back into the tunnel somewhere.

He stood up, started to follow her. Boots Mena's voice stopped him. "Strike a match!"

A match whizzed on a pants leg, flared up an orange glow. Wick held his breath, hoping they would not discover the rifle and sodden pile of cloth. He could see match light mirroring from Mena's expensive boots.

They did not see the kerosene-soaked cloth. They came on, cautiously.

Wick decided they had passed his trap, gave the string a gentle tug.

Pow! The powder blazed out of the Winchester barrel and ignited the cloth. Reddish flame leaped as high as a man's head.

Against the glare, the potential killers were outlined clear as camera silhouettes.

Blue-jowled Ole Bates fired a six-gun he held before Wick pressed the trigger.

Wick shot him in the right leg. He shot another man in the chest. Then he leaped sidewise and killed Boots Mena.

The bawling thunder of guns seemed to tear his eardrums apart. Lead filled the bedlam with whistling squeals and mad buzzings. Rock fragments knocked loose, spattered like hailstones.

Wick tumbled a fourth man-outline to the tunnel floor, then flattened and reloaded his six.

While he was doing that, one of the survivors scooped up Boots Mena's lifeless body and dumped it atop the burning cloth, smothering the flame.

Wick stood up. Lead shocked against his shoulder, pivoting him, reeling him backward. He dropped his gun, found it with his other hand. It jumped and boomed in his fist.

A man grunted sickeningly and made threshing sounds. Two survivors! Both ran back up the tunnel.

Their horses were grouped on the north side of the shack. They had almost reached them when Wick shot. He shot again. The men threw away their guns and put up their hands.

Wick dragged and rolled himself away from the tunnel mouth, then spurted words past his clenched teeth, "Get back in that hole! Bring the girl out! An' if she's hurt, damned if you'll ever come outta there alive'"

The pair backed, shaking of knee, into the dark hole in the canyon- side.

But ash-blonde Fay O'Reilly appeared almost immediately under her own power. She was unhurt. She pitched her slender form against the door of heavy timbers, got it shut. It had a bar as big as a fence post, still serviceable. She hefted the bar in place.

Anxious-eyed, she flung to Wick's side. "Your shoulder!"

Wick rubbed at the crimson stringing from his bit lip, winced, said, "It's actin' up. But I'll hold out while you ride for the sheriff. I'll watch the door to that hole."

She tore open his shirt, looked, sighed a jerky breath of relief. "The bullet just broke the bone. You'll be all right." She put on a makeshift bandage.

"Now you better ride for the sheriff," Wick said. He hesitated as though he had something more to say, but didn't know how to get it out.

She waited, and when she saw he was not going to say anything, murmured, "Are you—sure you'll be all right? Isn't there anything I can do to make you comfortable?"

He grinned more widely than it seemed possible any man could. "You might kinda—well give me a dose of my own medicine."

She acted puzzled. "I don't understand!"

"You know—when I kissed you—" The words threatened to choke him.

The girl laughed, murmured something, leaned forward.

Wick shut his eyes. He wanted to enjoy this.

• • • • •

The Devil's Ear

The Green River brakes of southwestern Utah made hot, lonely riding in August. Hardly a thing moved but the heat waves.

So when undersized Oscar "Big Plenty" Ruff slid off his buckskin bronc to get a drink at a waterhole, trouble was the last thing he expected.

It gave Ruff a shock to have a man jump from the concealment of a sagebrush clump and land feet-first on the small of his back.

The impact mashed Ruff into shallow water and gray mud like a stepped-on frog. His enraged, surprised squawk was a bubbling explosion. He drove his right hand hipward—did not complete the gesture when he felt his Frontier .45 stripped from the leather.

He rolled, flopping like a half-landed catfish. His fists flailed. One struck some part of a man—his eyes were too full of mud to tell what part. Cursing in a loud, braying voice, the assailant leaped clear.

"Cut it out, banty!" he snarled.

Ruff dropped to all fours, jammed his head into the water, shook it violently to wash mud out of his eyes. He glared at his attacker.

"C'mon out of your puddle, froggy!" directed the man.

He was big and solidly fat, one of the biggest men Ruff had ever seen. His dusty, faded clothes fitted him like skin on an elephant. His keg of a face was dourly expressionless, his small eyes alert and aglitter. His left hand held a single-action Colt.

"I'll froggy you!" Ruff gritted. "What's the idea?"

"The idea is that I got a cryin' need for your cayuse, peewee," rumbled the giant. "Not wantin' an argument, figured I'd just step on your spine an' peel your ironware. C'mon outta there!"

Ruff grimaced rage like a wet, mad bulldog. Under the turbid water his fingers curled, scooping up fistfuls of mud.

"You're gonna freeze to my buckskin, eh? Plain hoss rustler!"

"You've got a crust, runt!" The giant jutted his Colt forward a couple of inches. "I oughta salivate you. But I'll tie you across the saddle an' take you to the sheriff. The law'll handle you—and your pards, too. The sheriff of this county ain't finicky. He'll work on you until you tell where you're holdin' old Zeke McCann."

Ruff blinked, blew muddy water off his lips. "I don't know you. I'm just a ranny siftin' through. Name's Oscar Ruff—Big Plenty Ruff. Reckon you're makin' a mistake?"

"But Plenty Ruff ain't rough enough," chuckled the giant. "You tryin' to tell me you don't work for Stan Yonkel's Boxed-Y?"

"Never heard of the spread."

"I ain't seen you among the Boxed-Y hands, at that." The giant worked his huge shoulders. "Well, I ain't takin' chances. You'd lie, anyhow. Looks like you jaspers will do anythin' to get hold o' that Devil's Ear."

"Devil's Ear—what's that?"

"You'll find out when I get you to the sheriff. Quit lallygaggin'! Get outta that mudhole."

"I ain't no Boxed-Y hand. Look at the brand on my cayuse."

"That don't prove nothin'. You're probably a gunslinger Stan Yonkel's foreman, Silky Ed Crowder, brought in from somewhere."

Then the giant did what Ruff had hoped for—he looked at the buckskin. "Nope. Ain't branded Boxed-Y, but that don't—"

Ruff threw both fistfuls of mud. The stuff splattered the giant's face, blinding him. Before the man recovered, Ruff was out of the water and had kicked his gun arm. The .45 flipped upward without exploding.

Ruff leaped, trying to catch it. But the giant managed to lash out a foot instinctively and trip him. Snarling, the fellow leaped.

Twisting onto his back, Ruff drove both high-heeled boots into the giant's middle. The man lost air out of his lungs with a gusty roar. They tangled in a gouging, mauling pile.

"You little snort!" labored the big man. "You sure raise a stew for your size!"

Muddy water worked down out of Ruff's bristling hair into his eyes. He tried to rub it out, saw a fist coming—and the world exploded.

Ruff did not lose consciousness. But for several seconds his arms and legs were limp as worn hackamore ropes. When he was able to see, the giant was backing away, blowing on his huge right fist. The fellow stooped, got his .45.

"You crawl me again an' I'll do worse'n bump your jaw!" he promised. "Boxed-Y hand or not, you're gonna ride behind me to the sheriff—tied hand an' foot!"

Ruff glowered. "That buckskin won't carry double."

"We'll break 'im to carry double, or my name ain't Titanic Harrison!" rumbled the huge man.

He sidled toward the buckskin. The bronco spooked and retreated, swinging front hoofs high to clear dragging reins.

"Whoa, you yallerhammer!" soothed the big man, and tried again. Once more the buckskin leaped away.

Titanic Harrison pointed his six-gun at Ruff. "You catch the crock-head! He's scairt of me."

Ruff got to his feet with alacrity.

"Don't try to ride 'im off!" warned the giant. "You'll sure be pickin' lead outta yourself if you do!"

Advancing on the buckskin, Ruff came within reach of the reins without much trouble. He lunged, got them, gave them a yank. The bronc reared—and for a moment Ruff had the saddled barrel of the animal between himself and the man with the gun.

"Keep away from the Winchester!" barked the giant.

The man could see the Winchester under the other stirrup, so Ruff had no fear of his shooting. Some seconds longer he roughhoused the buckskin. Then he led the snorting, blowing horse back to the big man.

"This bronc is mean," he puffed. "He's gonna pitch when you fork 'im."

Titanic Harrison took the reins. "I'll fog that outta 'im! You keep back. There ain't no bronc I can't ride, even if you did spook this'n up on purpose."

Ruff retreated meekly.

The giant swung lightly onto the buckskin, settled in the rig. He rammed his gun into the holster, swept off his battered gray John B. and smacked the bronc's ears smartly.

Down went the buckskin's head. Skyward sailed the animal for more than half his own height. He hit the ground with a stiff-legged, shocking crash. Titanic Harrison lost his hat.

The buckskin took off again. Twice he sunned his sides. On the next buck, both saddle and rider left the animal and piled in a tangle a dozen feet away.

Running to the stunned giant, Ruff drew back his fist and punched the fellow in the jaw. He seized the man's gun and his own Frontier .45.

Hunkering down, he slapped the giant's face, first with his left hand, then with the right. He slid fingers inside his shirt and brought out a heavy-bladed knife.

Seizing the end of the latigo strap still attached to the cinch, he shoved it under the giant's nose. The latigo had been practically severed by a knife slash at the spot where it had broken.

"Cut it while I was roughhousin' the bronc!" he sneered.

"You—you tricked me!" gulped the giant. "Fixed it so the saddle come off!"

Ruff threw both guns and knife several yards away, hitched up his pants, tightened his belt. He made knotty fists of his hands and spat on each in turn.

"My Christian friend, I'm gonna do worse than trick you!" he growled. "I'm gonna teach you the error of grabbin' broncs off pilgrims you don't know. Then I'm gonna get to the bottom of this mysterious Devil's Ear business. I've always wanted to whip a gent your size. And now—"

"And now—" crackled a new voice. "And now—you'll put your hands up and stand still!"

Ruff spun. His eyes popped. Sagging jaw pulled his big mouth to a gaping circle.

The giant got up, swung a fist. Ruff made a belated effort to duck, failed. The blow flattened him.

The giant straddled him, lifting a monster fist for another swing.

"No need of that, Titanic," said the girl.

She advanced from beside the sage clump which had sheltered her furtive approach. She carried a cocked Winchester.

Her sunburned brown hair would come about to his shoulder, Ruff decided. That made her a rather small girl. She was twenty or so. Her mouth was full and glowing, her eyes large and brown and hot. She was a beauty, and she was both uneasy and angry.

"What're you doin' here, Miss Dawn?" muttered the big man. "You're takin' an awful chance."

"I wanted to make sure you got away safely." She eyed Ruff frostily. "Is this runt one of the Boxed-Y outfit?"

The giant stroked his jaw gingerly. "He may be pint size, but he's all man when you get hold of him. Sure, he's one of 'em!"

Ruff began, "I ain't—"

"Shut up!" snapped the girl. "You're going to catch that buckskin and not argue about it!"

Ruff eyed the Winchester barrel. He wet his lips.

"All right," he grumbled.

"Get going!" ordered the girl. "We'll follow you. We've got to stay under cover, but we'll keep you in sight. Try to pull one of your tricks, and you'll find that out!"

Ruff hesitated briefly, then strode after the buckskin. Dragging reins had stopped the horse a hundred yards distant. The animal saw him coming, began to sidle away.

Homely face disgusted, Ruff quickened his pace. The horse backed through a cluster of scrawny pinions, negotiated a gully. Ruff looked back, saw no sign of the girl and the giant, and fronted his eyes. He was barely holding his own with the fleeing buckskin. The bronc was wily at handling the dragging reins.

"Dang that educated critter!" Ruff growled.

The buckskin stepped on the reins, nearly somersaulted. Ruff sprinted, seeing his chance to catch the horse. The chase had covered full half a mile. Lunging, he captured the reins. A glance back disclosed no trace of his two captors. He debated forking the buckskin bareback and trying to make a getaway, wrinkling his forehead as he considered various angles of the thing.

"Guess I'll string along with 'em an' see what happens," he decided. "Dang me! It'll be worth it to get another look at that gal!"

He started back, leading the bronc. The girl and the giant still had not appeared.

Suddenly four men swelled up out of the sage around him. They pointed guns at him.

CHAPTER II

NECKTIE PARTY

Ruff put up his hands without being told.

Saying nothing, the four stalked grimly forward. Three were bandy-legged cowhands with nothing unusual about their appearance.

The fourth, their leader, came to a stiff-legged plant before Ruff. The fellow was tall, a bit dog-faced. He wore a green silk shirt and a lemon-hued silk neckerchief. The band on his black hat was lemon silk.

The man rifled Ruff's clothes in search of weapons, eyed Ruff's empty holster, then looked at the buckskin.

"Musta lost his gun when the bronc throwed him," he growled. "Sure, that's what happened. He sneaked away from the dang girl's ranch carryin' a bridle an' caught this stray bronc. He couldn't ride the cayuse bareback."

"Couldn't ride—" Ruff choked off his snort. He had discovered the Boxed-Y brand worked with silver rivets into the dog-faced man's leather chaps.

He began to understand. These were Boxed-Y riders. The dog-faced man must be Silky Ed Crowder, the outfit foreman.

Ruff flicked a glance across the sage and pinon-carpeted brakes, saw no trace of the girl and the giant. They must have seen these men.

"What kind of a hoorah is this?" he demanded.

Silky Ed Crowder ignored the question, jerked an order at his three men. "Tie the little squirt up!"

Ruff swore explosively, backed away. A lasso rope looped toward him. He failed to duck the noose and was yanked off his feet. The three punchers swarmed atop him, tossed half-hitches over his ankles and wrists and yanked them tight.

Silky Ed Crowder came over to glower down at him.

"Figure you're one of Miss Dawn Lorde's Broken-Stirrup hands," he grunted. "We're gonna find where you're holdin' old Zeke McCann. And if you've learned where the Devil's Ear is, we're gonna make you tell us that, too. First—how'd you get away from the Broken-Stirrup?"

"I'll be damned!" Ruff gulped. "This business is gettin' crazier every minute. An' you sure got me wrong. I don't—"

Silky Ed Crowder tossed his head at the buckskin. "Make a surcingle around that bronc with a rope. Tie the other end of the rope to this runt's feet. We'll make him think crazy business when he's dragged through a few cactus beds."

Ruff reared to a sitting position, his homely face shocked. "Hey—you ain't gonna do that to me? I'm just a ranny siftin' through on the scout for a job. I don't know nothin' about no Zeke McCann or Devil's Ear or anythin' else!"

"You don't, eh?" Silky Ed Crowder showed coffee-colored teeth in an ugly leer. "In that case, you're just outta luck, because we think you do. You'll be ready to beller the truth when you're full of cactus stickers. Did you leave the Broken-Stirrup alone?"

Ruff lunged against the ropes. "What you're gonna do to me ain't human. I tell you, I don't work for no Broken-Stirrup outfit."

"Our milk of human kindness has plumb curdled," sneered Silky Ed Crowder. "Havin' the Broken-Stirrup salivate two of our rannies soured it a-plenty. That, an' grabbin' old Zeke McCann to find out where the Devil's Ear is. We've had Broken-Stirrup watched close for a week, hopin' to get our hands on one of their waddies."

"I tell you—"

"Throw a surcingle around that buckskin's barrel!" ordered Crowder.

Ruff rolled his eyes in the direction of the waterhole, where he had left Dawn Lorde and the giant Titanic Harrison. If they were looking on, there was no sign of it.

Doubling backward like a contortionist, Ruff found his spurred boot heels with numbing fingers.

"Hey— lemme show you something!" He made his voice terrified.

Silky Ed Crowder came over, bent down, said, "Well, what—"

Ruff reached up both hands—magically freed of ropes—and gripped Silky Ed Crowder's throat. He jerked the man sprawling atop him, seized the fellow's guns, pointed them at the others.

"High like a house!" he snarled.

Up went their hands. Ruff knocked Silky Ed Crowder away, then twisted his spurs so the man could see them. The lower edge of each spur tine, between rowel and heel-band, was ground to a razor edge.

"Got dragged with a foot hung in a stirrup one time," he said harshly. "Since, I've kept my spurs sharpened like that so I could cut myself loose if it ever happened again. Now—"

He let it trail off. Hoof-hammering sound was reaching his ears.

Ruff fanned his captured sixes at the four.

"Unbuckle your belts!" he rapped.

They obeyed, snarling, reluctant. And hardly was the last belt and holster on the hardpan when a sorrel bronc and rider popped around a hill perhaps two hundred yards away.

"'Who's that?" Ruff demanded, and held his guns so the horseman could not see them.

"The boss—Stan Yonkel," Silky Ed Crowder admitted.

"Call 'im!"

The foreman called. Stan Yonkel started, neck-reined toward them. He pulled up a few yards distant, a withered monkey of a man near sixty years of age. A moustache of hairs which stuck out stiffly gave his face the look of an inquisitive mouse. He saw something was wrong. "What's goin' on?"

Ruff produced his sixes. "Plenty. Skin off your hardware an' climb down."

Stan Yonkel blew explosive profanity from under his bristling moustache. But he complied.

Ruff shifted his bound ankles until he sat so he could watch all of them.

"This dog-faced foreman of your'n got off on the wrong foot," he told the rancher. "He was actin' nasty because he figures I'm a Broken-Stirrup rider. I ain't. Now I wanta know what this is all about."

Stan Yonkel scowled at the gun muzzles. "We're tryin' to find old Zeke McCann."

"Who's he?"

"The best dang friend I got," Stan Yonkel said earnestly. "He's a great old jasper. And it's gonna go plenty hard with them Broken-Stirrup skunks who kidnapped 'im!"

Ruff squinted at the old rancher. "What's this mysterious Devil's Ear business?"

Silky Ed Crowder growled profanely. "Better not tell 'im that, Stan!"

Stan Yonkel frowned at his foreman. "Won't hurt nothin'. If he's a Broken-Stirrup rider, he already knows. If he ain't, we gotta explain things so he'll turn us loose."

He eyed Ruff steadily. "Like I say, old Zeke McCann is maybe the best friend I got. He's a prospector. Me an' that dang Dawn Lorde gal who owns the Broken-Stirrup has been grubstakin' him for years. That makes us partners of his'n."

He paused to glower wrathfully. "Well, a week ago old Zeke McCann showed up at my Boxed-Y. He was plenty excited. Said he'd made his big find, but it wasn't no gold mine. He called it the Devil's Ear. Swore it a wasn't gold, but wouldn't tell us what is was, said there would be four partners, this Dawn Lorde, a grandson of old Zeke's from over in Arizona, old Zeke and myself. He had been to the Broken-Stirrup to tell Dawn Lorde and was comin' by to tell me on his way to file—"

"You sure he didn't tell you what he'd found?" Ruff interrupted.

Stan Yonkel glared at him, said nothing.

"I got reasons for bein' interested," Ruff said tightly. "You see, I'm that grandson of old Zeke's from over in Arizona."

Stan Yonkel wheezed a long, surprised breath through his moustache. "The hell you say! You gotta have more proof than your word."

Ruff fished a letter out of his vest pocket, tossed it over. "There's what he wrote me. Just says come over—that he's got somethin' for me."

Old Stan Yonkel read the letter. "That's Zeke's writin', all right. He don't tell you anythin' more about this Devil's Ear than he told us, except that it ain't silver or copper or other metal ore he's found."

"He was plumb cautious," Ruff admitted. "But go ahead with your story. What happened to Zeke?"

"He started off to town with two of my riders. Out here in the brakes they was drygulched. One of my men was killed. The other got away. Old Zeke was kidnapped. My man who got away winged one of the gang and saw the drygulchers were from the Broken-Stirrup. Well, we rode over there. One of their hands was sportin' a new bullet hole in the shoulder. We accused 'em of grabbin' old Zeke to make 'im tell where the Devil's Ear was."

Stan Yonkel growled angrily. "We had a shootin' scrape. Silky Ed salivated one of their rannies, but they run us off. Since then we been kinda holdin' the Broken-Stirrup in a state of siege. By Harry, they may have old Zeke, but it ain't gonna do 'em no good!"

"She's all clear now." Ruff nodded soberly. "That big Titanic Harrison was makin' a break when he grabbed me a few minutes ago."

"Huh?" exploded Stan Yonkel. "What's this?"

"Talk low. The big jasper an' the gal are watchin' us now, afraid to show themselves because I got a gun. Don't let 'em hear us."

Then, rapidly, Ruff explained the happenings at the waterhole, up until his capture while pursuing the buckskin.

"Goin' for the sheriff, huh!" snarled old Stan Yonkel. "They're figurin' on tying us up with the law so they'll have a chance to make Zeke take 'em to that Devil's Ear."

"What they told you about tryin' to find Zeke themselves was a pack of damn lies!" Silky Ed Crowder grated. "We figured they'd try that stunt. That's why we was gonna drag you—to make you confess."

Ruff fiddled absently with the guns he had taken from the foreman. His gaze found a huge pinon tree a hundred yards distant, rested there. "We gotta use skullduggery in this. I got an idea."

"What?" asked Stan Yonkel.

"That tree over yonder—it's got a limb stickin' out just right to hang a man on. You fellers put me on my bronc, put the bronc under that limb an' run a rope from my neck over it to the tree trunk. Tie it to the tree with a knot that'll slip if any weight is put on it, so there won't be no danger of me stranglin' if the bronc jumps."

"You mean us ride off like we'd left you to hang?"

"Yeah. The big gent an' the girl will cut me down. They'll be sure I'm an enemy of your'n. I'll roar like I want your blood, an' they'll maybe give me a job. If they do, I'll learn if they've got old Zeke."

Silky Ed Crowder rubbed his hands. "That's a good idea. Gimme back my guns an' we'll do it."

Ruff shook his head. "What d'you take me for? Might as well tell you now I ain't trustin' nobody too much until I find out what's what. I'll keep your hardware in my shirt. If one of you jaspers tries to pick up his gun, it's gonna be too bad. I ain't forgot you was gonna drag me through cactus beds."

The foreman scowled uneasily.

"One of you grab this rope on my ankles," Ruff directed. "Pretend to capture me. But be dang sure it don't go no further'n pretendin'!"

Instantly a Boxed-Y ranny seized the rope which they had intended to surcingle around the buckskin's barrel. He yanked. Ruff waved his arms, fell backward. Old Stan Yonkel leaped upon him.

"Careful!" Ruff grunted. "Tie my hands in front where I can reach the gun in my shirt!"

His wrists were tied. They boosted him on the buckskin, led the animal to the great pinon tree. A lasso rope dropped about his neck.

Casting alert glances about, Ruff was unable to discern a sign of the girl or big Titanic Harrison. He dampened his lips. Had they taken fright and fled? If so, this elaborate trick was wasted effort.

The rope snaked across the limb. Stan Yonkel himself waded into the dense brush around the pinon bole to make the end fast.

"Be dang sure that knot'll slip!" Ruff breathed.

Old Stan Yonkel let him see the knot as it was tied. "That all right? It'll come loose if your bronc jumps."

"Sure. I'll have the big gent and the girl cut the rope so they won't see it's a fake knot." Ruff twisted his head to ease the nose about his neck. "Drag it, you jaspers!"

They strode off, Stan Yonkel to his sorrel bronc, the others toward the spot where they had left their horses. They all disappeared in the jumbled brakes.

Minutes dragged. Ruff heard hoof sound of horses being ridden away, although no one appeared. The buckskin under him began to kick at biting flies, making him unpleasantly conscious of the noose about his neck.

"Whoa, boy!" he grunted. He looked closely at the rope knotted about the pinon trunk, to make sure it would slip in case of an accident.

After that he felt better. The knot would certainly slip. There was no danger of his hanging. Five minutes later, possibly more, he heard a rustle off to the right. It was repeated, as though someone were creeping through the sage.

"Help!" Ruff howled, and made his homely face register as much agony as possible.

He looked toward the sound, expecting the girl or huge Titanic Harrison to appear. But they did not. Nothing stirred.

The buckskin snorted, kicked violently at a greenhead. The tug of the rope at his neck moved him to glance at the knot again.

Horror flooded his face. It was no longer a slipknot! Someone had crept, unheard, through the brush to the tree trunk and shoved a small stick through the loop portion of the knot.

His convulsive start as he made the discovery excited the buckskin. The horse walked off.

Leaning over, Ruff took up the slack in the rope as gently as he could. But the shock was still ghastly. His windpipe closed as though poured full of molten lead.

Wildly he clawed for the gun he had thrust inside his shirt. But the stretching of his body as it swung by the neck pulled his shirt tail out of his pants. The gun eluded his fingers, slipped to the hardpan.

He swung like a rock on a string, began to strangle.

CHAPTER III

DEAD MAN

Bringing his hands up, Ruff sought to grip the rope and ease the throttling pressure. He succeeded only partially. There was absolutely no possibility of his climbing to the limb, or even high enough to free the throttling noose.

His ears began to roar. His eyes protruded.

Suddenly there was a crashing in the sagebrush nearby. Diminutive Dawn Lorde appeared. She ran to the pinon, tore at the knotted rope.

The hemp slackened abruptly, letting Ruff down in a pile in the sage. He felt the six-gun gouge into his hip, and had presence of mind to jam it into his shirt before the girl reached his side.

"We thought it was a trick!" she gasped. "It looked like a fake hanging— so we could rescue you."

Ruff kneaded his throat, groaned loudly to cover his surprise. So they had seen through the ruse! "Where's the big gent?" he croaked.

She pointed. "Over there. Watching."

Titanic Harrison had appeared atop a boulder some threescore yards distant, gripping a Winchester, staring about alertly.

Ruff scowled—not entirely because of the agony in his throat. The giant's position was such that he could have crept up, unobserved by the girl, and thrust the stick in the rope knot. It had been Dawn Lorde moving which had attracted his attention, Ruff decided. She had come from a spot near where he had heard the sound.

He squinted at her, wondering if she had pulled some sort of a grotesque practical joke on him. No. Her face was strained, serious.

"Let's hike outta here!" he grunted.

Huge Titanic Harrison got off his rock and came over. Together the three of them sought shelter in a nearby gully.

"Why did they do such a thing to you?" the girl demanded.

Ruff stroked his neck, worked his jaw gingerly. "You still figure me as a Boxed-Y hand?"

"No—not now."

"Well, I ain't. But what I told you about bein' a ranny siftin' through on the scout for a job wasn't exactly the truth. Old Zeke McCann is my granddaddy."

"Oh! You told Stan Yonkel that?"

"Uh-huh."

"Then that's why they tried to hang you!"

Ruff's homely face registered stark puzzlement. "Stan Yonkel claimed old Zeke McCann was about his best friend. Somehow, I believed 'im. Yonkel didn't seem such a curious hombre."

The girl stared at him curiously. "You say that—after what they did to you!"

Ruff blinked. He had almost betrayed the fact that the hanging was his own idea. He got a grip on himself.

"I wish you'd tell me what's behind this!" he said hastily.

"Zeke McCann is a splendid old man," the girl declared. "I have been grubstaking him for years. A week ago he came to me and said he had made his strike. He said it wasn't gold or silver or the usual metals, but wouldn't reveal more than that. He rode off, saying he was going to tell Stan Yonkel, who had also grubstaked him, then ride to town and file his claim."

She grimaced angrily. "Late that night one of my punchers went to the bunkhouse door and somebody shot him in the shoulder. A little later Stan Yonkel and his outfit rode up. They accused us of kidnapping Zeke. There was a fight. Silky Ed Crowder shot one of my men. Since then they've had my Broken-Stirrup ranch surrounded."

Ruff nodded slowly. This story dovetailed with the one Stan Yonkel had told him.

For the space of two minutes, Ruff thought deeply. He made a decision.

"Listen!" He pointed off to the right. "Don't you hear somethin'?"

The girl and Titanic Harrison looked where he pointed.

Leaning over, Ruff wrenched the girl's Winchester out of her hands. Pivoting, he jammed the octagon barrel against Titanic Harrison's expansive chest.

Titanic choked, fluttered his hands at his six-guns, then thought better of it. "What're you doin'?"

Ruff scowled warningly at the girl. Rage was in her eyes. She seemed about to spring upon him.

"Behave an' you won't get hurt!" he told her. "I'm gonna start bangin' this thing around. That hangin' was supposed to be a fake, like you thought. But somebody sneaked up an' tied the knot hard in the rope. It could've been one of you, but danged if I see why you'd do it. It could've been one of old Stan Yonkel's outfit. But that ain't reasonable because I'm bettin' Yonkel ain't the kind of a gent to do a trick like that. Anyhow, I don't savvy why they'd want to scrag me."

"You—you—" The girl was almost incoherent with anger. "You're one of Yonkel's gang!"

"Nope. I'm lookin' out for number one—Oscar Ruff." He eyed her steadily. "I wish you'd believe that."

"I don't!"

He shrugged. "Well, that's too bad. But it sure don't alter my intentions none. I'm gonna hold you two prisoner. Then I'm gonna grab old Stan Yonkel an' his foreman an' put you all together. Then I'm gonna work on you all until somebody busts loose with the truth about this. There's an African in the kindlin', what I mean!"

Huge Titanic Harrison sneered viciously. His big fingers curled and uncurled.

He cursed twice, violent oaths that made the girl go scarlet, then began:

"You little—"

Wham! Gunshot sound clattered across the brakes.

Titanic Harrison clipped his mouth shut tightly. He put fumbling hands to his chest, took an aimless sidewise stop. Then he doubled suddenly down on his face.

At the report Ruff leaped backward, slanted his Winchester at the spot from which the bushwhacker had fired and stroked the trigger. He saw nothing to shoot at—just fired blindly in hope of preventing a second shot.

"Duck!" he ripped at the girl. "That's the buzzard who monkeyed with the rope."

The girl dropped to all fours, scuttled down the gully. Flattened, Ruff waited for another shot. None came. When he thought it safe, he looked at Titanic Harrison.

The puncture in the giant's shirt front told him the man had been shot through the heart.

Furtively, Ruff wiggled up out of the gully. He speared his hat on the tip of a sagebrush. No bullets were drawn. He left the hat there, moved a dozen yards away and tossed a rock to make noise near the heat. That did not draw fire, either.

From down the gully where the girl had gone came a faint screech and struggle sounds.

Ruff leaped wrecklessly erect, flung for the spot.

Wham! Wham! The bushwhacker had not moved. His bullets made hot squawkings bare inches in front of Ruff's face.

The undersized ranny pitched down.

Twisting as he landed, Ruff exploded the Winchester in the general direction of the unseen marksman. There was no sign he had hit anybody.

An open patch of alkali lay between him and where the girl had screeched. He circled it scuttling on all fours, making slow progress, but not daring to straighten and run.

Into the gully he tumbled. A moment later he found jumbled bootprints, large ones and small ones. The girl had been seized there. Down the gully he sprinted, trailing.

The gash widened, deepened. From sand, the bottom changed to bedrock. Smaller gullies opened into it.

Ruff stopped, knowing he had lost the trail. He strained his ears. He began to perspire.

"Two of 'em!" he breathed. "Maybe more." He mopped his forehead with a sleeve.

All about him was heat and silence.

Back toward the body of Titanic Harrison he crept. He made sure the giant was dead. A bit later he found where the bushwhacker had stood, but he found no empty cartridges.

"Caught 'em in his hand," he decided.

He circled, cautiously at first, then more carelessly. Time after time he showed himself without drawing fire. The brakes were so rough as to be almost impossible for one man to search. To the southward they became the Badlands and the Grand Canyon of the Colorado, probably the most torn-up stretch of country in the world.

A quarter of an hour of that and he heard horses galloping. He sought a small pinnacle quickly.

Old Stan Yonkel, Silky Ed Crowder and the three Boxed-Y riders came into view. They thundered toward him as swiftly as the nature of the brakes would permit.

Ruff swore softly. "That about lets them out! They couldn't have done it—they was too far away when I first heard their broncs."

"We heard shootin'!" veiled Stan Yonkel. "What happened?"

Ruff let them come up. "Somebody bushwhacked Titanic Harrison an' grabbed the girl!"

He took them to where Titanic Harrison lay, told them what had occurred. He showed them where the ambusher had stood, where the girl had been seized. He told how nearly fatal the hanging trick had been.

Gathered around the body once more, Silky Ed Crowder whispered something in an inside to Stan Yonkel. The rancher whispered back to the foreman.

Ruff scowled at the byplay, started over.

Instantly they both drew guns and covered him.

"Get the six in his shirt!" grated Stan Yonkel.

Ruff gave the man who approached him a glare that stopped the fellow in his tracks. "What kinda horseplay is this?"

Stan Yonkel looked him up and down wrathfully. "I guess we savvy this whole thing, now!"

"Yeah," leered Silky Ed Crowder. "It musta been you who grabbed old Zeke McCann to learn where the Devil's Ear is, and laid the blame onto the Broken-Stirrup outfit. Dunno how you learned about the Devil's Ear. We'll find that out later. If you're Zeke's grandson, that'll explain it. Anyhow, you killed Harrison before we ever found you!"

"We're takin' you to the sheriff for killin' Titanic Harrison," growled Stan Yonkel. "Titanic must've learned your game."

"You're locoed!" Ruff protested angrily. "I tell you, somebody salivated Titanic Harrison an' grabbed the girl!"

"Girl probably wasn't around at all," sneered Silky Ed Crowder. "You heist your dewclaws!"

Ruff gritted, "I'll be—"

"I'm sure gonna plug you if you act funny!" Stan Yonkel warned earnestly.

Ruff shrugged, put his fists above his hat brim, let them tear the six-gun out of his shirt.

CHAPTER IV
BLASTING DEATH

When they had him disarmed, Ruff tried again; "You jugheads! That girl is in trouble! She was here. I'll show you her bootprints!"

"I saw them bootprints!" Silky Ed Crowder growled. "They looked to me like your own!"

"Let's measure 'em," suggested Stan Yonkel.

They went down the gully. Coming in view of the spot where Dawn Lorde had been captured, Ruff stopped. His face purpled. He cursed his captors loudly, bitterly.

"I'm seein' some things now!" he snarled. "Some of you walked on them prints, blotted 'em out! You're trying to frame this whole mess onto me. You've got some men in your outfit I ain't seen. You had 'em plug Titanic Harrison an' grab the girl."

"That's a lie!" roared Stan Yonkel.

Ruff glared at him. "You got more men in your outfit, ain't you?"

"Two," the old rancher snapped. "But they're at home."

Ruff gave a shrug that shook his entire head and shoulders. "All right! All right! You've got this mess hog-tied onto me."

"C'mon," Stan Yonkel ordered. "We'll take 'im to the sheriff."

Ruff began, "That girl—"

"Shut up about that girl!" yelled Silky Ed Crowder. "She wasn't here."

"Wait a minute," interposed Yonkel. "We'll make sure the girl is safe before we take this feller to the law."

Silky Ed Crowder scowled, then brightened. "Sure. We'll hold this jasper at the Boxed-Y while some of us rides over to the Broken-Stirrup to see if she's there."

Ruff ran a rowdy gaze over the group. He wasn't so sure now this gang was framing him. If they were going to make sure pretty Dawn Lorde was safe before they took him to the sheriff . . . .

"In case the girl is missing, this gink probably put her outta the way," said Silky Ed Crowder.

So that was it! Ruff crushed his teeth together so hard the enamel squeaked. He let them push him through the sage with Winchester barrels to his buckskin bronc.

"How about my saddle?" he protested.

They escorted him to the waterhole for his saddle. Not certain it would do much good, he displayed the slashed cinch.

"Hm-m-m!" said old Stan Yonkel. He looked at unmistakable evidences of a fight in the waterhole. "Looks like you maybe did tell part of the truth."

Silky Ed Crowder finished repairing the slashed latigo strap, swung the rig on the buckskin. "We'll leave him at the Boxed-Y an' some of us'll go see about the girl!"

Ruff scowled as he settled into the kak. This talk about going to see if the girl was safe had him puzzled. There was something back of it. Or maybe these Boxed-Y hombres were not framing him. It was baffling.

He mulled over the thing as they rode southwest.

The Boxed-Y was a horse outfit. Ruff learned that when he came in sight of the corrals and saw the chutes fitted with squeezers. The buildings squatted on the south side of a butte, baking in the afternoon sun, basted with the gray dust of the brakes.

Two punchers came out of the low bunkhouse door as the group rode up.

Stan Yonkel squinted at Ruff, spat.

"These are my other two hands. If that girl was kidnapped as you claim, they couldn't have had a hand in it."

Ruff surveyed the pair. One had his shirt off. The other was carrying a half-finished horsehair hatband he had been braiding.

"Listen, old-timer!" Ruff eyed old Stan Yonkel steadily. "You're either tryin' to, kid me, or you're kiddin' yourself. If you're on the up and up, you sure better fog over to the Broken-Stirrup an' see about that girl. Somebody grabbed her, I tell you."

Silky Ed Crowder shot a pointing arm at the sod-roofed log ranch house. "You hold 'im in there, Stan. Me an' the boys'll catch up fresh hosses for the ride to the Broken-Stirrup."

Stan Yonkel nodded, shucked out his six-gun. "Make it snappy. You—runt—into the house you go!"

Ruff stamped into the ranch house, went to a rocking chair with sheepskin tacked on the seat, planted himself in it.

He glared at Stan Yonkel. "I'm tellin' you—"

"You ain't tellin' me nothin'!" grunted the old rancher. "I'm tired of listenin' to you. An' I'm holdin' you here while Silky Ed an' some of the boys ride to the Broken-Stirrup. Maybe we'll know then what's what."

Ruff tilted back in the rocker, locked his fingers together and said no more. Silky Ed Crowder rode up to the door on a fresh horse.

"We'll be back in 'bout three hours," he called.

Wheeling his horse, he galloped back to the bunkhouse. A moment later came a roll of hoofbeats. The noise receded.

Ruff got up, failed to heed Stan Yonkel's growled warning, and strode to the window. He looked out in time to see Silky Ed Crowder and his companions top a knoll and disappear. He counted the riders.

"Say—" He didn't finish it—became silent and tense, ears strained. *All the Boxed-Y hands had ridden with Silky Ed Crowder.*

Stan Yonkel fingered his six-gun. "What's eatin' you?"

Ruff lifted a fist, smashed the glass out of the window.

"Hey!" roared Yonkel. "Them winders cost money!"

Ruff put his head out. He turned it from side to side. He sniffed. Then he jerked back into the room as though he had been struck at. He backed for the door.

"Quick!" he barked. "C'mon outside!"

"Stand still!" yelled Yonkel. "You ain't trickin' me!"

Ruff kept moving for the door. He put his hands up. "Quick! Outside!"

He passed through the door into the sunlight, made no effort to dodge away, and literally ran backward.

Old Stan Yonkel followed him, bellowing, "Stand still or I'll salivate you! Stand still or—"

In the door, the old rancher halted. He brought the hammer of his gun back, steadied the weapon. Deadly purpose was in his faded old eyes. He suspected somebody might be hiding behind the house, ready to cut down on him when he came out.

"I'm not trickin' you!" Ruff rapped at him. "Under the house! There's—"

Who-o-m! Flame and flying timbers suddenly filled the interior of the ranch house. Old Stan Yonkel was blown out of the door like a paper wad from a school kid's bean-shooter.

The sod-covered roof sprouted upward, bloomed a great cloud of smoke. Dust and torn logs boiled, fell back.

Ruff, tumbled end over end by the blast, got to his feet as soon as he could. He leaped to old Stan Yonkel.

The withered frame was limp, pinned down by logs. Ruff boosted the logs aside, took the old man's wrist. There was pulse. He flexed Yonkel's bony arms and legs, lifted his head cautiously, pressed fingers to his ribs. No bones seemed to be broken. He was merely knocked out.

Ruff scooped up Yonkel's six-gun, sprinted to the bunkhouse, came back carrying the water bucket. He doused the rancher. The elderly man showed no signs of reviving.

Ruff stared in the direction taken by Silky Ed Crowder. He swore softly. Exploring, he found a sizeable knob in old Stan Yonkel's thatch of white hair. The skull did not seem to be fractured.

Flame was rapidly enwrapping the ruins of the ranchhouse. Somewhere in the burning tangle a box of cartridges started exploding. The slugs squealed about, knocking sparks, digging up dust.

Picking up old Stan Yonkel, Ruff ran to the bunkhouse. He had seen a writing tablet and pencil there. Seizing them, he wrote:

> Stan Yonkel:
>   Your foreman, Silky Ed Crowder, and your spread of punchers are behind this, I think. They must have put a keg of black powder under the house with a long fuse. I'm trailing them.
>
>   Oscar Ruff

Shouldering the old rancher once more, Ruff carried him to a freight wagon which stood near a corral, put him in the wagon bed, tucked the note in his pocket, covered him with a tarp.

"He'll wake up in time," he grunted.

Silky Ed Crowder had turned the buckskin into a corral with the other horses. Ruff ran to the enclosure, got a lass, spooked the buckskin into a corner and settled the noose on the animal. He saddled, mounted, spurred the trail Silky Ed had taken. Ruff was certain now that Crowder had the girl held prisoner.

Ruff flung along at a mad pace. Miles on, he slowed down and anxiously studied the gait of his horse. The animal's hide was a paste of lather and dust. It was blowing steadily, but not with the spasmodic force that meant exhaustion.

"Got a lot of miles in 'im yet," he concluded.

He pulled up, listened; far ahead he heard the distant rumble of hooves. Carefully he rode on. Rougher and rougher became the terrain. Sagebrush thinned. The knotted little pinons grew scattering and even more scrawny.

Conical buttes of grayish clay grew fewer, giving way almost entirely to stone. The sun, sinking nearer the horizon, sprayed colors in the rock formation with softened glare. It was an awesome waste into which he was riding, a region of scenic grandeur. But Ruff was blind and dead to everything but the clamor of hoofbeats he kept always before him.

"How much further can they be goin'?" he muttered uneasily.

Half an hour later he got the answer. They entered a canyon and the noise ahead died suddenly.

Dismounting, Ruff led the weary buckskin into a side gulch, left the horse there. Afoot, he went ahead.

He inspected old Stan Yonkel's six-gun. Yonkel had carried the hammer on an empty chamber, a common precaution with these single-action guns. It held five cartridges. And Ruff had no more ammunition.

He scowled. His quarry numbered six!

Abruptly he veered left, crept up toward the canyon rimrock. He had heard voices ahead.

Soon after, Ruff sighted the gang. Leading the girl, they wheeled into a sheer-walled, narrower cut. Two men remained on guard there.

Ruff scouted, discovered two more men on watch with the horses. He eyed the rimrock above his head, saw he was going to have trouble climbing it, and looked once more at the canyon into which the girl had been taken. No chance of passing the guards!

He went back to his buckskin and got the lass rope. With that he managed to surmount the wall-like rimrock. Creeping forward, he peered into the side canyon.

There was a shack below him, evidently erected by some prospector in the past. The structure stood on a shelf erosion had left above the canyon bed. Fantastic stone formation like huge spikes studded the slope from the shack to the canyon rimrock. And the rimrock itself was rent by a wash like a knife slash.

"Perfect!" Ruff breathed. He could creep, unobserved, to the very door of the shack!

He listened until he heard voices in the ramshackle structure. The words were unintelligible from that distance. He descended as silently as possible.

When he was fifty feet from the shack, he could understand what was being said.

"I'm tellin' you!" Silky Ed Crowder's voice rasped out. "We're gonna scrag the girl if you don't tell us where this Devil's Ear is!"

"You coyote!" The reply was high, squeaky, wrathful. "You'll sure decorate a rope for what you're doin'!"

Ruff advanced a couple of yards. He recognized that voice—his grandfather, old Zeke McCann. It had been ten years since he had seen the fire-eating old gentleman, but that high-pitched tone was unmistakable.

"So that's why they grabbed the girl!" he told himself. "They couldn't torture old Zeke into talkin', so they're usin' the girl to make 'im tell 'em what they want!"

Two ugly thudding sounds came from the shack. The girl gave a stifled gasp of pain, evidence she was being beaten.

Ruff gripped his gun, tensed for a reckless charge. Then he crouched back.

A man had appeared down the canyon, running toward the shack.

"If this Devil's Ear ain't gold or silver, what is it?" Silky Ed Crowder roared.

Before he got an answer, the running man reached the shack door.

"Hey, Silky!" he barked. "I went down the canyon a piece to keep a lookout like you ordered, an' I heard a bronc blowin'! It's the buckskin that dang runt was ridin'!"

Silky Ed Crowder popped out of the shack door. "Where's the bronc at?"

"I brought 'im up with the other hosses," said the man. "You reckon—"

"I thought the runt got blowed up in the house!" snarled Crowder. "C'mon! Let's look that bronc over!"

They ran down the canyon.

The instant they were out of sight, Ruff leaped for the shack door.

CHAPTER V

Trick Kill

A Boxed-Y rider stepped out of the shack, almost crashing into Ruff. He squawled in fright, pawed for his guns.

Ruff bashed the man in the face with Stan Yonkel's heavy six, knocking the fellow backward into the decrepit structure. The gunslick's spurs hooked the threshhold and he crashed down. Sailing into the air. Ruff descended on the man's stomach.

He swooped, got his victim's guns, gave the fellow's head two sleep-inducing blows.

Pretty Dawn Lorde, bound once more, was piled in the center of the shack. She had a livid bruise on one cheek where Silky Ed Crowder had struck her.

"You!" she choked. "They said you were blown up with the Boxed-Y ranch house!"

"Big Plenty!" howled old Zeke McCann. "The runt himself!"

The elderly prospector was spreadeagled on the dirt floor. Ropes stretched taut from his wrists and ankles to four pegs driven into the ground held him. His swollen, enpurpled arms spoke amply of the torture he had undergone. They must have kept him thus for days.

Zeke McCann was even more pee-wee in stature than Ruff. He had the physical build of a gnarled old ape. A wide, delighted grin twisted his homely, wrinkled face.

Ruff rolled the girl out of line with the door.

A bullet came in and clouted slivers off the wall. Ruff sighted Silky Ed Crowder and the man who had found the buckskin. The shout from the overpowered guard had drawn them back. He fired at them, missed, but drove them out of sight.

Rapidly he untied Dawn Lorde, then old Zeke McCann.

"They seized me right after Titanic Harrison was shot," the girl grasped. "It was two of the Boxed-Y hands."

Ruff nodded, told her he had guessed that. He tried showing his hat at the door, but drew no shot. He found a dusty Karo can about the color of his own sun-baked face, put it in the hat and tried again. *Clang!* The can banged across the room.

Instantly, Ruff fanned a shot back. He got a bark of surprise.

"They won't bite on that again," he decided.

He poked the chinking out of the logs in a couple of places to make loopholes. Then he saw old Zeke McCann still lay on the floor, spread-eagled as the ropes had held him.

"I'm sure petrified!" the old prospector groaned. "Kinda give me a start an' maybe I can get movin'."

Ruff pounded the stiffened, paralyzed muscles. Zeke McCann moaned through clenched teeth, became wet with perspiration. Ruff knew he was undergoing terrible agony.

When the elderly man could wave his arms feebly. Ruff left the limbering-up job to the girl and, not without some effort, pried a hole in the rear wall. He hoped they could creep out and escape the same way he had entered the canyon.

But a bullet screamed into the hole he had opened.

"We ain't outta this by a dang sight," McCann groaned. "I can work myself into shape now, Miss."

Dawn Lorde got up. "Give me one of those guns and I'll watch the back."

Ruff hesitated, then passed the weapon over. He watched her go to the rear wall, crouch and peer through a crack toward the canyon rimrock. His homely face slowly acquired a startled look, then one of great uneasiness. Suddenly he strode to her and took the gun back.

"You get over against the north wall an' stay there!" he said gruffly. "That'll turn bullets better'n the others."

"But why—" She peered at him wonderingly. "Why did you change your mind?"

He tried to scowl, became hot and uncomfortable. He pulled at his shirt collar, although it was open three buttons down.

"Daggonit!" he floundered at last. "Don't argue with a feller!"

For forty minutes nothing of importance happened. Then, up on the rimrock near the gash by which he had descended, Ruff saw a bit of white cloth fluttering.

"Now what the heck?" he grunted.

The cloth appeared and shook again. It looked like somebody's summer underwear.

Ruff hesitated, then waved his hat through the hole he had opened in the rear wall of the shack.

A man appeared cautiously on the rimrock and crept down through the gash.

"One of Silky Ed's gang," Ruff muttered. "I don't savvy this. But if he wants to palaver, we'll take a chance. We ain't got much to lose."

The actions of the descending man were strange. He took great pains to remain concealed from the canyon mouth.

Ruff gave old Zeke McCann a gun. "Watch the front close. They may be pullin' a shenanygin'!"

132   **LESTER DENT**

The Boxed-Y hand came within speaking distance.

"I'm gonna help you," he called in a low voice. "I plumb balk at killin' a woman. I got enough of this mess."

"Yeah?" said Ruff doubtfully.

"Silky Ed brought a keg of that gunpowder from the Boxed-Y," the man whispered. "He's got it planted on the rimrock so it'll blow the whole side of the canyon down on this shack. He left me there to light the fuse. But I ain't gonna do it. You sneak out with me, then we'll blow the canyon wall onto the shack an' he'll think you're all dead."

"Santa Claus!" Ruff gulped. "You mean that?"

"I sure do. Only—you gotta promise to let me hit for Mexico."

"Sure—we'll let you go free as the wind!" Ruff beckoned Dawn Lorde and Zeke McCann, seized the unconscious man.

They crept out, joined the Boxed-Y rider. The man looked nervous, worried. He passed over his six-guns as Ruff lowered the unconscious man clear of the avalanche the powder would cause.

"So you'll know I ain't trickin' you!" he said.

Carefully remaining hidden from the canyon mouth, they worked up the canyon rim. They reached the narrow, knifelike slash in the rimrock.

"Here's the fuse." The Boxed-Y hand indicated the grayish cord with its filling of black powder. The fuse protruded from under a boulder. Beyond the boulder it stretched several yards to vanish in a crack in the rock.

"I'll crawl up an' see if the coast is clear," breathed the Boxed-Y hand. "It's a long fuse. You light it an' come up together."

The man crawled upward, reached for the fuse. As a matter of precaution, he glanced upward.

The Boxed-Y rider was scrambling madly to get away from them!

Ruff grunted explosively. He kicked aside the boulder under which the fuse disappeared. A tin canister of black powder was revealed!

"The coyote!" he gritted. "Short fuse! The rest of the fuse was a blind. We'd a-been blowed up!"

He fanned a bullet at the disappearing Boxed-Y man, charged upward after the would-be slayer.

The fellow had a rifle concealed at the top. But in his wild haste the man had paused only to scoop up the weapon, then dash madly across the tableland.

Ruff shot the man in the left leg. The fellow fell, squirmed around and tried to use his rifle. Ruff's six bellowed again. The man slouched over slackly atop his Winchester.

A hundred feet away Silky Ed Crowder and two other men leaped from behind a boulder. Excitement over the failure of their evil scheme made them reckless.

Ruff dived, rolled. Lead made high barking squeaks around him. He got the Winchester from under the Boxed-Y rider's body, levered the empty cartridge from the ejector gate, and took his time aiming.

The rifle jarred his shoulder—one of the men with Silky Ed Crowder suddenly got down on all fours as though looking for something. The fellow coughed horribly a couple of times, then spread out flat.

Silky Ed Crowder and the other man leaped for cover. Crowder got out of sight, dusted closely by a Winchester slug. Ruff shot again and knocked

Crowder's companion against a boulder. His next slug felled the man.

Ruff charged. He could hear Crowder clattering down into the main canyon, trying to reach the horses. Gaining the rimrock, Ruff started down himself.

A gunshot filled the canyon with guttering thunder. Ruff lurched, nearly fell down the sheer face of the rimrock, managed to stumble back to safety. He sat down, stared vacantly at the hole in his right sleeve which welled crimson.

He tried the arm. No bones were broken. But he could hardly move it.

"Muscles torn!" he groaned.

Peering over the rim, he shot three times at Silky Ed Crowder and the surviving gunslick. They thundered around a bend as though bearing charmed lives, spurring their horses.

Pretty Dawn Lorde came up, assisting old Zeke McCann.

"They got away!" Ruff grinned wryly. "Not that I wasn't kinda tickled to see 'em go."

"Oh!" The girl's cry was anguished as she saw his reddening sleeve. She folded to her knees at his side.

Old Zeke McCann squinted at them owlishly, then, with a knowing look on his homely old face, hobbled to the rimrock edge. He started to glance back—but suddenly focused his gaze down the canyon.

The sheer-walled defile had abruptly filled with gun sound. Volley after volley of shots clamored. Then there was silence.

"Silky Ed an' his friend musta run into trouble," old Zeke chuckled.

Stan Yonkel rode into view down the canyon. He sighted them, waved his arms wildly.

"I followed you! An' I salivated both the coyotes!"

Old Zeke McCann tugged at his wrinkled jaw. "Well, where they'll be goin' it's too durn bad they can't take along some of that asbestos they was tryin' so hard to get."

"Asbestos!" Ruff ejaculated.

"Huh—sure!" grinned old Zeke. "That's what I found—a whole dang cliff of asbestos rock. Stringy stuff kinda reminded me of what I figured the fuzz on the Devil's Ear would be like, so I called her the Devil's Ear. Boy—howdy! If it ain't worth a million, I'll eat the whole works."

He squinted at approaching Stan Yonkel. "Guess it's lucky I mailed you that letter, Big Plenty, before I let Silky Ed overhear me tellin' old Stan I was gonna cut 'im on a fortune."

He waited for an answer, got none, and looked around. Ruff and Dawn Lorde had pretty much lost interest in the recital. Old Zeke grinned.

"Aw, heck! Reckon maybe I'd better go down an' kinda keep old Stan from interruptin'."

· · · · ·

The Haunted Saddle

The day Henry B. "Pocus" Hern rode his grulla bronc into Sunken City, he nearly scared a man to death.

That was strange. Pocus Hern was hardly a sight to spook a human. His Maker had apparently cut up old boot leather to fashion him a hide. His face was homely, very homely—so homely it made men chuckle. He looked peaceable.

His looks were deceiving.

When Winks Ellis saw Pocus Hern, he acted as if racked by streak lightning. Winks had a knife-carved cheek that twitched, winklike, at intervals. Now his whole face twitched.

"He was to be a ranny on a black bronc!" he wailed. "That's the one. And Henry B. Hern is *Pocus Hern!* Oh, dang! Why didn't I recognize that name!"

Pocus Hern reined the grulla bronc toward Sunken City's one livery stable. Winks Ellis quaked afresh.

"Headin' right for 'em!" he moaned. "They don't know what they're goin' up against! They'll crawl him."

He hunched behind the jut-boards of a Bain freight wagon, rocking from foot to foot as though he had caving rubber ice underfoot. There was a chance he might reach the livery stable ahead of Pocus Hern.

He slid away from the Bain, splattered out like a scared gopher in the shade of a pole corral, scooted fifty yards with his nose in the gumbo dust, erected and pounded up an alley at a dead run.

He saw then it was no use.

"Oh, dang!" he groaned. "If I just wasn't mixed up in this!"

Pocus Hern, blissfully unaware he had scared a man, tugged reins before the livery. He alighted, dusted and re-creased his Stetson, worked his toes in his Justins. He looked at the big man in the livery door. He grinned amiably.

"Howdy."

The big man had big ears. The tip of one lopped over, but the tip of the other had been missing a long time. He had little eyes and a scowly mouth.

He asked shortly, "Somethin' you want?"

Pocus Hern looked at the big man's lop ear, at his scowly mouth. He coughed politely.

"A lady," he said. "A lady named Dana O'Day. I'm lookin' for her."

The big man made no sound.

Pocus Hern thought he was hard of hearing.

"A lady by the name of Dana O'Day!" he repeated, more loudly. "I'm lookin' for her."

"Uh!" grunted the other. "You Hern?"

Pocus seemed surprised. He blinked, hitched his chap belt. He admitted he was in a puzzled tone. "Uh-huh."

The big man advanced out of the door, thumb-gestured an invitation inside.

"She's in there right now, waitin' for you," he said. "Go on in."

Pocus, seeming even more surprised, strode inside. He wore no guns. His spur bobs made loud, jangling music.

He tinkled into the livery office. A bearded man stood there, shoulders propped against the opposite wall. His nose was a bony peg in his mouse-colored beard, his neck a bony cane below it. He looked excited.

He was wiping a handkerchief over a single-action Colt .45. The gun muzzle waved absently in Pocus' direction. It cocked loudly.

Pocus whistled out breath shrilly, fell down with great effort and astounding speed. He landed on his right hand, eyes seeking behind him.

The big lop-eared man had drawn a six-gun. He held it upraised, club-like, above the spot Pocus' head had vacated. He gaped foolishly.

Pocus kicked both feet, mulelike.

The man squawked, reeled on peeled ankles. Pocus, rolling, shot up an arm, yanked the fellow down atop him, held him there as best he could. His best was pretty good.

The bearded man bounced about wildly, trying to get a shot past the big man.

Pocus strained, got the six away from the man atop him. He let the other look in its muzzle. "Leggo it, Whiskers!"

Whiskers let it go. The single-action bounced twice, rolled a yard.

The big man heaved up. He wore a wide rodeo rider's belt. Pocus put his foot on the buckle of that belt. The big man let out a lot of breath.

"My gun!" he labored at his associate. "I took the shells out so I wouldn't get shot if somethin' went wrong. 'Tain't loaded!"

The bearded man dived to retrieve his dropped six. Pocus glanced at Lop-ear's gun, saw it was not loaded, threw it at the bearded man. The fellow dodged it, went somewhat off balance. His clutching hand knocked his gun skating across the floor. Wildly, he pursued the weapon.

Pocus glided two paces sidewise, got his hands on a three-tine pitchfork. Jutting the fork out like a lance, he charged the scrambling man. The latter abandoned pursuit of the gun, reared up, tried for the door.

Pocus cut him off, horned him with the steel fork tines. Squealing, the man backpedaled. Pocus prodded him to the big, lop-eared man, jabbed the latter to his feet, herded them both into a corner.

They cursed him in chorus, fell silent before the menace of bayoneting fork tines.

"What was the idea of jumpin' me?" he demanded.

They both gave him silence.

He eyed one, then the other. "What's your names?"

"Whiskers Bloomburg," mumbled the bearded man.

Pocus threatened the other with the fork. "Your'n?"

"Fice."

"You had a father, didn't you?"

"Uh-huh. Sure."

"Didn't he have a name?"

"Lacy," snarled the man.

"Why'd you jump me?" Pocus tried again.

Flop-eared Fice Lacy gritted, "I'll show you why!" and dived recklessly at the fork. He shoved it aside at the expense of a lightly speared arm, drove a blow. Pocus whammed the floor with all his length.

He reared half up, was flattened by the concerted plunge of the two. They all boiled across the floor. Blows rapped. Breath labored gusty explosions. Bodies beat a rumble on the plank floor.

In swift succession, Fice Lacy caught a fist in the throat, another on the jaw, and flipped out senseless on the floor.

Whiskers Bloomburg began to understand just how deceiving were the looks of the man he was up against. He got scared, fought blindly. Pocus pummeled him to angle of floor and wall, mauled him until the man vented wheezing pleas for mercy.

Pocus gritted, "Why'd you crawl me?" and kept pumping his fists.

The man rolled his eyes at the door. "We wanted that!"

Pocus slanted a hard glance at the opening, saw nothing but his black horse. He growled, "I don't get you!"

"Saddle!" groaned the other. "We was tryin' to get your saddle!"

The saddle on the grulla bronc was of black leather, big-skirted, double-rigged. It had a silver-capped horn, half a dozen gold and silver rosettes inset with semi-precious jewels. A fancy rig. Worth several hundred. But several hundred did not warrant this attack.

"Yeah!" Pocus knobbed up one hand, looked speculatively at the fist it made. He hit his victim lightly in the face. "Can the bushwa, fella!"

The bony man gargled pain sounds. "To get the saddle—"

Pocus' eyes lighted avidly. He tangled both hands in the mouse-colored beard.

"I ain't lyin' to you!" wailed the bewhiskered one. "Fice Lacy wanted it. I dunno why. I just work for him sometimes. He don't tell me nothin'."

Pocus scowled at Fice Lacy. The big man was still unconscious. Pocus said, "You start jumpin' around and I'll make me a hair mattress out of them whiskers," and got up.

He studied the saddle on the grulla, scratched his jaw, retrieved his Stetson from where it had fallen, gave his chaps belt a yank. From a pocket he took a letter, read:

Mr. Henry B. Hern
Tinta, New Mexico

In a newspaper recently, I saw your picture and a story that you were retiring as a rodeo performer after winning the national championship riding contest.

The story said you intended to supply bucking horses to rodeos in the future. I have a string of outlaw broncs I believe you will be interested in,

It will be worth your time to come up and look at them personally, and we'll talk terms.

Yours sincerely,

Miss Dana O'Day
Sunken City, Wyoming

"Know anything about that?" Pocus asked, replacing the letter.

"Not a thing," Whiskers Bloomburg denied emphatically. "Dana O'Day has a ranch north of town. I dunno much about her."

"She got a string of top bucking horses?"

"I dunno. Maybe."

Pocus eyed the saddle on the grulla, whistled through his teeth. His forehead held resentful wrinkles.

"I don't savvy this. That saddle ain't worth the stew you two jaspers raised. It's too easy identified."

"You had it long?"

Pocus gazed at the man on the floor with sharpened interest. "Traded a gent two saddle broncs for it a month ago. Why?"

The other looked like he regretted the question. "Nothin'."

"What's funny about that kak?"

"I dunno."

Pocus made two fists, blew on them. "You say 'I dunno' like it was your whole vocabulary. I'm gonna change your tune." He loomed over the bewhiskered man.

A newcomer, sweeping in from the outer sunlight, said, "Well, well! Merry Christmas!"

He was well-knit, handsome, thirtyish. He had an alert little mustache and the bouncing exuberance of a boy. He looked at Pocus, frank-eyed.

"You might be Santa Claus, because you've brought these two what they've been needing." He jerked his head at unconscious Fice Lacy and bruised, frightened Whiskers Bloomburg, then came forward behind extended hand. "But I suppose you are Henry B. Hern."

Pocus took the hand. "Mind reader?"

"Not exactly," said the man. "You wrote Dana O'Day you would arrive on this date. And your black horse is the one in the picture."

"Oh." Pocus squinted questioningly at the handsome man.

"I am Lee Spaulding, Miss O'Day's foreman," he elaborated.

"Oh," said Pocus.

"Dana—Miss O'Day told me she had written you about buying our string of buckers."

"Did she?" Pocus pointed at lop-eared Fice Lacy and bearded Whiskers Bloomburg. "Did she tell you why these two should try to take my saddle away from me?"

Whiskers Bloomburg gave a gasp like cloth tearing, shrank back, paled.

Cold flame lunged into Lee Spaulding's eyes. He stared at the two on the floor, hard-mouthed. But his voice was calm. "No, she didn't. But I presume she can tell you if you ride out to the ranch with me."

Pocus studied Whiskers Bloomburg's mouse-hued beard. "I think I can learn a little right here."

"No, no!" Spaulding looked around wildly, moved his shoulders, pointed at a man at the far end of the street outside. A broad, bowlegged man in black vest and black hat. "Sheriff. Keeps his horse here and exercises it every day. He's coming for the bronc now. We better drag." He bobbed his head at Whiskers Bloomburg and Fice Lacy, added in a voice so brittle it clinked. "These two can be settled with later. We better drag now."

Pocus nodded. "Maybe we had, at that." He seemed very puzzled.

Hat in right hand, Pocus Hern slapped at hordes of mosquitoes. Marsh ground and a spring lay to the right, a hill and grazing whitefaces ahead. He pointed at the brand on a yearling.

"The Neckyoke—that Miss O'Day's brand?"

"Yes." Lee Spaulding drew on a cigarette, doused mosquitoes with smoke. "Bless these mosquitoes! They get thick in August. Yes—the Neckyoke spread is just over the hill."

The horses clouted through sage, rattled rocks, crunched over a cactus bed, topped the hill. The Neckyoke lay below them. Sheds, bunkhouse, house, windmill, a couple of pole corrals; it looked meager against the vastness of the range.

Pocus sized it up with a practiced eye. "Not bad. But it don't look much like a boss outfit."

"It's not, entirely. Broncs running on the west range. I'll have the boys hustle them in." Lee Spaulding pointed. "There's three of our hands. We got four."

The three punchers—one tall, two short—were greasing a hay wagon near the ranch house. Pocus appraised them, saw they were strangers, returned their lifted-hand salutes.

Lee Spaulding dismounted. "Miss O'Day will be inside." He lifted his hat, smoothed black hair that made a shiny skullcap, replaced the hat, smirked. "Dana—Miss O'Day and I are to be married next month."

"Yeah." Pocus' tone was politely interested. "I guess that happens to everybody, sooner or later."

When Lee Spaulding stood back courteously, Pocus entered the ranch house first.

Dana O'Day was there.

Pocus looked at her—and folded forward on his face. Pain jabbed at his eyes, sound blasted resonantly at his ears. He growled, fought off unconsciousness.

Twisting, he jammed fists feebly upward at Lee Spaulding. The handsome, boyish man discarded the gun with which he had felled Pocus. He ground Pocus' face to the floor, crashed his knees on Pocus' neck.

"Rope!" he barked. "Quick, Honey! He's hell on wheels!"

Pocus fought a little, but did not prevent himself being bound hand and foot. The tying done, Lee Spaulding backed away.

Pocus rolled over, looked bleakly at Dana O'Day.

She was tall, well-muscled for a girl, sinewy under satin-brown skin. She was pretty and twenty or thereabouts. Sun, besides browning her skin, had made her brown hair a faded khaki hue.

"So you're in it with Fice Lacy and Whiskers Bloomburg!" Pocus' tone was more curious than angry.

The girl glanced sharply at Lee Spaulding. "What does he mean, Lee?"

"Search me." Lee patted down his black skullcap of hair. "He had some kind of a row with Lacy and Bloomburg in Lacy's livery stable."

The girl bit her lower lip, shook her head. "I don't understand that. Lacy and Bloomburg are lice." She came over to stare down at Pocus.

Utter hate pinched her eyes and small mouth, made her cheeks hot with color. She stared thus for about a minute. Then tears came and wet her eyes.

"My full name is Dana O'Day Norton," she gritted.

Pocus said nothing in a puzzled way.

"Wes Norton was my brother!" she hissed.

Pocus shrugged. "And so what?"

"You killed him! You killed Wes Norton!"

Pocus frowned at her. She rubbed a hand across her eyes and the back of the hand came away damp. He said, "I don't know a thing about this."

"Go get that black saddle, Lee," she ordered.

Spaulding strode out jaunty of gait, handsome face grim. The girl backed away from Pocus until a table stopped her.

"No doubt you're wondering why I'm known as Dana O'Day and not Dana O'Day Norton," she said. "I'm a rodeo rider myself. I always ride as Dana O'Day. Everyone knows me by that name. That is why I knew my letter about the bucking horses would decoy you here, and you wouldn't connect me with Wes Norton, whom you killed. I haven't any buckers to sell."

"I traded that saddle off a man a month ago," Pocus advised shortly.

"That story is as good as any. I don't believe it."

Pocus scowled wearily, rolled to look out through the open door. His eyes narrowed. His mouth hardened. He raised his head to see better. What he saw made his face flush.

He said. "Don't, then!" and jerked angrily at the ropes.

A saddle slapped on the ground outside. Men's voices made low murmur. The windmill pumped slowly. Somewhere, a horse nickered.

"You killed my brother!" the girl said beratingly. "We're going to prove it, then see that the law does what it's supposed to do."

Pocus was silent.

"You know where my brother was killed—in the Lightning Flats country, a hundred miles from here. They found him with a Winchester slug in his head. The bullet had keyholed. It had done that because of a flaw in the rifling, which made it strike crosswise. It was a .45-70. I've got it. You carry a .45-70, don't you?"

"Thirty-thirty."

"You took Wes Norton's saddle. I recognized it in that picture of yours, published when you retired. So I decoyed you here."

Pocus moved a little on the floor, jerked his wrists against the ropes. "You went to a lot of trouble for nothing."

A man came in carrying a saddle. He was squat, unfirm of chin. His faded eyes looked everywhere but at Pocus. His cheek, knife-scarred, twitched winklike at intervals.

Winks Ellis dropped the saddle. It was the black kak with the silver rosettes and silver-capped horn.

"This bird is poison." Winks Ellis dabbed a finger at Pocus. "You wanta watch him, Miss Dana. He's a flash when he gets goin'. Poison!"

"Rat poison." Pocus' lips warped scornfully. "We met last at Frontier Days in Cheyenne, didn't we, Winks? Somebody who had a bet up paid you fifty dollars to put acid on my cinches, so they'd break."

Winks Ellis said, "That's a damn lie!" and kicked Pocus angrily in the side.

The girl said, "Stop that and get out!"

"How I hate this galoot!" Winks kicked Pocus again.

The girl ran over, shoved Winks alongside the head with her open right hand. "You get out of here. I'm running this show!"

Lee Spaulding came in jauntily, carrying a .45-70 Winchester and two saddlebags which had been on the black saddle. He put these on the table with a flourish.

"Just look what I found!" He opened the saddlebags, shook them. Two spurs fell out. Elaborate spurs of steel and gold and silver, each had been mounted with four jewels. The jewels were gone, pried from their settings.

"My brother's diamond-mounted spurs!" shrieked the girl.

"Exactly!" Lee Spaulding towered over Pocus. "The buzzard! He had them with him! He's pried out the diamonds and sold them."

"Frame-up!" Pocus looked at the girl, at Lee Spaulding, at Winks. The venom in his eyes made Winks pale and back outside. "Frame-up!"

Lee Spaulding snorted, picked up the .45-70, said, "He had this in his saddle scabbard." He went to the door, raised the Winchester, sighted. The gun filled the room with roar.

Putting the rifle down, Lee Spaulding went out, came back in a little while with a stick of pine stove wood. The .45-70 bullet had entered the stick flatwise, making a hole not unlike a keyhole. He split the stick with an axe to recover the slug.

The girl compared the bullet with another she took from the table drawer.

"They're the same. I don't need an expert to tell me that."

Pocus said hoarsely, "A swell frameup!"

"Why you—" Lee Spaulding started forward irately, then pulled up and shrugged his square shoulders. "It don't matter much what you say."

"These were my brother's." The girl passed her hands over the spurs from which the jewels were missing. "He pried out the diamonds and sold them. They were worth about fifteen hundred."

She wandered to the saddle, twisted at the silver horn plate. It resisted. She used both hands.

"What are you doing, dear?" Lee Spaulding was eyeing her curiously, interested in her movements.

"This should come off." She twisted more forcibly.

The silver horn plate gave, came off. The horn was of tubular steel. Removal of the plate exposed a cavity into which three or four cigarettes could have been forced. The girl explored this with a finger.

"It's gone!"

Lee Spaulding bounced to her side. His voice sounded surprised. "I don't get this, honey! What's gone? What were you looking for?"

The girl pivoted wrathfully on Pocus. "You took it!"

"Of course he did!" Lee Spaulding said hatefully. "But what was it?"

"My brother kept things in the hollow horn of that saddle." She laced her fingers together, tightened them until the wiry muscles ridged on her arms. "Money, sometimes. But it wasn't money I was looking for."

Lee Spaulding made impatient gestures. "What was it?"

The girl moved two paces to the right, put her right arm around Lee Spaulding. She looked up at his face. Her eyes were contrite.

"I haven't told you everything, Lee. I guess I should have, but I didn't. I'm sorry."

He patted her shoulder. "You're a sweet." But his eyes were questioning, his handsome lips set.

"My brother—you were foreman of his ranch up in the Lightning Flats country." The girl was looking fixedly through the door. "Did you ever notice anything unusual about his actions?"

Lee Spaulding considered, wrinkling his high forehead. "No. Except that he had been going away from the ranch alone a great deal just before he was—found shot to death."

"That's it." She moved her eyes from the door to the hollow horn of the saddle, to the spurs from which the jewels were gone, back to the saddle horn. "He wrote me. He told me what he was doing, what he had found."

Pocus rolled a little toward the table. The Winchester .45-70 lay near the table edge closest him. It was a light table. He could shove it easily. The rifle might fall off—and his hands were tied in front of him. Shaking his wrists had made a little slack in the ropes.

"The killer must have learned the secret," continued the girl. "My brother's horse was not found for several days, you know. It was twenty miles from the body, had been shot, had run a long ways before it dropped. And the saddle was gone."

Pocus squirmed a few inches more. He could nearly reach the table now.

"I think the murder was to get the location of what my brother had found. A map. He would probably keep it in the hollow horn of that saddle."

Lee Spaulding's teeth made a click coming together. "Gold?"

She shook her head. "No."

Spaulding opened his mouth, clipped it shut. Horses were galloping up outside. Two animals. They stopped. Voices murmured.

"What—" Spaulding shook his shoulders angrily. "Wait! I'll see who this is!" Stirrup leather squeaked outdoors, spurs clicked, as two men alighted. Spaulding swung for the door.

Pocus kicked the table. The Winchester fell off into his upraised, bound hands.

Spaulding, in the door, half-turned back. In the outer sunlight, a six-gun bawled.

The half-turn saved Spaulding. He gyrated out of the opening, ragged punctures in his left sleeve between shoulder and elbow. The sleeve began turning red around and below the punctures. He snarled, clawed for his gun, eyes on Pocus.

Pocus tilted the .45-70 at him. "Don't, you!"

Spaulding hesitated, took his right hand from his gun, gripped his left arm wound. He began to curse.

The girl ran for a .30-30 on wall pegs.

"Keep away from it!" Pocus roared.

She threw, "Don't be a sap!" and wrenched down the rifle. She knocked out a windowpane with the Winchester, exploded it, worked the lever, exploded it again.

Outside, gun-sound heaved against the ranch house walls and men yelped excitedly.

The girl bounded over, sawed through Pocus' bindings with a pair of scissors.

Spaulding stopped cursing to run around and point his six-gun at Pocus.

"Lee!" snapped the girl. "Can't you see this shows he didn't do it!"

Pocus got up, blind to Lee's big revolver, went to the window and bobbed his head briefly before the opening. In came a storm of lead which made ragged a Navajo blanket on the wall across the room.

Hunkered on the floor, unhit, Pocus rumbled, "Fice Lacy and Whiskers Bloomburg. Winks Ellis and your other three hands have thrown in with them."

"It looks like a party," Dana O'Day Norton choked.

The girl was scared, trying bravado. Her voice had a rattle of fright.

Gunfire outside eased slightly. A single bullet made a hollow slap against the Navajo rug. Someone was swearing excitedly and clicking the lever of a jammed rifle. Boots hammered around the house.

Pocus reared up, brushed along a wall, slammed into a back room—the kitchen. One man was already half across it. Another covered his charge from the window.

Pocus flung back so abruptly his feet, skidding, let him down on his knees. He got out of sight of the man in the window. The one crossing the kitchen fanned three times, using both hands to do it. The door jamb beside Pocus vibrated twice—the third bullet did something jarring to his left side.

Weaving, Pocus got partial balance. *Boom* went the .45-70 that keyholed its slugs. The man in the kitchen lurched rigidly erect. He opened his mouth as if to scream, shut it, let fall his gun. He groveled down on his knees, arms wrapped across his face.

"Don't!" he shrieked. "Don't shoot me again! I'll help you! I'll do anything!"

Silence fell. The man on his knees breathed sobbingly, whimpered in terror.

The kitchen quaked with a revolver shot.

The man on his knees, shot through the skull by the man in the window, lay down without a sound. He was a Neckyoke puncher.

Pocus snapped lead at the window. The man there—Fice Lacy—jerked back, ran around the house.

The girl and Lee Spaulding stumbled into the kitchen.

Pocus yelled, "Damn it—the other windows!" angrily, spun, lunged for the door through which they had just come.

Blasting sound and air knocked him back. Splinters, boards, a couple of timbers came through the door. The shape of the kitchen became strange, awry, as though it were about to collapse.

"Dynamite!" Lee Spaulding wailed.

Up from the floor where he had been knocked, Pocus jumped into the outer sunlight. A great mushroom of smoke and dust was squirming above the ranch house. The building was two-thirds a wreck. No one was in sight. But, around in front, Fice Lacy was yelling orders to cover the rear and to throw another bomb in.

The girl and Lee Spaulding came out. Spaulding's left arm was banged up. The girl was white, scared.

Pocus gestured. They all ran away from the house, toward a feed shed. Crunching agony was in Pocus' side. A rib was broken, maybe two.

They were fired on rounding the shed, but were unhit. Beyond the shed, sheltered from the wrecked ranch house by it, was a corral and horses.

Bullets clouted splinters off the shed, tore long rents in the corrugated tin roof as they caught three of the horses. Saddles and bridles were perched on the corral rails. They used the bridles, but passed the saddles up for lack of time. They mounted. The horses ran wildly out of the corral when the gate was opened.

They lay flat along the necks of the broncs, offering as small targets as possible. Pocus took off his shirt, wadded it against his side inside his undershirt. They reined into a draw, followed it half a mile. The horses climbed out with jerky jumpings.

Five pursuing riders bobbed behind, closer than they had expected. The five gained. Riding bareback was not easy. A mile. Another. The five behind dismounted suddenly, used their rifles. Jacketed lead squeaked.

Pocus' horse leaped wildly, flailed down.

Thrown three times his own length in the fall, Pocus heaved erect teeth set grittingly. The girl was lightest, had the biggest horse. He vaulted up behind her.

They rode on less than a hundred yards before Lee Spaulding's horse plunged down. They were targets of good shooting.

The girl had clung to her .30-30. Pocus took it, slid off. "Get her out of here, Spaulding!"

He sighted the .30-30, fired. The five shooting at them flattened lower in the sage, but kept shooting. Bullets hissed, ricocheted squawling, knocked gray leaves from the sage.

The girl's horse squealed, bucked, as a bullet stung it. Lee Spaulding, trying to mount, was thrown away. The animal pitched until the girl was spilled, then ran away, crazed by the wound.

"There's an old dipping pen over here," the girl gasped.

They crawled away, keeping below the knee-high sage. The dipping pen was a sheep layout, long disused. Of lambing sheds, nothing remained but spidery cottonwood pole framework. Slab pens had mostly fallen down.

Grass grew high on the sheep-manured ground around the pens. It was dry.

Pocus searched and found the old dipping vat. It was a concrete tank set in the ground, three feet deep, six wide, twenty or so long. They took shelter there.

Rain water stood in the vat, ankle deep, coffee colored, sour.

Pocus fingered his side, grimaced, breathed in and out carefully. "I can't understand this!"

"Simple." Lee Spaulding was letting the girl tie up his arm. "They think we've got that map. They're after it. They tried to plug me and sashay right in."

"But where'd they get their information?" Pocus sat up more straight to keep the sour water from his side.

"Winks Ellis. He worked for Wes Norton on the Lightning Flats place. He and the others drygulched Wes. The horse got away and they thought the map was somewhere in the saddle. They shot the horse, but it evaded them before it dropped."

Pocus said, "The jasper who sold me the saddle must have found it on the dead bronc."

"I oughta be kicked!" Spaulding grated. "While I was tying you up there in the ranch house. Winks Ellis put that .45-70 in your saddle scabbard and put those spurs in your saddlebags."

The girl was looking over the vat rim. She stiffened, asked, "Do you want to shoot a man?"

"You're damn right!" Lee Spaulding and Pocus lurched to her side. Spaulding got there first. He took the .30-30, sighted, stroked the trigger. A man leaped erect in the sage. Winks Ellis. Spaulding shot again. Winks Ellis fell backward with the rigidness of sudden death.

Pocus said, "Four of them left."

Winchester slugs searched about the top of the vat for a time. The futile shooting finally ceased.

The silence was tedious. A quarter of an hour became unnerving.

"They're up to something." The girl peered over the vat rim, through the rotting ruins of the pen. "I thought so."

Pocus looked. Fice Lacy and the others had slashed one of the dead horses, were dragging the carcass at the end of a rope in a big circle about the pens.

"Going to burn us out!"

Lee Spaulding muttered under his breath. The girl's cheeks burned hotly. They knew what it meant. The dragging of a butchered animal was an old trick to make a fire line. Fice Lacy would put flame to the grass in the circle. And the dipping pens were dry, the rank grass about so much tinder.

Pocus pulled off his boots, used them as buckets to throw water on the pens and grass about the concrete vat. Spaulding and the girl joined him. There was no noise but their breathing and the slosh of water.

Smoke, gray-black, sprouted off the range, came snaking toward them. There was breeze enough to sweep the flames along. The fire spread. Winchester lead began to snap through the pall.

Pocus coughed as the smoke pressed upon them. He wet his bandana, put it over his nostrils. The odor of the water was almost as bad as the smoke. The fire began to roar as it sprawled out and gained headway.

Low hissings came as sparks fell in the vat. Flame lunged up before their eyes as the taller grass around the pens caught. It was hotter. And they didn't notice the bad smell of the water now. They were grateful for its wetness.

The girl began to cough in spite of the handkerchief over her mouth and nostrils. She choked, laughed shrilly, wildly.

Pocus punched Spaulding, said, "Quiet her."

Spaulding did not take his eyes from the smoke pouring over the vat. "She'll be all right." His hands were clenched white on the Winchester.

Pocus moved over, put an arm around the girl. She was grateful, and quieted a little.

"It's a big price to pay for some water!" she said hysterically.

"We'll be all right." Pocus thought she was raving. "These grass fires ain't much. It'll burn out in five minutes."

"That map they're after—it shows where there's water." She was not raving. "Artesian water."

"Water!" Spaulding was beside them. "Water!"

"My brother sank a deep prospecting shaft and found it—an underground river. Enough to irrigate thousands of acres of that Lightning Flats country. It's worth a fortune."

"Water!" Spaulding seemed dazed, wet his lips.

"Wes wrote me about it. He was keeping it secret until he could get hold of the land it would irrigate." Her voice lifted wildly. "And they thought he had a gold mine or something. And they killed him!"

Spaulding said, "Water!" again. His voice sounded a little wild.

Men suddenly came through the smoke astride plunging horses. They had discarded rifles. Six-guns battered noisily over the hissing, snapping flames. The horses pranced, leaped, trying to keep off the hot, seared ground all they could.

Pocus grated. "Knew they couldn't burn us out! Figured they'd rush us while we're blinded by the smoke." He stood up with the .45-70 that keyholed its bullets.

Lee Spaulding hunched low in the vat, pallid, muttering. Pocus swore at him. He got up, floundering, eyes wild, jumped to the rim of the vat. He was brave enough.

The girl started to follow. Pocus pushed her back. He shoved the dazed Spaulding toward the oncoming four horses.

"Gotta get out in front of the smoke so we can see!"

They got out in front. Fice Lacy and his trio had not expected that. They were on excited horses, unstable seats to shoot from. The jouncing about made it hard to hold down a six-gun, and some smoke was in their eyes.

Lee Spaulding's .30-30 banged. Pocus, a pace behind him, kneed down. The .45-70 boomed. And the slug buried itself flatwise somewhere in the mouse-hued beard of Whiskers Bloomburg. The body slouched out of the saddle, hung in a stirrup and the frightened horse dragged it away.

Spaulding fired the .30-30 again, levered a new cartridge in, shot once more. The horse of the Neckyoke rider at whom he aimed abruptly bucked away. The rider hung on two-handed, hit somewhere in the body.

Fice Lacy's gun was empty. He got off, tried to make his horse stand and shelter him while he reloaded. The animal, spooked to a frenzy, swirled, kicking, and wrenched free.

Pocus aimed at Lacy, pulled trigger. The .45-70 clacked, empty. He threw the weapon at Lacy, rushed. Lacy sidestepped the rifle. He threw down his six and a fistful of cartridges, opened his arms bearlike to receive Pocus.

They struck with explosive impact, rolled end over end.

To the left, the remaining Neckyoke puncher emptied his six. Lee Spaulding emptied the .30-30, tore frenziedly at his pockets in search of cartridges. The Neckyoke hand spilled off his horse to reload quicker.

Fice Lacy fastened his teeth in Pocus' neck. Pocus yelled, wrenched. The teeth sheared through slack skin, came free. They mauled each other. The side wound had weakened Pocus.

Lacy got a throat hold, lost it. He struck with his teeth, weasel-like, missed. He got the throat hold again. He tightened down, tongue clamped between his teeth, eyes bulged out with the effort.

There was pounding in Pocus' head. Blood thundered against his temples. He could hear Lacy's big hands and arms creak and crack with the effort. He tore at Lacy's wrists. They were like cedar posts. His hands flippered. One fell into a burning sage, was showered with cooking embers.

Heedless of burn, Pocus scooped up embers, threw them into Lacy's protruding, murderous eyes.

The big man wailed, loosened his grip. Pocus threw more smouldering red coals. Lacy shrieked in agony, heaved upright. Blind, he kicked at Pocus. Rolling, Pocus got out of the way.

Lee Spaulding raced to them. The Neckyoke rider sprawled motionless on the charred, smoking range. There had been no shot. Spaulding had evidently clubbed him down with the .30-30, clubbed him with a killing blow, because the .30-30 barrel was bent badly, almost parted from the stock.

Making gibberish noises of mad rage, Spaulding scooped up Lacy's discarded six, some cartridges. He charged the cylinder, rocked the hammer back, aimed at blinded, pitiful Fice Lacy.

"Nix!" Pocus lunged, knocked the gun up as it quaked.

Spaulding screamed, "Damn you!" and arched the six muzzle around at Pocus. He got the gun cocked.

Pocus wrapped his hands around the six-barrel, shoved it up. It went off harmlessly. Forcing, Pocus levered the barrel up and over until it pointed at Spaulding. Spaulding took his finger out of the trigger guard then, devoted all effort to wrenching the weapon free.

They fell down, fighting for possession of the weapon.

Back at the concrete vat, tall Dana O'Day Norton came stumbling out of the smoke. She saw them scuffling, screamed shrilly and ran for them.

Spaulding jammed the muzzle away from his head. He cocked the weapon, put his finger back in the trigger guard. He gathered himself for supreme effort. Murderous purpose distorted his face.

Pocus levered down. The gun bellowed. The bullet caught Spaulding in the right cheek, ranged upward, found a lodgment somewhere in the brain. In a way, it was an accident.

The girl shrieked again as Pocus stood up. She veered to the Neckyoke puncher Spaulding had clubbed to death, got his gun and worked frantically at reloading it.

Pocus reached her just as she snapped the cylinder in. He got the gun out of her hands, shoved her sprawling from him when she tried to claw his face, and ran away from her with the gun, calling, "Search him!"

Blinded, Fice Lacy was trying to escape by running. He had covered a hundred yards. Pocus overhauled him.

Lacy could see a little through pain. He dodged a couple of times as Pocus struck at him with a six-barrel, then went down under a skull blow.

Black grass ash squirted from under his slamming form. His unconscious breathing continued to blow more squirts of the dark ash.

Pocus went slowly back to the girl.

She was standing over Lee Spaulding's dead form. Her arms hung stiffly at her sides; her fists were clenched. She seemed not to be breathing at all.

Pocus dampened his lips, said regretfully, "He was working with Fice Lacy and the others to get that map."

The girl seemed paralyzed.

"I saw him through the door, back at the ranch house. Just after he tied me up. He took the map from the saddle-horn. He put those spurs with the jewels missing in my saddlebags."

The girl did not move.

"I didn't tell you. I figured you and he were framing me." He made vague gestures with both hands. "After Lacy came, I kept quiet. Spaulding was plenty willing to help us fight Lacy, and we needed his help. Lacy and the others were double-crossing him. He knew that when he learned Lacy had jumped me in the livery stable. And Lacy knew it, too—knew he would have to get the map from Spaulding by force, if he got it at all. That's why he came a-shootin'."

The girl's chest expanded as she breathed in.

Pocus said, "I told you to search him. He's got the map on him."

"I did." The girl shuddered, opened her clenched fists. Jewels glittered there—diamonds—eight of them.

"From the spurs." She shivered. "Spaulding had them . . . . He must have—killed my brother—"

Pocus went over to her. She seemed grateful for his coming.

• • • • •

Trickery Trail

A lot of cowhands dream of riding along and finding a fortune—but would be plenty surprised if they did.

Zack Riggs was no exception. He was surprised. His eyes almost fell out.

The money lay on the trail, near the wriggly shade of an *ocotillo* clump. It was a sheaf thick as a deck of cards. Numbers on the top bill read 1,000—1,000.

Zack Riggs breathed an explosive, "Damn me!" and snapped his fingers like a dice roller after a natural. Then, instinctively, he looked for the catch in it. Things like this usually had a catch.

It was there, all right.

"Well, love us!" Riggs leaned over the neck of his bronc to stare down. He was a big puncher, burly. His face, otherwise homely as sin, had many little wrinkles as though he laughed and grinned a great deal. His clothes were nearly worn out and made him look a little seedy.

The trail followed a canyon bed, as most Arizona border trails did. Shaggy stone walled up on either side. Hot winds had brought white sand into the canyon. The stuff lay like drifted snow, a foot deep, and horse or man tracks should remain visible many days, unless there was rain.

It had not rained in months—yet there wasn't a track in the sand.

But marks there showed the sheaf of money had landed very recently.

Thrown from above? Of course! Zack Riggs looked up.

"Man alive!" He had received shock number two.

The girl up there was probably pretty. The sun slanted past her into Riggs' eyes, made it hard to tell. She stood beside a jut of rock twenty feet down from the canyon lip.

"Hey!" Riggs called tentatively. "Ain't you kinda careless with your *dinero?*"

"Sh-h-h!" she hissed sibilantly, and made frantic silencing gestures.

He grinned up at her. "What for? Been two days since I saw a soul—"

"Not so loud!" Her voice, low, was one Riggs liked. "Do you want to make a hundred dollars?"

"What a question! Everybody wants to make a hundred dollars."

"Then take that money, ride into Line City and put it in the bank there. Keep out a hundred."

He swallowed twice, as if her astounding request had choked him. He heaved over, got the sheaf of money without dismounting, fanned one end to see the bill denominations. His jaw fell.

"Lady!" he said. "Quit kiddin' me and take your money."

"Please!" she pleaded wildly. "I'll give you two hundred—"

He tapped the currency. "There must be thirty thousand here—"

"There's forty-seven thousand dollars. Put all but two hundred of it in the Line City bank in the name of Lida Southern."

Riggs winked owlishly. His grin was gone, his face ludicrous. "Lady—you never saw me before!"

"I know—"

"And you want me to ride off with forty-seven thousand dollars of your money?"

"Please! I'll pay you—"

"Lady!" His voice was solemn. "Come down here and let me see you. I think you're crazy."

"Oh—fiddle!" she snapped angrily. "Quit jawing at me and ride with that money. I know what I'm doing!"

"No, you don't!" he said. "Nobody capable of knowin' what they're doin' would trust a plumb stranger with—hey, wait! Wait a minute!"

She had spun, was scrambling up to the canyon lip. She went into shadow a moment, and he saw she *was* pretty. She was a blonde, tall.

He saw something else now—stark terror in her face!

"Hey!" he called. "What's this all about?"

She did not answer until she was on the canyon rim, then she gasped, "Hurry! And watch out! You're almost sure to have trouble!"

Then she was gone.

Riggs drove glances right and left along the canyon, saw the lower sides were too steep to climb here.

His bronc sneezed under the spurs, stormed down the canyon in a cloud of sand. Riggs rammed the money in a pocket, stood up in the tapped stirrups, watched for a place not too steep to climb.

The blonde girl's warning that he was likely to have trouble had slipped to the back of his mind.

That was too bad. He slammed into the trouble within a hundred feet.

A lass rope squirted a tan blur from behind a boulder, fore-footed his bronc, tightened. The horse flipped completely over.

Riggs sailed fifteen feet, hit, ploughed a furrow and half buried himself in the white sand. There was a couple of seconds when he was too stunned to move. Then he started to dig out.

A man piled onto his back. Another! A third! He took a blind backhand swing, made somebody grunt. A six-gun barrel parted his hair. He gave up fighting and concentrated on getting his head out of the sand so he wouldn't smother. He succeeded after a fashion.

"His bronc ain't hurt!" said a very calm, liquid voice. "Catch the critter, Dunce!"

One man got off Riggs' back to catch the horse.

Riggs began fighting again. Sand was in his eyes, as blinding as powdered glass. He landed a half dozen punches indiscriminately on the two atop him. But they slugged him at will, benumbed him, held him.

He let out a loud bellow for help, figuring it couldn't do any harm.

They poured a double fistful of sand in his open mouth. That silenced him.

The man called Dunce came back, saying, "I tied his bronc to your saddlehorn, Fancy."

Fancy, he of the calmly liquid voice, directed, "Give us a hand here."

They unbuckled Riggs' gunbelt, took it. They searched—got the money.

"This is him!" Fancy declared loudly. "His havin' the money proves it."

Then they all three laughed loudly. That seemed to be a big joke.

Riggs, sand nearly all out of mouth and eyes, glared at them. "What kind of a shenanygin is this?"

The liquid-voiced man said, "I'm Ed Fancy. I'm the sheriff."

Ed Fancy was tall, big-eyed, hook-nosed, a little too red in the face. He was twenty-five or so. The startling thing about him was his bald head. He was not old, but his head was bald as the nine ball.

Riggs spat sand, said, "Let's see your star!"

"I don't need one—everybody knows I'm the sheriff."

Riggs looked him up and down, reflected the fellow resembled a plucked owl. "The hell you're any sheriff!"

Ed Fancy laughed. Dunce and the other man chimed in. Dunce was a short, fat man whose mouth hung open. The open mouth made him look incredibly stupid. The other fellow was big as Riggs, perhaps not quite as burly.

"Watch him," ordered Fancy. "I'll go tell the girl it turned out all right."

That got another big laugh.

Riggs watched Fancy amble up the canyon and around a bend, then squinted morosely at Dunce. "You ain't tellin' me that blonde girl framed it so you'd catch me with that wad of money, are you?"

Dunce looked at his companion. They both laughed.

"Sure she did," Dunce said.

Riggs winked rapidly. His eyes still hurt. "Why'd she go to all the trouble when you couldv'e grabbed me any time and—"

"Swallow a cork!" growled Dunce. "You're too windy."

Understanding came into Riggs' homely face. "You're two damn liars! That girl didn't—"

Dunce flung a fistful of sand at Riggs' mouth.

Ed Fancy came swinging back down the canyon, showing a big-toothed grin under his hooked nose. He had covered his bald head with a *mostaza*-hued Mex sombrero. The mustard-colored hat gave his pallid face a vile tint.

"She was all right." He winked elaborately at Riggs. "She said you was kind of a nice feller, even if you are horse-faced. She said she'd have to get drunk as hell tonight to forget what she done to you."

"You're a liar!" Riggs fumed. "That girl didn't—"

"Tie him on his *caballo!*" rapped Fancy.

They prodded Riggs up on his horse, cut the strings off his saddle and whanged his wrists to the horn, his ankles to the stirrup leathers.

"C'mon!" Fancy swung aboard his mount. "We ain't got any too much time."

The canyon fanned out on a gravel flat within a few rods. They rode through sage and mesquite. Yucca shot up tufted crowns of spikes around them. Little gray lizards scampered everywhere with a speed that defied the eye.

Down a slope, the ground became sandy, the mesquite very thick and thorny and higher than their heads.

"This'll do." Ed Fancy pulled up. "Take his clothes!"

Riggs protested profanely as he was untied, hauled off, undressed down to his underwear. The fellow who was about Riggs' build made his clothes into a bundle.

"We're only takin' your duds so you won't get away," Ed Fancy smirked.

Riggs shifted from foot to foot in the fine sand. It was terribly hot. The thermometer must be a hundred and fifteen. "That's another lie! I see through—"

"I don't care what you see!" Fancy sneered. "You couldn't make three miles without your clothes, and that's reason enough for us takin' 'em. I'm leavin' Dunce here to watch you, too."

He mounted, rode away trailed by the man who carried Riggs' clothing.

Riggs churned his bare feet in the blistering sand for a while, glowering after them, then approached a yucca clump. He shook a couple of the dead, shaggy, treelike trunks that had fallen, to flush out possible sidewinders and gilas, then crouched in the shade.

"Listen, pardner, what's back of all this?" he asked Dunce.

"Swallow a cork!" grunted Dunce.

"Aw hell, you're funny!" Riggs dug peevishly at the sand to see if it wasn't cooler a foot or so down.

Dunce unslung a canvas water bag from his saddle, took a swig of the evaporation-cooled contents.

"Let's have some of that," Riggs requested.

Dunce sneered, poured some of the water in his hat, put the hat on, slung the bag back on the kak. "You dry up!"

Riggs, hunkered down in the inadequate shade of the yucca, began to feel like he was going to do just that. He had never realized before just how much blistering heat clothes kept off a man.

"Have a heart and loan me your coat," he requested. "I'm gettin' all sunburned."

"You shut up!" Dunce ordered. "Or I'll chase you out in the sun and make you sit there!"

"My pal!" Riggs gouged angrily at the sand. Judging from the rankness of the mesquite growth here, there should be a little moisture three feet or so down.

Probably a minute Riggs dug, then stopped very suddenly. He was dry—but perspiration abruptly stood as a sheen on his forehead. His face convulsed once before he carefully made it expressionless.

An arm length away, a sidewinder had shoved a stub-snouted head out of a hole in the sand. The snake played its tongue like an ugly little scarlet spark. The reptile, a night prowler in this desert range country, had been spending the day in the hole.

Riggs calmly tossed a double handful of sand over the hole, then looked at Dunce. The squat man, dampening the inside of his hat again, had not noticed.

Riggs heaved more sand, blocked the hole mouth, then continued digging. He dug very cautiously, not knowing what moment he would intersect the hole in which the sidewinder lay. The thing was one of the most deadly of the rattlesnake species. He didn't care to take chances.

"Whatcha doin' all the diggin' for?" Dunce growled.

Riggs sneered up at him, said, "I like to play in the sand, fat boy!"

Dunce swore at him, hunkered down in the shade of his horse.

Riggs unexpectedly uncovered part of the snake and fresh perspiration came. He dug a little more, decided he was about amidships of the reptile, and worked aft. The snake squirmed and he hastily slapped more sand on it. If the thing should rattle, his plans would be upset.

He was sweating prodigiously over the slow movements of his hands. He had no use for sidewinders. Their bite might kill a man unless the wound got immediate and expert treatment.

He decided he was ready, slanted a glance at Dunce.

"Hey—look out!" he howled.

Simultaneously, he snapped the rattler out of the sand, sent it gyrating at Dunce.

Dunce jerked up his gun, realized what the thing coming at him was, and ducked wildly. He got out of the way of the snake, but sprawled on all fours.

Riggs took a hop-skip, came down on Dunce. His fists made a couple of loud cracking noises. Dunce moaned, melted down in the sand. The insulted sidewinder coiled twenty feet away, buzzed some, then skidded into the mesquite with its characteristic sidewise movement.

Grinning fiercely, Riggs shucked off Dunce's boots, peeled his pants and shirt. He put them on, was stuffing the shirt tails into the too-big waistband of the pants when Dunce groaned himself awake.

Riggs sat on his bulge of a stomach, listened to the man's terrific groans, chuckled, "Now that's what I call sweet music!" He gouged Dunce a time or two to obtain louder groans. "When you're ready, you can tell me what's back of all this funny business!"

Dunce stopped groaning, began to curse him. His swearing was expert, very profane.

"Such naughty words!" Riggs slapped him a few times—got an idea, laughed violently. "You're the cookie who put that sand in my mouth, ain't you?"

He scooped up sand, forced it in Dunce's big mouth, roared, "You'll either swallow it or talk!"

Real terror came into Dunce's bleating.

"You ever see a man die because his craw was fulla sand?" Riggs asked fiercely. "It's a plumb awful way to go. I'll show you a sample. Swallow that! Swallow it!" He began to work on Dunce's throat, making downward movements with his big hands.

Dunce screamed in anticipation, blurted, "What d'you wanta know?"

"Everything."

"Ed Fancy has got five hundred head of crack saddle broncs," Dunce mumbled. "A Mex rancher a hundred miles south of the border is buyin' 'em. The Mex is named Don Feliz Metales. He is buyin' 'em through that girl, Lida Southern. She's a cattle broker from Tucson."

"I get it," Riggs grunted. "The girl is buyin' Ed Fancy's horses for Don Feliz Metales. Now—where does this funny business come in?"

"The girl and Ed Fancy got together and schemed to steal the forty-seven thousand dollars she got from Don Feliz Metales to buy the broncs. They needed a goat to hang the robbery on, so they grabbed you. They're gonna dress a man in your clothes, have him rob the girl in plain sight of the sheriff—then the feller was gonna come back here an' give you your clothes."

Riggs made a gritting sound with his teeth, grabbed fistfuls of sand. "You're lyin'! You been lyin' about that girl all along! She ain't—"

"She is too!"

"You tell the truth or I'll feed you sand until you choke!"

"Ed Fancy will scrag me," Dunce wailed.

Riggs funneled sand into the fat man's cavernous gullet.

Dunce gagged it out, squawled, "The girl's in it! But that wasn't all of her and Ed Fancy's scheme. They've arranged to take the horses across the line in the regular way, through the customs. Don Feliz Metales is a big rancher down in Mexico, so there was nothin' suspicious about that. But right after this fake robbery, Ed Fancy and the girl have arranged for this new Mex rebel, El Gordo, to steal the whole herd. Only El Gordo is payin' Ed Fancy for the privilege of stealin' the broncs."

"Then Ed Fancy is just pretendin' to sell the herd to Don Feliz Metales so he can get 'em across the line to El Gordo without smugglin'?"

"That's it. Five hundred broncs was too big a bunch to try to run past the Mex and American border patrols. El Gordo needs these broncs for his army. Ed Fancy has been schemin' to get 'em to him for months."

Riggs considered, frowning. "And the girl is up to her ears in it?"

"She sure is."

"Where's this fake robbery gonna be pulled—the one to get the money, I mean? And when?"

"In the pass at the border." Dunce shut his eyes tightly, was silent a minute. "The feller dressed in your clothes is gonna be hidin' at the foot of that needle peak halfway through the pass. The girl will have a couple of deputies with her—witnesses who'll identify your clothes. The deputies don't know nothing about the robbery, though."

"But the girl knows all about it?"

"She sure does. And you'd better bushwhack whoever is at the foot of that needle peak—plug 'em before you get close!"

"I dunno how much of what you've told is a damn lie!" Riggs suddenly stiffened Dunce with a swing to the jaw. "That's for the lyin' part."

He left Dunce limp in the yucca shade, went to the horse, took a drink from the waterbag, placed the bag beside the unconscious man. It would keep the fellow alive. But he wouldn't walk far.

On the bronc, Riggs spurred south to the border. Dust heaved up in the still, hot air behind him. To get rid of it, he reined over on low hills, where the ground was an expanse of bleak, weathered gravel.

He topped a ridge, saw much dust ahead. He worked closer, keeping out of sight in the mesquite. One of Dunce's saddlebags held a telescope, something a horse rancher wouldn't think of being without. Riggs used the glass.

Ed Fancy's men were throwing the horse herd through the pass into Mexico. A lot of men were about, U.S. border patrol and customs men, dark-faced Mexican *rurales* in khaki. Freshly clad Mex *caballeros,* evidently Don Feliz Metales' cowhands, were doing most of the work.

One of Don Feliz Metales' men sat his horse at the pass mouth, shifting pebbles from one pocket to another—one pebble for each horse that passed—a method of keeping herd count that about eliminated mistakes.

Riggs slanted the tapering cylinder of the telescope at the pass. Somewhere beyond there, in Mexico, El Gordo's rebels would be waiting to seize the horse herd. Riggs moved the glass back to the horses.

"They'll be gettin' some damn good broncs," he chuckled. "And they're usin' a slick scheme for gettin' the herd across the border!"

He waited patiently.

It was a long time—nearly three hours—before the last bronc was hazed through the pass. The border patrolmen, American and Mexican, rode away.

Riggs mounted, spurred south, veering a bit to the right to strike the bleak, brownish mountains a mile to one side of the pass. He reined into a gully that slanted steeply, crookedly upward.

"Ed Fancy's supposed to be waitin' at the foot of a needle peak halfway through the pass," he grunted. "Bet that was a dang lie."

He located the needle peak finally. But getting near it on horseback was out of the question. The ground was too rough. He left the bronc, scrambled up a slope hairy with candlewood and giant cactus, wormed over a ridge, eased laboriously down a rip in the stone that was hot enough to be the chimney of hell. He kept his eyes sharp.

"Huh—maybe it wasn't a lie at that!" He had discovered two men at the foot of the needle peak and it surprised him.

The pair crouched, alert, back of boulders. They had Winchesters trained on the pass floor. The pass was straight here—they could see everything for a mile up and down it.

Riggs examined Dunce's six-gun and Winchester, sighted a couple of times to get the feel of the weapons. Then he worked downward, very quietly, until he was positioned a dozen yards behind the watching pair.

"Up high!" he barked.

The two men became frozen statues, then flexed arms upward and turned slowly.

"Well, for—" Riggs' eyes popped. "So this is why Dunce wanted me to plug anybody waitin' here!"

The two men had vests decorated with big deputy sheriff stars.

Riggs hesitated, then ran to the pair and disarmed them. He jabbed a finger the badges. "What's the idea of them things?"

"Listen, hombre!" growled one of the men. "You ain't gonna get away with robbin' that girl, even if you have got the drop on us!"

"I ain't what?" Then Riggs swore with understanding. "Somebody tipped you the girl was gonna be robbed here?"

"You bet. She tipped us herself. Said she heard it was gonna happen right here."

"She, uh—" Riggs looked like he had found a tarantula in his coffee. "She told you that in person?"

"Not exactly. She sent a Mex kid with the dope."

Riggs grinned sudden relief.

"You've bit on a fast one. She never sent the kid. Somebody else did."

"Yeah?" They didn't believe him.

With three minutes of fast talk, Riggs told them what had happened from the moment he had ridden up to the money lying in the trail. He finished, "And I know damn well the girl ain't in on it."

"How d'you know that?"

Riggs shrugged, looked sheepish. "Aw, I saw she was scared when she gave me that money. She looked like—well, daggone it, she didn't look like the kind that would team up with that bald Ed Fancy."

"Ed Fancy has got the name of bein' plumb honest," objected one deputy.

"Sure. A lot of jaspers have had the name of bein' honest up until somebody caught 'em at their dirty work." He tossed them their guns. "I think I see through this whole thing. You gents stay here. I got some business up the pass."

The deputies strapped on their guns

They were average-sized men, looked honest, determined. One fingered his gun thoughtfully. "I figure you better stay here, fella."

"Nope." Riggs scowled at them. "Now don't start gettin' ideas! I'm handlin' this, and I'm willin' to have your help. But I'm handlin' it, see! You go interferin' and you or me'll sure get hurt!"

They frowned at him, not scared, but realizing he meant it. One frowned, said, "Damn if your face don't look kinda familiar. Just who are you, anyway?"

"Zack Riggs. Sure enough—that's the name my mom gimme. But lay off the silly questions. You gonna let me handle this my way?"

"Go ahead," one grumbled.

Riggs worked away from them, up the side of the pass. Once concealed from anyone lurking on the floor, he scuttled north along the rim. He saw a few gaunt jackrabbits, a fat and vile gila, many little gray lizards, but no other signs of life.

He crept down almost to the floor of the pass, waited.

He did not have to loiter long.

Shots clapped up the pass. Echoes made thunder that bounced on the bleak stone. Then horse hoofs beat a snare-drum rattle.

A dun bronc slanted around the pass bend, running madly. It was a fat, aged horse, could not run fast. Blonde Lida Southern rode it, belaboring with quirt and spurs.

Another horse and rider pursued her. The other horse was leggy, fast.

Riggs grinned fiercely over Winchester sights.

The man chasing the girl wore Riggs' clothes. A bandana mask obscured his face.

The fellow gestured with a revolver, fired. Riggs almost stroked his Winchester trigger—but didn't when he saw the girl's pursuer was shooting wide. The man loosened more lead, far to the left.

They were nearly in front of Riggs now.

The pursuer aimed his revolver again, more deliberately. He was not shooting wide now. He intended to kill the girl.

Riggs' Winchester whanged, gave a recoil jerk.

The rider wrenched up stiffly, waved his gun like a flag, aimlessly. He bounced with the leaps of his horse a few times before his dead body was thrown, a slack bundle, into the sand of the pass floor.

"Hey!" Riggs yelled, and came out in view.

The girl pulled up, then reined wide around the dead man and came to him.

"I got away from them," he grinned. "So that was their plan—tipped a couple of deputy sheriffs so they'd be in a nice place to see a jasper who looked like me kill you and pretend to rob you."

"Yes." She shuddered violently. "They wanted to lay my murder onto somebody—and they picked you. Ed Fancy has the money."

Riggs pointed toward the bend around which the girl and her murderous pursuer had come. "Any more of them there?"

"No. That—" she looked at the dead man, away. "That one brought me here. He turned me loose, then rode out chasing me so it would look like he was a road agent after me."

"I figured it'd be something like that." Riggs studied her. She was very pretty. "You found out Ed Fancy was gonna turn the horse herd over to this Mex rebel, El Gordo, didn't you? That's why Ed Fancy wanted you—well, out of the way."

She nodded. "I thought he was acting queerly and followed him. I overheard him arranging things with some of El Gordo's Mexicans. But they learned I had been listening, and they chased me. They were after me when I gave you the money in the canyon. They caught me just as you rode out of sight. Then Ed Fancy came and said he had you—bragged about what he was going to do."

"Fancy—the schemes he pulls are sure on a par with his name." Riggs gave the rocky pass sides a black look. "He's got the money on him, eh?"

"Yes."

"Lemme ride behind you." He swung up on the fat dun. "Head this crowbait for Mexico. We're goin' after that money."

The two deputy sheriffs met them. They were not suspicious now.

"You stay with these gents," Riggs directed the girl.

She looked at him, saw he was determined, slid off the pudgy dun.

The deputies listened with interest to her story.

"I'd never have thought it of Fancy!" one muttered.

"We'll pick up that Dunce monkey on our way into Line City," said the other.

"Fine." Riggs tightened the cinches a little on the old dun. "And I'll go after Ed Fancy."

"You're crazy!" protested a deputy. "We can grab Fancy when he comes back across the line. He went over with the horse herd."

"Fancy will more'n likely cache that money in Mexico." Riggs grinned queerly at them. "Anyway, I got schemes."

"You're a queer cuss." The deputy squinted narrowly at him. "And I can't get rid of the idea there's somethin' familiar about you."

"I been around some." Riggs laughed. "Maybe you have seen me before. I got a face so dang ugly people don't forget it easy."

He vaulted up on the dun. The horse grunted under his weight.

"You don't have to do this, you know," the girl said abruptly.

"Don't you want that money back?"

"Yes." Then she corrected herself hastily. "No! Not if it means danger to—"

He said, "I'll be back in a couple of hours."

"*We'll* be back, you mean!" interrupted the deputy who thought he remembered Riggs. "I'm goin' along."

Riggs chuckled. "So you've got around to thinkin' maybe it was on a reward poster you seen my beauty, eh? You figure you'll just be sure the money does come back. All right—get your bronc."

The man took nine or ten steps after his horse when gun sound filled the pass.

The thumping roar of shots came from up the pass, down it, and gobbled down the sheer, bleak sides. It lasted only a minute, then silence fell.

Ed Fancy's voice—it was almost above them—called: "I got fifteen men around you. They was shootin' in the air then to warn you. Throw down your guns."

The two deputy sheriffs searched wildly for cover. There was none nearer than a hundred feet.

"Drop them guns!" Ed Fancy roared.

"We better do it!" Riggs growled savagely. "They'll plumb salivate us if we don't."

"They will anyway!" groaned a deputy.

"Aw—use your head!" Riggs snapped. "He won't for a while—or he'd have done it already. He figures he'll dope out some slick scheme of gettin' rid of us so he won't look guilty himself."

They shed their arms.

Ed Fancy's gunhands closed in. Fancy himself came swinging up, mustard sombrero on the back of his head, a nasty grin under his beak of a nose.

"I was waitin' down the pass," he sneered. "I wanted to show up from the opposite direction right after the girl was killed. Now ain't it lucky I took that precaution?"

Riggs sneered back at him and couldn't think of anything to say.

Ed Fancy dispatched two men up the pass to find what had happened to the unfortunate Dunce. Then he had horses brought up, tied the girl, Riggs and the two deputies behind four of his riders.

They galloped south, toward Mexico—into Mexico a quarter of a mile.

"I wanta talk this little emergency over with El Gordo," Fancy told them maliciously. "These Mex rebels always know a lot of nice little tricks."

Riggs said to the girl, "Don't worry too much about this."

"Sure—it won't do any good," Fancy snorted. "I figure El Gordo will loan me some of his men for villains. We could make it look like they was the hombres who got the money—and killed all four of you in the fight while they was gettin' it."

The pass erupted the cavalcade, an irregular string, onto wide alkali flats. A mist of dust still hung there, raised by the horse herd that had passed a couple of hours before.

A ridge shoved up beyond the alkali flat.

Sound of a shot jumped over the ridge and down at them. Then more shots. Processions of roaring volleys. A lot of powder was being burned.

Ed Fancy laughed loudly, increased the pace to the ridge hump.

Another flat, much more vast, lay beyond. A new group of riders had the horse band now. A scatter of Mexicans, Don Feliz Metales' men, were spurring madly south.

"El Gordo's gang just grabbed the broncs!" Fancy chuckled. He squinted, discerned no dead or wounded men in evidence. "Hell! They done a lot of shootin'—but it don't look like anybody got killed!"

Mexicans raced horses to meet them. These men of El Gordo, the rebel, were heavily armed, better dressed than the run of *pastors* and *caballeros*.

Ed Fancy spoke with them in bad Spanish, gesturing, telling them what he wanted.

The Mexican who seemed to be in charge, bigger, more flashily clad even than his fellows, squinted curiously at the prisoners, His eyes rested on Riggs' sober face. He spat elaborately.

"Si, si," he told Fancy. *"Eso no es imposible.* It is not impossible. But we must consult El Gordo himself."

"Where's he at?" Fancy demanded.

"Not far, Señor Fancy."

"Take us to him. And make it snappy."

A dozen resplendent Mexicans escorted them westward. They worked through foothills, into a canyon, up it, and abruptly came to a spring.

An adobe house stood near the spring. Many fresh adobe bricks were stacked to one side, together with the ladderlike forms with which they were made. The house itself had been freshly built.

A thorny corral of *ocotillo* held many horses. Mexican rebels swarmed about.

The four prisoners were untied, urged into the adobe. It was big, clean, the furniture crude.

The gaudy Mexican leader drew a knife suddenly, cut the bonds of the girl, Riggs and the two deputy sheriffs.

"Hey!" Ed Fancy yelled. "What's the idea?"

The Mexican grinned at Riggs. "What shall we do with them?"

"Well—"

Ed Fancy knew something was wrong. He whisked a wild gaze about the adobe interior. In one corner were stacked automatic rifles, the latest type. Guns, drum-magazined, capable of four hundred shots a minute.

"Break for it!" he screeched. "Grab them machine guns!"

He clawed for his six-gun.

Riggs bolted sidewise, hit the table with both hands, skated it into Fancy, jammed the bald, beaked man to the wall. Fancy scraped down between table and wall, got under the table, heaved up. The next instant Riggs was flat on his back with Fancy and the table atop him.

Blonde Lida Southern ran over, screaming, and tore Fancy's gun out of his hand. She danced back, shrieking, "Hands up! Hands up!"

The flashy Mexican, grinning widely, grabbed the gun out of her hand and shot one of Fancy's punchers.

Some of Fancy's men had not come into the adobe. One of these, in the door, let out a bawl of alarm, unleathered his six.

Somebody got one of the machine rifles. It tore into the uproar in the adobe. Lead streamed and goosed clouds of adobe off the walls. A Mexican shrieked as the metallic torrent cut him half in two. Then somebody killed the gunner and the man fell, but kept his finger on the latch so the gun kept on vibrating thunder.

Riggs squirmed about under the table. Fancy, bellowing, got on the table and jumped up and down like an enraged ape. But he was not heavy enough to keep Riggs down. The homely puncher erupted table and man like a volcano.

Fancy fell down in his wild frenzy to inflict damage, Riggs bear-hugged him, banged him against the wall.

In the adobe, three or four six-guns were punctuating the mad clamor of the machine rifle. Outside, guns and men were making a lot of noise.

The girl, against the wall, dodged as lead loosened a rain of adobe down on her head.

Riggs heaved dazed Fancy at the fellow who had shot at her, tumbled them both in a pile. He dived over, got the girl, veered with her to a window.

He whipped the glass out with a fist, heaved the girl bodily outside, not very gentle about it.

The two deputies had them a Fancy puncher apiece, were doing damage aplenty.

Riggs got to Fancy as the bald man untangled from the fellow he had been heaved into. Fancy went down under a roundhouse swing that whistled like a Winchester slug.

The other man tried to shoot Riggs, was not quite quick enough. Riggs tumbled onto him, beating, hammering. Fancy revived a little, and Riggs divided his fistial administrations between the two of them. They were both tough, desperate, and it took fast work to keep them both down.

Riggs was glad enough when several of El Gordo's Mexicans took the job off his hands.

The blonde girl ran in, excited, anxious. She looked relieved when she saw Riggs.

Riggs was exploring a bullet hole, shallow, in his hip. He didn't have the slightest idea when he had gotten it. He winced, indicated Ed Fancy and his punchers who still lived. "Tie 'em up. Take 'em out!"

"Hey!" protested one of the deputy sheriffs. "They're our prisoners!"

"You're in Mexico, fella!" Riggs grunted. "They're El Gordo's prisoners. They'll get a regular trial. It may be kinda swift, but it'll be fair."

The girl was staring at him, round-eyed. "You're El Gordo?"

"Me—heck no!" He chuckled. "El Gordo and Don Feliz Metales are one and the same, though. El Gordo was kinda surprised when Ed Fancy come to him and wanted to sell him Don Feliz's horses." He laughed heartily. "El Gordo was already figurin' on stealin' the broncs from himself. He needed them, but he couldn't get them across the border as El Gordo without trouble."

The girl persisted, "Then who are you?"

"Zack Riggs, soldier of misfortune and a general in El Gordo's army. I was the general in charge of this horse stealin' expedition, to be exact.

I was comin' across the border to keep an eye on Ed Fancy when things kinda come bangin' down around my ears."

One of the deputy sheriffs snorted. "I remember where I seen your face now. You was ropin' in a rodeo at Phoenix—"

"Sure," Riggs grinned. "Well, I'll be ridin' back across the line with you. I'm quittin' El Gordo to take a whirl at the cow business."

He looked sidewise at the blonde girl. She seemed to like what he had just said.

• • • • •

The Frozen Phantom

Fingers had burrowed down in the snow and found Constable Andy Frost's throat. He knew that as he awakened.

Frost dashed a fist upward. The rabbit-lined sleeping bag impeded him. Snow had drifted over the bag three feet deep. It got in his eyes. He wore a fur parka over his Northwest Mounted Police tunic. It hampered his arms.

Frost was short, thick of shoulder and neck. He was built like a runt bull buffalo. His face ran too much to mouth and ears. His looks were not helped by the soot from the bottom of his tea kettle, which he had smeared below his eyes the day before to guard against snowblindness.

His groping hands found the parka hood of his attacker. He dug into it and clutched a greasy face. The face owner barked gutturals of pain. It was as though a bear trap had his features.

Frost recognized the voice!

Bill-Bill Oon! His Eskimo guide from the Coronation Gulf country! Frost, between blows, wondered what had gotten into Bill-Bill. The Inuit had always been reliable, although a little superstitious. One fact was certain—it was no ordinary thing that would cause the Eskimo to attack Frost. Bill-Bill had stood in awe of Frost since the day he had seen the little, homely constable grasp a large icicle and squeeze it to a frosty powder in one iron-tendoned fist.

The flexible sole of a *muck-a-luck* smashed against Frost's head. Frost trapped the foot in his hard, bearlike arms. Bill-Bill Oon spun like a top. He sprawled in the snow.

The Inuit might have been in a steel frame, so rigidly did metal-hard hands hold him. He had an *ooloo* thrust in his belt. Frost appropriated the small half-moon skinning knife and threw it away. An *oonapik* was stabbed into the snow nearby, and Frost kicked at it. The short hunting spear nipped twenty feet distant.

Bill-Bill Oon's features held a ghostly pallor. His stocky limbs trembled.

Frost frowned. The Eskimo was in the grip of a mortal terror!

"What's wrong, Bill-Bill?"

"Takuva-tongak!" moaned the Eskimo.

"You saw an evil spirit!" Frost shook him. "Speak English! Why'd you try to grab me?"

The Inuit rolled his eyes. "The evil spirit give Bill-Bill warning we should go back. Bill-Bill know you only laugh. He hope grab you and take you back tied to sled."

Frost exhaled from a corner of his mouth so breath-steam would not be in front of his eyes as he peered at the guide.

161

"When did you see this evil spirit? What'd he look like?"

"No man!" muttered Bill-Bill. "It woman! It Flame Maiden! A young woman, most good to look at, but with head of flame!"

Frost jerked upright. Breath expelled from his lungs, spurted a steam plume nearly to the snow-blanketed ground. He raced an alert glance about the spruce-walled clearing in which they had camped.

No living thing moved in the pale gloom of the Arctic night. Not even the dogs of their team. The huskies were asleep under the deep snow. Their sled stuck, curved end up, in a nearby drift.

"Is this Flame Maiden story the truth, Bill-Bill?"

"By the King of *Nakroom,* the great space beyond, it is!" Bill-Bill was a Christian. That was the strongest oath by which he could swear.

Frost's thoughts raced. He was near the end of his trail. Near the source of the fantastic legends of the Flame Maiden!

Constable Andy Frost had been sent to investigate the weird and terrible stories that had come out of this region for the last year. Stories of such horror that native trappers had fled their homes in the district!

The Flame Maiden appeared to travelers, whispered tales had it, and warned them to flee. To those who did not flee, ghastly things happened. Some vanished, never to be heard of again. Others were found, aimless wanderers—hopelessly insane.

The gibberings of these madmen were always the same—they had seen the Flame Maiden, then an awful monster of the night had carried them away into the sky and there destroyed their brains!

The Frozen Phantom, the strange brain-destroying demon was called. Too many men had been found in this region with deranged minds to longer regard the tales as superstitious prattle. The Mounted Police had become suspicious, curious—and here was Constable Andy Frost.

A black scowl contorted Frost's homely little face. "When'd you see the Flame Maiden?"

"As I gathered dry wood for the fire, just after we made camp." Bill-Bill pointed at the spruce that made a sombre, sinister wall around them. "It is true! By all that the missionary father said was holy, it is—"

"You stay here!" Frost grunted. "I'm going to look at the tracks this Flame Maiden left! And if I don't find tracks, I'm coming back and pull off one of your arms and use it to beat some sense into you!"

"There were tracks!" A fit of terrified trembling seized the guide. "But when I followed them, they vanished as though she had leaped into the sky."

Frost nearly laughed. But the abject fright of the Eskimo kept the mirth off his lips.

"What language did she speak to you in?"

"English," mumbled the guide. "Her head—it was all a flame. Her voice was beautiful. She was the flame of death!"

Frost turned thoughtfully away. The Eskimo's manner had driven home a puzzling belief. Frost thought Bill-Bill *had* seen something!

The spruce pressed gloom upon Frost as he entered the thicket. The snow had been made sand-hard by the intense cold. It rasped underfoot.

Frost followed Bill-Bill's plainly discernible tracks. He carried his Ross rifle with the bolt mechanism in the slight warmth of his armpit, to be sure the fulminate in the cartridge did not freeze.

A half dozen reports like gunshots cracked angrily against his eardrums. He stiffened, then relaxed. Ice noises from the lake! It lay a quarter of a mile to his left. It was several miles in area, he had noticed from the last ridge they had crossed. It was dotted with rocky islands.

Halting suddenly, Frost stared at the snow. Here were the tracks of the Flame Maiden!

She had been real after all! In a spot where the snow had not drifted, tracks were implanted clearly. A woman's foot, undoubtedly!

Frost wet the edge of his oversize mouth, steam curling from his tongue as he did so. He stood as though congealed by the cold.

"Aw-w-w!" he growled at last. "She's human enough, or she wouldn't leave tracks!" He followed the footprints of the Flame Maiden.

A breeze, sighing through the spruce, made low sobbing sound. Rapping ice cracks came from the lake. The frigid wilderness seemed alive. The snow groaned a tortured dirge as he stepped on it.

Toward the lake the trail led. It entered a clearing, to the right of which lay a sheer cliff of stone some forty feet high. This was the beginning of a narrow canyon, it seemed.

Frost's nerves were taut—far more so than he would have believed possible. For, when the Flame Maiden suddenly appeared on the top of the cliff, he all but jumped out of his parka!

After his first spasmodic start, Frost nearly shouted his relief. The girl did not have a head of flame! She simply had a tremendous wealth of brilliant red hair, which she had let down around her shoulders.

She was pretty! Even in the half-darkness of the Arctic winter night, he could discern a cameo quality to her features. The bulky fur garments did not entirely conceal the rather entrancing curves of her form.

Frost grinned. "You sure handed me a start, miss!"

The beautiful girl with the flaming hair did not answer. She stood motionless, silent as an apparition. Frost's spine began to feel strangely chilled. Now that he thought of it, he had not seen the girl appear. She had just materialized, as though by magic.

"Well—say something!" The runty policeman was surprised by the hollow quality of his own voice. For a long minute no sound came from the strange feminine figure.

"You must go!" She spoke in a small, bell-like voice. "Go at once! It may not be too late to avoid the horrible fate of those who linger!"

"Cut out the play acting!" Frost had decided she was deliberately trying to frighten him as she had Bill-Bill Oon. "I'm sticking right here. Furthermore, I've got some questions to ask you."

"No!" Her voice was a frightened shriek. "No! You must go. Go and come back! You are of the Mounted. Go and return with many men and machine guns and cannon. Only in that way can you hope to penetrate the lair of the Frozen Phantom!"

The stocky redcoat stood slack-jawed through the speech. "What are you talkin' about? Why do we need cannon?"

The red-headed girl seemed about to answer. Then, instead, she put fingers over her lips and screamed piercingly through them. Once, twice, three times, her shrieks ripped the Arctic cold.

Then she wheeled and disappeared.

Frost grunted explosively. He pitched for the low cliff. Its sheer wall defied him. He ran along it.

His mind tossed in turmoil. This beautiful girl! Was she mad, like the others found wandering in this part of the north? The thought was ghastly.

It took Frost many minutes to find a spot where he could ascend the cliff. He lost other minutes locating the Flame Maiden's footprints. He followed her trail.

Down into another steep canyon it led. The frigid wind, compressed by the sheer, blank walls of stone, was a near gale. It scooped the snow along in boiling clouds.

The tracks were already filling. And suddenly they ended!

Eyes popping in sheer unbelief, Frost stared. There was no getting around it—her trail simply stopped. He looked up. The sombre sky was like a long, ragged strip of lead stretched over the crack of a canyon. Fully four hundred feet of sheer, knotty stone reared on either side!

"Somebody could've pulled her up with a rope!" Frost muttered.

Moving down the canyon a few yards, he took off his snowshoes and spiked the ends upright in a drift. He proceeded to climb the cliff. It was a torturous job. Had his muscles been less than steel, his runty frame less monkey-like and adapted to climbing, he wouldn't have accomplished it.

At the top, he made an unnerving discovery. The Flame Maiden had not been hauled to the canyon rim by anybody with a rope! The snow was more than waist deep—at times Frost was forced to lie prone and roll to keep from going in over his head.

Had anyone visited either canyon rim within hours, he would have been able to tell the fact. And no one had!

Frost peered over the edge.

"Whew!" he muttered. "The cut of a canyon looked bottomless from up here. Gloom swathed the lower reaches, so deep was it.

"No sign of a shelf or a hole to be seen!" he commented. "Anyway, her tracks vanished near the center of the canyon!"

By peering steadily, he could barely see the spot where the Flame Maiden's footprints disappeared.

Stripping off an armload of spruce branches Frost tossed them over the canyon lip, one at a time. He watched the twigs float downward like green parachutes. It took them a long time to reach bottom.

Frost swiveled a gaze about. He could see out across the lake from this high perch. The many islands hulked up darkly in the white waste. None was more than a few hundred feet across. Most were sheer of shoreline, little more than gigantic stone blocks.

"Fella would need wings to get on a lot of them islands!" Frost decided. "This piece of country is plumb interestin'."

He clambered back down the cliff-like canyon wall. He put on his snowshoes and returned to his camp.

The Eskimo guide was not there!

"Bill-Bill!" Frost called loudly. His deep voice sounded like a pair of heavy drum taps as he shouted the name.

No answer! Frost ran to the tree where they had cached their supplies to keep them away from wolverines. One man's share was gone! Bill-Bill Oon had skipped out.

"I'll bet I shake some sense into that blubber ball!" Frost gritted.

He set off in pursuit of the deserting Bill-Bill Oon—only to halt within a score of yards. There was sound to the left. A man staggered out of the spruce thicket.

"A redcoat!" the man gasped wildly. *"Dieu!* You are gift of heaven!"

The stranger was tremendously tall and so gaunt as to seem a walking scarecrow made of bones. His eyes were dark-pupiled, red-flanked globes. His parka and *muck-a-lucks* were worn to the point of falling to pieces. The skin of his face was blue-gray where it was not covered with a coarse, blue-black beard.

When he spoke, it was out of the left side of his mouth. The entire right side of his face was apparently paralyzed.

"Who're you?" Frost had a hand inside his parka, cuddling his revolver.

The tall, disheveled man fawned like a delighted dog.

"Jules La Suede is my name," he mumbled. *"Dieu!* I am most pleased to find you. I have been wandering for weeks, barely existing on what ptarmigan I managed to kill with a club, and for a while on a caribou from which I chased wolves that had just killed it. But the next time I tried to chase away wolves, they turned on me and—"

"What became of your outfit?" Frost interposed.

The scarecrow shivered and peered furtively about.

"The Frozen Phantom, *m'sieu!"* he muttered. "The Flame Maiden appeared to me with a warning. I did not heed. That night a monster, a great and horrible thing of black, pounced upon me. I managed to escape. But when I crept back to my camp, my dogs, gun and supplies were gone. *C'est tout!* That is all! I have been a half-mad wanderer since!"

Frost studied the man. A frosty look was in the little constable's eyes. "What were you doing in this country?"

"I am a trapper, *m'sieu.* I was hunting new fur country."

Frost chewed a lip. "Do you know what this Frozen Phantom is?"

"Non, non!" The other was suddenly seized with terror. "I do not know. No one knows. A monster, a great werewolf of a—"

"Bunk!" snorted Frost. His eyes narrowed. "We'll go hunt this—"

"Non!" shrieked the Frenchman. The dead half of his face gave him a repulsive aspect, *"Merci, non!* We must flee!"

Frost was bleak-eyed. Back in his head, thoughts were clicking around and becoming a chain of knowledge that led to—understanding.

Abruptly he pointed off to the right. He said, "Look!"

The scarecrow man with half his face paralyzed turned his head.

Frost swung a fist. *S-s-wap!* The blow felled the man.

As the bony man crashed his length in the snow, the redcoat sprang atop him. He tore open the fellow's parka and crammed searching fingers inside.

He brought out a big Enfield revolver.

"Unarmed, were you?"

"Non, non! I meant—"

"Don't lie to me!" Frost sat on the man's chest. "It took me a minute to remember your face. I saw it on an old reward poster back at the post.

Your name isn't Jules La Suede! It's Half-a-Face Pontois! You're wanted for
murdering two men in a Dawson bank holdup!"

The prisoner shook his head violently. But there was an ugly light in
his enflamed eyes. "You are wrong, *m'sieu!* Gladly will I accompany you
to your post—"

"Sure you would—not!" Frost sneered. "I'm wonderin' why you showed
up here, Half-a-Face Pontois? It's got me plumb puzzled!"

"Mon Dieu! I tell you I am not—"

"So I'm going to scout around a little," Frost said dryly. "It wouldn't
surprise me a bit to find you were mixed up with this Frozen Phantom
and Flame Maiden business."

Frost handcuffed the man's arms around a small spruce. He tossed his
rabbit-lined sleeping bag over the fellow so he wouldn't freeze to death.
Then he set out on the trail of the Eskimo guide, Bill-Bill Oon.

Snow jarred off branches and showered Frost's parka hood and spilled in
clouds off his shoulders. The Eskimo's tracks kept to the open ground.
They were far apart, showing Bill-Bill was running.

Frost came to a large clearing. There he jerked up rigid. Ice seemed to
clutch his spine.

Bill-Bill Oon had met some kind of a horrible fate in the clearing!

Over an area a score of feet across, snow was whipped and torn with
the marks of a gigantic struggle. Frost gave those marks an incredulous
stare. He could imagine no human agency that might have made them. It
was as though—and he berated himself for a fool as he thought of it—some
feathered monster had beaten the earth with great wings.

Frost leaped headlong across the torn snow. He found tracks.

Tracks! The runty redcoat's throat tightened. He tried to fight off the
superstitious terror that wanted to seize him.

Such tracks these were! That any human agency could have made them
seemed preposterous. They were circular, big as small barrel-heads. In the
deep indentations were narrow lines which Frost's eyes kept telling him
were imprints of folded talons of gigantic size.

"C'mon out of it, guy!" Frost shook his shoulders impatiently. He made
himself follow the tracks.

The weird tracks—they were spaced only a couple of feet apart—
ascended a steep slope where spruces were less abundant. They crossed
a ridge.

Standing on the ridge. Frost stared about.

"Well, I'll be danged!" he muttered.

On the right, he could look across to the spot at which Bill-Bill Oon had
been seized. And this was the same side upon which the Flame Maiden
had stood when she screamed so strangely and terribly.

Had she seen Bill-Bill Oon's fate and screamed because of the horror
of what she witnessed?

Shrugging, he went on. The gloom of the spruces enveloped him. Sombre,
throbbing with the knelling dirge of the wind, the place had a reek of cold
death. The breeze made whispering siren voices that seemed everywhere.
They breathed words, threats, pleas into the redcoat's straining, nervous ears.
And when he ignored them, the frigid snow moaned horribly underfoot.

"Andy Frost!"

The undersized constable jerked up. His name! The whispers were breathing his name. He wet his lips and shuddered. Was he going insane?

"Constable Andy Frost!" This whisper was distinct!

Then Frost saw her—the Flame Maiden!

She stood to his left, almost invisible in the gloom of a spruce thicket. Off toward the Pole, the borealis fanned weird rods of tinted light in the heavens. The glow danced across the ghostly form of the Flame Maiden, making wondrous gleamings in her flaming hair.

Frost took a step forward. She did not recoil. He saw her face more distinctly. It was a nice face. But it bore—and he could hardly repress a shiver as he saw—a stamp of utter terror.

"You know my name?" Frost's voice was squeaky.

The Flame Maiden nodded. "Yes. Your guide—I heard him tell the Frozen Phantom you were Constable Andy Frost of the Mounted."

Her low belling voice had a quality of music that was muted rhythm.

"My guide!" Frost's voice was a crash of relief. "He is alive?"

He saw her slender, shapely limbs flutter like wind-punished plants as she shuddered.

"He is—alive. But it would be better—if he were not. The Frozen Phantom is putting him—in the Coffin of the Mad."

Frost's thoughts were divided—more than half of them on this entrancing bit of feminity before him. He was close enough now so that he could have touched her.

"The Frozen Phantom? What is the thing?"

"I am allowed to warn those who come near," she choked. "That is all I can do. If they do not flee, they are seized."

Frost made an impatient gesture. "What is the Frozen—"

"I'm here to warn you!" she interposed in a frightened rush. "It may not be too late. I warned your guide. Then I came again to warn you. There on the cliff, I saw the—Frozen Phantom—stalking your guide. I knew the fate that was meant for the guide. It was so horrible I screamed. Then, fearing the Frozen Phantom, I fled."

"You are in danger?" Frost demanded.

"I don't—think so," she said hesitatingly. "They haven't—haven't harmed me—yet."

Frost stepped to her side, took her arm. She made no effort to draw away. He felt immeasurably thrilled at the throbbing firmness of her.

"You're real enough!" he grinned. "Now cut out this ghost talk! Tell me what's behind the whole—"

He swallowed the rest. The girl had pointed over his shoulder with both hands. "The Frozen Phantom!" she shrieked.

Frost gripped his Ross rifle, twisted. But even as he spun, something seemed to fill all the gloom about him with swishing sound. His arms and head and shoulders were entrapped in something that was resilient, and yet which held him with an unbelievable strength.

In the murk, Frost could hardly see what it was. It was like—and the thought was too incredible for his brain to grasp—he was wrapped in a great spider web. He tried to lift his rifle, could not.

Frost saw, flinging toward him, the Frozen Phantom!

A monster that seemed nothing but a black, tumultuous cloud! The thing was almost upon him. It was a ghastly, unreal apparition in the half-darkness.

The flame-haired girl screamed again.

A yell ripped past Frost's teeth. He dropped his rifle, fought to get at the revolver inside his parka.

Blows from the black monster began to rain on him. Terrific smashes that left frozen, ghastly numbness where they struck! He was battered down.

He took a blow on the temple. A howling blizzard of Stygian darkness seemed to gather in the distance and rush down and envelop him.

Frost's awakening was slow, fraught with exquisite tortures. He tried to move his arms. They were bound. A jarring pain burst in his side. Another! He was being kicked.

"Get up!" snarled the voice of Half-a-Face Pontois.

Frost weaved to his feet. Then his eyes flashed wide with surprise.

A sizeable black cloak lay nearby, together with a pair of vicious clubs, and weird, round, barrel-head-like snowshoes.

"Oui!" sneered Half-a-Face Pontois. "I am the Frozen Phantom!"

Four bearded men stood close. They held the red-haired Flame Maiden.

No doubt the quartette had also released Half-a-Face Pontois by shattering the cold-brittled handcuff links. The steel circlets still hung to the scarecrow man's wrists.

"You fool!" Pontois leered at Frost. "You had your chance to leave peaceably! The girl pleaded for your life. But now—we have no choice. You will be put into the Coffin of the Mad—and made insane!"

Frost gave the dead-faced man back leer for leer. He was wondering what was behind all this.

"Walk!" commanded Pontois.

Frost was propelled away. Half-a-Face gathered up his cloak-and-club rigamarole—and a square of ordinary fish netting. That net showed Frost what had trapped his arms in such mysterious fashion. Half-a-Face had merely cast it over him!

The four thugs with the red-headed girl brought up the rear.

Down into the slanting floor of a canyon they went. Frost blinked. It was the same canyon in which the girl had seemingly vanished. Ahead, he could see the spruce branches he had tossed from the canyon rim high above.

"So we're going to disappear?" he said dryly.

Half-a-Face Pontois glared at Frost. "So you figured that out? I didn't think you was smart enough to do it!"

"I dropped branches from the canyon rim," Frost advised him. "I saw one bounce in midair, and knew it had struck a fine wire stretched between the two rocky walls. It couldn't be larger than a thread, or it could be seen. You use it, and a pulley system, to haul a stouter rope across the canyon when you want to leave the hidden tunnel in the rock—"

"You got it all, didn't you?" grated Half-a-Face.

"I had to guess about the tunnel," Frost retorted. "It's mighty well hidden. I couldn't see a sign of it. But it had to be there."

Even now the fine wire high overhead was pulling a rope across the canyon, through a concealed pulley, and back. A sort of block-and-tackle fitted with a chair ran out on the rope. The chair dropped downward. Frost was forced into it.

He was hoisted upward, then along the rope to a yard-sized hole in the sheer stone. This was closed with a stone door, so cleverly fitted that even a telescope from the canyon rim would not discern it among the many other cracks veining the vertical surface.

Two shaggy men held Frost under gun muzzles. The girl was lifted in the strange cradle that so simply explained her earlier "disappearance."

Then up came Half-a-Face Pontois and the others.

"I'm so sorry—" the girl started to tell Frost.

"Shut up!" ripped one of the gang.

They went down a crude, darkened tunnel, not unlike a mine bore. Half-a-Face Pontois lighted the way with a candle. For hundreds of yards they walked.

Frost realized they were heading out under the lake floor! The tunnel was taking them to one of the little, steep-walled islands! They came out into the Arctic night at last—on the crest of a castle-like island!

The center of the rocky islet was a cuplike depression. In it were rough buildings. The structures huddled close together. The party pulled up before one of them.

Half-a-Face Pontois thrust his features into those of Frost.

"You will be placed immediately in the Coffin of the Mad!" he leered. "In only a few hours, your brain will be gone!" He snapped his fingers, "Like that! Your Eskimo guide is already in the Coffin of the Mad!"

Frost's snarl made breath steam squirt through his teeth. But before he could speak, there came an interruption.

"Drop those guns!" rapped a voice from the window of the log shack.

The window instantly magnetized all eyes. The barrel of an ancient Snider carbine projected through the aperture. Back of the weapon, a man glared grim threat.

He was white of hair, seamed of face. He had a wasted figure. An elderly man, his features were intelligent, but intense suffering, probably mental rather than physical, had put grooves around his mouth and a haunted look in his eyes.

Suddenly, with a wild leap, Frost sailed for the door of the log shack. This man was a friend, no matter who he might be. He plunged through the door.

A man, obviously one of Half-a-Face Pontois' gang, lay unconscious in the middle of the floor. The white-haired man had knocked him out.

Boom! The old Snider spoke thunder. Outside, a man screamed and dropped—a man behind whom Half-a-Face Pontois had leaped.

Then whiskered thugs poured into the door. Frost's bound hands handicapped him. He was borne down by sheer force of numbers.

The white-haired man fired again, missed, and was knocked sense-less with a clubbed pistol. He fell beside the guard he seemingly had kayoed.

Half-a-Face Pontois, having kept clear of the action, came lumbering in breathing noisily from the live side of his mouth. He was dragging the girl. She clawed at him, dug at his eyes. He dodged his head from side to side and captured her hands.

"You little spitfire!" he gloated. "Tried to make a break, you and your dad! Well, I'm glad of it! I'm tired of playing along with you. I don't need to do that now, because we can do the work your old man has been doing!"

Understanding cracked in Frost's brain. This elderly man was the girl's father! Half-a-Face Pontois had been forcing him to do some sort of work using the welfare of his daughter as a club.

"What is your name?" Frost asked.

Before Half-a-Face Pontois could prevent her, the girl replied, "Loy Wynne! That is my father, Dave Wynne!"

"Why, you're the two who—" But a kick folded Frost in a gulping heap, the rest of the identification blasted off his lips.

Dave Wynne was a mining engineer. More than a year ago he and his daughter had been reported missing. But that was some hundreds of miles to the south!

Half-a-Face Pontois had kidnapped them. That was it!

"Lock up this little *singe!*" roared Half-a-Face. "When the brain of the Eskimo is destroyed, remove him. Then put this redcoat in the Coffin of the Mad!"

Frost was hauled out. A dozen yards away stood another cabin, windowless, more ramshackle. He was pitched into this. The door slammed. A bar rattled.

Frost sat up and looked around. The place was absolutely bare of weapons from dirt floor to log ceiling. It was bitterly cold. The cracks were big, unchinked.

Frost, cooling from the heat of the struggle, beat his arms against his sides and stamped his feet for warmth. He went through his clothing hastily, but found not a single article he could use for a weapon.

Laughter pealed outside. He squinted through a crack, saw a bottle of reddish liquor passing between two guards stationed near his prison.

"Damn them!" the redcoat gritted savagely. "That poor girl!"

He began to work on his wrist lashings. They were of walrus hide, stiff, tough. He freed himself at last, however. But he was little better off.

The door bar rattled abruptly. One of the gang came in. He had food—a filthy mush of stuff on a tin plate.

"Your last meal as a sane man!" he leered. "Eat it! Enjoy it! For henceforth, you will dine on bark and grass and on pebbles and dirt. For you will have no brain to tell you what is fit to eat and what is not!"

Knowing he was being baited out of vile cruelty, Frost started to curse the fellow. Then he swallowed his invective. A wily glitter came into his bleak eyes. He tried to keep his homely face expressionless.

"That's fine of you," he said. "Thanks."

The guard was disappointed. He made a move to throw the food out of the door, then sneered and hurled it at Frost. The stuff sprayed over the policeman and the floor.

"There you are!" leered the guard, and backed outside with the tin pan.

Frost stifled a bark of delight. He began gathering up the dirty, wet mess of food as though it were so much wealth. There was a moose hash in a mushy gruel of rice.

He balled the stuff. Then he placed it near a large crack. He made three balls, each about the size of his knotted fist.

He left them lying before the crack—in the bitter cold that swept in from outdoors: Five minutes, ten—he waited. Then he strode to the window and tested the balled food.

The soggy stuff had frozen solidly. He now had three missiles almost as effective as half-bricks!

Several times Frost went through the windup of a baseball pitcher. Sure his throwing arm was limber, he positioned himself against the wall opposite the door. There was no time to delay if he was to save Bill-Bill Oon.

Frost's homely face was a welted mass of taut muscle—some indication of the physical tension he was under. He knew only too well how slender his chances were.

"C'mere, one of you!" he shouted, lifting his voice.

Getting no answer, he repeated the call. He was cursed for his pains.

Frost scowled. He groped in his brain for another ruse. This one wouldn't work. He hefted the frozen food balls. Then he got an idea. He attracted the guards outside, enticing them near a crack.

"I have money," he breathed. "It was not found when I was searched. I will pay you to let me escape!"

"I'll be right in!"

Frost waited. He knew the guard, an ape-browed brute, had no idea of being bribed. The fellow merely intended to appropriate the money the others had missed.

The door bar rattled. Frost backed hastily across the room.

Behind the gaping snout of an ancient Enfield revolver, the apish guard crowded into the room. He saw Frost against the wall opposite—too far away to attack with a sudden leap. That lulled his suspicions. He turned carelessly to secure the door.

Frost had kept his hands out of sight. He produced them now, gripping his two frozen food missiles. The third was in a pocket of his scarlet tunic.

He lobbed one like a baseball. It caught the guard squarely in the head. It burst like a snowball. The fellow slapped against the door, slid down it to the floor.

Frost leaped. He scooped up the dazed guard's Enfield revolver.

Clank! The Enfield barrel sounded like wood-against-wood as Frost slammed it on the man's head. The apish fellow went down. It would be an hour before he awakened, at the least.

Frost yanked open the door. The second guard was just reaching for the latch. He tried to get his gun up.

But runty Constable Frost functioned with the bewildering speed of electrical apparatus when he went into action. He lobbed another frozen food ball.

It connected with the guard's mouth. His jaws filled with dislodged teeth. He bawled. He waved his arms. Frost charged him.

The man shot, but wildly. Frost let him have another ball of frozen food between the eyes. The mean orbs were lost behind slow-shutting lids. The fellow was out on his feet. They were effective, those frozen balls. No Kerry man with a brick could have done better.

Frost grabbed another big Enfield from the fellow's slack fingers. The man wore a shabby cartridge belt, well laden with shells. Frost seized it, yanked. Leather parted and it was in his fingers. He belted the stunned man again to make the sleep semi-permanent.

With a flying plunge. Frost went around the shack. He almost speared a man on the snout of one of his two captured revolvers.

The fellow was a stocky, evil picture of fat and whiskers. He yanked back the hammer of the rifle he was carrying.

Frost stroked trigger. His Enfield roared like a brass cannon. The man of fat and whiskers lay down slowly, as though tired of it all. The bullet had coursed through his brain.

The man had come from the largest of the collection of cabins. This was no more than twoscore feet away. Since no one was in sight anywhere else, Frost made for it.

When he was less than two yards from the door, a man popped out of the cabin in which the girl's father, white-haired Dave Wynne, had attempted his short-lived bid for liberty. The fellow came out as though driven by explosive. He threw up a rifle. But, at that range, no rifle could have been aimed and fired in time to catch Frost.

The runty constable whipped to cover inside the large cabin. He started to whirl and take a snapshot at the rifleman. Then he stopped. His eyes widened. He forgot all about the rifleman.

"The Coffin of the Mad!" he muttered.

He did not know what he had expected, but sight of the thing surprised him. It really looked like a coffin!

It was of some blackish-brown, massive mineral with a tarlike lustre. In size as well as shape, it resembled a receptacle for the dead. There was a cover, perforated with holes for breathing, secured with stout hasps.

The whole thing bore certain crudities that told Frost it had been made here in the northland! It had been mortared together roughly out of many blocks of the blackish-brown stuff.

The room held something else. Frost stared at it.

"Gold milling machinery!" he grunted.

The machinery, a small mill for crushing the rock, and mechanism for extracting the precious metal, was such as could easily be transported to this remote spot by dog team.

Stray lumps of ore lay on the packed earth floor. It was high-grade stuff! The wire gold was plainly discernible.

Frost understood the whole thing now!

Half-a-Face Pontois had brought the mining engineer, Dave Wynne, to this spot and forced him to conduct the technical operation of extracting the gold from the rich ore. Beautiful Loy Wynne's welfare had been the club that had driven the mining engineer to obey.

Half-a-Face, since he was wanted for murder, could not appear openly and lay claim to this rich lode. So he had been working it secretly, and by building up the terrible legend of the Frozen Phantom and the Flame Maiden, had sought to frighten away all that ventured near.

Only one thing remained unexplained. What was the nature of the gruesome Coffin of the Mad? Frost tore at the hasps. He got the black, grisly lid up.

Bill-Bill Oon lay inside. Wrists and ankles were bound. His eyes protruded. His face was purple. He looked like a man with a great fever.

Frost's heart sank. The Inuit might already be beyond help, his mind ruined. Frost peered at the strange, blackish coffin, wondering what ghastly quality it held to cause this terrible thing.

But loud yelling outside called him back to ugly reality. Half-a-Face Pontois was squawling for his men to get to work with their rifles on the Mounted Policeman.

Frost hauled the Eskimo out of the fearsome box of a coffin. He worked frantically over the man's tyings. A knot gave, then another.

Bill-Bill Oon said no word.

Frost got the bindings free.

Suddenly Bill-Bill Oon struck savagely at Frost. He raved a wild gibberish. He frothed.

Frost's heart sank. The Eskimo was beyond help! He was already insane, a gibbering idiot! With the greatest of difficulty, Frost evaded the Inuit. He dashed for the door. One of his two Enfields came up, banged.

A man—the rifleman—racing for the door hardly stopped his headlong charge as a bullet slugged him. He ran wildly a distance of twenty feet, then became a tumbling tangle of arms and legs.

"Four down!" Frost gulped. He had no idea how many men were here. There had been eight or ten at first, he suspected.

He hit the ground outside. Digging up snow, he whirled around a corner.

The string of a violin seemed to snap in his ear as a bullet went past. The slug screamed as it ricocheted from a stone somewhere. Frost threw up a revolver, sight-nocked the man who had fired and nursed the trigger back.

He missed. But the fellow who had tried to shoot him ducked from sight.

"Loy!" Frost roared. "Miss Wynne!" He wanted to know where the girl was.

"Here!" Her voice pealed from cabin to his left.

Frost ran for the sound. Ten feet from the door, he sailed into the air. He hit the door feet-first, a hundred and seventy pounds of bulleting force. With an explosion of rending wood, the panel caved.

Frost sledded inside atop the falling panel.

White-haired Dave Wynne was there, tied to the upright post of a built-in bunk.

Flame-haired Loy Wynne was there also. She was flushed, disheveled. Half-a-Face Pontois had been deviling her.

Pontois himself stood wide-legged, lifting an Enfield revolver. Scratches on his face, a split in his lip, one eye badly gouged, showed the girl had so far succeeded in repulsing his advances.

Half-a-Face's Enfield banged. He had hurried, and his slug split the door on which Frost coasted.

Frost pulled trigger. *Click!* Empty! He brought up his other gun. Then pretty Loy Wynne, flinging across the room, knocked aside Half-a-Face's gun just as he prepared to fire a shot that almost certainly would have finished Frost. She jabbed her fingers into the boss killer's eyes.

Frost got up off the door. He staggered to the struggling pair. He struck a blow with his empty revolver that broke Pontois' gun arm between wrist and elbow. He tried to land another blow that would have crushed the murderer's skull.

But Half-a-Face dodged. He twisted free. He tried to reach the revolver that had fallen from the slackening grip of his broken arm. But he saw Frost would certainly belt him on the head before he could get it. Straightening, he ran out of the door.

Frost, seeking to follow, got tangled in the wreckage of the door and fell down.

Fighting clear of the door ruins, Frost threw his empty gun and the cartridge belt to Loy Wynne.

"Load it! Keep it for yourself!"

He scooped up the weapon Half-a-Face Pontois had dropped. He swiveled to the door, boiled outside—a squat, homely-faced runt with the ungainly gait of a gorilla. A compact human fighting machine imbued with a recklessness the equal of which is rarely attained!

In one sense, he had gone completely amuck. He had shed every atom of caution. That he could have barricaded himself in the cabin and picked off his foes—with good luck—did not occur to him. The only thing he was seeing at the moment was the horrible, mad face of Bill-Bill Oon and the picture of pretty Loy Wynne in the hands of Half-a-Face Pontois.

Ten seconds later he bulleted between the eyes an incautious breed that thrust head and shoulders around a cabin to aim a rifle at him.

At the shot crack, Half-a-Face Pontois turned his head. Sight of the gnarled, red-coated little nemesis bounding across the snow after him seemed to lend him wings. He popped into a cabin, seized a rifle off pegs, saw it was empty and threw it down. He ran for his life. He dived out a rear door, fanned with cold air from a bullet that kissed nap off his shirt collar.

Into another cabin he popped. He slammed the door. Frost saw this structure was long. It had the marks of a bunkhouse. He jumped feet first against the door. It tossed him back. He knew then it was too solid to smash down in a hurry. He raced around it.

A man hung half out of a window. Crimson leaked from his nostrils. He was dead.

Frost gaped. He had not shot *this* one!

But now he became aware of low, shuffling sounds from within the long building. They loudened. Came a bawl of terror. Yells! Blows! Then shots! A volley of them!

Frost rammed head and shoulders in the window. Awesome was the sight that met his eyes.

Bill-Bill Oon was locked in mortal combat with Half-a-Face Pontois. Face to face, they strained across the floor. Half-a-Face Pontois had drawn a pistol. It exploded. The Eskimo jerked as the slug bedded down in his body somewhere.

Then, with a shriek, Half-a-Face was forced to drop his gun.

Bill-Bill Oon must have come directly to this cabin after Frost released him. The insane Eskimo had brought along the first thing that came to his hands—an ordinary steel crowbar.

The work of that crowbar lay spread on the floor. Three dead men!

They were piled in grotesque shapes, crushed heads staining the packed earth floor. Bill-Bill Oon must have come through this back window upon them.

Suddenly Bill-Bill discovered Frost. The insane contortion smoothed off his face to some extent, leaving it peaceful. He released Half-a-Face Pontois. He picked up his heavy crowbar. Like a big, gentle dog that has sighted its master, the poor idiot came toward Frost. He smiled vacantly. He did not know what he was doing.

Half-a-Face Pontois staggered about after being released. Then he pounced on his revolver. Bill-Bill was between Half-a-Face Pontois and Frost. Frost could not fire.

Half-a-Face Pontois shot the insane Eskimo in the back.

With a gibbering squawl, a ghastly sound that ripped through the frigid Arctic air, the Inuit whirled and sprang. Pontois' gun roared again. The bullet seemed to halt the Eskimo in midair. Then he came on. He was a violent maniac, made thus by the fiendish Coffin of the Mad! He seemed not even to feel pain. That was merciful.

His crowbar traveled a terrific arc. It brained Half-a-Face Pontois.

The Eskimo made an attempt to swing his club again, although it was not necessary. Then he seemed to go asleep on his feet. He swayed. He pitched forward across the body of Pontois and the life left him.

Frost jerked his head out of the window of that cabin of death. He raced around in front, eyes alert. But a sepulchral quiet had descended upon the castle-like rock of an island.

Ice out on the lake made ghostly pop-pop-booming noises.

Flame-haired Loy Wynne and her father ran up.

"'There's nine of them dead or laid up, includin' Pontois!" Frost barked. "How many's left?"

"Why—nine of them—that's the whole gang," Dave Wynn said wonderingly. "There's nobody left."

"Your Eskimo guide?" asked pretty Loy Wynne. "What about him?"

Frost shook his head slowly. "The Coffin of the Mad got him. But he went out like a hunter of his people would be proud to go. He accounted for Half-a-Face Pontois, and three of the others."

Frost looked sharply at Dave Wynne. "That Coffin of the Mad—what makes it work like it does. What is the thing?"

"It is made of pitchblende," Wynne explained. "It contains a rich quantity of radium. That explains its grisly operation. Radium in close proximity to the human brain is capable of doing great damage. All doctors are aware of that."

"But where—"

"Where did Half-a-Face Pontois get it? He merely stole it from a concern that is producing radium far south of here. I think he worked for the company and stole bits of rich ore until he had enough to make the Coffin of the Mad."

Frost shuddered, visioning again that awful, sleek black coffin. The Coffin of the Mad.

That nightmare faded, giving way to a picture that was real and infinitely more pleasurable. A picture of a flame-haired girl with haunting eyes. The Flame Maiden!

And from the look in the Flame Maiden's eyes, Constable Frost of the Mounted rather had a hunch he would have that picture with him for a long time.

• • • • •

Snow Ghost

Six men hunkered in the snow and talked of murder. Like six shaggy devils, they were. Like devils with their horns and spike tails frozen off, who had grown a coat of thick hair for protection against an Arctic cold which had shrunk the red line in the thermometer to thirty-five below. The giant of the crowd was growling words. In size, he was a monster among men. His sealskin parka would have housed any three of the others. He had a voice that gritted and thumped like floes of the polar ice pack piling on a lee shore.

"*C'est bien!*" he rumbled. "That right! De redcoat will get here soon. An' he mus' die before he find out a t'ing about us! *Oui, M'sieu* Ferrick! Yo' bes' let Le Chinois feex heem!"

The giant lifted mittened hands nearly as large as the body of a sled dog. The mighty paws made a gesture of seizing and breaking something. "Le Chinois do heem like dat!"

The other five shivered. They shrank deeper into their parkas. Even such hardened fiends as they got jittery at the idea of killing a constable of the Royal Northwest Mounted Police. It was about the most unhealthy thing a man could do in the Northland.

And maybe they were more than a little scared of the monster, Le Chinois. They didn't doubt he could break a man's back as easily as he had made that sinister gesture in thin air. They had seen him pick up a sled dog that had bitten him, and with his two hands tear it bodily apart.

The wind hooted down off the polar ice cap. It made frozen limbs of the spruce whine like tortured things. It stacked and unstacked the sand-hard snow. It shoveled snow into the fire about which the devilish six huddled, and the stuff made sickly sizzlings on the hot coals.

"Nix!" clipped the man called Ferrick. "Croakin' a Mountie is bad business, even if the Alaska border isn't far away. Them redcoats is worse'n dandruff! They've got a way of gettin' in your hair years after you thought you was rid of 'em. Lemme think!"

Ferrick had a face like a bunch of bones and some yellow hide jammed in his parka hood. He smoked a pipe. The wind from the pole kept sucking sparks out of the pipe bowl.

Two sledges stuck, curved-end-up, in the snow. A third sledge was farther from the fire. It had not been unloaded. The big bundle on it was done up in a waterproof oiled tarpaulin.

"I got it!" Ferrick rapped suddenly. He had a way of speaking as though he were always excited. "You grab this redcoat pest, Le Chinois. Bust his leg. Bust both his legs. I don't give a damn. Then let him pinch you for assaultin' him! Let him take you to his post. That'll get him away from here while we take care of the damn girl's reindeer drive!"

"Sacre Dieu!" growled Le Chinois. "Me—I no like dat idea."

"You'll like it less if you croak the redcoat and get hung for it!" sneered Ferrick. "The outfit that's hirin' me to take care of the girl's reindeer herd will hire you a lawyer. You'll only be fined for beatin' up the redcoat. They'll pay your fine. They'll pay you a bonus for your trouble—say five hundred bucks. How does that sound?"

The monster Le Chinois considered. Breath steam raced out a long, foul gray plume from his cavernous mouth, plucked by the chill wind.

"De five hun'ert buck sound dam fine," he rumbled. *"Oui!* I do heem like yo' say! Me—I don' keel heem unless I have to."

"That's bein' smart!" chuckled Ferrick. "Lookit! You can see him now—mushin' across the lake!"

Six pairs of eyes, watering in the frigid wind, peered out on the lake.

The man they saw mushed a four-dog team. It was a small team. The sledge was tiny, the grub pack on it hardly more than an armload.

The smallness extended to the corporal of the Mounted who plugged along in the sled tracks. He looked like a toy man, with a toy sledge and dogs.

"How'd a little geezer like that ever manage to get in the Mounted?" Ferrick snorted around his pipe.

Ferrick didn't know it, but he wasn't the first who had wondered about that. And some of them had damned well found out the reason.

The policeman left the snow-covered lake. He mounted the slope, wending through scrub spruces. He reached the devil's half dozen about the fire. His four dogs stopped without being told to.

"Hy'ah, gents," he said, so low his words were hardly heard.

He sounded like a Yank, a former Wyoming cowhand, judging by the whang of his words. He wore dark, nearly black, snow glasses. Below them, his face looked scrawny, like the features of an old man.

The devil's half dozen greeted him jovially. They grinned at him. They couldn't keep their grins from being evil, though. But the policeman seemed not to notice.

"Seen anything of the reindeer drive?" he inquired. His voice was so low as to be almost torn away by the howling wind.

"Not a thing," Ferrick said amiably. "Didn't know there was one."

"There is," whispered the policeman. "Young lady named Ida Thorne bringin' in a few thousand head from Alaska. Canadian government bought 'em to stock this part of the country. Kinda reminds me of the old cattle-trailin' days in Wyomin'. I was up in this neck of the woods, so figured I'd look the reindeer drive over an' see how they handle the critters."

He fell silent. Borne upon the booming wind came a mournful, hideous sound. It rose and fell in a yowling bedlam and finally died away as though stifled by the frigid gale.

"Wolves," grinned the undersized policeman. "Reckon the reindeer drive must be close, from the wolf tracks I've seen an' the howlin' I've heard. Guess the wolves follow a deer herd like they used to tag after a cow drive."

He seemed like a tired and homesick little man. Even his voice seemed played out.

"Might as well camp here and use our fire," Ferrick suggested.

The human monster, Le Chinois, got to his feet. The hulk of him was like a hill heaving up.

"By dam', I show yo' fine windbreak where yo' can feed de dogs," he rumbled.

"Thanky, pard," murmured the little policeman.

The two moved off. They were lost to sight in a nearby spruce thicket.

The other five of the devil's half dozen exchanged knowing leers. There was no windfall back in that spruce thicket. Le Chinois had drawn the diminutive corporal away. The others would have an alibi. They had not known Le Chinois hated policemen, they would say. And they would be very careful not to answer the constable's screams for help in time to save him from becoming a broken, helpless thing.

Le Chinois' great rumble reached their ears. It was angry.

"By dam'! What yo' mean by shovin' me? *Sacre Dieu!* Me— I teach yo' not to shove Le Chinois!" Le Chinois was picking the quarrel.

A terrific blow resounded. A loud crashing of spruce boughs followed, then grunts, groans, wailings, whimperings. Over it all rose the soggy smackings of awful fists striking. Twice, distinct and ghastly crunches denoted bones breaking.

"I hope that slug-silly Le Chinois don't croak him!" Ferrick said, half delighted, half uneasy.

An ominous silence fell in the spruce clump.

A bit later, two figures appeared. One was limp, quite helpless. The features of that man leaked crimson streams that froze hard and crusty the instant they touched the snow. The second man carried the first. He carried him lightly as he would a marten fresh from a trap.

The mouths of the five watching men fell open and steaming in the frigid Arctic twilight.

Surprises they must have received in their checkered past—but never such a shock as now.

The beaten, broken man was the human monster—Le Chinois. The man who carried the giant so lightly was the little policeman.

The officer looked no bigger than before. Indeed, he seemed smaller. For his parka and the tunic he wore beneath had been torn open. His shoulders and arms were bare to the polar chill.

Eyeing that chest and arms, the five onlookers began to revise their opinions. The small officer's body was the faintly tanned color of a catgut fiddle string that has been used a lot. And tendons seemingly made out of those same fiddle strings stood in great bundles and knots and gullies on his torso.

More amazing even than the inhuman physical strength the little policeman obviously possessed was his hair. There was a great shock of it. Like the plumed helmet of an ancient Roman, it waved erect. And it was the striking hue of burnished silver.

Ferrick spat his pipe and a choking oath out together. He dived a hand for his gun. But hissed words from a breed at his left stopped him.

"Non! Non!" gulped the breed. "Dat man ees de Silver Corporal."

Ferrick hastily pretended he had been reaching for the ground to shove himself onto his feet. He'd heard of the Silver Corporal somewhere.

He must have heard of him over in Alaska, for that had been Ferrick's stamping grounds for years. And for the reputation of a redcoat to penetrate into Ferrick's part of Alaska, it must be a reputation indeed. Ferrick got cautious.

The little policeman dropped his burden. Steam squirmed from Le Chinois' wounds. Both the monster's arms were broken. Most of his teeth were gone. Never again would his nose be the same.

"Reckon you gents could loan me a pinch of tea?" asked the Silver Corporal and his voice was so low as to be nearly lost in the gale. "My supply has plumb played out on me."

Ferrick and the others gulped. They swallowed uneasily. They had expected the policeman to at least get tough, ask questions. But he was absolutely ignoring Le Chinois' attack, acting as though nothing out of the ordinary had occurred. He was asking for tea! It bothered Ferrick and his breeds.

"We don't know Le Chinois very well!" Ferrick began hastily to explain. "He just lately joined up with our prospectin' outfit. We didn't know he was goin' to jump you—"

"Oh, him?" The Silver Corporal's tiny voice seemed nothing but a sorrowful whisper in the wind. "There's lots of fellers like him who want to hit a policeman whenever they see one. Funny, ain't it?"

Ferrick and his men didn't think it was funny. But they laughed like it was.

"Sure, sure," cackled Ferrick hollowly. "Here— I'll loan you the tea!"

The Silver Corporal fastened his clothes. He said no word. He made his tea in a little black kettle over the fire. The kettle was tiny. It might have been a utensil in a small girl's playhouse. Nor did the strange, small man speak again while he brewed his beverage.

Ferrick and his breeds looked on. They wondered where the Silver Corporal kept his gun. They hadn't seen any.

They'd have been surprised to know the truth—that the Silver Corporal didn't carry a gun. They'd have been tickled to know that. Or maybe they wouldn't have—if they had known the whole truth.

"Thanks for the tea," came the little policeman's wispy voice at last. "Reckon I'll turn in."

He faded into the spruce clump. His going was strangely soundless. But maybe that was because of the way the wind bawled down from the Pole.

"That gink gets my goat!" Ferrick shivered.

"*Sacre Dieu!* Yo' ees not firs' one whose goat hees get," muttered a breed.

"What d'you know about him?"

"Not ver' much, *M'sieu* Ferrick. De Eskimos call heem a *tongak,* a spirit from de other worl'. Dey more scared of heem dan of hell. De talk t'rough de north ees that hees do many wonderful t'ings. Dey say hees run down an' catch de caribou, jus' like de *loup*—de wolf. Dey say hees whip one whole tribe of bad Indians, jus' wit' hees two bare hands. Dey say hees no can be killed. Hee's man of magic!"

"A pack of damn lies!" But Ferrick shivered again, as though he had found an icicle inside his parka.

The Silver Corporal reappeared. He made no sound this time, either. It was as though a puff of furry smoke had squirted out of the spruces. He carried his rabbit-lined sleeping bag. Ferrick and the others watched him.

Near a great drift, the Silver Corporal got into his sleeping sack. He removed none of his clothing. He faced the drift. He drew the mouth of the bag shut over his head. His small form doubled low, then snapped upward from the earth.

The leap was prodigious. Fully a score of feet he seemed to sail. Then he shot feet first into the huge drift and vanished from sight. In a trice, the booming wind had smoothed the drift and there was nothing to show where he had disappeared.

The Silver Corporal had gone to bed.

Muttering, Ferrick and the others revived the wreck of a human monster, Le Chinois. They splinted his arms and bandaged his hurts. They asked him how he had come to be so grievously injured.

"A mon insu!" whimpered the suffering giant. "Me— I don' know. I grab heem. Den—*alors*—eet happen! De worl', she go plentee black!"

Ferrick cursed him up and down the range of an extensive fund of cusswords. Then he drew his breeds aside. They talked in low tones.

That their conversation boded no good for the Silver Corporal was evident from the furtive glances they cast at the great drift where he had vanished. But the drift surface remained undisturbed

Their sinister powwow ended. They gathered up their arms. They crept silently away in the Arctic twilight.

The Silver Corporal saw them go.

They knew little of the ways of the Silver Corporal, did Ferrick and his crew of evil breeds. If they had, they would not have spent so much time watching the drift where the strange, small policeman had vanished. They would have looked elsewhere. Perhaps they would have looked at a spot a hundred feet away, where the drift poked its tapering end into the spruce thickets.

The Silver Corporal often leaped into a drift as he had tonight. But he rarely slept at the same spot. Tonight he had tunneled, never disturbing the surface of the snow, to the spruces. He had been resting there, warm and comfortable in his rabbit-lined bag, watching Ferrick and the others.

Their sneaking departure told him they contemplated no good. He eased out of his bag. He rolled the sleeping accouterment, silently climbed a spruce and dangled it by a strap from a limb. Wolverines had a habit of playing havoc with a man's equipment in this Arctic waste.

He was about to take up the trail when he saw movement near the spot where he had leaped into the drift. They were sharp, those pale blue eyes of the Silver Corporal. They saw things even an old he-wolf, wily from years in this northland, might have missed.

The object he discerned resolved into a man. Crouching, the fellow worked nearer the drift. He carried a rifle, stock thrust up into his parka so his body warmth would keep the mechanism of the gun from freezing. He stopped, aimed.

The man's rifle muzzle guttered flame. Salvos of powder noise battled the wind. The gun was an automatic. It drove a stream of lead into the drift. With mad haste, the man clipped in fresh cartridges.

Traveling in his noiseless way, like a whorl of dark snow wafted sidewise by the frosty gale, the Silver Corporal approached the would-be killer.

He encountered bad luck—bad luck even he, the Silver Corporal, could not guard against.

A big Arctic snowshoe popped up underfoot. The rabbit was terrified. It ran wildly, flashing from one side to the other as nature had taught it best to avoid the foxes and wolves which preyed upon it. It made a racket among the spruce twigs.

The gunman heard. He whirled. He saw the Silver Corporal. His automatic rifle stuttered.

But the bullets only made zonging sounds through empty space and banged about in the spruces beyond. For the Silver Corporal was gone! Headfirst into a drift he had vanished, so swiftly that it seemed nothing less than magic.

The gunman dropped two cartridge clips before he got a third home. He shook as from the ague. He remembered what the other breed had muttered about this strange silver-haired man being immune from death. Terror got him. Whirling, he ran. He looked back.

The Silver Corporal had appeared like a diminutive genie, two-score feet from where he had disappeared.

"Sacre Dieu!" screamed the gunman. He put on more speed. Up a hill he fled, and down toward a wide stream beyond.

The Silver Corporal followed.

He went warily. He might be many things, but he was not bullet-proof. Besides, he wanted urgently to stay well and kicking long enough to solve this mystery. Something dirty was underfoot here. Just what it was—that question had him puzzled. And he did love to solve such puzzles. That was the reason he had taken to the Northland.

He neared the wide stream. His sharp eyes picked up a form. It was only a blur in the murk of the deep valley.

The form scudded across the ice. It vanished in stunted timber on the opposite bank of the stream.

The Silver Corporal hesitated. A man running on ice is about the best target there is, even if he doesn't slip and fall down.

Suddenly, there came a sound that decided him.

A woman's cry! It was shrill, piercing. It wasn't exactly a scream. It was more of a terrified, high-pitched shout. But the way it gargled off and ended in a stifled moan was awful.

That feminine cry sent the Silver Corporal out on the ice. With a speed almost blinding, he raced. He zigzagged, knowing shots might crash any instant.

But bullets were not his undoing.

With a deafening roar, the ice broke.

In possibly the space of time it takes to snap a finger, the Silver Corporal understood that he had been cleverly tricked. It was no man he had seen cross the ice! It must have been a dog, an animal light enough that the ice would not collapse. The canine had been decked with spruce boughs and a fur parka to give it the aspect of a man, so the policeman would follow it.

The gunman had left the dog leashed on the stream bank before putting on his shooting act. He had fled to the animal, turned it loose, and doubled back. The dog had dashed across the stream to one of the other breeds. The whole thing was a death trap to spring in case the fusillade of bullets into the drift failed to do their work.

The woman's scream? The Silver Corporal didn't know what to think about that. She must be a prisoner. Maybe they had let her scream at just the right instant to decoy him onto the ice. It didn't occur to him that the woman had lured him purposely. The Silver Corporal was a Wyoming cowpoke. To that breed, all women are good women.

Cold water hit the Silver Corporal like a sledge blow. Air was knocked screaming from his lungs.

The stream was running a mad torrent. This explained the thin sheet of ice through which he had dropped. At the freeze-up in the fall, the creek had been running high. But the cold had dried its tributaries and the level had dropped, leaving a thin, treacherous shell. The water that ran now was only that fed by great springs in the stream bed. The north country was full of such perils.

The Silver Corporal was battered about. The crushing force of the water made his struggles futile as the twistings of a limp rag. Pounding against boulders, the torrent lifted thunder in the ice-roofed cavern.

Helpless, he was borne ahead. The ice roof closed down. He sucked air into his lungs. Then he was swept under.

Although the ice had now thickened to a depth of four or five feet overhead, the current was still too swift for any man to swim against. Even this mighty little silver-haired man was unable to breast it.

Farther and farther toward his doom the Silver Corporal was tumbled.

The laboring water about him abruptly seemed to become tired. It rested. End over end, the Silver Corporal was tumbled across the bottom. His lungs already felt as though they were filling with hot sand, the result of holding his breath.

He pawed at the bottom, held himself there by grasping a water-logged stick, and pummeled his brain. He was sure-enough jam up against it. He couldn't swim against the current. There wasn't one chance in twenty million of finding a hole. Five feet would be a conservative guess at the thickness of the ice overhead.

Well, he wouldn't drown sitting still. He loosened his grip, let the waterlogged stick slide through his hand.

An instant after he let go the stick, he stroked madly back to it. He felt the end. The stick terminated in a sharp, conical taper.

The Silver Corporal nearly lost some of the precious air in his lungs, so excited did he become. The conical end on that stick meant—

Wildly, he stroked along the bank of the now idling stream. His head cracked the ice. He had his eyes open. It was dark. He could barely see the mud he was stirring up.

He continued to paw the bank, searching furiously. His lungs were entirely full of the ghastly hot sand feel now. Each beat of his heart seemed to throw a billiard ball against either eardrum. A few seconds more, and the fish would have the Silver Corporal.

Then he found it!

A beaver burrow! It bored straight into the bank.

The Silver Corporal jammed his way into it. Many times in his life, he had wished his Maker had seen fit to construct a bigger man when He came to this particular Wyoming cowhand. But now he'd have gladly been content with half his already diminutive size.

But beavers had a way of making ample-sized burrows. And the long-bladed, heavy-hilted knife the Silver Corporal hauled from inside his soaked tunic enlarged the narrow places.

The burrow turned up. His head topped the water. The air was black, nearly sickening with the castor smell of a beaver. But it was air!

The next instant a beaver attacked him. He had never heard of a beaver assaulting a man. But then, he had never heard of a man invading a beaver's domicile in this fashion. The teeth of the animal cut into his shoulder like knives.

He flung it away. Rearing up, he saw crazily colored lights when his head hit the roof. It wasn't a yard high. Then, with a *kerflug-g!* of water, the beaver was gone.

The animal would have no trouble finding sanctuary in other burrows nearby.

The Silver Corporal sagged down. The underground room wasn't large enough to stretch out in. So he curled, lay there drawing in great gulps of the musky air.

Unexpectedly, voices came to his attention!

Hauling himself up, the Silver Corporal put an ear to the frozen dirt ceiling of the tiny cell. It could not be many inches to the outside air. He heard feet thumping along the bank.

"C'est tres bon!" rasped a guttural voice. "Eet ees ver' good! Hee's feenished!"

"He sure is!" came Ferrick's clipped, excitable tones. "We've thrown rocks on that thin ice and broke it all the way down to where the water goes under thick ice. He didn't have a chance in that hell-tearing creek. He's one damn Mounted policeman we're rid of."

"Bien!" chuckled the breed. "Dat ees good! What do we do nex'?"

"You mean about our girl friend?"

"Oui!"

Ferrick swore a volley. He had a remarkable command of profanity. "To tell the truth, I ain't sure what we'll do about her," he rapped. "But it's sure her hard luck that she caught some of my boys gumshoeing around her reindeer herd."

"Yo' mean we mus' keel her?"

"Don't make me laugh, Frenchy. Sure we gotta kill her. The point is—how? When? Where? Before we pull our big stunt, or after?"

"Non," muttered the breed. "Me—I no like keel dat woman. She ver' pret'—"

"Horsefeathers!" snorted Ferrick. "With the money you're gettin' out of this, you can buy you a harem full of 'em like her. But if she gets loose— well, she saw us croak the policeman. They'll line us up on a board with ropes around our necks."

The pair moved out of earshot.

Cramped in the barrel of a beaver den, the Silver Corporal forked his waterproof matchbox out of his soaked clothing.

The den was floored with sticks, rushes, roots. The larger sticks were cone-shaped on the ends, where the beaver's teeth had gnawed them off. Smaller twigs had been clipped through as by scissors. The match went out.

With the knife that had proved so useful in enlarging the beaver burrow, the Silver Corporal went to work on the den roof. The first inch or so was easy. After that, the frozen earth got hard as a brick.

But the knife had a blade like a bayonet, heavy, thick. It chipped upward.

The policeman didn't hurry too much. He cut a circle until he had sort of a lid. Opening this, he peered out cautiously. No one was in sight.

A bound and he was outside. He landed running. He kept going at a headlong pace, but as silently as he could. He knew what would happen if he stopped. His saturated garments would freeze solid—cake him in an icy armor. He would be about as agile on the ground as an old-time knight.

He neared the camp. He saw figures about the fire. He counted. Seven of them!

That meant Ferrick had more of a gang than the five breeds who had been around the fire when the policeman arrived. The other villains must have been prowling about the reindeer herd.

Halting, the Silver Corporal lay down. He rolled in the snow. The stuff stuck to his moist garments. He gave it time to freeze there. When he stood up, he was white as a polar bear.

His small form blended with the snow now. He made for his sleeping bag.

In the darkest depth of the spruce clump, the Silver Corporal whipped his sleeping bag open. Standing beside it, with the thermometer at thirty-five below and with a howling gale from the Pole moaning like werewolves about his bare shanks, he stripped off stark naked.

His little, tendon-wrapped body was a remarkable thing. It had not changed a whit from its hue of long-used catgut, despite the terrific cold that would have turned an ordinary man blue, then the grisly white of frostbite.

Every gigantic muscle stood out as distinctly as the hamstring of a sled dog. It was as though some mysterious compound had dissolved all parts of his body except the bones and those astounding sinews.

The Silver Corporal sprang into the rabbit-lined sleeping bag. He disappeared into it completely.

His distinctive shock of silver-colored hair was literally a block of ice. He thawed it with his hands, throwing the ice lumps outside. He writhed about in the bag, drying himself. The rabbit sack was bitterly cold, but it was like a furnace after standing naked in that wailing Arctic gale.

When he was dry, he shook out his spare set of garments. They were in the bag—simply because they always served in lieu of a pillow. Without leaving the bag, he donned the clothing.

He belted on no firearm, but he did produce an object that had been the kernel of the pillow of garments. He shook this in his hand. It seemed to come alive. It crawled along his arms and over his hands. It ran out into the teeth of the gale, snapping taut with a serpentine hiss.

A white rope! It was braided of some hard stuff that looked like violin strings. It had the springy quality of a rod of whalebone.

No ordinary lass rope, this! It tapered a little, somewhat like a bullwhip, but not as much. One end was fitted with a honda in the usual fashion. The other end, the smaller, terminated in a double-edged blade of steel, honed to a razor sharpness.

As though possessed of invisible wings, this blade sped out in the Arctic twilight. It traveled faster and faster, until the eye could no longer follow it. Fully thirty feet distant, a spruce bough thick as a man's arm parted as though by magic—and the strange white rope with its fang of steel was back and coiled around the little policeman's arm before the bough had hardly jumped away in the gale.

It smacked of wizardry. But many things about the Silver Corporal smacked of that.

He drew on gloves. They were of velvet. They had an outer easing of white silk to keep out the wind. They were warm, yet did not hamper his strangely flexible hands.

He glided toward the camp of his foes. The garments he had donned were made from the belly fur of snowshoe rabbits. They were perfectly white. He drew from a pocket a small jar. This held white grease paint that was impervious to the cold. He smeared it on his face.

He could now have dropped prone where he stood, and an unknowing wayfarer might have stepped over him without realizing it was other than a strangely shaped drift of snow underfoot.

The Silver Corporal was little less than a phantom of the white spaces.

Lost in the squirming clouds of snow that the gale shoveled about, he glided to within fifty feet of the camp.

Only two men were there now. Two breeds! They had opened the pack on the sledge. They lifted out packages.

Every package was done in a wrapping of glaring red.

These packages they loaded into tumpline packsacks. The breeds talked as they worked, never dreaming of the phantom listener near by.

"Dis ees las' load," one said.

"Oui," agreed the other. "Een another hour, our work here weel be done. De reindeer herd weel be destroyed."

"An' de girl, too," reminded the first.

"Oui, oui! She mus' die, too. Only her death weel leave us safe. *M'sieu* Ferrick ees wit' her now, ovair by de cliff. He ees try' to decide how she shall be keeled."

The pair emptied the last of the sledge load into their back packs. They heaved the burden of red packages on their shoulders, adjusted the tumplines over their greasy foreheads. They moved away.

They neither heard nor saw the white wraith that haunted their footsteps.

The first intimation they had of its presence was when a strange missile came hissing through the twilight. It was the Silver Corporal's weird rope. The heavy honda caught the rearmost breed on the temple. The man dropped without a sound.

The rope coiled backward from the man's head like a winged serpent. A hand encased in a glove of velvet and white silk arrested it in midair.

The other breed heard the squawk of snow, frozen sand-hard, as his companion fell upon it. He whirled, pawing out a revolver as he did so.

He saw the white blur that was the Silver Corporal. He lifted his gun, finger tightening in the trigger guard.

But the weapon never discharged. There came a metallic song—like a piano key touched softly. The strange white rope for an instant was taut as a rod. The steel blade on its smaller end all but passed through the breed's body. Then it sprang back out of the terrible wound it had made. The breed was dead before his form fell and steamed in the frigid twilight. There had been no sound.

The Silver Corporal bent over the packs, inspecting their contents.

His gasp of surprise at what he found shot a long plume of breath steam against the whooping polar gale.

He concealed the packs in the snow nearby. He switched the surface of the drift with his white rope so no trace of where he had hidden them would remain.

The unconscious breed seemed to lift on a weirdly distorted snow pile and rush away. A hundred yards distant, he was lowered. Hands, hard as steel because of the bone and tendon from which they were made, slapped him until pain awakened him.

"Where are the girl and Ferrick?"

The breed shivered as the tiny, wispy voice of the Silver Corporal throbbed into his ears.

"Non!" he snarled. "Me—I don' know!"

Awful fingers seized the breed. They inflicted agony such as the villainous fellow had never felt before.

"Cough up!" said the wee voice that was like a whisper of death.

But the breed had courage, such as it was. He was fully conscious now, too. His brain was working. He pulled what seemed to him like a clever piece of brain work.

"Ferrick ees got de gal een cabin down by de lakeshore." The breed pointed. "Over dat way!"

The Silver Corporal poised over him a while. Then he was gone!

The breed weaved upon his feet. His head whirled. The first time he tried to run, he staggered a crazy circle. Then he got lined out. He ran as though that strange little silver-haired hoodoo pursued him.

He even looked back to make sure this wasn't a fact. He saw nothing.

He should have looked to the right and a bit ahead. For the Silver Corporal was running there. He hadn't wanted to waste a half hour or so scaring the breed into telling the truth. He didn't like to torture men, anyway.

So he was letting the breed lead the way. The Silver Corporal's rope balanced easily in his hand as he raced along.

Down into a deep valley sprinted the breed. It was almost a canyon. The opposite wall was a sheer cliff nearly half a thousand feet high!

The man veered to the left. He waded through scrub willows, up to his neck in snow. So taut were his nerves that he let out a bawl of sheer terror when a covey of ptarmigan roared out of the snow about him.

He stumbled over near the hulking cliff. So steep was the precipice that it seemed to overhang and blot out the cold-congealed gray sky with its puny flickerings of Northern Lights that were like varicolored candle flames guttering in the frigid wind.

A ramshackle cabin poked its roof out of the snow and brush. The roof had been made steep to shed the snow. It had been shingled with slabs adzed off logs. But many of the shingles were gone and the rafters shone through like the boiled ribs of a skeleton.

The cabin door gaped open. It framed a man—one of the breeds. Firelight behind the man painted the door around him with shuffling scarlet, as though it were the lurid mouth of hades.

"What de hell ails yo'?" he shouted. He had heard his comrade squawl when the ptarmigan roared up.

"Sacre–" The running breed pitched into the cabin with such speed that he skidded half across it trying to stop. "De Silver Corporal! Hees keel man who ees wit' me! Hees almos' keel me!"

"Yo' ees nuts!" said the other breed expressively. But he hauled out a Webley automatic revolver. He wished Ferrick were here.

"Non, non! Me—I tell yo' de Silver Corporal deed not die under de ice! Hees alive an' ees hunt fo' de gal—"

No doubt the man had a lot more to say. But he had been watching the open door. He saw a blurring, tumbling mass of white seemingly fill the door. He screeched like a banshee.

He seized the Webley from his comrade. The weapon clamored at the door. Bullets blasted through the white mass outside the opening. Yet the slugs had no apparent effect. They brought no moan of agony. They drew no gushing streams of crimson as good bullets should have.

The white mass before the door simply faded away. It was like nothing so much as a curtain that had fallen to the snow in front of the aperture.

The breed goggled. He might as well have shot at a ghost.

Sound came from his side. A choke, a hiss! He whirled.

His companion lay dead beside him. Like a long and thin needle, the Silver Corporal's white rope stretched upward from the body.

The breed would have fired some more. But his Webley was empty. He sprang for the door. He hated to leave that way. But he liked less the idea of remaining in this cabin of fantastic death.

He took two bounds. From over his head, a white figure flashed down. It landed with both feet astride his shoulders. A little steel club of a fist swung.

The breed was senseless before he hit the floor. He had no time to realize that flurry of white he had seen before the door was simply snow the Silver Corporal had shoved off the roof.

For, to one of the Silver Corporal's agility, it was a simple matter to leap to the roof. It was even simpler to shove off the snow, then launch the blade on his rope, spearlike, into the vitals of the first breed, and a moment later to spring upon the last of the pair. The shingles gone from the roof had left big holes.

The Silver Corporal raced pale blue eyes about the cabin.

The girl lay in a corner. Ida Thorne—for she could be no one but Ida Thorne, who was bringing in the reindeer herd—was bound tightly.

The Silver Corporal retrieved his rope. He glided toward her.

Another man might have paused to drink in the ravishing beauty of the girl. Women of beauty were more scarce in the Northland than cases of heat-stroke. Women of Ida Thorne's exquisite attractiveness were scarce in any man's country. She would have been a knockout at either Pole, and in between.

The Silver Corporal cut her free. He didn't say anything. And that wasn't because he was trying to be the strong, silent man, either. He didn't know what to say. He hadn't spoken to a white woman in months. In truth, he was a bit scared of them.

The girl stood up. She was taller than the Silver Corporal. She rubbed her wrists and ankles—something a man other than the Silver Corporal would have done for her. She broke the conversational ice.

"Thanks," she said, and her voice had volume and music. "When I saw you break through that thin ice, I thought you were gone. I tried to scream and warn you."

The little officer grinned like a Cheshire cat. His face didn't look so thin when he grinned. The white grease paint on it made him resemble a pleasant little clown. The rope in his hand, one steel-fanged end wet and steaming with blood, took away his funny aspect, though.

"Supposin' you tell me what this is all about," his wee voice whispered through the cabin.

That was the Silver Corporal—all business.

"I don't get paid for these reindeer until I deliver them," said the girl. "Ferrick and the others were hired by an Alaskan mining company to keep me from delivering them. They don't want me to get hold of the money."

"Why?"

The answer was postponed.

Ferrick bounded in the cabin door. He discharged his pistol at the Silver Corporal's back.

The Silver Corporal heard Ferrick. He had time to turn a little. It was enough. Ferrick's bullet only goosed a tuft of rabbit fur off his white parka.

The deadly rope came alive. The steel-armed end licked hungrily through the air at Ferrick's throat.

But luck rode with Ferrick at that instant. He dodged successfully. The blade passed him.

It spiked into the chest of a breed that came through the door behind him. The breed folded down.

Five more evil-faced fellows hurdled his body on their way inside. They flourished arms. Ferrick had most of his gang along.

They closed in on the Silver Corporal, watching his deadly rope.

"Don't shoot the runt unless you gotta!" ripped Ferrick.

One threw a pistol. The little policeman dodged it. The weapon caromed off the wall and the girl pounced on it.

Ferrick ran to her, knocked her down. The blow he delivered came whistling from far behind his back. He didn't mind hitting a woman. In fact, he liked it. Their soft flesh didn't hurt his knuckles.

He liked the promptness with which the girl fell unconscious. It made him feel he packed dynamite in his fists.

The next instant Ferrick let out a screech. His dying wail wouldn't be louder, more terrible. With incredible speed, the Silver Corporal had built a loop in his white rope and snared Ferrick's arm. He jerked.

Ferrick's arm broke with a noise like a stopper coming out of a bottle. Ligaments were rent. Only by a narrow margin did the arm stay on his body.

Ferrick sailed across the cabin. His luck still held and he got his good arm before his head. That saved his brains from being dashed out on the cabin logs.

A little white ermine of a man who moved with dazzling speed, the Silver Corporal loosed his white rope, cast the noose again. Hissing, opening widely, the loop settled over two breeds, tightened on them. The caterwauling breeds thought for an instant they were going to be merged into one messy pulp.

"Kill 'im!" Ferrick squawled.

That wasn't necessary. A rifle stock swung. It made a sound like dry wood snapping on the Silver Corporal's head. He sagged.

A breed leaped feet-first onto the little policeman's midriff. The man struck with a pistol. He struck again.

He kept on belaboring until the Silver Corporal was only a white pile on the floor that welled steaming scarlet.

Ferrick staggered over. He was crying like a spanked baby, so great was the agony in his arm. He kicked the prostrate little form. But that wasn't very satisfactory. The tiny body was hard as iron, and hurt his toes through his flexible *muck-a-lucks*

"He ain't a stiff yet," Ferrick whimpered. "But he damn soon will be! Tie 'im up! Tie the damn woman up, too!"

The breeds did the tying. They used for the job a bundle of rawhide thongs of the type employed for filling snowshoes. They took many turns of the tough thews.

"That'll hold 'im!" Every one of Ferrick's words was a moan because of his pain. He splinted his arm after a fashion, slinging it to his chest inside his parka. He pointed at two of his breeds. "You guys stay here!"

"Oui," they nodded. But they looked uneasy.

"Aw, don't be so leery," sneered Ferrick. "He don't breathe fire!"

"Maybee not," mumbled a breed. "But dey say hees no can be keeled."

"The next guy who mentions that crazy story is gonna get my fist hung on his kisser!" Ferrick snarled vitriolically. "Now listen, you monks. Get this!"

They snapped to attention. Especially the two who were to stay.

"You two guys will stick right here. The rest of us will go stampede the reindeer herd. You'll be able to hear the roar of the herd comin'. That's your cue to knock the Silver Corporal an' the girl over the head. You savvy that—knock 'em over the conks!"

The pair bobbed their heads like Punch and Judy on a ventriloquist's knee.

"After you bang 'em on the bean," Ferrick continued evilly, "You cut off their bonds in a hurry. Make sure they're unconscious first, though. When they're untied, you two beat it."

He took time out to kick the little body of the Silver Corporal. He used his heel. That didn't hurt so much.

"The reindeer herd pilin' over the cliff will smash in this cabin," he concluded. "The shack is right under the edge. These two will be crushed under a few hundred tons of reindeer meat. Then, when their bodies are found, it'll look like they was caught when the herd stampeded."

The breeds grinned in nasty appreciation. This Ferrick was a smart devil.

Their idol saw their admiration. He got a hold on himself, and worked out his pipe with one hand, filled it and lighted it. The effort put a sweat-grease on his forehead. He blew as much smoke out of the pipe bowl as he drew into his lungs. He was suffering.

He went over and picked up the white rope, using two fingers, as though it were a poisonous snake. He leered at his men.

"Any of you cookies want this for a souvenir?"

They didn't. They'd rather have packed around a couple of nice rattlesnakes.

Ferrick threw the rope on the floor. It writhed like a thing alive and became a quiet, coiled pile.

"C'mon, pals," he clipped, and weaved outside.

The breeds followed, except for the two of their number detailed to remain behind.

These two breeds didn't like the job. When the Silver Corporal rolled over, they both jumped on him with their feet. They kicked him. He kicked back, but feebly. He did flounce about on the floor quite a bit, though.

When the Silver Corporal lay quiet, they desisted. They could tell by his open, roving eyes that he was still conscious.

Not once had his wee, whispering voice spoken.

The girl revived. She did not speak either.

The two breeds sauntered about and made remarks about the girl. They weren't nice remarks.

The breeds didn't know it, but the little pleasantries they were exchanging signed their death warrant. The Silver Corporal was a Wyoming cow waddy by breed. Down in his country, men died violently for making cracks like these.

The tiny policeman moved a little. His floundering scuffle with the breeds had brought him over to the rope. They hadn't noticed it, but he was lying on the coils.

And while they strolled around and talked big, the razor-edged fang of steel had sliced through the tyings of his wrists and ankles.

A breed came over to kick the little man again. And suddenly he seemed to acquire a gaping red hinge in his middle!

The only sound was a hiss, a thud. The man toppled.

The other breed bellowed and flourished his gun simultaneously.

The rope, weighted by the heavy blade, swung once around the little officer's silver head. It made a shrill squeal of a sound. Then, with an accuracy that had come from years of practice, it speared through the air at the breed.

The man dodged successfully. But he had no time to fire. The Silver Corporal rushed him. The white rope looped in midair, trapped the breed's gun arm. The weapon snorted lead into the floor. The rope honda swung like a rock on a string and caught the breed's head. He went down.

Over to the girl glided the Silver Corporal. He cut her free with the red blade; then, with what seemed like a single gesture, he coiled the strange white rope.

"C'mon!" he said. He didn't believe in wasting words.

She ran with him across the valley. He accommodated his pace to hers. She was a good runner, and didn't barge into deep snow often. Then she dragged back.

"My reindeer herd!" she choked. "Ferrick and the others are going to stampede the deer over the cliff! They're going to wipe out every animal. They—"

She stopped. She was talking to empty air. The Silver Corporal was gone, and she didn't quite know where.

Probably that was mean of him. He could have taken a couple of minutes and explained what he was going to do. But he wasn't used to arguing with women.

She wandered about. She didn't know what to do. She was unarmed. The Silver Corporal had not even bothered to take the guns of the breeds he had finished. That puzzled her, set her to wondering if the little silver-haired man was quite human after all.

She decided to go get those guns. She plunged for the cabin under the cliff.

Then, as suddenly as he had vanished, the Silver Corporal was with her again.

He carried the two huge packs that had been toted by the breeds he vanquished—the packs he had hidden in the snow. Under their bulk, he looked like a tiny white ant struggling with a couple of big brown crumbs.

"C'mon," he said briefly.

They found a place to climb the cliff. It took them fifteen minutes. And it was a climb that set their lungs on fire.

From the cliff top, they could see the reindeer herd. The deer were bedded down in a vast, open glade, which was buttressed around by spruce.

The Silver Corporal looked them over. An appreciative grunt shot his breath steam into the wind. There were thousands of the animals. Their antlers—both male and female had antlers—were like a thick, bare brush.

"Looks kinda like a Wyomin' dogie drive," his wee voice whispered.

"What did you say?" asked the girl. She hadn't caught his tiny tones.

He didn't answer. He was mean that way.

He could see, over to the right, the camp of the Eskimo deer drivers. They had thrown up a snow igloo. Not a man of the Inuit herdsmen was in sight. Doubtless they slept inside.

Beyond the deer herd, he thought he could see men scampering through the spruce. A match flamed.

For a long moment, the Silver Corporal hung motionless. Then he saw the match was being applied to Ferrick's pipe.

"Whew!" he murmured in his small voice. "For a minute, that had me worried."

The girl heard him this time.

"How are they going to stampede my deer?" she asked.

"I'll show you," he replied.

He raced along the cliff edge. The hooting polar gale had swept the rocky earth free of snow here.

He lowered his packs, opened them. Red packages came to light. He tore loose the wrappings of these.

Then he asked questions. "Why don't the gang that hired Ferrick want you to collect for the deer?"

"They own a mining company in Alaska." The girl's strong, musical voice was rapid. "They want some good placer mining leases I own. They'll have the chance to get them if I can't get the money to do the work necessary to hold them. The money I need was to come from these deer. Without it—I'm sunk! And they get the placer leases."

The Silver Corporal worked rapidly. He strung the contents of his packages along the rocky ground, very close to the edge of the resting reindeer herd.

The girl watched him. As she saw what the packages held, her attractive brown eyes widened.

"Oh!" she gasped. "So that's how they're going to stampede my deer! They were going to use—"

But the Silver Corporal had struck a match, and a deafening roar drowned out her words.

The roar came from a firecracker. The next instant gory blobs of flame jumped from a Roman candle and raced at the peaceful reindeer.

The packs had held ordinary Fourth-of-July fireworks!

The Silver Corporal handed the girl the Roman candle. He lighted another and gave that one to her, too.

"Keep'm goin'," he advised. He ignited a pinwheel and hung it on a tree. The sparks set the tree on fire. But that didn't matter. There couldn't be much of a forest fire in this country.

Excitement rolled over the deer herd. Antlers tossed. The animals milled.

Eskimo herdsmen popped out of their igloo. They ogled the fireworks. Maybe they had never seen fireworks before. Or maybe they figured the big *tongak* mainspring devil of their superstitious religion, had sent some of his pet fiends to pay them a visit.

Whatever it was, they turned tail and fled.

The deer herd heaved into motion. Panic seized the creatures. They stampeded.

Straight for Ferrick and his breeds, preparing their own fireworks in the spruces beyond the glade, the deer thundered.

Ferrick and his gang cut loose with rifles. That was useless. They lighted their fireworks, such as were in place. But they were too late with that.

The reindeer numbered thousands. They were worse than a cattle stampede to be in front of. The spruce were not tall enough to offer safe perches.

Ferrick and his gang tried a desperate plan. They made a human wedge. Rifles flaming, they tried to cut through the stampeding deer herd.

Animal after animal veered aside from them. But those behind and to the sides crowded in blindly.

Ferrick and his breeds were suddenly engulfed.

Where they had vanished, a heaving sort of a knot lasted for a time, as deer leaped their squirming bodies. But before long, the knot smoothed out as the men beneath became a gory pulp, and nothing disturbed the rushing torrent of antlers.

The Silver Corporal discovered abruptly that the girl was looking away from the ghastly sight.

He faced the other direction with her.

"The deer probably won't run far," he told her in his strange, soft voice.

"No—they probably won't." She choked on the words.

After that, her knees buckled slightly. She swayed a bit, and felt blindly for the little form of the Silver Corporal. It was instinctive, the way his arms got about her.

But he didn't know the thing she wanted was to be held in his arms and petted and comforted and maybe kissed some.

The Silver Corporal—the sap—led her to a rock and set her down and threw cold snow in her warm, pretty, inviting face.

He was scared of women, anyway.

• • • • •

Appendix A–

A Bonus Silver Corporal Story

Death Cache

A man stood spraddle-legged in the snow and shuddered again and again. The sweat of an overpowering terror steamed on his fat face. His teeth rattled.

He was stocky, well-fed, sleek, this man who stood too stricken by fright to move. He was a white man, yet native beadwork was plastered thick on his parka, on his bearskin trousers, and on his knee-high moccasins.

The man stared fixedly at a snow drift in front of him. Slowly, as if it hurt, he brought his rifle to his shoulder. No wind stirred the snow. Spruce boughs popped with the cold. The sky was gray, glazed, like the inside of an ice-cake igloo, a little smoked by clouds in the south.

He aimed his rifle at the drift—at a patch a yard across, where the snow was roughened, as though recently stirred with a stick. The rifle slammed a bullet into the drift. The shot sound collided with spruce thickets, with a nearby hill, and bounced back like a hundred lesser shots. Again the man fired, and again and again until his carbine was empty.

He drew a knife. Screaming madly, he sprang into the drift to stab and slash at the roughened snow. The blade dug deep, rasped on the frozen ground beneath.

Greater terror wracked the man as he found nothing in the snow. He reloaded his rifle and emptied it, shooting at many parts of the drift. But nothing happened—only the echoes that galloped around like roaring, unseen animals.

The man whirled and ran. He fell down in the deep snow, got up, fell again. It was as though he were living in a horrible dream, one of those nightmares in which the victim may try and try to flee, but cannot.

"He-l-p!" shrieked the man. Then he took to screaming madly at the bleak, empty wilderness about him. "Lemme alone, damn you! I ain't doin' nothin'! You keep away from me!"

The echoes mouthed the wild words faintly.

But there was no sign of the mysterious thing that had driven the fat man mad with fear.

The fellow floundered out of the snowdrift. He plunged away with headlong blindness. Through a spruce thicket, boughs rasping his beaded garments, he dived. He reached a little clearing.

Seven men waited there, breeds and whites. An evil-faced, puzzled group, every man gripped a cocked rifle.

"The Silver Corporal!" bawled the running man. "I just saw him!"

Out of the grouped seven stepped their leader—gaunt Le Bouc.

Le Bouc had chin-whiskers like those of a billygoat. They looked comical. But no one ever laughed. Not at Le Bouc!

He was a fiend, this bony man with the goat whiskers. Nobody was sure how old he was. The Indians claimed he'd prowled the northland for a hundred years, and that he'd never die, because when he did, he'd be sure to take charge of hell. And since the devil reigning down there didn't want that to happen, he took pains to see that Le Bouc remained alive on earth.

Maybe the natives exaggerated. But they knew Le Bouc.

"Sacre!" Le Bouc raged. "What thees t'ing you say, Beautiful?"

"The Silver Corporal!" The fat, scared man called Beautiful waved his arms and steam came from his mouth with his words. "I seen 'im, I tell you! He rose right up out of a drift not forty feet from me! He looked right at me. I saw the starved face of 'im, his silver hair, and a thing coiled in his hand that looked like a white snake fifty feet long! And then he was gone!"

Beautiful flung up a pudgy hand—snapped fat fingers. "Just like that, he went! Right into the snow! And I shot the drift full of holes, and jumped in and cut it to pieces with my knife. But there wasn't nobody there!"

"Wheech prove you ees crazy!" sneered Le Bouc. "You crazy wit' de cold!"

"I ain't nuts, Le Bouc! I saw him plain as I see you. A little shriveled guy. It was the Silver Corporal! Why, even that infernal thing in his hand crawled around like it was alive—!"

"Shut up!" Le Bouc swiveled slowly to glower at his men and his evil eyes widened with surprise. For on the faces of some of his men terror was stamped.

Two especially, the Tromso twins, had drawn apart. Back in their native Sweden there was a standing reward of many thousands of *kronas* for these Tromso twins. They were small-faced, slender weasels of men. They looked like two slim boys. One was minus all his teeth.

"Silver Corporal bane bad medicine," muttered the one who had no teeth. "Aye t'ank we bane go 'way."

"Canards! You ees start dis t'ing an' you ees got to go t'rough wit' it!" snarled Le Bouc. He began to stroke his goat whiskers. The Tromso twins turned deathly pale and stumbled over themselves to get back with the others. When Le Bouc stroked his whiskers—that was a sign of death.

"Who ees dis Silver Corporal?" growled Le Bouc. "He ees Mounted Policeman, *non?"*

"You ain't never heard of him?" asked Beautiful, with hanging jaw.

"Oui! I hear talk. But she crazy talk—talk dat not make sense. Dey say hees ghost of de snow, dat hees no can be killed, dat hees whip whole Indian tribe wit' de bare hands, dat hees no carry de gun. Such talk ees damn foolishness!"

"That's all true!" whined Beautiful. "It's a fact! Nobody knows any more'n that about the Silver Corporal, except that he's a Mountie. They say he can smell devilment, that he always turns up where there's trouble. Well, I believe it. He's found out what we're goin' to do to this Rhoda Dunsay girl. An' he's here!"

"Show us where you see heem!" rapped Le Bouc.

"Listen, I don't want to go back there—!"

Beautiful choked on his whimpering objection. For Le Bouc was again pawing his whiskers. Beautiful had seen men drop dead when that happened. Trembling and sweating, he led the others back to the drift into which he had plunged his bullets and his knife.

Le Bouc was canny. First, he circled the drift, following the clearing edge, hunting tracks. Leafless limbs jutted over the snowdrift, casting cold, pale shadows. Nowhere was there tracks, except those of Beautiful.

"You crazy!" sneered Le Bouc. "You no see anybody!"

"I did! I'm tellin' you the Silver Corporal has learned about this Rhoda Dunsay girl—!"

"Shut up! No dam' man can walk in de snow wit'out hees leave de tracks. You crazy an' t'ink you see sometting, an' you start shooting. Now let me tell you one t'ing—you act like dis again, and—!"

Le Bouc fondled his beard. Beautiful shook from head to foot, but said no word. He knew he was near death.

"We go make plan, catch dis Mam'selle Rhoda Dunsay!" leered Le Bouc.

They wheeled, strode off. Le Bouc didn't look back. The others did. But they saw nothing, and the snowdrift was soon lost in the spruce.

A few minutes later, something happened in the clearing that they would have found of great interest. A small upheaval occurred in the snowdrift, far from the spot where Beautiful's bullets and knife had probed. And when the upheaval was over, a strange little man-figure stood there in the snow. His face looked drawn and scrawny. His hair waved erect in a great shock, the color of burnished silver.

His fur garments were unusual. Parka, trousers, both were tailored from the white fur of snowshoe rabbits. His *muck-a-lucks* were dyed white; his belt was of white leather. His clothing was thin, light. It seemed entirely insufficient to cope with the bitter cold.

He made a weird, mysterious figure there in the snow. He was almost child-like in his smallness. And a passerby would have had to look with a sharp eye to see him at all.

But by far the most remarkable thing about him was the object he carried in one hand. This was nearly forty feet long, thin and white and tough as a violin string. A heavy brass lassrope honda weighted one end. But the thing was no ordinary lass rope, for it tapered in the fashion of a bullwhip, and the thin end terminated in a double-edged blade of steel, honed to a razor keenness on both edges.

The strange white rope seemed to come alive in the tiny man's hands. It crawled about. A loop, formed in the honda end, climbed upward and outward and settled snug on an overhanging limb.

With a bewildering agility, the mysterious little man climbed the rope. He reached the limb, ran along it with the ease of a squirrel, and with a swing across space that an onlooker would have sworn impossible, he reached another tree and was lost in the spruces.

There was left behind only a scuffed place in the snowdrift to show where the Silver Corporal had departed.

Goat-whiskered Le Bouc had halted his men a couple of hundred yards distant. He was giving them orders.

"De gal weel be along soon," he said. "We mus' mak' ready grab her. Now, de firs' t'ing ees—"

He never got to say what the first thing was. The Tromso twins had drawn aside, two weasels out of the pack. Suddenly they both drew pistols.

"You men bane put hands up!" snapped the one who had teeth.

Le Bouc's face turned into a terrible thing to witness. He reached for his whiskers.

"Aye bane shoot!" warned the Tromso twin.

Le Bouc left his whiskers alone. He choked, snarled. *"Sacre!* W'at ees you t'ink you doing?"

"We t'ank we bane go away," said the Tromso twin who was toothless. "Aye bane hear plenty about dat Silver Corporal feller. Aye not like little bit. We bane go long way from here, and do him damn quick. After that aye not know where we ben go. To hell, maybe, huh?"

Both Tromso twins laughed at this wit. They backed away. The spruces received them, and they whirled and ran.

Hissing his rage, Le Bouc lunged after them, only to pull up with a disgusted snort.

"Bien!" he grunted. "She just as good dat we get rid of dem feller. We handle dis job alone. Den we not 'ave to divide up so many shares."

Four of Le Bouc's five remaining men, all four stolid ruffians, gave lip-smacking, greedy nods. The fifth—Beautiful—only gave a mighty shiver and wiped sweat off his face. He was thinking of the Silver Corporal.

Le Bouc scowled at Beautiful.

"You ees no damn good to 'ave aroun'!" he clipped. *"Sacre!* Dat be jus' like you to holler an' scare away de gal! So you better go down de trail t'ree mile. At dat point, de trail, she go t'rough a narrow canyon. You watch dere. De gal, should she get pas' us, you grab her!"

Beautiful quailed, pawing his beaded garments nervously. "Do I have to go alone? Maybe two of us ought to go an'—!"

"Depechez-vous!" hissed Le Bouc. "Hurry up!" And he touched his whiskers. Beautiful plunged away, going to wait at the point where the trail entered a narrow canyon, three miles distant.

"We weel wait 'ere!" Le Bouc grinned at the other four. "Dis place, she good as any. De gal be along soon. We grab her. Den, *bien.* Everyt'ing she rosy color."

One of the breeds smirked and fawned. *"Oui!* An' we don' have split wit' dem damn Tromso brotters. Good t'ing dey go!"

Le Bouc and his breeds would have changed their minds had they seen the Tromso brothers at this moment. That precious pair had circled back to the trail, reaching it at a point by which the girl should pass.

"Le Bouc, he tank he bane damn smart feller!" chuckled the Tromso brother who was without teeth. "He ain't smart as he bane tank he is."

"Yah," agreed the other. "We bane fool him. We make him tank we bane two scared fellers."

The first Tromso swept their surroundings with an involuntary glance. "Yumpin' yoe! You tank maybe Beautiful see Silver Corporal after all?"

"Naw. Beautiful bane coward. He no good for nothin' but play around with squaws. He bane go nuts."

Both twins stared along the trail, shading their eyes.

"Gal not in sight," said one. "Aye reckon it best we hurry, anyhow."

One Tromso now produced a piece of paper. He scribbled a note, using the snout of a .30-30 cartridge for a pencil. He had a lot of trouble with the note, neither twin being able to write much English. Afterwards he stuck the note in the split end of a stick and stabbed the stick upright in the middle of the trail.

"It bane easiest for us to grab gal here," suggested the one without teeth.

"Yah, sure!" snorted the other. "And dot Le Bouc feller would get us. Le Bouc bane bad monkey. Our other plan bane best one."

They moved away, seeking spots where no snow lay, so as not to leave tracks. Soon they were lost to sight.

From a boulder beside the trail stepped the tiny figure of the Silver Corporal. His strange, springy white rope with the razor-sharp blade on one end, the heavy brass honda on the other, dangled over one arm. It seemed a living, squirming thing.

A leap took him to another rock, a second leap to a fallen log, a third to the trail. He left no tracks. He inspected the note, and read:

> Miss Rhoda Dunsay,
>   Le Bouc and his breeds bane wait three hundred yards down trail for to grab you. Maybe it bane good idea to go around them fellers.
>
> A friend

The Silver Corporal replaced the note. His hands were bare to the bitter winds, yet they seemed flexible, impervious to the cold. He spoke suddenly to himself:

"This thing is gettin' to be a regular dang mystery!" His voice was strange—a wee, wispy, whispering thing, a sound as small as the man himself. But his words had a whang that smacked of the Wyoming cow country.

He glanced about. A couple of hundred feet away, a spruce tree towered. He moved to it, not once leaving a track. His weird, white rope looped upward, and a moment later he was perched in the tree, well-concealed among the evergreen boughs.

He watched the trail with eyes that were the same striking silver color as his hair.

Half an hour later a girl swung down the trail. She was wiry, long-limbed, athletic, young. Her eyes were large, brown. They swept warily from side to side. She carried a light tumpline backpack with the manner of one accustomed to it, and she gripped a short .30-30 carbine with both hands.

She discovered the note, but looked around alertly before approaching it. Then, after she read it, she stared about even more sharply.

The girl stepped off the trail. Her going was silent, expertly swift. She circled wide of the spot where Le Bouc and his breeds were supposed to be hidden, then returned to the trail, since the spruce grew very thick and the going was rough.

But the Tromso brothers had been wildly wrong on their distance count. Le Bouc and his gang were waiting more like half a mile down the trail. When the girl returned to the path, they saw her.

"Sacre!" Le Bouc bellowed. "Catch dat she-fox!"

The girl heard his roaring voice. She turned and fled with long, deter-mined strides. As she ran, she tied a scarf across her face, to keep the bitterly cold air from freezing her lung tissue.

Once she stopped.

"You won't get it!" she shrieked at the men behind. "I won't give it up!"

She jerked her rifle to shoulder, aimed to the left of the five pursuers, and fired. Le Bouc and his four took to shelter, but came on, although not as swiftly. They kept hands over their mouth, breathing into cupped palms to protect their own lungs from the freezing air.

"Beautiful weel get 'er!" gritted goat-whiskered Le Bouc. *"Bien!* Dat was lucky t'ing I did, sending heem on ahead!"

The chase lead on and on. A mile, then two. Once the fleeing girl wrenched the cloth from face, smacked it against a spruce limb to knock off the ice her breath had formed. Her features were Nordic. She had a large mouth and enough jaw to look determined. She had some freckles, but not too many.

She replaced the cloth and ran on. A ridge swelled up in her path. It was matted with spruce. Plunging into this growth, the girl was lost completely from view.

Le Bouc's men approached the thicket warily. They were excellent targets, should the girl be waiting with her Winchester. But no bullets met them, and they worked through the matted spruce.

The running figure of the girl was now not more than two hundred yards ahead. The trail angled down into a canyon.

"I 'ave tell Beautiful to wait een dat canyon!" hissed Le Bouc. "Hees damn well bettair be dere!"

"Hees dere!" shouted one of the breeds. "Look!"

The fleeing girl had passed between two large boulders. A man was concealed behind them. He sprang out, took two lunging jumps. With both arms, he swung a clubbed rifle. The blow hit with a thud that reached Le Bouc's ears. The runner dropped like a shot rabbit, face-down in the snow.

"Cochon!" screamed Le Bouc. "You ees strike too hard! We don' wan' keel her until she ees tell us de t'ing we wan' to know!"

"Aw—hell! My foot slipped!" Beautiful whined back.

Le Bouc galloped up. He stared frantically at the body. Crimson was puddling about the head jammed in the snow. It steamed in grisly fashion from the scarf-swathed head.

Le Bouc dropped to his knees and grasped the hand of the fallen form, apparently with the idea of shucking off the scarf. But his hands seemed to become paralyzed, and he slowly kneaded the head under his fingers—it was horribly shapeless, like a broken egg.

"You 'ave bust her skull!" he screeched at Beautiful. He lurched to his feet. He yelled. He made mad gestures with his arms. He cursed. "You 'ave keel her! You damn fool! Dis a pret' kettle of feesh! Everyt'ing ees spoiled!"

And then Le Bouc grabbed at his goat whiskers.

Beautiful screamed like a hurt child. He knew what this meant. "Jeeze! Please don't! Please—!"

Out from under Le Bouc's beard came a nasty little black derringer. He kept it in a necklace-like sheath on his upper chest. He pointed it at Beautiful.

What came next surprised everybody. There was a strange sound, an abrupt, serpentine hiss of a sound. Le Bouc's gun arm jerked to the right. He was wrenched entirely off his feet. For an instant, he sailed through the air like a piece of paper on the end of a string. Then he slammed to the snow.

Came a low swish, and the uncanny thing that had seized Le Bouc's arm disengaged itself, slipped away through the snow. They all saw it—a thing like a thin, racing chalk line! A white rope!

"De Silver Corporal!"

Beautiful whirled and ran. Head down, breath tearing shrilly through his teeth, he plunged away. The breeds shot hateful stares in search of their phantom foe. One thought he saw something, lifted his gun. But there was a swishing sound, and a thin white snake seemed to strike from behind a boulder, a snake fanged with a razor-sharp sliver of glistening steel. The stroke ended with a *chuck!* The breed bleated in agony for his right hand was suddenly hanging to his arm by only a hinge of hide.

"Rush heem!" bellowed Le Bouc.

His men charged the boulder, bounding around it from their side. But there was no Silver Corporal behind.

Another breed piped out in pain. Blood poured steaming from his shoulder. There had been no swish that time, no warning

"You no can see heem!" the man wailed. Then he turned and fled, along with his cohorts.

Le Bouc chased after them, howling, *"Cochons!* Cowards! Why you run away? De Silver Corporal don' even carry a gun!"

But Le Bouc showed no wish to remain and fight alone.

About the time the fugitives were lost to view in the spruce, the Silver Corporal appeared from behind a boulder. He ran to the form Beautiful had clubbed down. He wanted to see if the girl was really beyond help. He shucked off the wet red scarf.

"Hell's little tinkle-bells!" he gulped.

The dead person was not the girl, but the toothless Tromso twin.

The Silver Corporal reached up absently and finger-combed his shock of silver hair.

"Wearin' the woman's rig," he mused, the whang of a Wyoming range waddy more than ever in his wee voice. "Changed with her somewhere durin' the chase—probably in that spruce patch back a piece."

The weird white rope of a thing writhed on the Mountie's scarlet-coated arm, as if seized by rage. Wheeling, the strange little trooper ran from the spot. He did not follow the fleeing man, but went in the opposite direction, deeper into the canyon. His eyes searched alertly.

He soon found what he half expected—the end of a cord hidden beside the trail. He considered, then pulled it.

Instantly there was a roar high up on the canyon wall. Thousands of tons of rocks, snow and gravel poured down loosened by dynamite. Had anyone been coming along the trail, he certainly would have met death.

Many things became clear.

"The whole gang is after somethin' the girl has got," the Silver Corporal told himself in his small voice. "The Tromso twins double-crossed the others and left the note to get the girl ahead of Le Bouc. They knew he'd eventually follow her. The Tromsos grabbed her in that spruce patch, and one put on the girl's outer duds and came ahead to lead Le Bouc and his breeds into this death trap. Yeah, sure. But the Tromsos didn't know Beautiful was hidin' ahead."

The Silver Corporal knew all these men, their names and reputation. He knew most of the crooks in the North country. They, in turn, were not aware that he knew them, did not know he spent a lot of time just tagging them around. The couldn't understand the uncanny way he had of turning up just when they were in the middle of some devilment.

He was a man of mystery, this Silver Corporal. His ways were strange, the things he did even stranger. He hadn't been in the Northland long. But men who walked outside the law were beginning to curse the mention of his name, and shake in their moccasins when they heard he was in their vicinity. And sometimes they were seized with a wild madness on days when the wind went whispering across the snow and through the spruces and made sounds like the phantom Mountie's wee, small voice.

The Silver Corporal climbed over the debris blown into the canyon by the planted dynamite. He gave the dead form of the toothless Tromo twin only one glance, then went on past it and entered the spruce thicket where he was certain the Tromsos had seized the girl, Rhoda Dunsay.

In the spruces, he found the other Tromso twin, the one who had teeth. The man sat against a tree. He sat as though asleep. But it was a sleep from which only the devil's pitchfork would awaken him.

A knife stuck like a thorn from the man's heart.

The Silver Corporal did something that was rare for him—he shuddered. The eerie white rope of a weapon coiled over his arm seemed to shudder with him, as though it lived with him, exulting when he was pleased, suffering when he was pained.

The Silver Corporal was a Wyoming product. Down there, they put their women on pedestals, and all of the sex were considered sweet and good. It shocked the strange little man to think that one of them would stick a knife in a man's heart.

Of course, the girl might not have knifed the Tromso twin. The snow was too scoured by feet to tell a story. Prints made by the girl and others made by men were mingled together. Le Bouc and his breeds might even have come upon the Tromso twin and his young woman prisoner, killed the twin and taken the girl.

The Silver Corporal began to circle the spot, his metallic eyes roving alertly It would be no trouble to trail everyone who had been near this spot. But he followed no trail at the moment.

The Mountie's eyes were sharp. They missed little of what went on about him—they missed so precious little that the Indians had taken to claiming it was not human eyesight at all which he possessed, but thousands of eyes scattered all over the north so they saw everything all men did, even things done in the privacy of a cabin, tent or igloo. The Indians, however, are addicted to tall tales and legends.

The Silver Corporal saw the blue-black snout of a rifle crawl from behind a tree. He moved so quickly that he seemed to vanish momentarily and reappear a couple of yards from where he had stood. The rifle coughed a bullet that missed him.

Hunkering down, he sped to the nearest snowdrift and went into it headfirst, as a diver enters water.

Out of the surrounding spruces popped Le Bouc, Beautiful and the four breeds. Beautiful was still shaking and sweating, afraid to flee from the gang. The breed whose hand had fallen victim to the Silver Corporal's strange, deadly weapon staggered pitifully along in the rear. He had torn off his hand, thrown it away and bound up the stump. It was a wonder he was able to walk.

"After heem!" bawled Le Bouc. "Get heem!"

Le Bouc had, by curse and threat, pursued his men to come back and fight the Silver Corporal. They scattered to the far side of the drift. Shooting into the snow, stabbing with knives, they advanced.

But the Silver Corporal had expected that. He reappeared only a few feet from where he had entered the drift. None of the men saw him, for he scooted along, half buried in the snow. The spruces took him into their shelter.

He halted there to watch.

"Sacre Dieu!" gritted Le Bouc, right hand always on his goat-like whiskers. "We must keel heem!"

Bullets ripped through and through the snow.

Suddenly, in front of Le Bouc, there was a commotion in the snow. A figure stood up unsteadily.

"Don't shoot!" screamed Le Bouc as his men leveled rifles.

The figure was that of the girl, Rhoda Dunsay. She was bound hand and foot with hide thongs; a wad of handkerchief silenced her jaws.

Le Bouc pounced upon the girl with a gleeful gurgle. *"Bien!* The Bon *Dieu* ees treat me swell!"

He seized her bound figure and threw her down. The others crowded around.

"What ees happen?" Le Bouc demanded of the girl, ungagging her.

"The Tromso twins seized me," she said in a voice coldly steady. "One of them stabbed the other to death, so he would not have to divide the loot. Then he took my outer garments and went off to lead you into a death trap."

The girl wore fuzzy brown woolen trousers, a woolen sweater, the garb that had been under her fur clothing.

"You fellers hunt de Silver Corporal!" Le Bouc rapped at his men.

They scattered, leaving the girl bound in the snow. They hunted fifteen minutes, but found nothing. They never even noticed where the Silver Corporal had entered the spruce—for the ghostlike lawman had a way of swishing his strange white rope over the snow behind him, smoothing it out until there remained hardly a trace that it had been disturbed.

Le Bouc came back and leered at the girl. "You mus' tell me where de cache is, *mam'selle!"*

The girl looked at her scurvy captor. She shivered. "I'll tell you. I don't want to be tortured."

Le Bouc wasn't fooled. He sneered at her. "You t'ink de Silver Corporal weel help you, eh? *Non!* He weel never get you from Le Bouc!"

"I said I'd show you the cache," Rhoda Dunsay repeated.

"Bien! We weel keep de gun pointed at you head, an' should de Silver Corporal show heemself, de brains weel be blow' out of you pret' head!"

Le Bouc said this loudly—fairly screamed it. He wanted the Silver Corporal to hear that threat.

Taking the girl, leaving the body of the Tromso twins behind to freeze solid, they went down the trail. Two miles brought them to Le Bouc's hidden camp—to his sled and dog team.

They tied the girl on the sled, bundling her in furs. They didn't want her to die of cold before they were through with her.

Le Bouc indicated the breed that had lost a hand.

"You stay wit' sled an' guard de gal. Keep you gun press' tight to her pret' head. Should de Silver Corporal come, you shoot de gal. Savvy!"

The breed nearly fell over when he nodded. The loss of the hand had about done him in.

"Now we go take one more look fo' dat Silver Corporal!" rumbled Le Bouc.

They made a thorough job of the looking. They tramped the trail, the adjacent wilderness, hunting for tracks. They saw none.

Back to the sled they went. But the instant the sled was in sight, Le Bouc emitted a howl.

The one-handed breed was sprawled face-down in the snow.

Le Bouc sprang forward, crying, "De Silver Corporal ees get de gal!"

Then, observing a form squirming in the bundled furs on the sledge, he sucked in a sigh of relief

"Non! De gal still dere." He bent over the motionless breed, picked up the fellow's wrist, dropped it. "De dam' fool, hees pass out from dat hurt hand."

Le Bouc considered further, than announced they'd leave the breed there for the wolves. It'd be one less to share. He addressed the sled.

"Where ees de cache?"

Muffled, made barely understandable, a faint, shrill voice came out of the bundled furs. "Five miles along the trail, a cabin on the right. I'll tell you the exact spot when we get there."

"Bien!" said Le Bouc, much pleased. "We go to dat cabin!"

They hooked the dogs to the sledge and departed swiftly, callously leaving the wounded breed behind for the cold and the wolves.

The fat man called Beautiful brought up the rear. His beaded garments rasped together faintly as he trotted. An ugly hate burned in his eyes, flaming hottest when he looked at Le Bouc. His eyes held something else, too. Suspicion: a suspicion that the girl, Rhoda Dunsay, wasn't in that bundle of furs on the sled. Le Bouc had not looked inside them.

Beautiful, a leer on his round face, decided that the Silver Corporal had kayoed the breed guard, freed the girl from the sledge, and taken her place.

A horrible thought: It hit Beautiful like the palsy. But he said nothing about what he suspected. He, Beautiful, the white man who liked to play around with the native squaws, would hang back, let the Silver Corporal vanquish Le Bouc and the others. Then Beautiful would shoot the Silver Corporal and have the contents of the cache for himself. He had a gun, a revolver. Le Bouc hadn't taken it. Le Bouc had apparently forgotten he had been on the point of killing Beautiful.

The cache! There should be a fortune there—wealth in furs and gold dust. Five trappers had been returning from the new gold country to the west, carrying their fur catch—and the cleanup from a rich placer gold stream they had found.

They had camped, unknowingly, in a cabin whose last occupant had died of smallpox. All five had been taken down with the dread disease. Four had died immediately. The fifth, father of the girl, Rhoda Dunsay, had reached the settlement to the south. But pneumonia had seized upon him in his weakened condition, and he had succumbed. But before passing on, he had told Rhoda Dunsay the gold and furs were cached, and told her where the cache was.

Beautiful scowled. All this information had come to him from the squaw who had been nurse to the Dunsay man. The squaw was one of Beautiful's lady friends. But she hadn't heard exactly where the cache was.

Beautiful—he rasped his teeth at the memory—had gone to Le Bouc, told him the story—and here they were.

He plodded on, busy with his plotting. The cache belonged to him, not Le Bouc. And he'd get it. He'd let the little devil on the sled take care of Le Bouc and the others. Then he'd shoot the Silver Corporal. The girl wouldn't be hard to find. He'd kill her, too, and play safe.

Beautiful was feeling good. He even ceased to shiver and sweat.

The men came finally to a cabin and turned toward it. Very substantial was this cabin. The logs were big, the roof of split slabs.

They pulled up before the closed door.

Le Bouc addressed the sled. "Where ees dees cache?"

"In the inner room, under the floor," came a prompt reply from the bundled furs. The voice was shrill, but very faint.

"Come!" boomed Le Bouc, and shoved open the cabin door.

Beautiful hung back, whining, "I'll stick our here and watch the dame!"

"Bien!" agreed Le Bouc. "Dat ver' good idea."

Le Bouc and his breeds swaggered eagerly into the cabin.

Promptly, Beautiful wheeled and ran. He'd watch this from the brush. The Silver Corporal would come out of that sledge and vanquish Le Bouc and the breeds. Then Beautiful would shoot him down—in the back, if he could.

Reaching the nearest spruce thicket, Beautiful whirled to watch.

Sure enough, the fur bundled on the sledge opened. A figure stood erect.

Beautiful nearly choked. It was the girl. The Silver Corporal hadn't taken her place!

Beautiful shook, began to sweat again. Suddenly he seemed to hear a viperish swish of a sound—the sound of the Silver Corporal going into action. It must be his imagination, he thought in terror.

But it wasn't. There was a sharp rap as the heavy brass honda on the Silver Corporal's strange rope of a weapon hit Beautiful's temple. The fat man dropped, the beadwork on his garments grinding into the snow.

The Silver Corporal came on as silently as he had crept upon the fat dandy. He sped straight for the cabin door.

Passing the girl, he winked solemnly at her.

A volley of terror-stricken screams came out of the cabin. They were the cries of Le Bouc and his breeds. Their feet thundered for the door.

And they found something horrible in the cabin rear room.

The Silver Corporal reached the door first. He slammed it. There was a stout hasp. He clipped the leaf over the staple, thrust in a hardwood peg which, strangely enough, he had ready in his hand.

Le Bouc and his breeds hit the door. It held. They poured bullets into it. The wood was very thick; some of the bullets did not even go through.

The Silver Corporal ran to the girl, caught her arm and hauled her into the spruces. They stopped where they could see the cabin and still remain hidden. He beamed his little imp-of-mirth grin. Ordinarily, the bantam-sized Mountie was shy of women, and never spoke to a strange young lady without an introduction. But he'd been introduced to this one, back there where he had knocked the one-handed breed out and cut her bonds free and told her to bring Le Bouc and his men here.

The girl was puzzled. "What did Le Bouc find in the cabin?"

"The thing that scared him and the breeds, you mean?" the Silver Corporal queried in his tiny voice.

"Yes."

"That's the smallpox cabin. Your father left a warning sign on the door. I took it off and put it in the inside room. Le Bouc saw it when he got in there."

"You knew the sign was there—when you talked to me back yonder?"

"Sure. I looked this cabin over weeks ago."

There was no more yelling and shooting from the cabin. The quiet was ominous.

"They'll get out!" said the girl bitterly.

The Silver Corporal's dry chuckle sounded like a wee, elfin thing in the cold silence. "I reckon they'll try!"

Rhoda Dunsay glanced at this strange little man wonderingly. She'd heard talk of him. Weird tales, they were. Tales that said men who fought the Silver Corporal had a way of dying in traps of their own making.

She wondered if the cabin that held Le Bouc's gang could be such a trap.

The Silver Corporal abruptly spoke words that made her sure the cabin was indeed a trap.

"Le Bouc and them breeds have all been in jail a lot of times, and it didn't reform them," he said, speaking so low the girl could barely hear. "That sorta proves they're the kind of jaspers who don't ever reform. There's only one way to handle them kind."

The girl didn't shudder; she felt no horror at all. This mysterious little man was right. His way might be grim, terrible, but such was the way of the north.

She decided that she liked this little man, even if she hadn't known him long. She liked especially his homely, wrinkled grin.

Whur-r-room!

The cabin seemed to turn suddenly into a red-streaked monster of flame and smoke and debris, and jump a hundred feet in the air, stirring the snow, making boulders jump down slopes, making spruce boughs shuffle together. The wreckage settled slowly, in a tired way, stacking itself together with deafening crashes.

"That got 'em," said the Silver Corporal with simple certainty.

"What—what—?" The girl finished her query with a shiver.

"There was a dynamite case with two sticks, fuse and caps in it," the Silver Corporal murmured dryly. "It was on a shelf. But two more cases, plumb full of dynamite, where hidden under the floor, right by the door. They tried to blow open the door, an' the boxes under the floor let loose."

The girl shut her eyes tightly. She had to ask a question.

"Did you—plant the dynamite?"

"Nope. Believe it or not, it was just where I found it when lookin' the cabin over a few weeks ago."

The girl studied him. "You're a strange person. How did you happen to get on Le Bouc's trail in the first place?

The Silver Corporal shrugged. For a moment, he thought he wouldn't answer. He had already talked more than he usually did. The girl must be the cause of that. Ordinarily he was scared of women. But, somehow, he wasn't scared of this one.

"I just crossed their trail," he grinned. "Figured so many bad actors couldn't be together for no good reason, an' tagged along to see what devilment they were up to."

She did not speak at once.

"The furs and gold are cached behind the cabin," she said finally. "If you'll help me take them back, I'd like it—a lot."

Long ago the Silver Corporal had made himself a rule. It was a rule to always steer clear of women—especially the pretty ones. So far, he'd stuck to it. This hadn't been hard, because he was scared of women. But here was one he wasn't scared of. He looked into her brown eyes, felt himself slipping, tried to count the freckles on her nose to get his mind on something else—and failed.

His rule was the same as broken.

· · · · ·

Appendix B–

Articles

Hogleg Facts

Some Interesting Points of Six-Gun Savvy

The deadliest gunfighters in the West never touched a finger to a trigger. Few even owned a six-gun with a trigger. The old-timer who was there and knows can name the good ones—like Wyatt Earp, "Bat" and the other two Mastersons, Ed and Jim, Jack Bridges, "Doc" Holliday, Bill Tillman, "Mysterious Dan" Mather, Billy the Kid—and cite the best in the collection to prove it.

About the first formality after the purchase of a new six-gun was taking the trigger out. In the single-action six there is a bit of metal called a "dog" which holds the hammer at cock. Sometimes the "dog" was only filed off. But the usual thing was to take the trigger out, too. Triggers had a habit of catching in clothes or on strings and one thing and another.

The front sight was something else to be dispensed with. Front sights wore holes in holsters and occasionally the sight hung when somebody wanted his ironware in a hurry. So off the sights went. Incidentally, a sight gone wasn't something greatly missed. The gunfighter who waited to look for the sight on his lead pusher generally never saw it—or anything else, either.

Aiming was by pointing, sometimes with the forefinger, sometimes with the thumb. The thumb pointers claimed the adherents to their method managed to die of old age more often than finger pointers. That the thumb was busy while in the act of pointing didn't seem to make much difference. The forefinger was busy, too, for that matter. It was all a business of "feel." Kind of a developed instinct.

And that forefinger wasn't inside the trigger guard. It was wrapped, with the other three fingers, around the grip of the flame-thrower. And the fingers were really *wrapped.* They gripped the butt as tightly as possible.

The butt of a single-action frontier six was a man-size handful. Nor was the hammer a little thing, by any means. It stuck up where a man could get at it. A real hammer. A waving thumb couldn't handily miss it.

When a beginner tries to demonstrate the business of fanning on an ordinary double-action gun, he misses that hammer and big butt. When he unraveled cartridges, a good gunfighter used the second joint of his thumb to fan the hammer back. He didn't use the end, or ball, of his thumb. That was liable to slip. He made a hook out of his thumb and the second joint hit the hammer.

By the very nature of the beast, the single-action six was made to be fanned. As it came from the factory, two separate motions were necessary to fire the single-action gun. It had to be cocked. That turned the cylinder and put a fresh cartridge behind the barrel. Then the trigger had to be pulled. With the "dog" filed off, all that was necessary was to get the hammer back and let it go.

On the double-action guns, pulling the trigger brought the hammer back and turned the cylinder, and the hammer was automatically released at the right time. That was the difference.

Some fanners held the gun in one hand and stroked the hammer back by making passes with the other hand, but this had its disadvantages. It took both hands for one gun. It was a little awkward, especially when a man wanted to shoot at a target to one side or slightly behind.

Shooting was done from the level of the hip, of course. If a man thought, "I'll take a bead on this jasper!" it was liable to be his last piece of thinking.

This was largely because gun fights came on the spur of the moment. A ranny would round a corner or go into a saloon and see somebody he didn't care much for and guns were shucked and lead flew. The commonest battlegrounds were the saloons. Card table disputes stood high on the list of causes for gunning bees. Turning down a drink was a deadly insult. Failure to empty the glass of liquor might even cause trouble. It was a reflection on the drink the host was buying. Because of this, saloon-keepers had their whiskey glasses made with thick bottoms so they could be filled to the brim without holding so much.

Altogether, most fights started from what might be called no cause at all.

When a cowpoke came to town after a few months on the range, he was full of vinegar and bubbles and it didn't take much to get him on the prod. Sometimes he was so loaded with orneriness somebody just had to step up and let it out of him. It can be said, however, that they usually didn't have to look far for their trouble. Nearly every town had its local expert to handle these customers. Generally, this was the sheriff. The list of old-time Western sheriffs unquestionably contains the greatest collection of gun-fighters ever to live.

It was almost always an outfit of waddies that shot up a town. One man seldom cared to try it. More often than not they did the shooting-up as they left, when they had a skinful of liquor or a peeve. This pastime was hard on the nerves, but not much else. Most of the lead went into the air, but occasionally somebody couldn't resist the temptation of a window. And such capers, if pulled when they came into town, were liable to result in somebody getting swatted with a slug from some irate townsman's Winchester.

Incidentally, all rifles were called Winchesters, whether they were that brand or not. The sole exception was the big-bore buffalo gun, which was always called a buffalo gun. Shotguns were scatterguns and held in contempt by every cowboy. Sheep herders used them to scare coyotes. Shotguns were mightily respected, though. Bartenders usually kept one, sawed off, behind the bar.

The single-action six-gun did not gain its favor because there were no double-action guns. Double actions aplenty were for sale, and the green-horn was rather more than apt to choose that type. But the man in the know took a single-action, which was not as liable to get out of order. The single-action was simplicity itself.

An accomplished fanner could pour out five slugs in one big roar.

Always five bullets. Never six. Because, although the single-actions were "sixes," the hammer was kept resting on an empty chamber. Five cartridges in the cylinder and one empty chamber for the hammer to rest on. Otherwise, the gun-toter was liable to lose a leg or a foot in case the honda of his lass rope or a bush rapped the hammer.

And speaking of shooting from the hip, put a six-gun in the hands of a man who never held one before and he can usually shoot straighter from the hip than he can by taking his time and aiming. The faster he shoots, the more liable is his hip shooting to be better. Try it and see.

The talking iron was carried in an open Mexican holster low on the hip. The holster was called Mexican because it, like the cowboys' saddle, was adopted from the Mexican *vaqueros*. Swinging low that way, the gun could be gotten at handily. There were other reasons, too. Those cannons were not toys. They weighed something. And one belted tight around a man's tummy was something to think about on an all-day ride. Down on the hip that way, the weight of the gun was distributed where it wouldn't be felt so much.

Nobody courted suicide by having a flap on his holster top. Holsters were usually tied to the leg with a buckskin thong attached to the lower end, but not always. Tying down helped to prevent accidents when accidents meant a seven-by-three-foot bit of freshly turned sod.

The bottom of the holster was usually cut off to allow the end of the barrel to stick through about an inch. Dirt had a habit of collecting in the bottom of the holster. Too, sometimes a man wanted to shoot without shucking his gun. These were the hombres who didn't tie their holsters down. The through-the-holster shooters were always fanners, too. When the six is in the leather, a trigger just can't be pulled with any degree of success.

A tied-down holster did not necessarily mean a bad hombre. Tying the holster kept it from flipping around and throwing a good gun out in the dirt when a bronc was bucking. And a bronc always bucked when he was first hairpinned. If he didn't buck, he wasn't worth his salt. Sometimes holsters were tooled or plain, to suit the vanity of the wearer.

Likewise the gun might have pearl or gold handles, and gold and silver inlay on the barrel and cylinder. Cartridge belts had loops all around, but cartridges were usually carried in front alone. Behind, they were hard to get at and rubbed on the saddle.

Cowhands used their six-guns for other things than throwing lead at each other. A .44 or a .45 was a first-class cow-scarer. Cow herds had a nasty trick of stampeding when a ranny sneezed or a jackrabbit jumped out from under his bronc's feet. Texas longhorns were pigs at that. Riding in front of a stampede, a ranny could blaze away under the noses of the leaders and turn them until he had the herd milling. Then he'd let the critters run in a circle until they had the run out of their systems.

Six-guns were nice to start fires with. When a waddy got caught in the rain without his slicker, or got a ducking swimming a stream, his matches naturally got wet. The hot sun would dry out the landscape and his clothes, but it wouldn't help his matches. He could pull the lead out of a cartridge with his teeth and fire off the powder and start himself a fire, provided he was careful his improvised blank didn't bang his kindling all over the scenery.

Practice made perfect with a six, as with everything else. To keep in trim, a man had to burn a little powder every day. Keeping a tomato can rolling was just a fair trick. Breaking poker chips tossed in the air was better. Silver half-dollars would do, but nobody wanted his good money all bent up. Shooting either the paper or brass end off empty shotgun shells thrown in the air was fair work. To do this right, though, a man had to be able to erase whichever end a bystander called for after the shell had been tossed. Lighting matches stuck in a fencepost was nice, too.

Twenty dollars was the standard price if a cowboy got hard up and wanted to soak his six to buy drinks or chips. Any saloon would advance him that. But no more, even if the six had pearl handles which had cost him fifteen dollars extra when he bought the gun. A good six sold for around thirty-five dollars in the stores.

Altogether, those single-actions were real hunks of death in the hands of a man who knew how to use them.

· · · · ·

Ridin' Sign

The "Sherlock Holmes" of the Cow Country

A stranger rode into a Black Hills mine town about noon. His long black hair was in beaded braids at the sides. That marked him as an Indian. He went into the bank. After a bit, he came out and rode off.

Half an hour later, the bank president came back from lunch and found his cashier on the floor with a bashed-in skull. Something like a hundred pounds in gold dust was missing.

It doesn't take much gold to weigh a hundred pounds. Evidently the gent with the Indian look about him had walked out with it under his coat.

The bank president called the sheriff. The sheriff learned which way the killer had ridden out of town, then directed a deputy to "Fork a bronc and get Skookum Charlie."

When you looked at Skookum Charlie, the things you remembered were a faded yellow moustache like a sorrel bronc's mane, a tremendous chew of tobacco and many wrinkles. Nobody knew how old Skookum Charlie was. Some said the Sioux had raised him. Charlie never said much about himself.

The posse rode out of town with Skookum Charlie a couple of hundred feet in the lead. The tracks of the killer's horse were occasionally plain enough for all to see.

But it was not long before Skookum Charlie pulled up. Although the tracks stretched away ahead, he said: "Nobody's ridin' that bronc now."

They went back to a stretch of rock near the trail. Skookum Charlie circled that, and soon set off. Before long, even the posse members could see a man's boot tracks indented in the sand of a creek bed.

Later they saw more plain tracks. Skookum Charlie pulled up, said: "He's got rid of the gold. Musta heaved it in that deep pool he passed back a piece."

The sheriff said: "Well—he'll head for his tribe now and expect them to keep him hid. There's some Blackfeet camped north on the Belle Fouche. We'll ride straight to them."

Skookum Charlie pointed at the tracks. "That ain't no Indian."

The sheriff took a closer look; said: "Sure enough—it ain't!"

They went on until the trail disappeared on a stony ridge that stretched for miles. Nothing to do but search the edges. But within half a mile, Skookum Charlie found more tracks. It looked like a second man had lately come from the direction of town and walked onto the stone ridge.

But Skookum Charlie said: "Gent who made them tracks was walkin' backward."

The sheriff scratched his neck. He said: "The hell he was! He's headin' back for town, then."

So they followed these tracks. Skookum Charlie opined: "He's about ten minutes ahead."

The trail led to a shack where a tin-horn gambler was just burning a wig of long black hair. They decorated a tree limb with the tinhorn that afternoon.

Now—you ask how Skookum Charlie learned all that? It was simple— when you knew how. Skookum Charlie was good at riding sign. One of the best.

In the first place, Skookum Charlie knew the killer had quit his horse because the fore part of the animal's tracks were not as deep as before. A ridden horse tends to accentuate the front of the hoofprint. By the same token, a trotting horse scuffs the ground a bit. And any amateur can tell when a horse is running by the lengthened stride.

Second, Skookum Charlie knew the killer had ditched his loot because a man carrying a load steps heavy on his heels. His heel marks are indented more deeply. The minute Skookum Charlie saw the heelprints of the man he trailed were not as deep as before, he knew the fellow had gotten rid of the loot. A little natural observation suggested the likeliest place—the deep pool of water. That tinhorn was taking no chances. He could come back and get it later—he thought.

The killer was fairly well disguised as an Indian. But by looking at his boot tracks, Skookum Charlie knew he wasn't an Indian. How? Simply because an Indian usually toes in when he walks. A white man usually doesn't.

Now, how could Skookum Charlie tell the man had walked backward off the rock? Because a man walking backward puts most of his weight on his heels after a few paces.

Then Skookum Charlie knew they were close on the tinhorn. How? He could tell the trail was fresh in a number of ways. The Black Hills are full of birds that might be scared away as the killer passed. Grass slowly straightens after it has been stepped on. Bits of disturbed dirt slowly topple into tracks. At creeks, muddy water clears away slowly. Or, if the print is in damp sand, it fills slowly with water. The underside of stones are damp. Overturned, they dry slowly.

Riding sign was a highly developed art in the days before telephones and automobiles came to the West. A sign rider was the Sherlock Holmes of the cow and mine country. Every sheriff, if he wasn't a good sign rider himself, had somebody handy who was. A sign rider drew down good money for his work, too. Cowmen hired him to track rustlers. The U.S. government hired him to track Indians and outlaws.

A sign rider could sometimes locate the trail of the man he tracked a mile or so distant, because bits of mica in rocks showed like tiny sparks in the sunlight after they were scuffed by a horse or a man. By the same token, disturbed snow showed scintillating crystals visible from a great distance for a time after it was disturbed. If a sign rider saw these crystals, he could be sure his quarry wasn't far ahead.

A man riding the owlhoot trail and expecting pursuit was inclined to flatter himself about what he would do to his pursuers when they came up. So he was likely to practice drawing his gun. The flash of sun from a six being rolled in practice has betrayed many a badman.

A man with a limp left one deeper track and a twisting easily detected. A drunk took steps of unequal length. Of course, a horse or a man bent grass forward, plainly indicating the direction of travel when the tracks themselves were too faint to show that.

Dropped objects could be felt to see if they were still warm. If they were, they hadn't been there long. Wet cigarette butts meant the same thing. Fires of dry wood didn't give much smoke, as everyone knows, but they did exude an odor a good tracker could detect for miles, if there was any kind of a breeze.

Western broncs were rarely shod, and the hoof rims were nearly always chipped and broken. So most horses left hoof marks about as individual as fingerprints.

So you see, Skookum Charlie's performance was very simple!

· · · · ·

Bronc Twisting

The "How and Why" of Four-Legged Dynamite

Let's start this on a certain day a few thousand years ago. On that day, a jaguar crouched on a limb that overhung a trail. The giant cat's eyes glittered yellow-green with hunger.

A horse came along the trail, making for water.

The jaguar leaped onto the back of its quarry. Front paws drove down, crooked spikes of claws unsheathed and sank in just behind the horse's front legs. Teeth gripped the horse's neck. Holding on thus, with awful, kicking strokes of rear claws, the huge cat sought to disembowel its victim.

Down went the horse's head to tear off the terrible grip of those teeth. It shot into the air and hit the ground stiff-legged, leaning sidewise, trying to jar the cat loose. It swapped ends suddenly, hoping to twist the jaguar off. Rearing, it fell over backward in an effort to crush the killer feline. It was a battle for life.

Finally the horse got away and lived to produce offspring. These had more offspring.

But we'll skip that and come up to date.

On a Western ranch, a man is cinching his saddle on an unbroken bronc. The man is a cowboy, who specializes in breaking broncs, a "bronc twister," "snapper," "peeler," "buster," "bullbat," "buckaroo," or a plain "bronc breaker."

When the twister saddles up, the cinch goes around the bronc about where the front legs of the jaguar gripped his ancestor. When the twister swings aboard, his weight in the saddle might be likened to the position of that jaguar long ago.

So instinct tells the bronc what to do. Down goes his head. He "sticks his bill in the ground." He "swallows his head." He sails skyward, and when he comes down, he's stiff-legged and leaning at an angle, "sunning his sides." He swaps ends, he back-shuttles.

The bronc thinks he's fighting for his life. He "bellers" like a spanked kid. He turns inside out the bag of tricks he's inherited for getting rid of things on his back. It's instinct for him to buck, instinct handed to him by his ancestors.

For that reason, the buckaroo on the back of the bronc takes about as agonizing a shaking-up as it is possible for a man to get. Unless he knows very well how to make his ride, the man's hat flies off. His shirt tail comes out. He may begin to bleed at the nose, the mouth and the ears. It goes red and black in front of his eyes. His insides feel like there's a catfight in there. Eventually he may be thrown so high he "lit a-runnin'." He may just topple off and "sun his moccasins."

Or possibly he's a good bronc peeler and sticks. Or maybe the unbroken horse has been "sacked" and "handled" until he don't "wild up" so violently.

"Sacking" is the act of shaking a saddle blanket, gunnysack or dried cowhide around an unbroken bronc until the animal ceases to go into a frenzy. Of course, the methods of different buckaroos vary a bit. Some use a saddle for the "sacking."

However, the first job of a bronc fighter is to teach the animal what a rope means. The horse is corralled, usually with a bunch to be broken.

The buster goes into the corral with his rope. He does not swing the loop around his head. This spooks the animals. He lets the loop drag in the corral dust behind him, from time to time giving it a gentle flip with his wrist to keep it open. When he sees his chance, he throws with a single quick flip of his arm, which creates little commotion.

Maybe the roped bronc drags the fighter around the corral a few times. But eventually the man gets the rope looped around the "snubbing post," a stout post set deeply in the center of the corral. The bronc, by dashing to the end of the rope and throwing himself a few times, will soon understand it is futile to fight the "string." The violence of these first lessons is usually attested by deep brown grooves the rope has burned into the snubbing post.

Later, when the bronc is older, he probably learns the trick of stopping and dropping his head between his front legs when he sees the rope coming, and will seek to remain in the back of the bunch when he sees a man around with a rope.

When the buster has the bronc resigned to the rope, he probably will haze the animal out of the corral and stake him on a picket rope. Often a bronc fighter will have several animals he's breaking out on these "putto" ropes.

At all times, the buster lets the bronc know who is boss. Gentle words and caresses will not break a jug-headed bronc, unless the process is spread over a period of many months. However, the man doesn't fight the horse—unless he wants to deliberately make the animal an "outlaw."

Incidentally, some ranches specialize in making outlaws. These buckers fetch big money from producers of rodeos. All cowtowns worthy of the name have a rodeo every year. Bucking horses for the rough-riding contests are hard to get. Some of the worst outlaws, animals that can be depended upon to furnish a spectacular ride, occasionally bring a price ranging into the thousands.

But usually the buster doesn't want to make an outlaw, and he is calm, but very firm in handling the bronc. He moves around the horse as much as possible, talking or swearing in a gentle tone, getting the animal accustomed to his presence.

When the bronc is broke "to lead," the buster starts "sacking." He fans a saddle blanket quietly about, eventually dropping it on the bronc's back many times. The blanket may be a felt "corona," shaped to fit under the saddle, but more often, it will be an ordinary thick "Navajo," which is folded to the size of the saddle.

The saddle goes on next. A blanket is not generally used on the first ride or so. Sometimes the saddle is a double-cinch rig, "double-barreled." Sometimes it is "single-barreled," or has only one cinch.

When a cinch is tightened, it seems to be instinct for a bronc to suck air into himself until he's swelled up like a tickled toad. Like putting his head down when he sees a cowpoke with a rope, this "blowing up" is a habit that becomes more aggravating as the cayuse gets old and wise.

The waddy can prod the bronc gently in the side with his thumb to cause the critter to let out the wind. Or he may haul off and kick the bronc in the slats. It depends on how he feels.

But if the cinches are not tight, the saddle will "turn."

At first the bronc is allowed to buck with the saddle alone. That helps convince the animal the rig is on his back to stay. Once the bronc is in this frame of mind, the breaking is made a lot easier.

Saddles are many and varied. The bronc fighter usually uses a "swell-tree." That is, the saddle has a pronounced bulge on each side of the horn. This swell assists the rider in staying on, furnishing something to grab with his knees when the cayuse starts him skyward. If the saddle is not swelled, the peeler often ties his slicker in a thick roll across the pommel to get the same result.

The saddle tree is usually of beechwood, sheathed with canvas, with iron plates riveted to head and cantle for added strength. The best covering is pigskin. Cheap saddles have a cherry red color, a gaudy hue that is apt to fool a greenhorn. The leather may be plain or tooled. Possibly the saddle is elaborately "mounted" with silver. "Whang-strings," long strings attached to the saddle for tying on things, may even be wide as reins and a different color from the saddle on fancy rigs. The twister probably has no rope on his saddle on the first few rides, since there is always a chance of a rope hanging on a spur.

The stirrups are usually "tapped." That is, they have a leather covering on the front to keep the foot from sliding through. To ride with "open" stirrups is to invite having a foot slip through, in which case a ranny is almost certain to be thrown. Many a twister has been dragged to death this way. It is to prevent a foot slipping through a stirrup that cowboy boots have high heels.

Stirrups may be tied under the bronc's barrel. But this reflects somewhat on the ability of the twister. It is akin to "pulling leather," or hanging onto the saddle horn when the going gets "high and wide." Most cowhands would rather be thrown than do that.

Bridles are varied. Some are kept on the animal by a "throat-latch," which buckles under the throat. Others have merely a hole in the head-stall for one of the bronc's ears, or maybe both ears. "Blinkers," leather tabs to keep the animal from seeing anything except what is ahead, are seldom used on a cowboy's riding bridle.

Sometimes a "martingale" is employed, an arrangement of straps from the cinch to the bridle to prevent the horse throwing its head up, but this is not a common practice.

Bridle bits are varied, too. Some are simple snaffle, a bit with smooth bars, usually jointed. Others are "tool chests," curb bits calculated to effect the most exquisite torture. A curb bit has a chain under the bronc's jaw. Most cowhands use a curb bit with a "port," or a raised part for the horse's tongue. Sometimes this port is equipped with a ribbed or fluted roller. In between are various kinds of straight bar and bribboon bits, the latter being snaffle bits without bars. Bits are often inlaid with silver, and sometimes gold and jewels.

These bits are apt to impress the uninitiated as awful things when, as a matter of fact, they are not cruel. The bronc is taught to guide by "neck-rein" early in his education, by pressing the reins against the neck, and not by pulling the reins, as a plow horse is turned. And the reins are not yanked to stop. Even the most churn-headed bronc will halt at the word "whoa."

These "tool chests" in a bronc's mouth are what make him stand when the reins are dropped. When he tries to walk and steps on the dragging reins a few times, the bit punishes his mouth severely and he learns it is best policy to stand.

When the bronc-twister gets aboard the animal he is breaking for the first time, he probably grips the saddle horn with his right hand and puts the thumb of his left hand over the bronc's left eye. This thumb over the bronc's eye gives the cayuse something to think about while the twister settles himself in the kak with a quick, light swing. He cannot see what is happening until the man has "took root" in the saddle.

Incidentally, broncs are sensitive about their eyes. When blindfolded, they are apt to stand still and tremble and snort, instead of bucking. Hence outlaws are blindfolded in the chutes at rodeos while being mounted. A runaway bronc can be stopped if the rider leans over and puts his hat over the animal's eyes. Once in a while a cayuse falls down when that is done, though.

The twister may ride "slick-heeled," without spurs. Or he may wear just one spur, or two. Usually the spur wheels have huge blunt spikes and bobs which make clicking sounds that are company on a long ride.

Once in the kak, the twister does his best to keep the bronc's head up. Once the cayuse "sticks his bill in the ground," it's "good night ears."

Broncs rear and fall backward quite often. When this happens, the animal is slow toppling over and the twister simply drops out of the saddle, steps clear, then gets back on as the cayuse climbs up.

Sometimes the animal will lie down gently. Peelers cope with that in different ways. Most get off. Occasionally there's one who stays in the kak and lets the bronc lie on his leg. This is all right if the bronc doesn't take a notion to roll. But if they're the type who stay in the rig, they usually have their legs protected by heavy chaps.

As for the chaps, the serviceable kind are made of plain, heavy leather. Ornaments, if any, are of metal. These chaps are intended to protect the wearer's legs in brush country. If there's a lot of surplus leather sticking out behind, they are "batwing" chaps.

Fur chaps are more showy and are usually made of mohair, the hide of an Angora goat. However, some are made of bearskin, dogskin, calfskin, deerskin or plain canvas. When made of Angora, the fur is dyed whatever bright color the owner happens to prefer. However, cowpokes usually steer clear of red shirts and chaps. This mohair is very fine and silky—so much so that punchers sometimes call a young woman a "mohairrie" because of her fine hair.

A bronc can be broken of the lying-down habit if the twister simply alights and pulls the cayuse's head off the ground. The horse cannot get up then. The peeler holds the bronc's head up until the animal concludes it's a bad policy to lie down.

If the bronc-snapper is thrown, he is pretty certain to immediately crawl back on the animal, if he is able. It gives a cayuse bad ideas to leave an impression the rider can be gotten rid of by being bucked off.

In case a bronc tries to "tromp" a twister who has been thrown, the horse can be "dusted." That is, a handful of dust is thrown in the bronc's eyes, blinding him temporarily.

The bronc is quirted during the time he bucks in order to "whip the buck out of him." On the first ride, though, the peeler is usually too busy staying on to do much quirting. Sometimes a wide strap is used for this quirting. The strap makes loud reports with each blow, which scares the bronc more than it hurts. The idea, of course, is to show the animal bucking doesn't get him anywhere.

When the cayuse "gentles down," or stops bucking, the peeler "fans" him with a hat, or gives the horse a belt over the ears. That "spooks" the animal into renewed effort so he will buck until he "has it out."

After the first ride, the twister unsaddles slowly, and possibly rubs the bronc's back a bit with a gunnysack. Either then, or a bit later, he "pulls" the bronc's tail, cleaning out burs. Unbroken horses usually have their tails full of burs and are called "broomtails." A broke cayuse, with his tail "pulled," is called a "shavetail."

A cowboy almost never curries his bronc. The back, under the saddle, is rubbed clean, of course. But this is done with the palm of the hand as often as with a currycomb.

A few twisters do their riding with a hackamore. Hackamores can be terrible things if fitted with a "ghost cord." A ghost cord is an instrument for inflicting ghastly tortures on a cayuse that starts bucking. Instead of "whipping the buck out," the buster uses this ghost cord to inflict pain on the animal as a punishment for pitching.

Ghost cords are of many forms. Some twisters have a secret style of ghost cord all their own, and guard its nature jealously.

Another gruesome instrument used by some busters is a "twitch," or "twister." This is a cord looped on a stick and employed to squeeze the horse's upper lip. It is from this the term "bronc twister" was derived. Now it is commonly applied to all breakers, whether they use a "twister" or not.

However, most ranchers frown on peelers who use a "ghost cord" or a "twitch." They ruin broncs, make outlaws.

After the bronc "has the rough taken off," he may prove to be dumb, in which case the animal is a "churnhead."

By much riding after being "broke," the cayuse is taught to "cut" cattle by throwing himself against the animal. A good "cutting horse" can and does take a cow out of a bunch of stock with hardly a command from the rider.

The highest trained animal is a "rope horse." A good rope horse does about everything but toss the rope. A mediocre roper on a good rope horse can shame a highly expert loop twirler on a churnhead.

A "top" hand is a good cowpuncher. By the same token, a "top" horse is any good horse.

Every ranny has a "string" of horses that nobody but himself rides. Each string has a few top horses, some churnheads, and some broncs, or practically unbroken animals.

A string of horses may be "rough" or not, depending on how many unbroken animals are in it.

Every good cowhorse is a bit "kinky" when first forked in the morning, and maybe bucks a little until he has the "kinks out of his system."

On roundup, all the "strings" are herded together in a "cavvy," or remuda. A day wrangler, or "wrangatang," herds the horse cavvy in the daytime, and a "nighthawk" does the job after darkness. The nighthawk sleeps in the chuck wagon during the day, or, if the camp is not moved, in the shade under the wagon.

At the home ranch, saddle stuff is usually kept in the "horse pasture," except for one "'kept up" or wrangling horse, usually an old and very wise animal.

If trail-herding, or holding a bunch of cattle on roundup, each puncher usually keeps up a "night-horse," sometimes saddled. The animal may be picketed, or hobbled. If the bronc has learned to hop along at a good speed when hobbled, he may be "side-lined," a front and back leg hobbled together. If the cayuse is particularly expert at wandering off, he can be "cross-hobbled," or hobbled crosswise from front to rear feet.

Of course, night horses are kept up to cope with stampedes.

The twister usually breaks broncs at so much a head. The price may vary from three to twelve dollars a head, depending on the thoroughness with which the animals are to be broken. Usually the price is around six or eight dollars. Most twisters are young chaps getting money for a start at ranching. After they've been at it a while, they get crippled and torn up inside. They're like prize-fighters, usually too old for the game at thirty. And it's no job for a waddy hunting the soft spots.

Some twisters make a business of catching wild horses, breaking them "to lead" or "to ride," and selling them to the ranches. These men are called "mustangers." A mustanger may make good money—if he can catch enough wild horses. The animals are captured by several men chasing them in relays until they are exhausted, or by enticing them into corrals erected for the purpose far from ranches.

Incidentally, wild horses are still plentiful in the West. They run in the brakes, country so rough it is nearly impossible to "relay" them down and get them alive.

The latest dodge is to use airplanes to herd the animals out into the open.

· · · · ·

Cold Facts

What the Waddies Do When It's Forty Below

A cowpoke usually takes his bridle to bed with him in the winter. Not that anybody cares much for a bridle as a bedfellow, for the average bridle bit is quite a tool chest and makes something of a hill under a man's ribs. But then, a ranny does a lot of things in winter that he doesn't care much for.

He goes to bed with his bridle so his body heat will keep the bit warm. Ever touch your tongue to a piece of metal that's been out in zero weather? Wondered how you'd get loose, didn't you? Well, a cold bit will just about ruin a bronc's mouth. Of course, a fire in the bunkhouse stove would warm the bit, but it's a rare event when anybody but the cook builds a fire in the morning.

Another thing a bronc peeler does when the first cold snap hits is throw his high-heeled boots under the bunk and leave them there until spring. Those boots are tight, thin and natural refrigerators. The waddy replaces them with German socks. A German sock is made of wool, is almost half an inch thick and reaches nearly to a man's knees. Over these are worn overshoes. High ones; six buckles, if they can be gotten. One or two buckle overshoes are lowly things like overall pants. Sheep herders wear them and no self-respecting ranny will if he can get any other kind.

More often than not, the big hat decorates a bunkhouse nail through the winter, too. A fur cap with ear flaps which tie under the chin replaces it. Muskrat fur is the accepted material for the cap. Occasionally a waddy will shiver through with his hat on, and every district has a local freak who goes through the winter in his shirt sleeves. But these are exceptions.

A cowpoke puts on two, three or four pair of pants, depending on the temperature and his wardrobe. A man riding doesn't move his legs much, so they're mighty susceptible to frostbite. A sweater, a mackinaw or a sheepskin-lined coat goes on over the vest. Add to this fur-lined mittens, and the ranny—resembling an Eskimo—is ready to fork his bronc.

When he's been out in the snow a few hours, he's liable to go snow-blind. When a man is a dozen miles or so from nowhere, that going snow-blind is no joke. People like to say a cowpoke merely has to give his bronc its head in cases like that and the crock-head will take him home.

The answer to that is maybe yes and maybe no. It depends on whether that bronc is being fed oats at the home ranch. If the cayuse gets to thinking about an oat dinner, it'll take the blind waddy in. Otherwise, it's liable to wander around until the said waddy is frozen so solid he'll ring when you tap him.

Colored glasses will keep a man from going snowblind. In case a ranny has lost his smoked specs, black horsehair shoved under the sweatband of his cap or hat and hanging down over his eyes is a big help to keep out the glare. Sorrel horse hair is better than nothing, but hair off a gray or a white bronc is not much good. If he isn't riding a black or a moderately dark crock-head, the puncher can help save his eyesight by burning matches and smearing the black off the sticks under his eyes.

Winters are the terror of the cowman. If an outfit can get its dogies through the winter without a heavy loss, everything is hunky-dory. It snows in the north cow country. And it gets cold. Real winters, they have. Forty below excites nobody in Colorado, Wyoming and Montana. Weeks occasionally pass when it gets no warmer than twenty below zero.

Snow covers about everything but the cottonwood trees along the creeks. Wind packs the snow until it has a crust that will hold a cow. So the dogies often as not eat the tops off the cottonwoods, starting on the bark and leaving the wood for an emergency.

With the first deep snow, feeding of hay and cattycake starts. The hay is put up off the creek bottoms, every cow outfit having some hay land fenced. During the summer, before the fall roundup, the bronc peelers all pitch in and pitch hay. This is the one thoroughly detested job of ranch life. A waddy will do almost anything to get out of "hayin'."

The hay is stacked in barbed wire lots, and hauled out and spread on the snow as it is fed. Jackrabbits haunt these hay lots by the thousands when the snow is on, affording some nice six-gun practice. Cattycake is the name applied to all cottonseed feed preparations. It is freighted to the ranch during the summer.

Incidentally, any kind of hauling is called freighting. Special, very big, wide-tired wagons with built-out beds to allow heavy loading are used. Up to sixteen horses draw a wagon, or sometimes two wagons coupled together. The driver is called a freighter. Instead of lines, he uses a stout cotton cord called a jerkline and drives only the lead team by yelling "Gee!" and "Haw!" and what cusswords he knows. He walks alongside the wagons, or rides on a board that sticks out on the left side of the first wagon, low enough so that it can be hopped on and off of conveniently.

The winter's grub is freighted in before the first snow, too; because snow means the outfit is "holed up" for the winter. There's no going anywhere with a wagon. The women go to town and stay and send the kids to school.

Cows drift with the wind, falling into snow-filled gullies if they're not watched, or leaving the ranch range. Ice has to be chopped out of water-holes. Sometimes the cow critters will crowd onto the ice of a waterhole and when the waddy rides around the next day, a bunch of horns and tails sticking up out of the ice will be the only sign of a hundred or so head of stock.

A chinook usually takes the snow off. A chinook is a hot wind that removes the snow in a few hours, leaving a sheet of water covering everything. After that, the range turns green in a few days. Cows, if very weak after the winter, are apt to lie down and starve rather than undertake the effort of getting up. So cowpokes have to "tail" the critters up. "Tailing" is rubbing the animal's tail between two boards or two rocks. It's the only thing that will bring a defeated dogie up. Once on their feet, the critters usually decide to stay up and eat.

Riders go onto the range and skin dead animals on the shares. A waddy would no more do this work than he would herd sheep. Later in the summer, hilltops are apt to look white from a distance, so thickly have animals died up there where the snow was thinnest over the sage.

Maybe horns, frozen during the winter, drop off. If so, the dogies have "hollow horn." This only happens after a very hard winter.

After the chinook, a bronc peeler can put on his boots and hat again and let his bridle hang on a corral post all night and otherwise start being a human again.

In other words, she's thawed out.

· · · · ·

Appendix C–

Letters to Western Trails

Letters from Lester Dent

April 1932

Howdy, All:

This Powder River Bill bronc-snapper was jawin' kinda longin'-like about a hossback ride one of his *Western Trails* outfit is figurin' on. From New York to the west.

Fella, that's a swell idea. Only, me, I wouldn't hanker to ride no crock-head between New York and the place where the fences stop. There's too much concrete road and too many automobiles in between. Them and broncs don't mix extra good.

But after you was out there! That's some different. If this hombre with the itchin' feet was goin' into the north range country, and could get as far as the Dakota badlands and buy himself two jugheaded broncs there, that'd be keno. Hosses are cheap out here. Pack his bed and grub and hoss hobbles—and a big canvas waterbag—on one and cinch his kak on the other. Then he could meander through the Black Hills, pannin' a little gold on the way. There's gold in lots of places and a fella can make day wages a lot of the time. There'd always be a chance for a big strike, too; but if he didn't hit lucky, he'd have his fun. What I mean, it'd be fun. There's no mosquitoes in them Black Hills.

On west, he'd cross the Belle Fouche and Powder River country. My stompin' ground. I've got a couple of cousins, Paul and Ted Norfolk at Moorcraft and Gillette, Wyoming, who'd be glad to chew the fat with him. That's range country. He might get himself a job cowpokin', but they've had three of the dryest summers that ever came out of hell up there, and he'd be lucky if he caught on with a cow outfit. Goin' farther west, he'd hit the Big Horn mountains. Real hills, them.

After that, he'd better fill his waterbag plenty full, because between the mountains and the Big Horn river, there's as dry a streak of country as a man ever saw. The "Honeycombs," some calls it.

If I was doin' it, I'd keep goin' west into the Rockies, north of Yellowstone and the Jackson Hole country. I'd lay in a cache of grub and winter there. Do some trappin' and huntin', gettin' a cabin built in time to put out bear bait. There's plenty of game and scenery. It's a fact that a white man has never seen some of that country.

A fella could get his meat off'n the country from the time he hit the Black Hills badlands. A little lard, some flour, baking powder, coffee and salt is about all the groceries he'd need. And some canned tomatoes to eat when he'd been ridin' all day in the sun.

And he better take him a pair of pliers, the kind made for pullin' staples. Once in a while he's liable to hit a drift fence. He could pull the staples, let the wire down and lead his broncs through. But he better not cut no wire, or he'll get run ragged. Them's the only fences he'd hit, and not many at that.

Fella, this *Western Trails* hand has got himself an idea that is.

But I wouldn't ride no bronc from New York. No sir.

Lester Dent

June 1932

Hi, all:

I once heard about stunt like the little moharrie in "The Gun Quest," pulled on Praying Squent. It happened over in the Black Hills badlands of eastern Wyoming. Did the cock-eyed scheme work? It did! And the hombre who got rooked had it coming to him. Was his neck red when he got wise? It must have been, because the jasper who told us about it laid down and laughed until we had to put him in his bedroll.

You'll notice "The Gun Quest" yarn is laid in them same badlands. I've pinned a cayuse all over that country. If you've got a good map of Wyoming, look in the northeast part and you'll find a place marked "Pumpkin Buttes." Well, this yarn happened right in the shade of them buttes, on the head-waters of the Belle Fouche.

I learned a little about shooting by popping away at them mud swallow nests under the eaves. The birds weren't such pests, but what they carried were. Things that made a fella scratch himself to beat hell, if you get what I mean. Only I missed so many shots that the roof got full of holes and when the fall snow came, I got some orders to leave them nests alone.

Anyway, writin' this yarn kinda got me to smelling sage and I've about half decided to spend next summer in that country. She's a great bailiwick. And she's layin' there right now just like she is in this "Gun Quest" yarn.

Just to make her ring right, Long Shorty Sims is a buckaroo who drifted through the Four-J one day. That fella just didn't have any meat on him, what I mean. One of our Four-J waddies swapped a rifle off him. He only stayed one night, then rode off toward them Pumpkin Buttes. And he wasn't no more than out of sight when a posse of sheriffs from Caspar showed up.

This long, skinny gent had robbed banks and trains and what not. The sheriffs mentioned a reward big enough to start spurs rattling and broncs bucking as every Four-J ranny hit that jasper's trail. Seems I recollect my mother even stood a shotgun in the corner of the kitchen.

Anyway, they didn't catch him. But a few weeks later, up in Montana, somebody tried to rook that long jasper in a poker game. He just naturally beat hell out of the card sharp. Broke both his arms and hammered his nose down with a six-gun barrel. They clapped the long gent into the local bastille—and found out who he was. I made some inquiries last summer and learned he's still in the Wyoming state pen.

A cultus hombre for a hero, you say? Maybe. But that long gent kinda struck my fancy. He could shoot the paper end off a shotgun shell tossed in the air and not touch the brass, or wipe off the brass and not tear the paper much. And that's shootin', fella. He talked quite a bit, and held his own in the augerin' around the bunkhouse that night. But—he slept with his guns.

Lester Dent

May-June, 1933

Hello, Folks:

Let's sorta figure you've already read "Snow Ghost."

Doin' that, you met the Silver Corporal. He's a strange, mysterious cuss. In some ways, he's kinda like the stuff nightmares are made out of, 'special on cold nights when the bed tarp has got a hole down toward the foot. Anyhow, some cultus gents has felt that way about him.

Powder River Bill slips me the word he'd like to know somethin' on the side about this ranny who goes trompin' around in the snow workin' bad hombres over with a doojigger that's a cross between a bullwhip, a lass rope and a Mex toad-stabber. And he don't pack none of Colonel Colt's product! Imagine a cowpoke without hardware, says Bill. And how come! Bill orates as how he's wonderin' if there ever was such a gent.

There was.

It was in northeast Wyomin', fifty miles south of Gillette. It was January and about thirty below. Pumpkin Buttes sloped up to the west. The daggone wind and snow seemed to take a runnin' start down them buttes and slam right through a sheepskin coat. It blew hay away fastern' four frosty cow nurses could heave it on a hayrack.

A ranny came ridin' in from the line camp twelve miles up the crick, where a dab of cows was winterin'. He had a toothache. He'd have to go to Gillette and get that tooth fixed.

He'd hired a gent who just happened along, to take care of the dogies. Ordinary, the foreman done any hirin' and firin'. But the waddy claimed this was an emergency or somethin', and he'd hired the stranger, and if the foreman didn't like it, he knew the place he could go to, which sure wasn't the North Pole. The toothachy ranny rode off toward Gillette, wrapped in his whole bedroll like a Sioux buck and with three plugs of Climax for his affliction. It was sure as hell cold.

Curiosity was the cause of some of the spread ridin' up in a few days to look the new hand over. They got they eyes full.

It was this Silver Corporal jasper. Only the cowhands right off took to callin' him Nickelplated Poison, which was more descriptive.

They thought at first his voice had frozen, he talked so low. He looked starved and he sure was little. His hair wasn't white. It was more like a skullcap hammered out of Uncle's silver dollars. And he carried that funny white rope with the sharp blade on the end, all the time. He even ate with it across his lap.

He didn't drink, swear, smoke, play poker or tell lies. He didn't carry guns, not even a rifle. As a cowpoke, these things made him a dead loss.

With that funny bullwhip-knife-rope jigger, he was a whiz. He could flip the blade the length of the line shack and cut in half flies sittin' on the wall. Of course, the flies had been sittin' there all winter, frozen solid, but that didn't make them any bigger. The honda in the other end was big, heavy, might easy have popped open a man's skull. The things he could do with that rope contraption was plumb scandalous.

What really scared our rannies, though, was seein' this strange jasper widen out a horseshoe with his bare hands so it'd fit one of the broncs. The rannies had heard of that stunt, but this was the first time they'd ever seen it done. Their eyes stuck out like the pods on jimson weeds.

Nickelplated Poison could tear a deck of cards in halves, which is some stunt.

The rannies didn't get to know him any too well, 'cause the assistant foreman told the little feller that in view of his unofficial way of bein' hired, he wouldn't get no pay. This assistant foreman figured he'd save the outfit a few dollars. He'd also been heard to boast he could lick a wildcat.

Well, he got his chance to try. And when he woke up, Nickelplated Poison was gone.

Before the peewee gent rode off, though, he was heard to whisper that Wyomin' was gettin' to be a hell of a place, what with one thing and another, and that he was goin' up north and join the Mounted.

He did. We heard about it—yarns that sifted all the way down from the Arctic.

Them yarns was—well, another story. I'm basin' these Silver Corporal tales on 'em.

If you like 'em, brand 'em in the ballot at the end of this department and let Powder River Bill see same. If you don't like 'em, here's hopin' your fingers is rope-burned or your pencil breaks. What with the price of cows like it is, nobody wants any knockin' goin' around that might hurt his meal ticket.

S'long,

Lester Dent

Appendix D—

From Lester Dent's notebook—
Story submission records

AUTHOR OF FICTION
IN MORE THAN FIFTEEN
MAGAZINES, AND RADIO
DRAMAS BROADCAST BY
OVER SIXTY STATIONS

WESTERN
DETECTIVE
WAR-AIR
LOVE
AIR
GENERAL ADVENTURE
MAGAZINE ARTICLES

LESTER DENT

The letterhead of Dent's stationary in 1934 embraced his rugged, western heritage.

Story submission notes

Original, working or alternate title	Published as/date
Rip 'Em Up Ranny.. originally entitled The Bust 'm Up Ranny Finished October 26, 1931 Delivered October 26, 1931 Bought November 5, 1931. Check for $60.00. to appear as "Dusty Trant—Bank Robbers"	Dusty Trant—Road Agent *Western Trails,* January 1932
The Sudden Disaster Gent... Finished November 22, 1931 Delivered November 23, 1931 Sold January 10, 1932 Paid February 1932 $50.00	The Sudden Disaster Gent *Western Trails,* April 1932
Gun Key	The Gun Quest *Western Trails,* June 1932
Medicine for Wick... Finished June 27, 1932 Delivered June 28, 1932	Trigger Trap *Western Trails,* October 1932
The Bag of Tricks Gent	The Haunted Saddle *Western Trails,* December 1932
Death Cache, Skull Cache...............................	Snow Ghost *Western Trails,* June 1933
Cold Facts .... Finished January 18, 1932 Delivered January 18, 1932	Cold Facts *Western Trails,* September 1933
Bronc Twisting.. Finished June 15, 1932 Delivered June 15, 1932	Bronc Twisting *Western Trails,* July 1933

PUBLICATION HISTORY

"Dusty Trant—Road Agent" Copyright 1932 Magazine Publishers, Inc. From WESTERN TRAILS, January 1932. No notice of copyright renewal.

"Gunslick Roundup" Copyright 1932 Magazine Publishers, Inc. From WESTERN TRAILS, March 1932. No notice of copyright renewal.

"The Sudden-Disaster Gent" Copyright 1932 Magazine Publishers, Inc. From WESTERN TRAILS, April 1932. No notice of copyright renewal.

"The Gun Quest" Copyright 1932 Magazine Publishers, Inc. From WESTERN TRAILS, June 1932. No notice of copyright renewal.

"Hell's Hoofprints" under the psuedonym Cliff Howe Copyright 1932 Magazine Publishers, Inc. From WESTERN TRAILS, June 1932. No notice of copyright renewal.

"Fear Ranch" Copyright 1932 Magazine Publishers, Inc. From WESTERN TRAILS, September 1932. No notice of copyright renewal.

"Trigger Trap" Copyright 1932 Magazine Publishers, Inc. From WESTERN TRAILS, October 1932. No notice of copyright renewal.

"The Devil's Ear" Copyright 1932 Magazine Publishers, Inc. From WESTERN TRAILS, November 1932. No notice of copyright renewal.

"Haunted Saddle" Copyright 1932 Magazine Publishers, Inc. From WESTERN TRAILS, December 1932. No notice of copyright renewal.

"Trickery Trail" Copyright 1933 Magazine Publishers, Inc. From WESTERN TRAILS, January 1933. No notice of copyright renewal.

"Frozen Phantom" Copyright 1933 Magazine Publishers, Inc. From WESTERN TRAILS April 1933. No notice of copyright renewal.

"Snow Ghost" Copyright 1933 Magazine Publishers, Inc. From WESTERN TRAILS, June 1933. No notice of copyright renewal.

"Hogleg Facts" Copyright 1932 Magazine Publishers, Inc. From WESTERN TRAILS, June 1932. No notice of copyright renewal.

"Ridin' Sign" Copyright 1933 Magazine Publishers, Inc. From WESTERN TRAILS, June 1933. No notice of copyright renewal.

"Bronc Twisting" Copyright 1933 Magazine Publishers, Inc. From WESTERN TRAILS, July 1933. No notice of copyright renewal.

"Cold Facts" Copyright 1933 Magazine Publishers, Inc. From WESTERN TRAILS, September 1933. No notice of copyright renewal.

Letters to *Western Trails*—April 1932, June 1932, June 1933

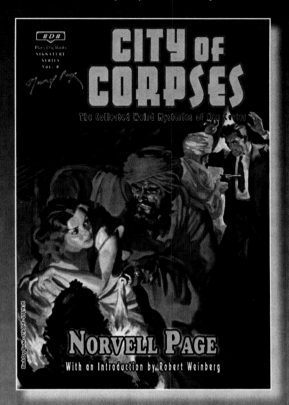